A city-loving book addict and peony obsessive, **Katrina Cudmore** lives in Cork, Ireland, with her husband, four active children and a very daft dog. A psychology graduate, with an MSc in Human Resources, Katrina spent many years working in multinational companies and can't believe she is lucky enough now to have a job that involves daydreaming about love and handsome men! You can visit Katrina at katrinacudmore.com

Helen Lacey grew up reading *Black Beauty* and *Little House on the Prairie*. These childhood classics inspired her to write her first book when she was seven, a story about a girl and her horse. She loves writing for Mills & Boon True Love, where she can create strong heroes with soft hearts and heroines with gumption who get their happily-ever-afters. For more about Helen, visit her website, helenlacey.com

Also by Katrina Cudmore

Their Baby Surprise
Tempted by the Greek Tycoon
Christmas with the Duke
Resisting the Italian Single Dad
Second Chance with the Best Man

Royals of Monrosa

Best Friend to Princess Bride
Christmas Encounter with a Prince

Also by Helen Lacey

Three Reasons to Wed
The Cowgirl's Forever Family
Married to the Mum-to-Be
The Rancher's Unexpected Family
A Kiss, a Dance & a Diamond

Discover more at millsandboon.co.uk

SUMMER FLING WITH A PRINCE

KATRINA CUDMORE

THEIR SECOND-TIME VALENTINE

HELEN LACEY

MILLS & BOON

First Published in Great Britain 2021
by Mills & Boon, an imprint of HarperCollinsPublishers,
1 London Bridge Street, London, SE1 9GF

Summer Fling With A Prince © 2021 Katrina Cudmore
Their Second-Time Valentine © 2021 Harlequin Books S.A.

Special thanks and acknowledgement are given to Helen Lacey for her contribution to *The Fortunes of Texas: The Hotel Fortune* series.

ISBN: 978-0-263-29898-7

0121

MIX
Paper from
responsible sources
FSC™ C007454

This book is produced from independently certified FSC™ paper to ensure responsible forest management.

For more information visit: www.harpercollins.co.uk/green

Printed and bound in Spain
by CPI, Barcelona

SUMMER FLING
WITH A PRINCE

KATRINA CUDMORE

To Liz, Treasa, Susan and so many other wonderful friends, for all your support, belief and encouragement during my writing journey.

CHAPTER ONE

HIS SILVER-GREY GAZE flicked over her and then away from where she was waiting for him in the reception area of the open-plan office. His first acknowledgement of her arrival. Seated midway around the conference table positioned at the centre of the converted warehouse, he was listening intently, a slight nod or frown his only feedback to what was being said by the others around the table.

The group of fifteen were speaking in English but, given their accents, they were from a wide mixture of nationalities. Their exuberance and passion for whatever they were discussing was what united them, as was their body language that said they were trying to impress him. Their boss. Prince Ivo of Monrosa. Former international athlete and now Private Investment Management CEO.

His staff, those taking part in the meeting and the twenty or so others who were working on laptops at long communal tables, were casually dressed to suit the laidback vibe of the office interior that housed break-out areas with low-slung armchairs and lavish barista machines, modern artwork hanging on the exposed stone walls. But Ivo stood apart, his exceptional height, proud stature, immaculate grooming and astute, watchful presence making it near impossible not to stare at him. He had a hardness, a sharpness in every feature that made him strikingly handsome but also incredibly intimidating.

His crisp blue open-necked shirt and navy trousers were bespoke. His wavy brown hair, cropped at the sides, was swept back from his forehead. With high cheekbones and tight, glowing skin, he still had the bright-eyed energy of an international athlete. And with a royal title, wealth, a distinguished sporting career and now a reputation in the financial world for killer analytical skills, no wonder he was aloof. He didn't have to impress anyone.

Admit it, Toni Clarke...you find his cool self-possession inspirational...and sexy as hell. And the way your heart is thumping...well, it's not just due to your nervousness over this interview, is it? Nope, it's seeing him again that's throwing you off balance.

Unable to bear sitting any longer, she stood and stared out of the window to the rejuvenated and historical dock area on the harbour front of Monrosa town. She had so many ties with Ivo, but had only met him the once—when she was bridesmaid at her best friend Alice's wedding to Ivo's brother Prince Luis. Ivo had been best man. And it was through Alice that she had become friendly with Kara, Princess of Monrosa, who was married to the eldest royal brother, Prince Edwin, now monarch of Monrosa, having inherited the crown when his father abdicated.

She had known they'd invariably bump into each other this weekend at the christening of Kara and Edwin's firstborn child—Princess Gabriela. She would have been able to handle that, as there would have been other people around for her to chat to. But now…thanks to Kara, she was about to spend four whole days in his company. The wedding had been eighteen months ago…but she was still mortified about how she had sobbed in his arms…and how horrified he had seemed.

You have this under control. Yes, the timing is terrible and, yes, he's seen you ugly-cry, but the man's an icon and this interview has the potential to change everything. Okay, so he might be the most unnerving man you have ever met but he's still human…isn't he? The Machine—his nickname when he won a gold medal for rowing, his expression never changing, whether it was on the starting line or on the podium, always the same unsettling, penetrating seriousness. Ivo never gave interviews. He was known for being intensely private. Other journalists would give their right arm to be able to interview him…for an hour even, never mind getting to spend four whole days with him. The simple fact is that you need this interview. You need it to be a success. Back yourself. Don't give in to your self-doubts. At least you know something about his life and you're not going into this interview completely blind like you usually do.

How on earth had she ever let Kara persuade her that she shouldn't know who it was she was going to interview until the very last moment? Yes, this tactic led to honest and raw interviews where she learnt about the individual at the same time as the listener. There were no scripted questions, no time for her to enter the interview with any preconceived ideas about the person. But it was a nerve-racking process…especially as the podcast also involved her moving in with the person for four days. The interviews were garnering great feedback for their unique and intimate style. She and Kara had agreed that the initial interviews should be low-key, a way to experiment and learn from the process. And she had assumed that Kara, whose team organised the interviews, would keep it that way for another few months. Instead she had thrown her right into the deep end with an interview that would test the nerve of even the most seasoned of journalists. What had Kara been thinking? Kara knew she wasn't in a good place right now…your ex's surprise wedding splashed all over social media tended to have that effect.

She was over Dan. It wasn't as though she had spent the last eighteen months pining over him. She had got on with life, determined to make something of her new, if unexpected, independence. But his wedding *had* thrown her. It had brought back all the memories of the hurt and shock and disappointment of him leaving her…but also the regret and shame that in their later years together she had stayed with him not for love but because he made her feel secure. Regret because she had clung to the embers of their relationship for all the wrong reasons. Shame because she should have known better. For her entire childhood she had watched her father come and go from her life. She had known that love was unreliable. But instead of learning from that, instead of being wary and making sure to protect her heart, aged nineteen she had jumped right into a ten-year relationship with Dan, desperate to feel safe and secure. And when their relationship had started to go wrong, when Dan had grown distant and remote, she had fallen into the same trap her mother had fallen into with her father. Time and time again her mum had taken her dad back even after months or sometimes years of absence, always hoping that one day he would change and give her the love she needed and deserved.

She should have been braver in her relationship with Dan. Ended it long before he had walked away. She shouldn't have been so willing to stay in a flawed relationship, compromising her own happiness and self-worth because she didn't know how she would cope on her own.

Now she knew that she needed to protect herself, be tougher and not be so emotionally vulnerable. In the past she had always worn her heart on her sleeve, overly confident of other people's loyalty and friendship. But all of that had been shattered when in the aftermath of her relationship with Dan ending, colleagues—who she had considered friends—in the television production company they both worked in had distanced themselves from her. It shouldn't have been such a surprise. After all, Dan was the global star of riveting historical documentaries and the reason why the production company's fortunes were growing year on year. She, as a producer, was much more replaceable. Even if it was her who introduced Dan to the production company in the first place when they had been searching for a presenter of their new documentary series.

Never again would she allow herself to be hurt. Yes, she dated guys but she kept them at a distance. She had no interest in anything serious and was instead pouring her energy into her career as a podcaster.

This *YA Together, Person Unknown* podcast was everything to her. It was her way of re-establishing her name and reputation. It was the thing that gave her a purpose in life. She could *not* mess up this golden opportunity.

Along the marina, office workers finished for the week, and, no doubt celebrating the fact that it was a long weekend in Monrosa, as Monday was a national holiday, sat outside the bars and cafés, sipping cocktails and eating tapas. Her stomach grumbled. She hadn't eaten since she had grabbed a croissant in her local café this morning on the way to the airport. But she hadn't even managed to eat that in full, thanks to Kara's phone call. Kara had excitedly announced that she had set her up with an interview for the weekend. Toni had argued that she was in no fit state to interview anyone but Kara wasn't having any of it. Kara wouldn't even listen to her protests that she had been looking forward to spending the weekend getting to know Gabriela. Instead Kara had ended the call saying that as usual the driver who was to collect her at the airport would inform her of her interviewee once they were approaching the interviewee's place of work. She had binned her croissant and run home to collect her portable recorder and microphones.

'Miss Clarke?'

She swung around, her heart pounding. She hadn't heard him approach.

'My apologies for keeping you waiting.' He gestured in the direction of the refreshment area. 'Can I get you something to drink?'

He was so polite, so formal. So unperturbed at meeting her again. Blood rushed to her cheeks. His voice, deep and accented, had her heart thumping in her chest.

'No, thank you, Your Highness.'

He asked her to follow him and, grabbing her laptop bag, she followed him into one of the glass-walled offices to the side of the warehouse. He sat behind the desk, a huge window behind him giving a view of the row of mega-yachts lining the marina, the ferry that ran between here and Monrosa old town creating a white ribbon wake in the ink-blue Mediterranean.

She took a seat on the opposite side of the desk.

He fixed those silver eyes on her. Seconds passed.

He continued to stare at her. Was this a test? She smiled in the hope he might respond in kind. He didn't. She felt herself redden again, her heart really pounding now under the force of his gaze, the aura of power that surrounded him, his comfort with the silence between them that was making her want to start babbling. And what really scared her was that one very crazy and inappropriate question kept going around her head and she was terrified of blurting it out.

Do you like having sex standing up?

What was the matter with her? Why was she sitting here trying to erase the image of Ivo holding her against a wall, that deep voice whispering into her ear?

'Four days seems excessive.'

Was he thinking about sex too? She swallowed hard. 'Four days?'

He frowned. 'Yes, the interview. Kara said it would take four days.'

'Oh…yes… I'm afraid so.' She took a deep breath, knowing she needed to focus. She was used to this. Interviewees having second thoughts about agreeing to the interview in the first place. 'But I promise to be a good houseguest. I don't have any bad habits…that I know of anyway. Although one of my interviewees did reckon I hogged the bathroom too much in the morning, but then she did live in a one-bathroom apartment, not a palace.' She gave a laugh. And then cringed when his expression tightened.

It was time to start again. She held out her hand.

'Sir it's really nice to see you again and thank you for agreeing to the interview. As Kara may have explained, I do not know who I am interviewing until I arrive, so it's a great pleasure and surprise to know that it's you.' Surprise, yes. Pleasure…that she wasn't certain of.

He leant across the table and took her hand. His grip was as strong and encompassing as she remembered. Breaking away, he asked, 'Why a pleasure?'

His stare was uncompromising. As though he was assessing every detail about her, storing away every fact in order to decide whether he was going to go ahead with this interview. And instead of meeting him head on and persuading him that this was something he wanted to do, her brain headed off in a completely different direction.

Well, pleasure might be pushing it. Yes, I could watch you for eternity—you have the face and body of a Greek god—but in truth you kind of terrify me. Quiet people unnerve me. I like chat and banter. I like connecting with people and knowing where I stand with them. I don't want complications or awkwardness. But with you… I'm not sure I'll manage any of those things.

She sat more upright in her chair. It was time to pull herself together and do her job. 'Your appearance on the podcast will help us to reach an even wider audience. People will want to hear your story.' She paused, a sense of purpose grounding her. 'This podcast, *Person Unknown*, is a gateway for people to learn that Young Adults Together is there to support them with any mental health problems they're facing. After each podcast, there's a spike in people contacting the helplines. But lots of young people either don't know of the service or are too nervous to make contact—in having prominent people talk about their lives and what they have learnt in both good and bad times, listeners can realise that they aren't alone in facing challenges. I am certain that your interview will be immensely powerful in helping others.'

He didn't respond to her answer. His gaze shifted away to a point over her shoulder, a tiny movement ticking in his jaw. Outside, in the main office, staff were leaving for the day, their chatter and laughter in stark contrast with the silence between them.

She needed to take this situation in hand. Unzipping her laptop bag, she said in her best cheerful voice, 'But before we talk any further, let me set up my equipment. As Kara will have explained, I always hold my first interview at the person's place of work so that listeners get a glimpse of their professional life. And I begin recording as soon as is feasible so that the listeners get to hear our interactions from the very beginning. We want them to feel immersed in the whole experience.' Placing the recorder on the table, she plugged the two microphones in and, positioning them in their mike stands on the table, she stood and leant across the desk in order to put the mike close to him. Raising her head, she met his solemn silver gaze. For long moments neither of them looked away. A buzz of attraction danced in the air between them. 'Are you ready for me?'

He raised an eyebrow.

Heat blasted her cheeks. 'I mean, are you ready for me to start the interview?'

A single small diamond around her neck swung as she waited for his answer. The top three buttons of her yellow dress were undone, her pale yellow bra beneath visible. Her perfume hadn't changed—it was still that light, floral scent. He inhaled an irritated breath, admitting to himself that ever since Luis's wedding he had been subconsciously keeping tabs on her life, alert to any conversations Kara and Alice had about her, lingering over the media reporting of her split with her ex, newsworthy because he was a famous and much in demand TV historian.

Frowning, as though wondering just when he'd answer her question, she pushed her long brown hair back behind one ear. It was the same light chestnut colour as her eyes. Her nose was pert, her lips full. Her skin lightly tanned. At Luis and Alice's wedding she had worn a gold sequinned bridesmaid dress that emphasised the swell of her breasts, the curve of her narrow waist, and when she had walked down the aisle, her hair tied up, tears in her eyes despite her wide smile, he had been unable to tear his gaze away from her. She had a soft, gentle beauty that was utterly captivating. He had told himself that he followed any news on Toni with just the same interest and concern he would have for anyone who had an association with the family. But some nights, alone in the silence of his *finca*, the idea of contacting her would bubble inside of him…but that idea had never become more than a fleeting thought, as he had never been sure of what purpose it would serve, and anyway, the complications of contacting her were too great, considering her ties with both of his sisters-in-law.

But now she was back in his life…and he wanted to end all of this. Now. He had zero interest in talking about his life…or sharing his home and privacy with anyone.

But Kara had pleaded with him to do this interview and deep down he knew it was the right thing to do for the charity. He would take part in the interview but he would control it at all times. And shut it down whenever he wanted to. He would only talk about the things he was comfortable discussing—his sporting and financial careers. There was plenty of material and life lessons in both. Enough to fill the hour-long podcast. 'Before we start I think I should make it clear that I'm not given to overthinking or self-inspection—I will answer your questions but please don't expect any great insights.'

She sat down, still frowning. Went to speak, stopped, studied him some more, but then with the slightest of shrugs said, 'How about we just give it a go? People are sometimes surprised at how much they learn about themselves by taking part in the interview.'

He made a disbelieving sound. Her response was

yet another shrug and with a hopeful smile she said, 'Here we go,' before pressing the 'record' button.

'Hi and welcome back to the *YA Together, Person Unknown* podcast, where we meet the person behind the fame and explore their life lessons. I'm your host, Toni Clarke.

'So guys, this week I am beyond thrilled with who I'm getting to interview. But before I introduce you, let me give you some teasers to see if you can work out who it is. I'm on a Mediterranean island that I reckon should be famous for its three Bs: beauty, beaches and banging cocktails. Right now, I'm sitting in the coolest office I have ever visited, a brilliant blue summer sky visible out the window, and we're surrounded by art galleries and bars and restaurants. It's Friday evening and people are out partying. The vibe here is amazing. And across from me is my interviewee. An international gold medallist and now successful CEO. I think it's fair to say that we all know *of* him, but not many of us know him, the real man. Oh, and did I mention that he's also royalty? Can you guess who it is? Yes, it's Prince Ivo of Monrosa. Welcome to my podcast, Your Highness.'

'Thank you.' Her style was upbeat, intimately chatty, and he guessed well suited to her young audience. It left him dreading what was to come. He had to hand it to Kara. She was a master at picking her moments in persuading people to commit to things. Last night she had brought Gabriela to visit him in his apartment in the palace, on the pretence of discussing his role as Gabriela's godfather at her christening on Sunday. But as he held Gabriela, terrified but in awe of just how perfect every tiny detail of her was, Kara had asked him once again to take part in this podcast, arguing that people would be inspired by the struggles he had faced to achieve sporting success. For a while he had wavered, knowing he should provide more support to the charity, given that he hadn't been able to commit fully to his role as its ambassador in recent years as he'd built up the business and taken over his role as special advisor to the treasury, at Edwin's request. But then Kara had admitted that it would entail the interviewer, Toni Clarke, moving in with him for four days. The thought of being all alone with the beautiful Toni Clarke for four days had been a tempting proposition…but his home was his sanctuary. Sharing that with anyone was a step too far. He had been about to say no but then Gabriela had started to cry. And, as she paced his apartment with a fretful Gabriela, Kara had described her concern for Toni.

At Luis's wedding, Toni had been an exhausting, exuberant and excitable chatterbox. But when they had danced he had seen a different side to her. A more vulnerable, troubled side.

'Of course, this isn't the first time that we've met—as some of you know, my best friend is Alice O'Connor, who is married to Prince Luis. When they married, I was bridesmaid and Prince Ivo the best man.' She met his eyes, her cheeks growing warm. 'The wedding day was incredible, wasn't it? But we didn't get to spend much time getting acquainted.'

'No.'

She waited for him to say something else. But what was he supposed to say? That in fact when they had danced, thrown by her silence, he had attempted to make conversation with her and asked her if she was enjoying herself. She had answered, 'I'm trying to,' and her eyes had held such a sadness that he had without thought murmured, 'Everything will be okay.' He had followed her when she had bolted away. Horrified that he had somehow upset her. And when he had apologised out in the palace gardens, she had sobbed, soaking his shirtfront in the process. Not able to get any sense from her what the matter was and at a loss how to help her, he had simply held her until she said she needed to go and call her boyfriend. He hadn't realised that she was in a relationship given that she didn't have a partner attend the wedding with her.

'It was an emotional day. Gosh, I think I cried more in that one day than I did in my entire life. They were all tears of joy of course. Weddings are such moving affairs and Alice was such a beautiful bride.' Pausing to draw a deep breath as though to say that drew a line on what had happened between them at the wedding, she tilted her head to the side and continued, 'You're variously described as being the youngest of the three Monrosian Royal Princes and an international rower. But if you were to describe yourself, what would you say?'

See, it was questions like this that he hated. How was he supposed to answer it?

I keep to myself. I don't overthink things. I get on with life and I don't spend too much time navel-gazing.

'I like to work hard.'

'And outside of work?'

'I have my royal duties and in particular my advisory role to the Treasury.'

Shifting back in her chair, she frowned and silence fell between them. Raúl, the Director of Royal Communications, had attempted several times to counsel him on the art of interviews, but Ivo couldn't see what was wrong with a blunt approach. It avoided wasting time. He had zero interest in the personal lives of others, so he never understood why anyone would have an interest in his.

'Your company Pacolore Investments has become incredibly successful in a very short space of time. What do you think is behind that success?'

At last. A question he was comfortable answering. 'I set up Pacolore before I retired from rowing, so I had a clear view of what my business plan would be from the very start. But the key I believe to our success is that I recruit a wide diversity of people. I want people who think differently, who come from different backgrounds and life experiences. We see opportunities that other investment companies miss.'

'Where does that policy come from?'

He knew the odds stacked against those who operated outside the usual social norms and expectations. It was a bugbear of his that the confident talkers, those from a certain background, those who followed a conventional path in life were snapped up by employers. Those who were different left behind. Which was why he never followed the normal process of interviewing but instead made his recruitment decisions based on past performance and their completion of an online skills assessment. He judged people on their actual skills, not on how well they could sell themselves. 'I studied Financial Maths at university and after graduating I heard about how some of my brightest classmates didn't thrive in the more conventional investment firms—if they managed to get in the door, many didn't even get beyond the interview stage. I ran Pacolore for many years on my own while I rowed, investing my own money, making mistakes and learning from them. Through that work, I joined online investment discussion groups and I realised the wealth of talent out there…hugely intelligent and lateral-thinking people who just because of the fact that they didn't go to the right university or lived on the other side of the world, never got the opportunity to work in an investment firm. I was determined to recruit as diverse a group as possible. I like difference.'

Her expression intrigued, she asked, 'Why?'

'Because it is those who are different, who don't fit the mould, who often live on the periphery of groups and wider society, who are the true innovators and change makers.'

'Do you see yourself as being different?'

He heard it in her tone, the suggestion that he couldn't be different. How could a person born into such privilege, class themselves as being outside the norm? But in truth he had always felt separate from those around him. 'In ways.'

She waited for him to expand, her expression growing more quizzical but when she grew tired of waiting, she asked, 'Before university, where did you go to school? What was your childhood like?'

Confusing and lonely. Terrifying at times. Not that he'd admit that to anyone. 'I was sent to boarding school in England when I was ten.'

'Did you like it there?'

'I grew to like it.'

Her eyes took on a softness that made him shift in his seat. 'You went to boarding soon after your mother, Princess Cristina, died. It must have been a tough time for you.'

CHAPTER TWO

IVO PUSHED BACK in his chair. 'I don't remember a lot about that time.' He waited in dread for her to ask about his mother, to describe her, to talk about her death. It was well documented in the press that he was alone with her when she died. Would she ask him to recall that day and the nightmare that unravelled in the days that followed?

His father's initial shock at her death had almost instantly morphed into fury—he had raged against the stable staff, the bodyguards who hadn't accompanied them on the trek even though he knew his mother always insisted on trekking with the horses alone. Sick with guilt, unable to process what had happened, Ivo had tried to tell his father how he had begged her to go riding with him even though she had said she wasn't feeling well, how he panicked and ran for help when he should have stayed with her so that she didn't die alone, but his father had shut him down, too angry to listen. In his grief, Ivo had ached for the safety and comfort of his family but it was as though everything he knew and understood in his life had imploded. His family had changed out of all recognition. His father had been furious with the world, Edwin constantly preoccupied and trying to act like a buffer against that anger, while Luis had found refuge with his friends, disappearing from the palace for days on end. His mother had understood him, his innate quietness and need for time alone, but when she had died that understanding had disappeared from his life and, though he had so desperately wanted privacy to grieve, had wanted to keep a low profile throughout her state funeral, his father had insisted he play a central role in the proceedings. And as he faced the other mourners' stares he had wanted so desperately to cry himself but knew to do so would be unacceptable. To survive he had closed himself off not only from the outside world but also from his own family. And that detachment had become even more necessary when he had been thrown into the bewildering world of boarding school, where there was no escape from others, where the only way to survive was to single-mindedly pursue the challenge of getting onto the school's first rowing eight, where he had little time to think. Rowing had given his life structure…and the perfect excuse to avoid the emotional entanglement of friendships. The rowing team had accepted him, making no demands on him other than wanting his physical skills and unrelenting drive to win. They never questioned his silence. Unlike his own family, who could never hide their bafflement and disappointment with him. He never measured up to what they thought he should be. They never accepted that he had little interest in socialising, in indulging in small talk and that he abhorred being in the limelight.

But instead of asking any further questions Toni pointed to the microphone and said, 'I need you to stay close to the mike. I should have explained that before we started. And don't worry about any of these asides, I can edit them out…and of course I will edit out any questions or answers you aren't happy with. This is your podcast… I won't release anything you or the Palace aren't happy with.' Pausing, she gave him a quick smile before asking, 'What are your ambitions for the future?'

Her change of tack away from the topic of his mother and childhood was deliberate. Why had she done that? A lifetime of knowing people wished you to be different had made him wary of what lay behind even the most innocuous of actions. His father's bribes and threats when he spent too long in his bedroom. The summer camps he had been forced to attend, the camp leaders watching his every move, no doubt under instruction to do so by his father. Edwin's poorly disguised suggestions that he socialise more. Luis's visits to him at university and later on at rowing training camps, insisting they go to the most crowded and noisiest bars and clubs in town. Luis, who thrived on chaos, could never fathom his preference for more private bars and restaurants. 'For the immediate future I want to embed Pacolore's success.'

'You don't want to expand the business?'

'Perhaps, but now isn't the time.'

'I had thought, given how successful you have been, you'd be keen to have the business grow. Are you a risk-taker or cautious by nature?'

'I'm a calculated risk-taker. And rapid growth isn't my motivator.'

'What is?'

'Obviously a certain level of financial gain is paramount, but it's the analysis, reading the markets and making the right call that gives me the greatest buzz. I like seeing my team thrive and develop.'

She nodded several times as though considering his answer, before she asked, 'And what are your ambitions for your private life?'

'In what sense?'

For a moment, a shadow of annoyance flittered in her eyes. If she was hoping for a free-flowing conversation she was interviewing the wrong person. With a shrug, as though it weren't a significant question and she didn't particularly care what his answer would be, she asked, 'Do you want to marry? Have children?'

'I have no plans to do so.'

'Are you in a relationship now?'

He had dated in the past, but it never worked out. He wasn't blind to the fact that women were attracted to him because they thought he offered a world of glamour and success. But few were prepared to accept the reality. That he worked as hard as he had trained as a rower, that he had no interest in partying or having a high profile. He inhaled a deep breath, now irritated with this questioning. 'No, I'm not in a relationship.' He glanced out into the main office. All of the others had left for the weekend. They were now alone. And would be until Sunday when they travelled to Gabriela's christening. He really did not know if he could do this.

'Why have you agreed to this interview?' The tone of her question was curious but, meeting her gaze, he saw uncertainty and doubt. She leant towards him, resting an arm on the desk, her eyes taking on a soft gentleness as though imploring him to trust her.

'To support Kara and her work with YA Together. I am a goodwill ambassador for the charity but, due to my work in recent years, I've not been able to work as closely with the charity as I would have liked. This interview is part of my contribution to make up for that.' He hadn't needed the tiredness in Kara's eyes last night or the short and pointed phone call from Edwin today to know that Kara needed extra support now that Gabriela had arrived. He knew how important the charity was to Kara and though he was a reluctant participant he could see how impactful and wide-reaching this podcast could be.

She frowned, as though uncertain what her next question would be. 'Have you ever personally had mental health issues?'

He knew the answer he should give—the one he had settled on overnight, knowing that the issue would eventually come up. But something about the softness of her voice, the gentle enquiry in her eyes, stole his answer away. And for the briefest of moments he was tempted to admit how separate he felt from the world…until good sense and the need to protect himself kicked back in. 'Being an athlete is as much about psychological strength as it is physical. There have been times when I've struggled with injuries, been dropped from the team and of course lost races. I have learnt to accept where I am at the moment, not project negativity into the future, and try to be content with what I have already achieved.'

Her nose wrinkled as though she was trying to unpack his answer…which even he had to admit was more ambiguous than he had intended. 'Where's your happy place…where do you feel most at home?'

'I own a *finca* in the north of the island. I spend as much of my free time there as is possible.' The last time he had brought someone to stay at the *finca* it had been an ex-girlfriend who had been unable to conceal her horror at its simple structure and remoteness. Was the same thing going to happen this weekend with Toni? Would she judge and criticise the life that made him happy? He picked up his phone. 'I have calls I have to make before we leave.'

This was a disaster. She wasn't getting to know him. Yes, it was only the first interview but the flow was all wrong. Her questions were meandering and without focus. And even without listening back to the recording she knew that they sounded both stiff and uptight. She needed to inject some fun into the interview. Break down some of the tension between them.

She grabbed her notebook from the laptop bag and opened it to the list of questions that she had decided to keep in her back pocket in case any interview went as pear-shaped as this one was going.

'Of course. I'll leave you to your calls but first can I ask you to take part in a rapid-fire interview quiz?'

'Why?'

She needed to counteract his wariness with a healthy dose of enthusiasm. 'Because it will be fun!'

His gaze narrowed. 'Only if I can ask you a round of questions too.'

Why would he want to do that? She couldn't say no…but the feeling of not being in control of this interview escalated at the prospect. 'No problem. Do you want to share my list?'

'No, I'll think of my own.'

'Okay…this will be interesting. I'll start first. Apple or orange?'

He folded his arms, as though to say *Seriously…? Is this the level of interview you are going to subject me to?*

She winced, waiting for him to call a halt to the interview. But, raising one of those thick, straight eyebrows that emphasised the hard, masculine intensity of his face, he answered, 'Orange.'

'What couldn't you live without?'

'My dogs.'

He had dogs. She smiled warmly. 'Ah, how sweet!' She wanted to ask more about them but this was supposed to be a quick-fire session. 'When was the last time that you lied?'

'Last night.'

Her heart sank. *Please don't have hurt someone.*

'What happened?'

'I said that I was okay with Princess Gabriela spewing on my shirt.'

She laughed in relief. 'I haven't seen her yet. Is she as gorgeous as she is in the photos?'

'Even more so.'

Her heart kicked at the tenderness in his voice… maybe he did have a soft side after all. And for a moment he held her gaze and she was transported back to Alice's wedding when they had danced together. The gentleness, the empathy in his voice, when he had asked her if she was enjoying herself, the way he held her gaze, not looking away, had jolted her into realising that Dan never looked at her that way any more. And everything she had been trying to deny, her loneliness, how unattractive she felt, how she didn't know herself any more, had all collided and she had ended up uncontrollably sobbing in his arms. She looked down at her list of questions, found the next one. 'What irritates you?'

'People who do not accept or respect other people's choices.'

She studied him, but the tightening of his mouth told her not to follow up what he meant by that… not yet at least. 'Your most embarrassing moment?'

'Catching a crab while competing in the world junior championships and ending up in the water.'

She frowned. 'An actual crab made you fall out of the boat?'

He stared at her and then the most wonderful smile played on his lips. 'No, it's the expression used in rowing when the oar blade gets caught in the water.'

'Oh.' She rolled her eyes. And was rewarded with the pleasure of seeing soft amusement glisten in his eyes. 'Beer or wine?'

'Wine.'

'Do you have a motto?'

'No.'

'If you did, what would it be?'

He rolled his neck, considering this. 'I guess... be true to yourself.'

'Have you ever been heartbroken?'

He rubbed his hand along his jaw, shrugged. 'Upset...' he paused, his eyes holding hers, his voice dropping a notch '...but not heartbroken.'

She was glad. For his sake. 'What makes you happy?'

'Walking with my dogs late at night in the olive groves surrounding my *finca*.'

'Why?'

'I don't know... I guess the silence there and the fact that there are no expectations or pressure on me at that time.'

Was he talking about the pressures of work, or those that came from his royal duties? There was so much more she wanted to ask him, but she knew she had to bide her time. Ivo was the most reluctant interviewee she had ever had. She needed to build his trust in her. She needed to be patient. He was deep and complicated, a man you might never fully know. She shut her notebook. 'That's all my questions—now it's your turn.'

He nodded, frowning in thought before he asked, 'Pear or pineapple?'

'Pear to eat, pineapple in a cocktail.'

'Town or country?'

'Definitely town.'

He shrugged at her answer as though he had expected as much. 'What one word would you use to describe yourself?'

'Curious.'

'Olive oil drizzled on ice cream—yes or no?'

She pretend-gagged. 'Definitely no—is that even a thing?'

'You haven't even tried it? I'll make it for you this weekend.' Ignoring her look of horror, he continued, 'Cocktails on the beach or hiking in the mountains?'

'That's an easy one—cocktails on the beach.'

There it was again, that shrug that said she wasn't surprising him. Did he disapprove of any form of slacking? What did she expect—he was an ex-international athlete and now an investment manager. That profile wouldn't exactly suggest someone who could chill out easily. Did he enjoy life? Party? Find ways to escape from reality for a while?

'What second word would you use to describe yourself?'

Without thinking she answered, 'Thin-skinned.'

She gave a laugh, trying to pretend she was kid-

ding, but Ivo didn't even crack a smile in return. Instead he asked, 'What do you like about yourself?'

What did she like about herself? She went to say
something glib, like her hair, but then he smiled, an
unexpected and gently encouraging smile, and she
heard herself say, 'I do keep trying…even when I
don't want to.'

Well, that probably made no sense to him…but
it made sense to her. After Dan had split with her,
some of her ex-colleagues, awkward with the whole
situation between herself and Dan, had distanced
themselves from her. In the end she had decided to
search for another job, the awkwardness with her
colleagues and having to face Dan every day proving too stressful.

But she had picked herself up and got on with life.
That had to count for something, didn't it?

To her amazement he smiled. Her heart danced
to see his grin. 'I like determination in a person.'

Her belly flipped at the soft intimacy in his voice.
'I hope you're still saying that in four days' time… I
really want to get to know you.' Pausing, she knew
she should clarify what she meant by that for the
sake of the listeners, but a charge, an intimacy, ran
between them at her words.

He lifted an eyebrow. And her heart slammed to
a stop, this almost playful, teasing side to him even
more disarming than his usual reserved demeanour.
'Dinner with friends or dinner for two?'

'I guess dinner for two can be special…depend-
ing on who it's with, of course.'

Oh, God. She wasn't supposed to be flirting with him.

He considered her answer, a glint of what possibly might be amusement in his eyes again. Whether he was laughing with her or at her was, of course, debatable.

'What do you fear the most?'

Being too scared to do the right thing to protect myself...like how I should have ended my relationship with Dan long before he left. How I should have ended all contact with my dad much earlier than I did, knowing his unpredictability, how he came in and out of my life to suit himself, was damaging me. It wasn't only my mum who time and time again fell for his apologies. I would ignore all the evidence of the past—how he would turn up on our doorstep after months of little or no contact—and instead cling to the hope that this time he would stay. That finally we would be a family, that the sparkle in Mum's eye would last for ever. She was unable to resist him. She would go through a ritual of pretending not to want anything to do with him, but even as a child I saw the chemistry between them that skewed my mum's judgement so terribly.

She had learned from her father that love was unreliable, commitment only a word, but her biggest fear was that she had inherited her mum's lack of judgement and ability to protect herself. She *had* to be tougher. Less emotional. She needed to move through life with a more cautious but less invested approach to relationships. She needed to wear relationships lightly—enjoy them but not get emotionally involved.

But there was no way she was admitting any of that to him. So instead she answered, 'The possibility of being forced to eat olive oil ice cream this weekend. Talking of which, I will be staying with you until Tuesday morning. What do you have planned for the weekend? Of course, we have Princess Gabriela's christening on Sunday, which I'm very much looking forward to. But am I going to experience Monrosa's nightlife again? Regular listeners will know I'm a huge fan of the local cocktail, Paradise City, which I got to try when I was here for Alice's wedding.'

'There isn't any nightlife where we're going.'

What on earth did he mean? There were numerous exclusive bars and clubs suitable for a royal close to the palace. 'Aren't we staying at the palace?'

'No. We're staying in my *finca*, San Jorbo.'

She tried not to look shocked. This wasn't how she saw the weekend panning out. Should she protest? But on what grounds? She was his guest. She had to fall in line with his plans. Even if it was away from the assurance of knowing Kara and Alice would be near by. 'Great, it will be wonderful to see more of Monrosa, and I have heard that the towns and villages in the north are stunning.' Flicking off the recording, she disconnected the microphones. 'So, your *finca*—what town is it close to…and will there be others staying there too?'

'There's a town on the opposite side of the harbour, and we'll be alone.'

She stopped packing her bag. 'How about your security team?'

'They patrol the area but don't worry, they won't disturb any of the interviews.'

That was not what she was worried about…and, though his expression was deadpan, she was certain he knew that. All alone for four days with him…what was she walking into? Would she somehow overcome just how unsettled he made her feel? Would she ever manage to get him to relax and have the spontaneous and free-flowing conversations that she wanted to give to the listener? And what about the sparks of attraction between them…were they even real or just in her imagination…but if they were real, what on earth was going to happen when they were all alone?

'If you'd prefer to stay in the palace, that can be arranged. We can talk again on Sunday when I'm there for the christening. With today's interview and a longer one again on Sunday I'm sure there will be enough material for a podcast. In fact, you can send me your list of questions tomorrow and I can prepare in advance.'

She winced at the enthusiasm in his tone. She obviously wasn't the only one not relishing the prospect of four days together. She plastered on a smile. 'That's not how these podcasts work. I have to spend time with you.' She stopped and cringed. That sounded all wrong…it sounded as though she was contemplating a prison sentence rather than it being the part of her job she usually loved the most—having the privilege to peek into another person's life and really connect with them on a deep level. She was still in contact with all of her ex-interviewees. Somehow she got the feeling that that might not be the case with Ivo.

Even though she was standing, Ivo remained seated, studying her closely, which was only making her even more jittery than she already was.

'I know things have been tough for you. Stay in the palace. Spend some time with Alice and Kara.'

She zipped the bag closed, shame keeping her eyes averted from him. Oh, God, he obviously somehow knew about Dan's wedding. Did he pity her? The whole thing was embarrassing enough…and now she had the man who was nicknamed *The Machine* feeling sorry for her. 'Make your phone calls and I'll go and get myself a Paradise City in the nearest cocktail bar. Come find me when you're ready to leave. I'll treat you to a Friday night drink before we disappear into the wilderness.'

She walked away, knowing she was leaving one unimpressed prince behind her. She knew she was being glib and perhaps even a little disrespectful, but the thought of four days alone with him was making her irritable…and a whole lot nervous. And when she was like that she needed noise and activity and as many distractions as she could find.

CHAPTER THREE

THE SUV THAT had trailed them all the way from Monrosa city didn't follow them past the heavy wooden gates and security lodge that marked the entrance of Ivo's *finca*, San Jorbo. But what did follow them were two wildly yapping dogs, who only calmed when Ivo drew his car to a stop and opened his door. A little grey-haired terrier was the first to jump in, but he was swiftly shunted across the car and onto her lap by a much larger dog who vaulted himself onto Ivo. She patted the terrier gingerly, praying the short-haired monster on Ivo's lap wouldn't decide to spring across to say hello to her too.

Ivo murmured in low Spanish to the dogs, stroking them both, his arm inadvertently brushing against her chest in the process as he stroked the terrier on her lap…and she liked the press and warmth of his bicep a little too much for her own good. She was tempted to leap out of the low-slung car. Give up her space to the two dogs, who were getting more of his attention than she had received for their entire fortyminute journey here. Okay, so maybe some of it was her own fault…she should have realised that she had misplaced her phone much earlier. They, and Ivo's security, who had been stationed behind his sports car in their SUV when they had left the cocktail bar, had had to turn around fifteen minutes into their journey north in order to search for her missing phone.

She had hoped their journey would be relaxed and an opportunity for them to get to know each other a little better, but he had answered her questions in his direct, unembellished way and that had been as far as their conversation had gone. The silence had been awkward and she had found herself running a one-sided stream of observations on the mountainous landscape they had passed through. But there were only so many times that you could ooh and aah over the spectacular views of the coast from the narrow mountain road, the towering pines and eucalyptus trees clinging to the craggy, sun-bleached terracotta earth or the narrow laneways of the whitewashed villages they had passed through, locals sitting on terraces in the evening sun, nodding their heads in respect as they spotted Ivo's convoy pass by. She had eventually run out of steam and, reluctantly giving in to his silence, she had wound down her window and allowed the scent of the mountain forests in. And after a while her whirling mind had stopped racing, the wind blowing against her hair, the ancient beauty of the landscape that looked as though it hadn't changed in thousands of years, and Ivo's assured and calm driving skills even on the endless hairpin turns allowing her the first moment of calm in a week she'd rather forget.

But now she was firmly back in the reality of knowing that she had a job to do. On his command both dogs hopped into the rear seat of the car, which was barely big enough to contain them both. Reaching for her phone, which she had eventually located under the cushion of a seat in the outdoor terrace of the bar, she asked, 'Is it okay if I record our arrival at the house? I always ask my interviewees to give me a guided tour of their house so that the listeners can get a sense of what their homes are like.'

Ivo eyed her phone wearily.

'A quick tour is all I need,' she added by way of encouragement.

His answer was a curt nod.

She opened the recording app and pressed play. 'So, we've now arrived at Ivo's *finca*. The surrounding countryside is mountainous and we are approaching the house along a steep driveway in a valley that runs down to the sea, terraces of olive trees on either side of the drive. And we got a surprise welcome when we entered Ivo's property—his two dogs came to say hello and are now excitedly sitting in the back seat of the car.' Turning, she pointed the phone at them, 'Say hello, doggies.' She giggled when both dogs barked in response. Ivo even cracked a smile.

'What are their names?'

'Paco and Lore.'

She laughed. 'Which came first, the business or the dogs?'

He drew the car to a stop at the side entrance of a traditional single-storey sandstone *finca*, topped with a terracotta roof. He looked back at the dogs, and despite his smile she could see worry in his eyes. 'Paco is twelve years old. I adopted him five years ago when I was living in Seville. And soon after I adopted Lore. I'm not sure of her exact age, somewhere around fifteen.'

He was worried about losing them. Something solid lodged in her throat as he climbed out of the car and pulled his seat forward, both dogs bounding out to receive even more vigorous rubs from him, Ivo's eyes twinkling in delight. His bond with his dogs transformed him...lightened him.

Stepping out of the car, she held her phone out, wanting to record the cicadas in full song, and wondered if she would manage to capture the crash of the waves on the shoreline below them for her listeners too.

'I'll show you to your room.'

Had he forgotten his promise to show her around? She doubted it. 'Are all of these olive trees yours? They seem to stretch on for ever.'

He nodded. 'There are over five hundred trees in total.'

'That's a lot of olives for one person to eat.'

He raised an eyebrow at her feigned innocence. 'My neighbouring farmers harvest them. I get some olive oil in return.'

'You don't keep it all for yourself?'

He shrugged. 'They do the work. Life is not easy

for olive producers on the island, so they need as much support as they can get.'

Unable to help herself, she walked to a nearby tree, placing a hand against the warm, gnarled trunk. 'The earth here seems so parched, it's miraculous that they survive.'

'Some are over three hundred years old.'

Her attention caught by a group of different trees, she moved towards them. 'And you have lemon and fig trees too.' Wandering up some steps to a flat terrace, she added, 'And a vegetable garden. Do you have many staff working for you…a housekeeper, a gardener?' He had said they would be alone, but maybe he hadn't factored domestic staff into that equation.

Standing on the steps, the fading evening sun creating a long shadow of him on the dry earth, he answered with a hint of wariness, as though he didn't trust her reasons for asking the question, 'I have a housekeeper who comes in during the week. I take care of the garden myself.'

'Wow, really?' Her only attempt at gardening was a tomato plant on the windowsill of her apartment kitchen…she hadn't realised that too much watering wasn't a good thing. Moving further into the plot, she said, 'There are chillies, peppers, cucumbers, broad beans…' she reached across and from a vine plucked a glossy red tomato, adding, 'and an endless supply of tomatoes. And now I'm going to try one.' Biting into it, she sighed at the warm sweetness of the fruit before turning in Ivo's direction. 'Wow, that tastes amazing.'

He didn't smile. It was as though he was trying to figure her out.

And she hadn't ever thought of him as someone who would garden. 'I didn't think you'd have the time to garden...or the interest.'

His expression tightened for a moment before he gestured to the miles of coastline in either direction of the *finca*. 'I need to be self-sufficient here.'

Following him back along a path that ran around the house, she shielded her eyes when they arrived back at the entrance of the house, the westerly sun dipping lower and lower. In the far distance she could just about make out a cluster of houses set low in the mountainous coastline, boats in the harbour below the town. 'Is that the nearest town?'

'Yes. Laredo.'

'Wow. You really are isolated here.'

'Yes, and I like it that way.' His tone carried an impatience and, not waiting for a response, he opened the door to the *finca* that was painted in the same pale blue as the open shutters on the windows.

She rushed after him, conscious to keep their dialogue going for the sake of her listeners. Inside, the entrance hallway was cool in comparison to the intense heat out on the terrace, shafts of sunlight falling on the stone floors. 'How often do you stay here?'

'Four or five nights a week.'

Stopping to study the bright oil paintings hanging on the whitewashed walls, she asked, 'Why did you choose to live here in particular?' The *finca* was small. A fraction of the size of the palace apartments.

'It suits me perfectly—I live alone and don't need or want a lot of living space. It's the outdoors that is important here.'

She followed as he walked away and into an open-plan kitchen and living room, embarrassed that her surprise at the *finca*'s size had shown through. Opening the terrace doors in front of a slightly faded yellow corner sofa, he stepped out onto a covered terrace, heavy with trailing vines, and pointed towards the Mediterranean. 'I bought San Jorbo for the views and access to the sea. I like to swim and sail.'

Joining him on a patch of grass beyond the covered terrace, she saw that a path ran from the terrace down to the sea. Standing on tiptoe, she could see golden sand at the bottom of the path. 'You have your own beach…that's incredible. And is that your boat tied up at the dock?'

Bending over to straighten a pot that had tiny buds poking up from the soil, he patted the earth gently before finding a more sheltered spot for it amongst a cluster of other growing pots that were bunched together along the length of the low garden wall. 'It's a ten-minute journey over to Laredo by boat but a thirty-minute drive. The car has to negotiate the mountain roads between here and Laredo.'

Crouching down, he began to pluck some weeds from the pots, the gentleness of his movements so at odds with his size. His shirt strained across his back, the muscles beneath working as he reached and pulled. The sun caught dark copper tones in his hair and the very odd temptation to rest her hand on his shoulder grew in her. His silence moved something in her. He was as remote as his home was. In past interviews, recording the tour of the house had been fun and insightful...but with Ivo it just felt all wrong. Moving to sit on the wall near to where he was crouched, she closed down the recording app and placed her phone on the wall. 'I think we've covered enough for today—we can record more tomorrow.'

He paused in his work and they stared at each other for long moments, her heart pounding. She wanted to know him, she wanted to reach him. And not for the sake of the podcasts. She swallowed, realising it was because she recognised a vulnerability in him beneath all of that solid silence that at first she had mistaken for uncompromising self-confidence.

'I was brought up in London. I've never been to anywhere so remote...' She paused, the fear that she was falling into the old trap of oversharing making her hesitate for a moment before she admitted, 'I reckon there would be way too much thinking time here for me.'

Moving to sit beside her, their backs to the sea, he leant forward, his arms resting on his thighs, tilting his head to meet her gaze before staring towards the *finca*. 'You don't have to stay here.'

His tone was gentle...as though he was freeing her of an obligation. She went to speak but before she could he added, his hand gesturing towards the *finca*, 'The accommodation is basic. I like it that way. But I accept it's not to everyone's taste.'

She studied the pale stone and blue shutters of the house, the gardens beyond that a little wild but utterly in keeping with the surroundings. It was all a far cry from the glamour of the royal palace but Ivo's *finca* had a soothing stillness that somehow was already seeping into her bones. 'You have a beautiful home. I would like to stay…if that's okay with you.'

'Because of the podcast?'

The easy and perhaps right thing would be to say yes. To not expose herself. In past podcasts she had revealed few details of her own personal life, not needing to, as her interviewees had all been forthright and comfortable with sharing their lives, but with Ivo she had to do things differently to reach him…and every instinct told her it had to be by being brutally honest about herself. Even if it flew in the face of her pledge to protect herself by being more closed. 'For the podcast…but for myself too. It might do me good. This week has been difficult…seeing the photos of my ex marrying…it has brought back memories I'd have preferred not to think about.'

She dropped her head, embarrassed at how exposed she felt to admit that to him, and waited for him to ask her for more details, but instead he said, 'I think you're right. Time here might help you. San Jorbo is a place of healing.'

Really? Ivo calling his home healing had to be up there as one of the most unexpected things she had ever heard. Yes, she had briefly glimpsed a softer,

more compassionate side to him at the wedding...
but she hadn't been certain if that had been a temporary glitch in his usual aloof demeanour. She studied him, but he would not meet her gaze. And she
got the distinct impression that he was annoyed with
himself for what he had just said. 'Does it heal you?'

He shrugged. 'I enjoy having time alone to think.
There's too much noise in the world. Silence is un-
derrated.'

She wished she could agree with him, but the
thought of staying here all on her own for days on
end would panic her. She didn't think she would
cope. She'd desperately miss chatting to people. 'Do
you know, I've just realised that I've never actually
lived on my own?'

His eyebrows shot up. 'Never?'

Oh, crikey...he *really* was handsome. Of course,
she had recognised it at Alice's wedding, had felt
flustered around him in fact, but she had compart-
mentalised it away because she was with Dan. She
jumped up from the wall and tried to gather herself
as she bent to pat Paco and Lore, who were lying in
the shade. 'I know that sounds strange, now that I say
it...but I've always lived with people. I moved in with
my ex while we were still at university. And when
we separated I moved home for a while...but now I
flat-share. My mum and I get on...but we drove each
other crazy when I moved back in with her. She reckons I'm too messy.' She came to a stop. Ivo did not
need to know about how perpetually disorganised
she was. Time to get the conversation back to him.

'So, what do you do apart from gardening, swimming and sailing when you are here?'

Stretching his legs out in front of him, he asked, 'How long were you with your ex?'

'Ten years.'

She saw his wince. And wasn't surprised. It was how most people reacted. And what usually followed was pity. She braced herself for Ivo to say something similar.

'Are you still in love with him?'

Taken aback by the bluntness of his question and the intense way he was staring at her, she garbled out, 'I'm not still in love with him but I miss him being around... We were good friends.'

He stood, his broadness making him look even taller than his six-foot-two height. He approached her, those grey eyes holding hers all the while. She swallowed.

'Friends don't hurt you the way he did.'

'Our relationship changed...that wasn't his fault.'

'And it wasn't yours.'

'I'm not saying that...'

'You deserved better, Toni. You didn't deserve him walking out on you after ten years without explanation...or the fact that he started dating someone else a week later. You didn't deserve him marrying in secret and not having the decency to tell you.'

She took a step back. 'How do you know all of that? Alice?'

He didn't answer except for the minute movement of one shoulder.

'No…then it had to be Kara.' She made an exasperated sound. 'Why did she tell you?' She held out her hand to stop him answering her question, even though he looked as though he had no intention of doing so. 'Don't tell me…so that you would do the podcast. I don't need your pity.'

He folded his arms. 'Good. Because you won't be getting it.'

How was she supposed to react to that? 'Yes… well… I'm glad to hear that.'

Cool as you like, he walked away, saying, 'I'll show you to your room. And then I'll prepare dinner while you go for a swim.'

She chased after him. 'I'll help you.'

He didn't respond and, picking up her suitcase in the hallway, he led her past a large study and then went into the next room along the corridor. He dropped her case by the double bed and turned to her. His expression was determined. 'Go for a swim.'

He studied the closing stock prices in New York and banged out an email to his North America team, inhaling deeply in a bid to concentrate and not give in to the temptation of staring out once again at Toni's black and silver bikini hanging from the branch of an olive tree. After her swim earlier she had entered the *finca* with a towel wrapped around her, her wet hair piled on top of her head. Stationed at the kitchen counter chopping peppers, he had almost taken off a finger, knowing that beneath the towel she was naked.

Paco, collapsed on the studio couch as usual, Lore tucked into a pillow beside him, lifted his head and made a throaty growl. And then he heard footsteps in the hallway.

'Hi, there you are. I was wondering where you had got to.'

He stood.

She stayed in the doorway, her bare feet at odds with her above-the-knee turquoise pencil dress. She looked great. He hadn't dated in months. Was that why he constantly found himself staring at her? Over dinner he had watched her tussle with a bread roll and they had both ended up laughing as she had frantically tried to clean the table of the confetti of breadcrumbs she had created by pulling the roll apart a little too eagerly. Their shared laughter had eased some of the tension between them and they had spent the dinner with him answering her questions on Monrosa's history and geography. He had even ended up drawing her a rough map of the island, highlighting Monrosa's hidden secrets she should some time visit.

'Alice said to say hello.'

She had spent at least an hour on the phone…even though she had said she'd be five minutes when she had excused herself after dinner to call her mother and Alice.

'Alice and Luis are going to a party in the city tomorrow night—she asked if we'd like to join them.'

He had learnt years ago that being direct and shutting down any expectations head on was the most effective way to deal with other people's judgement. 'I don't like parties. But I can arrange for a car to take you.'

As though she thought he was joking she laughed and asked, 'Is that just an excuse not to have to go with me? I know I chat too much and ask way too many questions, it's my nervous tic—and habit from my former career as an associate producer—but I promise to try to stop.'

'Are you nervous of me?'

Her eyes widened. 'Kind of...' but then, any hint of jumpiness disappearing, a playful smile grew on her lips. 'You are pretty formidable...and I'm guessing that it's an image you like to maintain...the untouchable Machine.'

Now it was his turn to laugh. Since he had left the world of rowing, where bluntness was part and parcel of a winning attitude, he had lived in a world where people constantly deferred to him. 'I'll admit that in some areas of my life I can be really formidable...' He trailed off, grinning as Toni's eyes widened even further and heat crept into her cheeks.

'You still haven't answered my question. Why won't you come to the party?'

'Small talk bores me.'

She gave him a curious look but then her gaze moved over to the table behind him, settling on his painting equipment.

'You paint?'

All through his childhood it was only his mother who had encouraged his painting, his love for creating. Meanwhile his father had said that he should be outdoors, doing something worthwhile. And in school his rowing team had teased him over it, calling him Rembrandt. He had stopped painting then, hating the attention and how different he had felt from his teammates. Hating that no one seemed to understand the comfort it brought to him. No one knew he was painting again. 'I was just about to take the dogs for a walk.'

She went and lifted the sheet of rice paper he had been working on last night, studying the monochrome painting of the chilli. 'This is beautiful... Where did you learn to paint like this?'

'A few years ago I saw an exhibition of Chinese ink painting in New York and I decided to try it.'

'Can I have a go?'

Thrown by her enthusiasm, he hesitated. Painting was his escape, a fundamental and deeply personal part of his life that he didn't want to share with anyone. After his mother had died he had found solace in painting toy soldiers, the precision and concentration required quietening his mind, until his father had sent him away to boarding school. When he had returned home after his first term, all of his paints had been binned, his father telling him he was not allowed to spend time alone in his room any more.

'The ink can't be washed out.' He nodded towards her dress. 'It may damage your clothes.'

Smoothing her hand over the material of her dress, she rolled her eyes. 'I guess I should explain why I'm so formally dressed—I packed thinking I was staying in the palace. I didn't think to pack anything casual.' Lowering his painting to the table, she added quietly, 'I would really like to give painting a go… I'll be careful with the ink.'

He searched her eyes, trying to understand why she was so keen, but all he could find was a gentle eagerness. 'I'll go and find something for you to wear over your clothes.'

When he returned to the studio, she studied the embroidered logo on the white T-shirt he passed to her. 'You must be very proud to have represented your country in sport.'

He watched her slip on the T-shirt, smiled as it engulfed her, reaching almost as far as the hem of her skirt. 'It meant a lot to the people of Monrosa— we had never won an international medal before.'

He pulled an extra chair to the table. They both sat and he lifted out the paint caddy, brush stand and two fresh sheets of paper.

'Do you miss rowing?'

'Not particularly. The training and travelling were gruelling. My life was a constant round of aeroplanes, training camps and hotel rooms.'

Her gaze moved out beyond the open terrace doors of the studio, the outline of the olive trees and the mountains visible thanks to a full moon. 'It must have been strange shifting from that world to this.'

He patted the fine goat hair of a brush clean. 'I slotted in straight away. This way of life suits me much better.'

'Why didn't you change careers sooner?'

He had thought about it endless times during his rowing career, particularly after their first failed international bid. Frustrated by injuries, exhausted by the constant change, he had questioned his commitment to the sport but ultimately he had loved the focus, the silent bond with his team, the hypnotic pull of the oar on the water as the sun slowly rose in the east. 'I wanted to win gold.'

'For yourself?'

'And others.' He had wanted to prove to his father and his brothers that there was more to him than the silent younger brother who so clearly puzzled them.

Moving the brush stand towards her, he said, 'Explore the different brushes.' Pausing, he placed a small amount of ink onto the ink tray. 'Lightly dip your brush into the ink and create shapes on the paper.' He demonstrated some brushstrokes, using three different brushes, showing her how different pressure created shadows.

They worked in silence, the roll of the sea on the rocks below the *finca* and Paco's restless movements on the sofa the only sounds. He waited for her to speak but instead she focused on her brush strokes, swirling patterns filling her paper. He drew out another blank sheet of paper from the cupboard, fetched a sculpture of a tern from the bookshelf. With his hand hovering over the sculpture he talked to her about the flowing shapes of the bird, moving his hand over to the paper to illustrate how she could capture its shape by curving the lines and playing with the space between them.

Her nose wrinkled unhappily with her first line that was to capture the curve of the tern from its head down to its proud, elongated tail.

Placing his hand on hers, he said, 'Have confidence, hold the brush more freely, feel the curves, don't think...just feel.'

He guided her hand, creating the breast of the bird and then the beak.

And when he drew back, he got why she looked away from him. Something unnerving was beating between them.

'Toni...'

She turned, those huge brown eyes troubled but also unable to hide the same spark of attraction that was in him.

'This is all...' He breathed deeply, hating how inarticulate he was.

She waited for him to speak but eventually said, 'Complicated... I know,' she dipped her head, her fingers running over the handmade rice paper, 'I'm here to do my job, but please know that when we're not recording the interview...everything is off the record. I hope you can trust me on that.'

He resisted the temptation to laugh and tell her that he hadn't truly trusted anyone for decades. Always attuned to other people's judgements, always knowing that when push came to shove people would always serve their own interests over his. He should call it a night on the painting and go and walk the dogs, but for reasons he didn't fully understand he wanted to turn the tables and see just how much Toni trusted him. He knew of some of her background, thanks to overhearing conversations between Kara and Alice, but would Toni share her past with him? 'You said that you used to be an associate producer, so why are you now doing podcasts?'

She grimaced at his question, running a hand over her cheek and back over her hair, which was tied back into a ponytail. 'When Dan broke it off with me, I left the production company we both worked for, as it was too awkward to stay working together. I became a freelancer working for a podcast advertising firm—I still work with them occasionally. Part of my job was researching podcast content and advising clients on their appropriateness as an advertising platform.' With a sigh she continued, 'Personally I wasn't in a good place. I felt overwhelmed by how my life had changed so utterly. But listening to podcasts, often when I went for long walks, really helped. I loved their immediacy… I'm naturally curious about people, not in a nosy way, but I love hearing their stories. Giving them a voice. There's so much power in sharing our stories. We can make the world a better place by connecting…' she held his gaze for long seconds '…in wanting to understand one another.' For a moment she paused and frowned before giving a disbelieving laugh. 'I say all that but sometimes I battle with the fact that I have a tendency to overshare. I'm a born chatterbox. My mum used to have to ask me to stop talking when I was a child. I was a nightmare at school. I know it has its downsides, oversharing, and believe it or not

I'm trying not to be so open...but admittedly I'm not doing a particularly good job right now, telling you all of this.'

They stared at each other for long moments, the air in the room vanishing, his heart beating faster. It would be so easy to reach out and touch her hand, move even closer towards her. 'I'm sorry he hurt you.'

She nodded, her slow, grateful smile catching his heart. 'When Dan left me, it felt like I had been hit by a truck. I suppose, like any relationship, ours had changed over the years, but we were friends. We made each other laugh. One night after he had left me I couldn't sleep, so I went for a walk. I listened to a podcast given by a singer who spoke about her marriage ending and she said that she had been too scared to end the marriage herself, even though she knew it wasn't right for her.' She picked up one of the paintbrushes, idly drawing a circle onto the page, its circumference growing wider and wider. Not breaking her attention from the drawing, she added in a low voice, 'And I realised I had been too scared to even contemplate leaving Dan, never mind doing it... even though I knew deep down I wasn't truly happy.'

'Why were you scared?'

'It meant stepping into the unknown.' She put down the brush. 'I like to feel secure...the unknown scares me.'

Dio! She disarmed him. Her beauty, her forthrightness, the endless unnerving chemistry between them. He needed to be blunt...he had no idea what the next few days would bring, but he knew he had to make sure Toni knew exactly what she could expect from him. 'I'm not good at relationships. I like being independent, living on my own.'

Again she shrugged. 'Given that I don't think I'll ever have the courage to trust someone again, I'm trying to embrace independence too.' Her attempt at a smile did little to cover her vulnerability.

Without thinking he placed his arm around her shoulders, pulling her towards him, and placed a kiss against her hair.

Just as quickly he pulled away. He stood up. What was he doing? He should be keeping all of this strictly professional...otherwise the boundaries between them would become a tangled mess. 'There will be fireworks in Laredo later—it's the *feria* week in the town. I need to walk Paco and Lore before the fireworks start.'

She twisted in her seat. 'I'll join you.'

He shook his head. Needing distance. 'Stay and paint.' He turned away from her disappointment, alarm bells that he was lowering his defences overriding every other desire in him...for her company, for her.

CHAPTER FOUR

SHAFTS OF LIGHT from the closed shutters fell across the bedroom. Outside came the frantic barking of dogs. Throwing back the bedcovers, Toni opened the terrace doors and flung open the shutters, squinting in the glare of the already hot morning sun. The stone of the terrace was warm under her bare feet. Following the barking, she ran down the path towards the beach. Were the dogs in trouble? She cursed as she stubbed her toe on a rock, hopping on one foot but still continuing her journey, unable to see what the crisis was, as wild and fragrant shrubs obscured her view of the beach.

She raced down and out onto the golden sand. Paco and Lore were scampering along the gently lapping waves, barking out to sea. Her gaze darted to the calm blue expanse. Was it Ivo? Was he okay? She called out to the dogs, who calmed for a few seconds before charging once again up and down the beach, their barks even louder than before. She followed them into the water, a hand shielding her eyes as she searched for him. Should she run and get her phone…even run to the security lodge and alert Ivo's staff? Was he even out there? Maybe he was still in bed? Maybe his dogs just barked at the sea for no particular reason. Her chest tightened. She knew she needed to stay calm, but she could feel her pores start to sweat, her heart race. What if Ivo really was in trouble? And then she saw a movement on the sea. An arm slicing into the water. And then another. A splash of feet. She backed away, collapsed down onto the sand further up the beach, relief wiping her out. She breathed in deeply, thrown by how panicked she had felt.

Both dogs quietened as Ivo swam closer to the beach, their tails swishing in anticipation as he stood and waded out of the sea. He was wearing dark green swimming trunks, his body a series of rock-hard lines of muscle emphasised by his dark golden skin. At the shoreline he paused and shook his head, a spiral of water arcing through the air, smoothed his tousled hair into order and then lifted a warning finger to both dogs, who instantly sat as though thoroughly chastised, but their wagging tails on the sand gave away their true feelings of glee to have their master back safely.

She stood as he approached, trying not to give away just how giddy she felt at his near nakedness, her fingers itching to follow the path of the water droplets slowly oozing down from the light dusting of hair on his chest, down over his pronounced six pack and disappearing into the band of the trunks that hung low on his narrow hips. Her pulse thundered in her ears. Did he have to be so disarmingly gorgeous? How was she supposed to breathe, never mind think straight when faced with so much testosterone?

He came to a stop a few feet away from her, his gaze briefly flicking down over her body. 'I'm sorry if they woke you.'

There was an intimacy to his voice that had her fiddling with the thin strap of her pyjama top and adjusting the legs of her shorts. 'I was worried something was the matter...' She trailed off, now embarrassed by her panic.

He shook his head, glancing back at the dogs. 'They go crazy like that sometimes,' then, pausing, he gave her the smallest of smiles, 'but thanks for being concerned.'

She grinned back, buoyed by the soft glimmer of laughter in his eyes.

An internal dialogue was screaming, *You are standing in front of a near-naked Prince Ivo—do you know how lucky you are? Make the most of every second of this. Memorise every detail of his body... memorise every smile, every look. You'll cherish these memories in the months and years ahead. An extraordinary weekend to look back on wistfully.*

'Can I interview you again this morning?'

Moving away, he grabbed a towel from the row of beach sunbeds behind them. They hadn't been there last night when she had come down to the beach for her swim. The door of the yellow wooden summer house perched against the cliff face was open, so she was guessing that Ivo had taken them out from there. 'I have to work—I spend Saturdays catching up on emails and paperwork.' He gestured to the sunbeds. 'I thought you might like to spend the day here on the beach. The summer house has a well-stocked kitchen. Help yourself to any drinks or snacks you might want.'

She got the distinct feeling work was just an excuse to avoid another interview. Her usual approach to interviews clearly wasn't going to work and instead she needed to adapt to Ivo's closed personality. 'How about we cut a deal—I won't interview you again until Monday if you agree to hanging out with me for the next two days?'

'Hang out?'

She laughed at the dubious way he said it. 'Yes, hang out. We can chill out here on the beach, go for a swim, chat, get to know one another. Sunbathe.'

As he walked towards her his eyes worked their way down her body and back up again. 'There are sun umbrellas in the summer house. Use them. Your skin is way too delicate for you to lie directly out in the sun.'

Something crazy stirred in her stomach at the heat in his voice. 'Well, I guess that's why sun cream was invented…and I like the heat. It's therapeutic.' She had no idea how to deal with the seductive chemistry that kept popping up between them…but, for now, light-hearted flirting instinctively seemed like the safest way to defuse its dangerous potential. 'I guess it's a good job that you'll be here to rub it on all those hard-to-reach spots.'

He held her gaze, a hint of a mischievous smile growing on his lips. 'If I'm going to forgo a day's work then it has to be for something worthwhile, not idling on a beach.' Shifting away, he moved towards the path back up to the *finca*.

She followed. 'Worthwhile...what do you mean?'

'I'll call the outdoor sports shop in Monrosa town—they can deliver everything you need within the hour. We can leave straight after to ensure we aren't hiking in the warmer hours of the day.'

Hiking! It was already baking hot. His towel slung over his shoulder, Ivo was powering up the path ahead of her, his long legs making short work of the incline. There was no way that she would be able to keep up with him. Her idea of a long walk was the ten minutes it took her to reach her nearest bus stop...this was going to be so embarrassing. She had to persuade him that it wasn't a good idea. She really should chase after him...and she would, but right now she just wanted another few seconds of watching his magnificent body at work, the pull of tight muscles across his upper back, the indent at the bottom of his spine, the hard round shape of his bottom... What would he be like in bed? Would he be gentle or demanding? Would she see a true glimpse of who he was beneath the closed veneer he showed to the world? Would the true man reveal himself to her?

A shriek cut through the air. Paco and Lore, who had been trailing close to his heels, bolted ahead, their tails between their legs.

Whipping around, he raced back to Toni, who was flapping her arms wildly and leaping in the air like a gazelle. 'Snake! A snake just slithered across the path. It went in there.'

He studied the dense undergrowth she was pointing back towards. 'Snakes play an important role in keeping our natural ecosystem thriving.'

Toni pushed past him, making a disgruntled sound. But then, coming to a halt, she twisted back to him, yanking off one of his old baseball caps. A trail of dirt smeared her cheek. 'You said the hike would be a short one—we've been walking hours.'

He checked his watch, holding back a grin. 'We've been walking less than an hour.'

'Uphill all the way, in the baking heat.'

Turning to survey the mountain forest below them, his beloved Mediterranean in the distance, he said, 'Yes, but look at the views. Wasn't the climb worth the effort?'

That earned him another heavy sigh. 'Yeah, they're fab.'

His lips twitched. So did hers. She tugged at the collar of her new T-shirt. 'This isn't helping—it's way too tight.'

Not in his eyes. Earlier when the outdoor store had delivered the hiking gear for her, she had tried it all on, grumbling that the sizing of the white polo shirt and khaki shorts were wrong, but he hadn't said anything, guessing that she didn't want to hear that he thought that the tight-fitting clothes revealed the soft curves of her body perfectly.

Reaching for the water bottle at the side of his rucksack, he offered it to her.

'I don't suppose it's a Paradise City in there?'

'Cocktails aren't recommended for hydration.'

She rolled her eyes and took a long sip of the water before saying, 'You do realise that we could be out having lunch in a restaurant with air-conditioning right now, or, even better still, lying on the beach.'

'Yes, but then you wouldn't be getting to see any of the hidden treasures of Monrosa you were so keen to hear about last night. Come on, we'd better go and find Paco and Lore—they ran off when you started screaming.'

Her eyes widened. 'Why didn't you say so before now?'

Before he could answer that it wasn't a problem, as he was certain they would find them further along the trail, she sprinted up the hill away from him. He caught up with her as she found the dogs lying in the shade of a giant pine.

Bending over, she patted them both. 'I didn't mean to frighten you.'

Dio! Those shorts were tight. He dragged his gaze away and stepped beyond her, gesturing that they should move on. They walked to the peak of the hill and then as the path dropped down and twisted inland he asked, 'Is there any other wildlife that terrifies you that I should know about? Where do you stand with lizards and spiders? The Monrosian Hairy-Back Spider thrives along this coastline.'

Her eyes widened but then, shaking her head, she

said, 'You're teasing me, aren't you? Who knew that the Machine had such a sense of humour?'

He laughed. 'I reserve it for those who are close to me.'

She studied him for a moment. 'I guess I should be honoured in that case. Who are the people close to you? Who are your support network?'

For a while he pretended to concentrate on crossing the wooden bridge suspended over the river that flowed down to the coast. He was tempted to change the subject. But something inside of him wanted to tell her the blunt truth. He wanted to see how she would react. Would she distance herself from him, back away from the attraction between them? Would she get that he was never going to form close attachments to anyone? 'I prefer to fend for myself in life. I don't have or need a support network.'

Toni watched as Ivo walked ahead of her. What had just happened? One minute the mood between them had been light and teasing and now it was as though she had touched a raw nerve with him. Did he really need no support…was he really that self-contained?

She knew she should just accept what he said. Wasn't she trying to emulate his detachment, after all? But her curiosity was too great. Her need to understand him had her chase after him and without much thought she admitted, 'I admire your ability to be self-contained. Sometimes I wish I could be more like that.'

He glanced in her direction, clearly perplexed.

Then he shrugged and gave a humourless laugh. 'You must be the first person who sees my preference to lead a private life as a positive thing.'

She laughed too, raising an eyebrow. 'Well, positive up to a certain point, of course, but I can see the merits of being self-reliant. Happy in your own skin, so to speak. In the past I have looked too much outside of myself for happiness—with Dan, in my social life, through work... I looked at all of those things for affirmation, but deep down I have struggled with truly believing in myself.' She paused, snapshots of memories from her life when she had felt overwhelmed by feelings of vulnerability looping through her brain. The times she had run home, only to find that her dad had disappeared once again. Her mother's withdrawal in the weeks that followed. The endless questions she asked herself as to whether there had been something she had done wrong to cause him to leave. The constant erosion of her confidence that had her cling to friendships and later Dan as though they were a lifeline of affirmation and safety. Her first year in university when everyone else had seemed so confident and she had just felt utterly lost. 'Sometimes I wish I was tougher, less thin-skinned, that I was someone who could brush off life easily. Someone like you, in fact.'

He came to a stop, his expression intense. He shook his head. 'No. Don't wish to be anything but what you are.' He stepped back, ran a hand through his hair and grimaced. 'Look...in the past I struggled with accepting who I am. In my teenage years,

I was always being compared to my brothers. I knew people wondered why I wasn't as gregarious as Luis, as charismatic and high-achieving as Edwin. But with time, I learnt that I had to accept who I am.' As he stepped back closer to her, his voice dropped a notch and his eyes held hers with a frank openness that had her heart turn over. 'Be true to who you are, Toni. Accept all of your qualities, use them to your advantage. My way of doing things…well, I accept that it's not for everyone. But it's right for me. I need privacy and isolation, the ability to focus… I guess that's why I'm an investment manager obsessed with hard facts and figures. You're a rising star in the podcast interview world for a reason and maybe that's tied up with what you call being thin-skinned, but I would call being empathetic.'

She laughed. 'A rising star—who told you that?'

He began to walk away. 'Kara…' Pausing, he turned and then added, 'Kara and I listened to all of your other podcasts.'

He had? She didn't know whether to be thrilled or worried. She caught up with him. 'You listened to them all? When?'

'Thursday night after I had agreed to take part in the interview—I thought I should find out what I was letting myself in for.'

She waited for him to say more, wanting to know what he thought of her work. She clinched her hands, her body tense with the need to hear his opinion on her work, until it dawned on her that silence was probably so natural and normal to Ivo that she would have to draw him out. She blew out a breath. 'So, what did you think of them?'

'The interviews? They're engaging. You're good at your job.'

'Do you really think so?'

He came to a stop. 'Well, what do you think? Do you think you do a good job?'

She winced. 'Sorry... I must sound pathetic.'

The most gorgeous smile played out on his lips. 'I wouldn't say that...' he tilted his head '...in fact, I would say that you have a passionate personality... you have an open heart and nature, which people obviously warm to. Don't knock yourself for being that way...accept it.' His gaze darkened. 'Accept your warmth, your openness...as I said before, be true to yourself.'

God almighty, did he have to stare at her so intensely, speak in such a low voice? It felt as if he was making love to her with his eyes and voice.

He tilted back her cap, his thumb rubbing against her cheek. 'By the way, you're looking a little grimy.'

Her heart somersaulted at the teasing in his voice, and for the briefest moment as his head dropped down she thought he was about to kiss her, but, as though catching himself, he straightened and instead led her along the path they had been climbing until it twisted to reveal a tiny village of white houses in the valley beneath them. A square stood at the centre of the village, several narrow alleyways that could just about accommodate a single car converging together at this heart of the village.

'This is our first stop—Almijara,' he explained.

Feeling light-headed from both the heat and the fact that she was certain that Ivo had been close to kissing her, she breathed out on a sigh, 'It's so beautiful.'

He turned and watched her, heat and laughter in his eyes. 'Like so many things around here.'

His mouth twitching, no doubt in response to her blushing so fiercely, he turned his attention back towards the village. 'A few years back Almijara was close to being deserted, but the remaining families came together and developed a co-operative.' He guided her down the track, pointing out the newly whitewashed houses that had been recently renovated in a bid to attract families back to the village.

The shade of the narrow alleyways was a welcome relief from the burning intensity of the sun. Pulling off her baseball cap, she slowed her pace, taking the time to admire the second-floor Juliet balconies at the front of the higgledy-piggledy assortment of houses, wondering just how ancient the cobblestones were. It was the utter silence that surprised her the most, and when they moved out into the square she asked, 'Why did people leave such a beautiful village?' She gestured to a now empty grocery store and the blank menu board next to what once must have been the village taverna.

'For a number of years the village was cut off because of a major landslide. To reach the outside world the villagers were forced to travel down to the coast to take a boat to get to the nearby towns. It was unworkable for those with children, as there's no school in the village. The road has now reopened but the lack of employment opportunities locally has kept people away. The co-operative is hoping to change that.'

She followed him when he led her down a steep, narrow alleyway, her already exhausted legs protesting at the sharp decline, and into a large building, its ancient and huge double doors painted in green. Inside he explained, 'The river we crossed earlier flows down into Almijara and used to power the mill that once was located in this building. Nowadays it's the headquarters of the co-operative.'

'Ivo!'

A woman emerged from one of the rooms off the entrance hallway and drew Ivo into a warm hug.

Turning, he said, 'Toni, this is Carmen, the instigator and now project manager for the co-operative.'

Smiling fondly at the immaculately groomed and elegantly dressed woman, he added, 'You should interview Carmen for one of your podcasts.' Turning back to Carmen, he explained why she was spending the weekend with him and Toni could see that Carmen instantly embraced the publicity opportunity participating in an interview would bring. Disarmed, she reluctantly followed Carmen when Ivo suggested that Carmen give her a tour of the mill. Did he not even think to mention any of this to her? But her misgivings were soon forgotten as Carmen took her on a whirlwind introduction to the other members of the co-operative. When Ivo had mentioned a co-operative she had envisaged craftspeople, when in fact the mill was home to an array of professionals—Irene, an architect, Alberto, an IT security expert, Salvador, a freelance graphic designer. She was blown away by their enthusiasm for the project to bring the village back to life and quickly realised that, while Carmen was the driving force behind the project, it was Ivo who was their financial backer.

And after half an hour in Carmen's company Toni could understand why Ivo had suggested that she interview the founder of the co-operative. Carmen's enthusiasm for the project, her tenacity in the face of many obstacles, her warmth and wit, her personal battle with breast cancer, which had been the catalyst for wanting to restore the place of her birth, were all truly inspiring.

Before they left the village to continue their hike, she and Carmen exchanged contact details, Toni excited at the prospect of coming back to the village to interview Carmen in the near future. And as they followed the road out of the village, down towards the coast, she glanced at Ivo. How would he react if she called to say that she was returning to Monrosa to interview Carmen? Would he be open to their meeting up, spending time together? Would she even want that?

'Carmen told me that you are the financial backer for the entire village rejuvenation project. I'm guessing it's a major investment, considering all of the building renovations and the broadband roll-out that it entailed. What was it particularly that made you want to support it?'

'We need to protect our villages. Up until fifty years ago Monrosa was a mainly rural country. If we lose our villages, and we have lost many here in the north of the island, then we will lose many traditions and ways of life.'

The sun was now at its height and, though mercifully her new hiking boots fitted perfectly, her top and shorts were clinging to her even more, thanks to the mounting heat of the day. She thought longingly of sinking her feet into soft sand...or, even better yet, the refreshing coolness of water. She eyed the sea below them. 'Can we go for a swim?'

He lifted an eyebrow. 'Did you pack a swimming costume?'

She hadn't thought about that. But there was no way she was giving in to his obvious teasing. 'No... but I can swim in my underwear...it's not against any law or royal protocol, is it?'

His brow furrowed as though he was seriously considering this. 'I don't think so. We're a pretty liberal society. In fact, it's perfectly acceptable to swim in the nude as per the Freedom to Nudity convention Prince Ferdinand passed in the seventeenth century.'

She stifled a laugh, trying not to give away just how perturbed she was by his suggestion or even worse still at how keenly he seemed to be embracing the idea. Ivo may on the surface appear reserved but beneath it there was a whole load of testosterone.

And as they continued their hike she wondered at the façade Ivo presented to the world. Why did he allow so few people to see his humour, his empathy towards others? She turned and considered him, wondering just how easily he would erect those pillars of self-containment around himself with her, if she pushed him to reveal more about himself. Should she leave well alone? Not push to know him better? But she owed it to her listeners to dig a little deeper into his personality. 'For someone who is as self-contained as you are, the so-called *Machine*, you show a lot of kindness and empathy towards others.'

He shrugged but didn't answer.

'Carmen also told me about your financial support for the local olive growers. You seem very willing to give to others, whether that's the co-operative, your staff, local farmers…but you don't ever want anything back. Is that about controlling the situation, not making yourself vulnerable to anyone?'

Pulling his water bottle from his rucksack, he took a long swig. She waited for him to respond but instead he just continued to walk on in silence.

She waited and waited and waited for him to say something. And eventually she said with a sigh, 'You really are a man of few words.'

He turned and regarded her, his shrug not matching the weariness in his eyes. 'I was thinking.'

'About what?'

'What you just said, of course.'

'And…'

He gave another shrug. 'You could be right.'

She waited for him to say something more, but they continued walking in silence. And then despite herself she started laughing, and when he glanced at her she said, 'You really are impossible.' Why she was laughing she had no idea, but there was something about Ivo's ability to fall into silence, to seemingly just accept something and move on, that was deeply refreshing in comparison to the constant chatter that went on in her own head.

Directing Toni through a coded gate that took them back onto San Jorbo land, they followed a path down to a private beach. He smiled at Toni's surprised laughter when she spotted a picnic blanket spread out on the sand, a cooler box positioned in the shade, and a jet ski out on the water, their transport home later, all delivered by his staff earlier.

Dropping his rucksack onto the picnic blanket, he folded his arms and with a raised eyebrow nodded towards the gently lapping waves. 'So, do you still want to swim?'

Toni had been right when she had asked if he didn't look for anything from others. Life was so much easier when he kept people at arm's length. When he was in control of the relationship and could maintain a safe distance. But somehow Toni was getting under his skin. Her chatter, her sunny nature, her empathy, the chemistry between them were all deeply unsettling. He could fight her on the emotional front, keep her at a distance...but with each passing hour his physical resistance was fading.

Considering his question, Toni tilted her head. 'Only if you join me.'

Dio! How was he supposed to resist that teasing smile, the quiet suggestion in her eyes?

But there were things that needed to be said.

'You're still hurting… I don't want you to regret anything from this weekend.'

She raised her chin, pride shining in her eyes. 'What I want right now is to have some fun.'

'Define fun.'

With a laugh she gestured around her. 'Well, this is all a good start. Glorious sunshine, a beautiful beach,' pausing to study him, she added, 'and good company. I'm not looking for anything serious, I just want to chill out and enjoy myself.' Then, tossing her hat down onto the blanket, she lifted her T-shirt slightly, exposing the smooth, pale skin of her stomach, merriment dancing in her eyes. 'So are you going to join me?'

He waited for her to lift her T-shirt even further but instead she left it hovering with just an inch of skin showing, her teasing smile catching in his heart. *Dio!* The world felt like a better place when she smiled.

Unbuttoning his polo shirt, he tugged it off, smiling at how her eyes feasted on his chest and abs. Desire punched through him. He folded his arms, waiting for her to make the next move.

She eyed him as though trying to decide the best plan of action. And then in one smooth stroke she whipped off her top, revealing a green and white lace bra beneath.

His pulse thundered in his ears as he took in the swell of her generous breasts cupped in the lace, his mouth drying out when she unbuttoned her shorts to reveal matching underwear.

Again she lifted her chin but there was a shyness to her defiance this time. His heart swelled with tenderness. Yes, she was doing this for herself but there was a light in her eyes that said she was doing it for him too.

Walking to her, he smiled as his hands cupped her face. She smiled back, her brown eyes glittering with desire...and fun.

His life was so serious, so controlled. Toni's energy and spontaneity drove that home with a force that was startling. 'I need some fun in my life too,' he admitted.

Her eyes shone even brighter. 'Good.'

Lowering his head, their eyes teasing one another, his mouth found hers. Her lips were soft and warm. A long sigh travelled through his body before he pulled her against him, desire then nearly having him stumble backwards at how glorious her body felt pressed against his.

Her hands crept around his neck. He deepened the kiss, all thought abandoned to the sweet heat of her mouth.

She gave a sharp inhale when he touched the bottom of her spine, his fingers stroking the top of her panties.

Her body moved in a slow dance against his. Within minutes he was in danger of rushing things, of giving in to the temptation of lying her down on the sand and fully knowing her body.

Reluctantly he pulled away. His breath unsteady,

he yanked off his own shorts and, taking her hand in his, led her to the water.

Breaking free, she challenged him to a race and when he caught up with her they kissed again, plunging beneath the water before they spluttered to the surface, laughing.

With her hair slicked back, her eyes glistening like the high sun reflecting off the sea, he kissed away every single drop of seawater on her face, her legs wrapping around his waist.

She gasped when his hand moved against the side of her breast, shuddered against him when his thumb flicked over her nipple.

He kissed her long and hard, her legs wrapping even tighter around him.

He couldn't get enough of her. There was something sweetly addictive about how she tasted and felt, the chemistry between them like a separate force.

Knowing he needed to slow things down, he guided her out of the water. Covering her with a towel, he patted her dry, drinking in her smiles, the soft wonder in her eyes, pushing away all the fears bubbling inside him as to the danger of this intense attraction.

They moved the picnic blanket into the shade and ate some food, but soon that was abandoned again to long kisses and gentle touches as they tentatively explored each other's bodies, the desire to rush things tempered by the slow, sensual seduction of wanting to do this right, even if it was only for a few stolen days.

CHAPTER FIVE

TONI WAVED THE tennis ball in the air. 'Come on, Paco, one more fetch.' But just like Lore, Paco ignored her and ambled away to carry out a sniffing inventory of the shoreline. With the dogs now bored of the fetch game and the light rapidly fading, she had no good excuse not to return to the *finca*. Apart from the fact that she was worried that she might very well make all the wrong advances on their master.

She couldn't stop thinking about Ivo…and everything his body was capable of. On the jet-ski ride back to the *finca* earlier she had buried her head in the gap between his shoulder blades, her cheek lying against his hard muscle, her insides melting at his heat, his musky scent. And over dinner she had been jumpy and awkward, hyper-aware of his every move, babbling in her nervousness, probably driving him crazy in the process.

She had sighed in relief when he had said that he needed to work in his office for a few hours, but afterwards had worried that it was just his way of getting away from her for a while. Was he regretting this afternoon? She hoped not. It had been wonderful and sensual…and yes, fun. She had to keep this light and unemotional…but when those silver eyes held hers, the regard and tenderness beneath the passion of his gaze could make it all too easy to fall for him.

Across the bay, yet another helicopter went to land on a property on the outskirts of Laredo. Yachts and speedboats had been arriving for the past hour too.

Following Paco and Lore, who were already heading back up to the *finca*, she knew that there was no way she was going to be able to spend the entire evening alone with Ivo. She needed to take a breather from what was happening between them and get some much-needed perspective.

She knocked on his office door but he was not there. Moving further along the corridor, following a hissing sound, she came to a stop at another doorway. Ivo was in the home gym on a rowing machine. Dressed in navy shorts and a T-shirt that clung to his damp body, he attacked each stroke with stern determination as though excising some internal demon.

She swallowed at the thick muscles of his thighs, the contraction of his biceps, the power and strength of his massive body. What would it be like to have him lie on top of her? She hadn't slept with a man since Dan. Was that why her hormones were raging? Was it simply by virtue of being in the prolonged presence of a young single male that was having her have sexual fantasies that were beyond anything she had ever contemplated before?

She had to stop this. She needed to get a grip.

She breezed into the room and perched herself on the edge of the treadmill. 'I'm exhausted just looking at you.'

He faltered for a few seconds but, regaining his rhythm, grinned at her. 'Would you like some one-on-one tuition?'

See, this was what she couldn't deal with, when he surprisingly flirted so easily with her.

'There's a lot of activity over in Laredo, with yachts and helicopters arriving at a property on the waterfront—what's going on?'

'The singer Federico has a villa in Laredo, and he throws a party every year on the night of the *feria* parade.'

'Federico! I had such a schoolgirl crush on him.'

Ivo frowned before coming to a stop in his rowing. 'He's a nice guy…it's a shame his plastic surgery went so bad though…he's almost unrecognisable.'

'You're kidding! He was perfect as he was—why on earth did he have surgery?' Pausing, she let out a disbelieving breath. 'You're winding me up again, aren't you?'

His eyes shone with amusement. 'When was the last time you saw him?'

'I've no idea. He disappeared from the music scene about ten years ago… How do you know him?'

'We sometimes meet in Laredo. It's a small place.'

'Have you been invited to his party?'

Placing the rowing handle in its holder, he unbuckled his feet, grabbed a towel and ran it over his face. 'Yes, but I have no interest in going.'

'Why not? It'll be fun. It'd be nice to get out and meet other people.'

He stood, giving an impatient shake of his head.

'Please, Ivo…just for an hour or two…what's the harm in going? It would be great to get out for a while…' She trailed off when he walked towards her. Reaching down, he pulled her to her feet, his eyes blazing down into hers. And then he was kissing her, pulling her against his damp body. Her senses went into immediate overload, his strength, the tang of fresh male sweat heady in its vitality, and instantly she was lost to everything but a hunger for him.

When he broke away from the kiss he kept one hand threaded through her hair, his other palm gently resting on her cheek. 'I want to spend time here… alone with you.' His voice was low and raspy. And then he was walking away, muttering that he needed to take a shower.

'Maybe that's why we should go,' she called out in frustration.

He turned and considered her for a moment, but with a shake of his head he gave her his answer, and left the room.

Scrubbing his scalp, Ivo turned the water flow up to maximum and let the pounding water drum into his skull. Unable to focus on work earlier, he had hoped an hour's rowing would ease his restlessness and it had worked until Toni had arrived at the gym. The sight of her perched on the side of the treadmill, her red wrap dress accentuating the gorgeous shape of her body, had all contributed to wrecking his attempts to try and get some perspective on what had happened on the beach earlier.

The chemistry between them, so raw and urgent, was unsettling in itself. But as they had lain together and kissed and touched and chatted and laughed, a dangerous connection had spun between them. A fondness even. Fondness…was that even the right word? It felt like an odd choice of word, but nothing else summed up the gentle teasing, the natural ease that was between them. An ironic ease, given that it troubled him so much.

In all of his previous relationships he had been able to maintain an emotional distance. None of his exes had challenged his status quo—he had managed to remain detached from them, had continued on with life in the way he wanted to pursue it. But Toni was different. He had a hunger for her, an uncontrollable need to touch her, to chat with her, tease her, which felt apart from his usual self-control and logic.

He needed to create distance between them. He needed to make it clear who he was and that he wasn't for changing.

Towelling himself dry, he pulled on chinos and a lightweight shirt. He found her out on the terrace staring towards the lights of Laredo. Dropping her feet from where she had propped them on the side of the outdoor coffee table, she sat up on the sofa and pulled out the earbuds attached to her phone.

He sat opposite her, his back to Laredo. 'I like my life. I don't need or want to go to parties.'

He expected questions and protests but instead she gave him silence. He arched his neck against the sudden burning need to talk. 'I have always been content on my own. It's other people who have difficulty in accepting that.'

She grimaced. 'I'm sorry…'

'It's frustrating having to justify the decisions you take, all of the time.'

'Is that why you prefer to be alone, because you feel you have to justify yourself to others?'

Why was he talking to her about any of this? What use could it serve? 'Yes…no…look, can you just accept that I am happy in my life? I work and enjoy life here in San Jorbo. I don't need anything else.'

She flinched at his words and he regretted the heat in his voice. But then, meeting his gaze she asked, 'What about your family? Don't you want to be with them?'

'We have a complex relationship. We were all sent to boarding school from a young age, so we aren't as close as other families are.'

'Do you wish things had been different?'

'I don't see the point in wishing for things that are already in the past,' he responded.

'I guess, but it's okay to admit that things have hurt you. We all have things in our past that we wish had been different or regret…at least, I do.'

Something caught in his throat at the gentleness of her tone. And without thinking he blurted out, 'I was alone with her when she fell.'

Dio! Why was he talking about this? He clenched

his hands. This was not what he had planned. He should just make his excuses and leave.

But instead he sat in the silence between them and as much as he fought it, his eyes kept being drawn back to her steady, soft contemplation. 'My mother— we were out riding. I had gone ahead, and when I turned back her horse, Cassini, was charging towards me without her. I found her lying on the ground unconscious.' He closed his eyes. How was it possible that that memory still invoked the same horror now as it did all those years ago? 'I tried waking her, but she was unresponsive. I ran for help. I should have stayed. She shouldn't have died alone.'

He waited for her to justify his decisions that day, or even, as his father had done, tell him to stop thinking about it, that it didn't matter. That there was nothing he could have done. His father hadn't understood… Ivo knew that he wouldn't have been able to save her, but the thought that she had died without someone by her side destroyed him.

Had she known that she was alone? Had she felt abandoned? Had that been her last thought? Why was she dying alone with no one to hold her hand, to speak words of love?

Toni moved over and sat beside him. He waited for her to speak but instead she rested her hand on his and he breathed against the instinct to take his hand away. This was not who he was. He didn't discuss his past. The pull to clam up, to withdraw from her, gathered strength.

'Were you able to talk to your family about how you were feeling?'

He laughed at that. 'We operate a *the least said, the better* policy.'

'Do you miss her?'

A heavy weight pressed down on his chest. Her hand shifted to wrap over his completely, the light, feminine weight undoing him in how she was trying to comfort him. 'She understood me. She understood that by nature I'm private and often need time alone.' He shook his head. 'Not the best qualities when you're born into public life, I'll admit.'

'I reckon Luis makes up for you on that front.'

She was right. Despite himself he laughed, but the weight on his chest still felt like a heavy mass. 'True.' And then he heard himself admit, 'I found public life tolerable when I was younger…but after she died…' he trailed off, not sure how to explain it all. 'I didn't want to leave my bedroom. I spent hours building fantasy worlds with my toy soldiers. It drove my father crazy.'

She exhaled slowly, her eyes holding his. 'You had a major trauma. It was your way of coping.'

'I needed space, I needed to grieve in privacy, but instead I had to publicly grieve in front of the entire world. I couldn't cope with the crowds, the television cameras.'

Shifting forward in her seat, she turned so that she was looking at him directly. 'I'm sorry that you lost your mum and that you weren't able to grieve for her in the way that you needed to.' She grimaced, shaking her head. 'I wish I could say, do something more than just say that I'm sorry.' She paused and he saw tears glisten in her eyes. 'I had never thought about it before tonight but I know that with my mum, when...' she stopped, clearly struggling to speak '...when she dies I'll want to be there for her, and I'm so sorry that didn't happen for you.'

He had no words. So he gathered her to him, laying her head against his chest, fighting back a heavy wave of emotion in his chest, her compassion, her understanding, overwhelming him.

And then came panic. The cool walls of logic and detachment he had erected around himself were melting in the warmth of her care. He couldn't allow himself to be vulnerable to anyone again. He didn't want heartache and disappointment, all of the conflict that came when you had to negotiate your way through relationships.

He pulled away from her and stood. Nodded in the direction of Laredo. 'Let's go to Federico's party.'

She considered him with a dazed expression. 'Why...what's changed?'

I can't do this. I can't grow close to you.

'You're right, it would be good to get out.'

On the road beneath the terraced gardens of Federico's villa, the feria parade marched from the harbour to the town centre, a statue of the local saint carried on a plinth leading the way. Following her were local girls dressed in flamboyant gowns, their dark hair smoothed into perfectly neat buns, proud men on horseback, fishermen pushing their boats on trailers, and a flotilla of cars, each packed with an impossible number of people, smiling and waving and shouting messages of good cheer to the watching spectators.

Toni bit back a smile when, at the baying of those in the procession, Federico, with false reluctance, stood on the terrace wall and began to serenade the crowd. The hairs on the back of her neck tingled as the crowd grew quiet, Federico's rich baritone voice filling the night air. He sang his most famous song and soon the entire party and the crowd below were clapping and singing along.

Toni beamed. This was exactly what she needed. A brilliant distraction away from everything Ivo was stirring in her. Federico's villa and gardens were jammed with exquisitely dressed guests, the noise levels from the chatter and music deafening. It was like an extreme version of any other party she had ever attended, more glamorous, noisier and spectacular in its excessiveness. Uniformed staff, who had an uncanny ability to anticipate her every need, were constantly topping up her champagne glass and the other guests were warm and welcoming. Federico, on learning that she was a friend of Alice's, had introduced her to Alice's new personal assistant, Carolina, who had taken her under her wing and had introduced her to a dizzying array of other guests. She was having an incredible night…she really was. She took a sip of champagne, stepping away from a group who had travelled from Madrid for the party to search the crowd. Ivo was standing up at the villa with another man, away from the bulk of the party-goers, who had crowded down to the parameter wall to watch the procession. Both men would occasionally glance towards the noise and activity but were preoccupied with whatever they were discussing.

She wanted to be with him. This party was amazing, everything she had thought she had wanted. But it wasn't working...no amount of noise and laughter and distraction could hide the fact that she was denying yet again her true feelings. She had done it all of the time when she had been with Dan, papering over the cracks in their relationship by being too busy in work and their social life to ever have to face up to the problems between them. And since he had left her she had been doing the same, always busy, busy, busy, never allowing herself to exist in silence, never allowing herself to truly admit and accept the loneliness inside of herself.

She knew she should stay and enjoy the party. Revel in the chatter and good company of others. Have a few more drinks. Forget about everything that made her feel incomplete. Avoid the temptation to connect with Ivo, to know him better. Ignore the pull inside of her to tell him who she truly was. She should be sensible and stay.

But instead she walked up the garden steps. Waited until Ivo saw her. Her heart thumped as his eyes met hers, a charge running between them. She waited while he excused himself and made his way to her. She breathed deeply at his staggering beauty, her fingers itching to touch the silkiness of his hair, the hard lines of his face, her body alive to the smooth, agile movement of his body that promised so much in bed.

When he reached her he tilted his head in question. The sudden blaring of horns on the road had her reach up so to be heard and whisper into his ear, 'Can we go home?'

The rib glided over the moonlit water, the sea air rushing against them a welcome break from the heat of the night. Toni had yet to explain why she had asked to leave and, given her silence, he wasn't expecting an answer anytime soon. He glanced in her direction. Her gaze met his, a heavy beat of chemistry playing out between them. His eyes drifted down over her red wrap dress, her hand grabbing hold of the material to cover thighs exposed by the wind. Her feet were bare, her high-heeled silver sandals discarded. The dress highlighted every delicious curve, the sweet valley between her breasts, the swell of her bottom. What would happen when they reached San Jorbo?

Steering the boat off the path he had been following, he headed instead towards the faint lights in a cove to the east of Laredo. In answer to Toni's quizzical look he said, 'Let's get a nightcap.'

Toni's laughter was an echoing twinkle when the bar's ancient jetty rocked as they leapt onto it. The clifftop bar was only accessible by water and as usual only a dozen or so locals were gathered there. He

introduced Toni to Antonio and Dolores, the own-
ers, requesting that they make her a Paradise City,
which neither had heard of, enjoying the scene that
followed as Antonio, who hadn't altered the bar's
offerings in decades, grew more incredulous when
Toni listed the ingredients. In the end Toni opted for
the simpler order of a beer, just like him, and when
they carried them out onto the terrace she gave him
an evil look, 'I'll get you back for that.'

He grinned. 'I'll look forward to it later.'

Her eyes widened and she darted for a free table
overlooking the bay. Fairy lights were strung around
the olive trees surrounding the terrace, candles
flickering on each of the tables. From Antonio's ancient gramophone the music of a flamenco guitarist drifted to blend with the sound of the breaking
waves beneath them.

He spoke briefly to the other customers on the
terrace, discussing the olive crop with Lidia, his
neighbour, enquiring after Ignacio's wife, who was
in hospital, before joining Toni.

Toni watched Dolores bustle out onto the terrace
to sit with Lidia, the women's eyes immediately
shifting to study them. 'Why do I get the feeling
we're the hot topic of conversation?' she asked.

He shrugged, the full consequence of what he
had done suddenly dawning on him. 'You're the first
woman I have ever brought here with me.'

'You should have explained that I'm a journalist,
that there's nothing more to it than that.'

Shifting back in his seat, he studied her, watched

as she drew her hair back and twisted its long length into a rope, the beauty of her eyes and mouth richer now that her hair wasn't a distraction. 'But then I'd be lying, wouldn't I? Because there is more than that to our relationship.'

Toni frowned. 'Why *did* you bring me here?'

He had thought it was simply to buy time, to cool that heat and desire burning through him. He didn't want to rush them sleeping together. He wanted to be certain it was what she really wanted. But now he realised he had other motives too for bringing her here. 'For a nightcap, but also for you to see where I like to go when I do sometimes go out.' He gestured around the rustic bar, the low murmurs of the other customers, the lights of houses on the opposite side of the bay. 'This is me. This is what I enjoy.' He shrugged. 'Some might consider it boring. Unglamorous. But it's what makes me happy.'

Her head dropped to the side, her forehead puckering in thought. 'Do you think that I'm going to judge you?'

'It's not what most people want.'

Butterflies dancing in her stomach, Toni tried to gather her thoughts. He was opening up to her again. Earlier he had told her about his mother and now this…she should be pleased and she was…but she was also scared. Not only of messing up by saying something that would drive him back into silence, but also as to what it meant was between them. She wanted honesty and openness, but it would make everything between them more intense and significant. And even harder to say goodbye. But she did want to know him…and he, her. She wanted a true connection with him, no matter if it was for only a few days. 'Maybe most people don't know what they want. Maybe they haven't stopped and really thought about what makes them happy and simply follow what society tells us what being happy looks like. When I was with Dan, if I was asked at the time, I would have said that I was happy. I had a great career, money, a nice home and a relationship. But now I realise that it was what I wanted to believe rather than what was true. At the start I did love Dan…but that had ebbed away years before we split.' She swallowed again, thinking about how their love life had been practically non-existent.

'So why did you stay together?'

'Habit.' She glanced away and cringed. 'Plus a little pleading on my part.'

His eyebrow shifted up in question. She couldn't believe she was admitting this. She hadn't even told Alice, too embarrassed by her own neediness. 'Dan broached the idea of us splitting up a few times but I laughed off the suggestion.' She clasped her hands against her burning cheeks. 'Where was my dignity? I used to make a joke of it all by telling Dan that we were destined to grow old together. I couldn't face being alone. It terrified me.'

He shifted towards her and gently asked, 'Why?'

For the longest while she could only stare at the hollow in his throat, the patch of dark skin where his shirt was open, and below that the long line of pale buttons of his shirt, a desire for his warmth, his touch making her light-headed. And then, cringing again, she met his eyes and answered, her laugh empty even to herself, 'Because sometimes I long for security…to feel safe. It's not great…but at least I now recognise that I can be that way and hopefully can avoid falling into the trap of an unhealthy relationship again.'

'Why did you stop loving Dan?'

She wrinkled her nose. It had just happened. She hadn't put much thought into it. 'He's incredibly smart and driven…but horribly disorganised and forgetful. Even worse than me. And as he became more successful, he became more stressed out. We used to have horrible arguments. I'd try to get him to chill out over whatever was worrying him, because in truth I couldn't handle the tension, and he'd just get more stressed out. The worse the arguing became, the more we socialised to forget about it all.' She shook her head. 'I hate arguments.'

'Why?'

She arched her neck, the low sounds of the flamenco guitar sending a shiver up her spine despite the warmth of the night. 'I…' she swallowed, tried to laugh '…I told you that I'm thin-skinned and I wasn't joking. I hate the idea of arguing because I have a morbid fear of upsetting others, that they might think less of me or might not want me around any more.'

'Would you really want those people in your life though, if they couldn't respect your point of view?'

She rolled her head side to side, trying to find a better way to explain herself. 'I guess what I'm trying to say is that I like feeling safe in my relationships, whether that's with friends, family or romantically. My mum always struggled financially when I was growing up. She's an artist but would take on temporary jobs to tide us over. I never knew when she'd get home from work. I spent a lot of my evenings alone. I hated being on my own. I guess that's why I struggle to be alone now. In my teens I used to hang out at my friends' houses and when I met Dan at university we immediately moved in together. In hindsight I can see that I was desperate to be with someone, to not feel alone.'

'What about your dad?'

She rolled her eyes. 'Oh, he came and went. He was an artist too. My parents met at art college. He moved around a lot. He lived in Italy and then France. He used to visit us sometimes and even persuaded my mum several times to give their relationship a go again. But it never worked out. They used to argue over money…and the other women in his life. Sometimes I'd go to bed and the next morning he'd have disappeared again.'

'And do you see him now?'

'He died five years ago in France. We only found out when his then partner wrote to my mum from France a few weeks after his funeral.'

Ivo grimaced. 'I'm sorry.'

She shrugged. 'I would have gone to his funeral

if we had known. He wasn't a great dad...but he was *my* dad.'

For a moment Ivo dropped his head as though studying his clasped hands that were lying on the table before him. When he looked back up she was undone by the compassion in his eyes. 'Wanting security, to want to feel safe in your relationships, is understandable.'

She gave him a wry smile. 'Yes, but not when it's the only reason to stay in a relationship. Dan and I were together for ten years...it should have ended long before it did.' Wanting to divert the heat of the conversation away from herself, she asked, 'How about you—have you had many relationships?'

'Nothing that lasted more than a few months.' Gesturing to their empty glasses, he said, 'Let's go.'

As they made their way down to the beach, slowly negotiating the dark path, he took hold of her hand. Her heart swooned at its reassuring warmth, how it sealed the intense connection between them. Nearing the end of the path, he pulled her to a stop and stared at her for long moments. Her heart began to pound, the beauty of the moonlit beach adding to the sense of magic whirling in the air. He gave her a tender smile. 'You should be in a relationship.'

Her heart in her throat, she desperately waited for him to say more. But nothing came. Why did he say things like that and not follow it up with details and explanations? How could he so calmly and un-emotionally make such a pronouncement while holding her hand, the memories of lying together on the beach today binding them together?

She pulled her hand away from his, her frustration with him spilling over. 'Why?'

And who with?

'With the right person you could find the security you want.'

'I thought you were against relationships?'

'For me…but I'm not blind to how happy being in a relationship can make others. My brothers, for example.'

She gritted her teeth. Trying to pretend that she was cool with this conversation. That it didn't feel as though he was stabbing her in the heart.

Toni, get a grip. You don't want a relationship now. And especially not with a man as complex and detached as Ivo. It would drive you crazy, never knowing exactly what he felt for you, what was going on in his mind. Why on earth would you want to be in a relationship with a man who has zero interest in being in one in the first place? Remember, this is about fun. Nothing more. A step on the road to discovering yourself and lightening your expectations of relationships. You cannot fall at the first hurdle by falling for the first guy you make out with.

'Maybe you're right…maybe not. I'm learning about myself all of the time right now. I want to learn to be happy on my own, before I consider a relationship again.' She backed away from him, heading towards the wooden jetty. 'Right now I'm finding myself and thankfully shedding some of my old insecurities.' She straightened her back, a sense of purpose and liberation taking hold. 'I want to be light-hearted, freer in my relationships.' She waited until he joined her on the rickety jetty, laughing as it moved under his weight, emboldened by her own words. 'I want to have fun. Pure and simple. With no expectations.' She paused and gave him an inviting smile full of flirtation. 'What do you think?'

He eyed her for a moment, but then glorious amusement and attraction brightened his dark gaze. He edged closer. 'If you're certain that's what you want.'

She nodded. And giggled when he drew her into his arms, the jetty bobbing beneath them as he kissed her, one arm holding her tight while the other lightly grazed against the side of her breast, her hip, her bottom. The dull ache at her core that was her constant companion when close to Ivo blew bright and fierce.

She sat close to him on the boat ride back to San Jorbo. Her legs were weak with longing when they climbed the path back up to the *finca*, her heart pounding in anticipation.

When they entered the *finca*, he shut the door behind him and they were enveloped in the near total darkness of the entrance hallway. She waited for him to switch on a light but he didn't move. She knew he was near by. She could sense the pull of his body, the powerful force of his personality. Every nerve in her body was drawn taut with anticipation.

He moved in front of her, those silver eyes shining down with heat and desire. His finger trailed over the fold in her dress, lightly touching the valley between her breasts. She couldn't quieten her loud inhale and he smiled in pleasure. With one tug he undid the bow at her waist holding the dress together. Now it was his turn to inhale sharply and her knees grew weak at the way his gaze devoured her red underwear.

His hand lightly trailed over her ribs and waist and she gasped when his mouth touched against her collarbone before moving down to her breasts. His tongue flicked over the material of her bra, catching against her nipple. She swayed backwards but his hands moved to her hips, steadying her. Kneeling, he ran butterfly kisses over her stomach.

She raked her hands through his hair, the intense heat in her core and restlessness in her pelvis forcing her to bite back pleas for him to hurry up.

She went with him when he led her to her bedroom. Pushing her dress to the floor, he kissed her until her head was swimming with need.

Lowering her to the bed, he opened the curtains and the terrace door beyond, allowing in the light of the moon and the crash of the sea.

He shrugged off his shirt and then his trousers, his assured, agile movements making her want him even more. Lying down on the bed beside her, he held her gaze while his hands slowly touched and stroked her. 'Are you certain you want this?'

She nodded, incapable of speech, the low sensuality of his voice stealing away her last semblances of control.

He kissed her tenderly and her body arched high

off the mattress. She pulled him tighter, needing more heat and pressure. He deepened the kiss, his hand moving over her breasts, rubbing against her nipples.

Removing her bra, he kissed her breasts and she thought she would break apart at any moment. And then his hand was on her panties, lightly touching her, exploring.

She breathed out, 'Please, Ivo... I need you now.'

For long seconds he searched her eyes and then, with a smile that touched something deep in her heart, he removed her panties and then his own shorts.

Her heart was pounding when he lay on her, his weight the most wonderful thing she had ever felt. Her world shrank and shrank until all she was aware of was pressing her hips against his, a dreamlike other-world sensation in her head as she lost herself to the pleasure of his kiss, the exquisite tightness of him moving into her.

She cried out long and hard when she climaxed, clung to him when he soon followed. Lay in his arms afterwards, dumbstruck that anything could be so perfect.

CHAPTER SIX

'Ivo, I SAW your note.' Her hair tied back in a high ponytail, the silver and black ties of her bikini top poking out from her T-shirt, Toni popped her sunglasses onto the top of her head and waded across the sand to him, her attention turning to the cooler box sitting on the low table between the two sunbeds. 'What's going on?'

He had woken early and, unsettled at how good it was to wake next to her, he had gone for a dawn swim. She smiled while she slept. Why did that get to him so much? He had to focus on what they had agreed. A few days of fun. Nothing complicated. Nothing that would threaten his world order.

'You said that you wanted to spend some time on the beach, so I decided we'd have breakfast and hang out here for the morning before we leave for Gabriela's christening.'

She folded her arms. 'I thought lying on the beach was your personal idea of hell.'

Walking to the cabin, he lifted two sunbed mattresses out of the storage room and put them onto the loungers. 'It depends on who I get to hang out with.'

Placing a bright yellow umbrella between the sun-beds, he opened it up and gestured for her to sit down. He sat opposite her and dropped the cooler box to the sand. Opening it, he said, 'I hope you're hungry.'

Her eyes widened as he unpacked the food. A platter of pineapple and grapes, drizzled with mint from the garden, and a tray of freshly baked crois-sants. Removing a flask and two cocktail glasses from the box, he popped a handful of ice into each glass and then the contents of the flask. Passing a glass to Toni, he raised his in a toast. 'My version of Paradise City...virgin, of course, given the time of day that it is.'

Her eyes sparkling, she grinned widely, and his heart kicked at her delight. They touched glasses, amusement shining between them, Toni's murmurs of pleasure when she tasted the drink a potent re-minder of her sighs last night.

But then her forehead bunched. 'Why are you doing this?'

'I've realised that I've never actually spent time here on the beach. Which even to me seems crazy.' He raised a teasing eyebrow. 'It's my way of saying thank you for last night...and I guess I enjoy spend-ing time with you.'

She dipped her head, almost shy for a moment, before she laughed and said, 'Even if I spend too much time talking?'

'I never said that you do.'

She rolled her eyes. 'Oh, please. At Luis and Alice's wedding your pained expression throughout the day whenever we chatted said enough.'

'You were pretty excitable.'

She picked up a grape and crunched down on it. 'I was nervous.'

He nodded. 'It was a very public role being bridesmaid.'

'There was that...' she shrugged '...but you unnerved me too.'

He did? 'Why?'

'You were so serious,' she said with a laugh and a shake of her head, 'and so handsome. I was a nervous wreck around you. You do know that you have that effect on people?'

He grinned at the playfulness dancing in her eyes, at the heady flirtation dancing around them. 'It comes in useful sometimes,' he admitted. 'And now...do I still make you nervous?'

She considered his question with pretend seriousness, a smile tugging on her full lips. 'No... I think it's safe to say that I'm growing immune to you.'

'Really?' Shifting forward in his seat so that there were only a few inches between them, he touched a finger against her knee. 'How about when I touch you—are you immune to that?'

He heard her intake of breath but she gave a firm nod yes. 'One hundred per cent immune.'

He shifted his hand to her inner thigh, his pulse upping a notch at the soft warmth of her skin. 'And now?'

This time she breathed out raggedly, heat forming in her cheeks. 'I… Shouldn't we be having breakfast?'

Unfortunately she had a point. Reaching into the cooler, he pulled out the tub of vanilla ice cream and placed it on the table.

'Ice cream for breakfast?'

He chuckled at her horror and, grabbing hold of the olive oil bottle, brandished it before her. 'But this isn't any ordinary ice cream…not when we add olive oil from the groves of San Jorbo.'

She made a gagging noise. 'You're on your own with this one.'

He drizzled some oil over the ice cream and scooped out a spoon's worth, reaching over to feed it to her. She backed away, grimacing.

He ate the scoop and then helped himself to another few spoons before asking, 'Don't you like ice cream?'

'I love ice cream, but not for breakfast and certainly not with olive oil.'

Lifting up the dark bottle of oil, he studied the San Jorbo label before fixing her with a stare. 'You can have a lot of fun with oil.'

Her eyes widened. 'In what way?'

'I might show you some time.'

Her mouth opened. She went to speak but stopped, her cheeks growing red. And then she laughed. 'There really is another side to the Machine, isn't there?'

He laughed too. 'It's rarely spotted, but you do seem to have the ability to reveal it.'

'Did you mind that you were called that? The Machine? How did it even come about?'

Pulling apart a croissant, he took a bite before answering. 'My school coach was the first to use it.' Tearing another chunk of the pastry off, he continued, 'In my final year, I made it on to the senior squad but he dropped me from the starting eight just before the racing season began.' Realising he was no longer in the mood to eat, he tossed the croissant away.

'And?'

He was tempted to give her a glib answer. To feign that he had taken it all on the chin. But once again, the attentiveness of her steady brown gaze, her keenness to understand him, had him admit, 'I was devastated. Being in the starting eight was everything to me. I had trained for years to get to that position and without any explanation he dropped me. For a few days I considered giving up but I decided to prove him wrong and began to train even harder. Midway through the season he gave me my position back.'

'Did you ask him why he dropped you in the first place?'

'No.'

'Why not?'

'I didn't see the point at the time, reckoning that he obviously had his reasons. With hindsight perhaps it was because I kept myself apart from the team to a certain extent. Perhaps he wanted me to prove just how committed I was to the team.' Rolling his shoulders, trying to ease a kink of tension at the base of his neck, he added, 'Once I was back on the starting eight he started calling me the Machine, and it stuck from there.'

'And did you mind being called that?'

He shook his head. It could have been so easy to have fallen into the trap of giving way to the bitter disappointment of being dropped by a coach he had idolised, but the experience had been a valuable lesson in digging deep and staying focused and determined. 'It was a useful reputation for intimidating the opposition...and for my own mind-set. Rowing is as much psychological tactics as it is physical.'

'And now in business?'

'Clients like it—they want an investment manager who runs on logic and not emotion.'

'How about your team at Pacolore?'

He gave a wry smile. She saw straight through to where his style came undone. 'Let's say that it's a work in progress... I try to remind myself to take time out to be supportive.'

'From what I saw on Friday, your staff hold you in very high regard.' She paused, frowning before she continued. 'Honesty and openness are the lifelines of any relationship—whether it's personal or professional. Maybe if Dan and I had been more honest with each other, the same with my dad, then I could have avoided so much upset. I used to pretend to everyone, including myself, that I was okay with my dad coming and going from my life. But maybe if I had been honest and said how much it hurt me, demanded more of him, then we could have had a better relationship.' Meeting his gaze, she added in a low voice, 'Sometimes the easiest option is to say nothing...but that doesn't make it right.'

After his mother's death he had tried to talk to his father but his father hadn't wanted to listen and had shut him down immediately. What would have happened if he had insisted on being heard and had spoken about the awfulness, the guilt of it all?

And perhaps the same could be said for all of his relationships in the world of rowing. He had kept a deliberate distance from everyone, only trusting in himself, uncomfortable with the idea of asking for even a semblance of help and support. Would he have felt less isolated, less apart from his teammates if he had had the courage to openly talk about his race-day nerves and how they had sometimes paralysed him? Or spoken about his frustrations and fears with the shoulder injuries that had been a feature of his entire career. It might be too late to amend the past but he could be honest with Toni. 'When you're unsure you talk. I go silent instead.'

Her head tilted to the side, her eyes silently asking him to explain what he meant. He swallowed, the irony of the situation not lost on him. He fought against his natural inclination to clam up, doubts as to what he was admitting holding him hostage. He went to speak, stopped, tried again. 'At Luis's wedding...you completely stole my voice. I'm not usually that silent.'

She blinked, those huge, soulful brown eyes sucking him in. 'I did?'

'You looked incredible.'

'I was a red-eyed emotional mess.'

'Not to me.'

'Oh.'

He grinned at her surprise, her slow smile freeing what felt like years of silence and caution and wariness of others. 'I thought you should know.'

'Well, thank you for your honesty.'

He laughed at her teasing gravity. Lifting the olive oil bottle, he asked in a low voice, 'So, do you want me to show you some other ways this can be used?'

For crying out loud, it was hard enough to resist him when he was all serious and cranky, but his sexy grin and the memories of all his touches and kisses and whispers last night were playing havoc with her self-control.

What would Kara and Alice say about it all? Would they worry for her? Perhaps, but somehow she reckoned that they would both be delighted that she was enjoying life again. And what was the harm? Both she and Ivo knew this was a fleeting moment in both of their lives. Nothing more than chemistry and opportunity playing out.

Yes, she had felt a pang of disappointment when she had woken earlier to find him gone, but she refused to dwell on the significance of it. They didn't owe each other explanations and she wasn't going to over-analyse his every move. Wasn't this the new type of person she wanted to be—laid back, care-free, not given to overthinking life?

Standing, she lowered the umbrella and, tossing a bottle of sun cream to him, she asked, 'Can you rub this into my back?'

She pulled off her top and then her shorts. Her heart hammered in her chest as his heated silver gaze moved down over her body. She lay down on her front on the sunbed, twisting her head to watch him.

Above her the hot morning sun beat down on her exposed skin, but it was nothing in comparison to the heat licking her insides as he moved to kneel beside her sunbed.

She jerked when he flipped open the top with his thumb, a devilish gleam in his eye. He squeezed a long trail of the white cream into his palm. Her eyelids closed involuntarily, a long, slow sigh moving through her body as the warm weight of his hand touched her collarbone, making circular movements down over her shoulder blades. She arched her back instinctively, pushing her groin into the thick cushion beneath her as his hand drifted down her spine, his other hand lifting up her bikini top to allow him to apply the cream there too.

She screwed her eyes shut even tighter, wishing he would say something to break the intense and ever-growing tension between them…wishing she could find something to say herself but knowing that if she opened her mouth a deep sexual purr would escape.

She pushed her hips even further into the bed when his hand moved down to the base of her spine, stifling a groan when he reached the scalloped edge of her bikini bottoms.

'Toni.'

Her whole body arched at his deep whisper and she opened her eyes, her heart fluttering at the playful desire in his eyes. His fingers danced over her lower back, skimming her bikini bottoms. And then a finger ran down over her thigh. 'I'll do your legs too…just to be safe.'

'It's okay, I can do it…' She trailed off, giving up any pretence that she'd rather do it herself. Who was she trying to kid?

His smile grew even darker, more devilish. He started at her ankles, his huge hands capturing both at the same time, performing some magical pressure. She bit down on her lip, thrown by how malleable she was in his hands, every inch of her self-restraint dissolving rapidly. Instead she felt an unburdened, delicious, innate hunger that made her body feel weightless except for the heavy pulse of desire in her very centre.

His hands worked their way up past the backs of her knees, over her thighs, and then his fingers moved to graze over the intimate space between her legs.

Unable to take much more, she flipped over, her cheeks blazing.

He blinked for a moment, their gazes clashing, hunger and desire obvious, neither of them trying to deny it.

He yanked off his polo shirt. She breathed in

deeply, the glory of his broad, rock-hard chest and moulded abs setting off tiny firecrackers of lust in her stomach. She grinned in approval, arching her back a fraction. She was rewarded with his gaze darkening even further.

He placed a finger at the base of her throat and very slowly and deliberately ran it down over her breastbone, into the valley between her breasts, her already hardened nipples bunching even tighter.

Down, down, down his finger travelled, skimming over her belly button until it reached the edge of her bikini.

He raised an eyebrow in question.

And her heart exploded in gratitude that once again he wanted to make sure that she was okay with every step of this. This wasn't dangerous…this was safe. Her throat tightened with emotion. And she nodded yes.

But his finger didn't move. Instead he lowered his mouth to hers and kissed her tenderly, his lips brushing over hers. The emotion in her throat tightened.

He pulled away, but his eyes remained glued to hers as his hand moved down over the fabric of the bikini and her hips rose automatically, her legs shifting ever so slightly apart.

She closed her eyes as his feather-light touch left her light-headed and disorientated. She groaned when his lips moved to her throat, her hands threading through his hair, curling down to caress the warm, broad stretch of his seemingly never-ending shoulders.

'Your body is incredible…so soft, so sensual.'

She tried to respond to him but she was incapable of anything other than nodding. In those moments she believed that her body *was* incredible, given the conviction of his voice. He did this to her all the time—looked at her with such regard and tenderness that it emboldened her, made her feel seen and treasured.

Opening her eyes, her heart flipped at the intensity of his gaze, deeply moved by how utterly seriously he wanted to give her pleasure. She shifted upwards, found his mouth, dragging him down with her, her entire body igniting at the firm heat of his lips.

She may have initiated the kiss but he soon took over the lead, his lips parting hers, his tongue exploring her mouth. It was a deep, lusty kiss that had her body arch, her nipples tighten, her breasts feel heavy and generous.

She gasped into the kiss when his hand skimmed over her stomach and up over her breasts, his hand cupping the tight swell, her nipple pressing hard into the softness of his palm.

She arched once again, her hands running over the bunched muscles of his back, his biceps, and the powerful and tight muscles of his waist, her hunger for him even more intense now that she knew what was to come, thanks to last night.

Crying out when his thumb flicked against her nipple, he somehow flipped them over in one smooth movement so that he was lying on the sunbed and she was on top.

For a moment she grew still, dazed by the shift, dazed at the freedom of lying on top of him but not sure that she actually wanted the vulnerability that came with lying half-naked on top of him. But there was something deeply sensual about the way the breeze was kissing her skin and she shifted her legs to either side of his wide thighs, anchoring her knees into the mattress. She gazed down at him, her mouth involuntary opening when his hands moved from her waist down over her bottom. Her head reared back, her nipples scraping over the solidity of his chest.

She kissed him again, deep and unapologetic, the movement of his hips under hers telling her that he liked what she was doing.

Long shivers ran through her as his fingers trailed over her spine. He was finding sensitive spots in her body she'd never known even existed—the indents at the bottom of her spine, the point where her neck ran into her collarbone.

He pulled the string of her bikini top, whispering for her to sit up. And when she did, he eased himself up too. Inch by inch he lifted her bikini up, his eyes drinking in the shape of her breasts. He pulled her closer, his hands resting on her bottom, his mouth closing over her nipple. She shuddered long and hard, the sensation exquisite.

He pulled away, desire tightening his expression. And she saw it in him too—bewilderment mixed in with demanding need. How could this be so powerful? What were they unleashing?

He eased down her top, reaching behind her to
retie the strings.

Unable to move, she stared at him in shock. Was
that it?

But, taking hold of her hips, he guided her until
she lay beside him, pulling her into his arms so that
her ear was pressed against his chest, his pounding
heart pulsing against her skin. He stroked her hair
and whispered gently, 'Later.'

CHAPTER SEVEN

THE DRINKS RECEPTION for the small group who had attended Gabriela's christening took place in the palace's garden room. Clusters of white roses, named in honour of her birth, adorned the room that overlooked Monrosa harbour.

Seated with his uncle Johan, Ivo tried to concentrate on his uncle's concerns over recent financial investments he had made, but his attention kept being drawn back to Toni, who was standing at the opposite side of the room, moving amongst the guests, introducing herself with ease, her cheerful demeanour, her natural enthusiasm, breaking down any resistance the other guests might have to a newcomer in their circle. Now that she was wearing a knee-length fitted pale pink dress, her hair held back with a tortoiseshell comb, it was hard to compute her elegance with the tousle-haired, sensual woman who had gazed down at him with such open hunger only a few hours ago. He didn't want this elegance, he wanted her raw and sensual. He wanted her naked and a bundle of sexual tension.

It had taken every ounce of his self-will to pull away from her on the beach. He had wanted to tear away those scant pieces of cloth and worship again her body that was so incredibly responsive. Her skin, her scent, the way her body uncoiled, her gasps, turned him on in a way he had never experienced before. She slotted against his body seamlessly, her femininity a perfect embodiment of everything that was amazing about life.

And that, right there, was exactly the reason why he had pulled away. He wasn't making sense any more...even to himself.

Moving to talk to Edwin and Kara, she glanced in his direction and frowned as though trying to figure something out. He looked away when she smiled at him, hating how much he wanted to be at her side. This was alien territory to him, to actively not want to be alone.

He breathed in deeply, rattling off some statistics to Johan on world market movements and central bank predictions, while he watched Toni chat to Edwin, who had grown in stature and unadulterated happiness since Gabriela's arrival.

Kara, holding Gabriela, was chatting with Luis, who was cooing over his new niece, Kara giggling over whatever Luis was saying, Gabriela staring at her uncle, no doubt as charmed as every other girl who had ever met his brother.

Edwin and Luis were working closely together now. Edwin's second in command, Luis was also the chair of Monrosa's tourism sector, which played a vital role in the country's economy. He had always felt apart from his brothers, but now more so than ever, not only because of their close working relationship but also their mutual delight in their marriages.

He stayed where he was seated when Johan excused himself to go in search of his aunt, Princess Maria, his attention once again drawn back to Toni, who was laughing at something Luis was saying to her. He tore his eyes away, fighting the empty sensation opening up in his stomach. And then the hairs on the back of his neck stood up. Instinctively turning, he saw his father, who was seated by the palace's permanent elaborate display of orchids that had been his mother's passion. His father was staring towards him, nodding at what Alice was saying to him, no doubt something to do with the latest of the Monrosian history books they wrote together detailing the trials and tribulations of his ancestors, which were proving to be huge international hits, but Ivo could tell that his father's concentration was in fact on him.

What did he want? Why the staring? His father was changing. Retirement and the arrival of his first grandchild were softening him, and Ivo didn't know how to deal with it. He especially didn't know how to deal with his father's awkward enquiries on how Pacolore was doing. Only last month he had unexpectedly arrived at the *finca* and they had spent an uncomfortable hour in each other's company, the sovereign investment portfolio the only topic of conversation that they had been able to settle upon. His father had left with the disgruntled expression of someone who had not achieved what he had set out to do. Ivo wasn't a fool. He knew his father was trying to patch up their relationship. But how do you heal twenty years of silence?

His father stood and walked towards him. He stood too, darting a glance in Toni's direction, intending to go and speak to her as an excuse to avoid his father. But she too was coming towards him, holding Gabriela, a brilliant smile lighting up her face.

His father was moving closer. Ivo stepped towards Toni. 'We should be leaving.'

She shook her head, handing Gabriela to him. 'This little lady would like some time with you first.' Then, turning to his father, she smiled in welcome and went and sat on the chair opposite him, a deliberate move in order to let the chair next to him be free.

How did Ivo manage to look so comfortable holding Gabriela? Wasn't he scared of dropping her the way she was? And God only knew how she would cope if Gabriela started crying. She had zero experience with babies. In truth, they terrified her. During the christening ceremony Ivo had lifted his niece from her father's arms and had held and cosseted her like a pro, performing a little jiggle to quell her whimpers when she had grown restless. Ivo set himself apart from his family, his silence even more pronounced in their company. But could Gabriela help heal the silent distance between them?

Now Gabriela's hand curled around Ivo's finger and he smiled down at her, truly enchanted with his niece. He looked so gorgeous… The Machine taken down by a cooing baby.

She caught Ivo's father's eye and cringed at his speculative gaze. Oh, great, he had spotted her mooning over Ivo.

'I understand that you are interviewing Ivo.'

Other than when Ivo had introduced her earlier, when it was obvious that he didn't remember her from Luis and Alice's wedding, this was the first time Ivo's father had spoken to her.

'That's correct, Your Highness.'

His father lifted an eyebrow. 'Are you having much success?'

Ivo looked sharply at his father and then at her, his expression tensing.

'Yes, it's…' She bit back a smile. 'Ivo is surprising me in many, many ways.'

She resisted the temptation to laugh at Ivo's horrified expression and turned her attention back to his father. 'It's the most pleasurable and thought-provoking interview I have ever conducted and your son is an amazing man.'

His father looked from her to Ivo, his expression astonished but then fading to what almost looked like sadness. 'I'll look forward to listening to the interview in that case. Maybe I'll learn something.'

Ivo frowned. 'You'll listen to it?'

'Of course I will.'

Ivo worked his jaw, looked down at Gabriela, who was staring up at him with rapt attention, and said, 'We still have material to record.' He held his father's gaze for a long, steady beat. 'Given that the purpose of the podcast is to raise mental health awareness, it's my intention to speak about Mother and the impact her death had on me.'

The air around them seemed to evaporate, a tight tension replacing it.

'That's private family business.' Ivo went to say something but his father waved away his interjection. 'But… I understand why you would want to.' Looking down towards Gabriela, he added, 'It's time we dealt with some of the past.' Shifting his attention towards her, Ivo's father added, 'I may not have always taken the correct decisions when it came to family matters and my children possibly paid the price.'

With that Ivo's father stood and walked away from them.

Ivo stared after him, his expression furious.

And then he stared at her, his expression darkening even further. She had done nothing wrong. Why, then, did he look as though he'd happily lock her in the dungeons beneath the palace and throw away the key?

'Care to tell me what's eating you up?'

Ivo gritted his teeth and pushed even harder down on the accelerator. Minutes passed, words bubbling inside of him, some words years old, others more recent. He gripped the steering wheel tight, pulling the car around corners.

Everything was changing. And he didn't know how to react. He prided himself on being cool and detached, thinking things through logically and burying anything he didn't want to confront. But all of a sudden he was feeling emotions that weren't part of him. Mostly anger.

'Can you slow down, please?'

He inhaled a breath and, though he wanted to press the accelerator even harder he eased back. 'I wasn't driving fast.'

Even to his own ears he knew he was being unreasonable, but he felt an unnerving need to be defensive and cranky…and to push Toni away.

'Why don't you let me drive?'

He let out an exasperated breath. 'No.'

'You're obviously upset about something.'

'I'm *not* upset.' He swallowed hard, aiming to say no more, but Toni's hand as it came to rest on his seat beside his thigh, the solidarity of the gesture, made him realise that he was bone-tired of leading a life of silence, of constantly keeping his emotions in check.

'I'm an outsider. I'm an outsider in every part of my life.' He paused, his words taking him by surprise. And yet he could not manage to contain them. Instead they spilled out of him like blood gushing from a wound. 'It feels at times that I'm standing outside my own life and observing it from a distance. How can I be so detached, even from myself?'

He let out another angry breath, frustrated with himself. Why was he telling her all of this?

'Has it always felt that way?'

What was the point in this conversation—what could answering her question achieve? Her hand moved closer, the warmth of her fingers touching his thigh. In response, the need to explain himself shunted his de-fault setting of silence right out of the picture. 'Before my mother died, I didn't feel that way...at least, I don't think so. It was such a long time ago. After she died I didn't know who to turn to, who to trust, and it felt safer to withdraw and rely only on myself.'

'You didn't feel safe with your father and brothers?'

'They had their own stuff to deal with.' How could he explain the suffocating guilt he had felt after his mother's death? Why he hadn't wanted to be a burden to anyone? How he had been terrified of crying in front of the thousands who had lined the streets for her funeral? Displays of such emo-tion would have horrified his family. And worse still he would have been letting his mother down by in-dulging in his own emotions instead of respectfully maintaining a dignified bearing.

'It must have been a very lonely time for you.'

He shrugged, a heavy weight forming in his chest, remembering the days when he couldn't bring him-self to leave his bedroom, watching his family come and go from the palace, desperately wishing some-one would come and sit with him. But instead his father would send an aide to try and persuade him out of his room.

'Maybe, given what your father said earlier, you can now work on your relationship with him.'

'Perhaps.'

'Why are you so afraid to talk, to express what you need and want from others?'

He was thrown not only by what she said, but also

by the soft emotion in her voice, and his cranky side reared its head again. 'Maybe because I don't want to.'

She waited until he had negotiated around a group of cyclists before she replied, 'I get that you are an intensely private person, but you need some connections in life, safe connections. You need to learn to trust people, know that they won't intentionally hurt you.'

He flicked a glance in her direction. 'Can I trust you?'

She blinked at his question and he cursed silently at her disappointed expression. 'I'd have hoped you'd know the answer to that already, without needing to ask me…but yes, you can trust me.' She inhaled a long, deep breath. 'But it's with the key people in your life, your family, that you need to open up. I know it's not going to be easy and that there's a lot of complicated history there, but I saw it in you tonight… I know that you want to be a part of your family. Maybe you're all in the right emotional place now for things to change.'

They were approaching the gates to San Jorbo. His anger had now turned to frustration. 'I wouldn't even know where to start.'

Not waiting to exchange some words with the security team at the gate as he usually would do, he drove straight through.

Toni twisted in her seat so that she was looking directly at him. 'Spend time with them. Invite your father here. Visit Gabriela. You're so natural and comfortable with her. A new generation can mean a new start for you all. Things can change, people can change.'

'Even me?'

'If you want to, you can. I guess it's down to what you actually want in life. Do you want to be part of your family and all of the positives and negatives that come with that? Or are you happier being alone, reliant only on yourself?'

He glanced at her and asked, 'Couldn't I be asking you the same questions?'

She shrugged. 'I have my mum and my friends.'

Pulling the car to a stop at the *finca*, he asked, 'And that's enough for you?'

'For now, yes, it is.' Reaching down to pick up her handbag from the footwell, she grimaced and on a sigh said, 'Can I be frank, just so that we are both straight on all of this?' She waved a hand to emphasise she was talking about what was going on between them. 'Even if I was looking to be in a relationship, you would be the last person I would want to date. Yes, you have a long list of incredible attributes—you're hot, successful, intelligent, et cetera, et cetera… But you're too complicated, too deep for me. You'd drive me nuts with your silences. I need someone who's upfront, who wears his heart on his sleeve. I'd be an emotional mess around you, I'd never know what you were really thinking, and quite frankly you'd exhaust me.'

How was he supposed to respond? Should he be pleased, insulted, relieved? Instead he went with puzzled. 'Why are you telling me this?'

'So that we both know where we stand.'

'Stand?'

'With us sleeping together... Why did you pull away down at the beach earlier?'

Irritated that she was so easily dismissing him as nothing more than a passing fling, he answered, 'Based on what happened last night, I wasn't sure we'd make Gabriela's christening in time if we continued... but I'm happy to make amends now.'

Oh, crikey. What had she started? Ivo looked seriously hacked off...and ready to pounce. She leapt out of the car, her heart hammering. She bolted for the front door and had to wait for Ivo to unfurl himself from the car, stretch as though he had all the time in the world and eventually saunter towards her, his expression giving zero away.

Her heart was now a loud drum in her chest, her breathing so shallow she was growing increasingly light-headed.

He came to a stop before her and considered her. She tried to keep up her pretence of nonchalance but with her head thrown back to meet his intense silver gaze, her body alive to every perfect detail of his formidable body, his silence truly unnerving, she had the ridiculous urge to run.

The next thing she knew, she was lying firefighter's-lift-style on his shoulder, and he was carrying her down the path towards the beach, jettisoning her sandals in the process. 'What are you doing?'

'I think we could both do with cooling off.'

Down at the beach he carried her to the water-front, where he dropped her onto the golden sand.

Without a word he twisted her around, to face the lights of Laredo, the thrum of far-off music and the break of waves the only sounds. He drew down the zip of her dress. She gasped as he twisted her hair away to kiss and caress her neck, his hands slowly running the length of her spine.

He pushed her dress down to the waist, his hand circling over her stomach, hugging her to his body, while his mouth continued its tender assault.

She arched into him as his hands captured her breasts, his thumbs skimming over the lace edges of her bra. His mouth moved to her earlobe, gently biting as he lowered her dress to the sand.

She inhaled a shaky breath. 'Will we be seen?'

He gave a teasing chuckle. 'It's much too dark. Are you having second thoughts?'

She gasped when his teeth bit down on her earlobe again, an erotic thrill almost cutting her in two. He didn't wait for her to answer but instead turned her around to face him, unbuttoning his shirt, flinging it to the ground, his shoes and trousers soon following. His white trunks were moulded to his body like a second skin.

He dropped to his knees. She stumbled backwards but he grabbed her by the hips and eased her back towards him, his lips touching her belly. He moved across her skin with a painful, reverential slowness, her heart giving way to a tenderness, a wash of affection overwhelming her. He eased the band of her panties down an inch, his lips grazing over her hips.

She dropped to her knees and her hands roamed

over the warm solidness of his chest, down over the steel strength of his stomach.

She parted her lips, wanting his lips on hers. Wanting him to take the lead. His hands cradled her head and his mouth found hers, the kiss light and teasing, his teeth nipping against her bottom lip, building up the tension pitch perfectly.

On her moan he gave her what she wanted. A full-on, deep and penetrating kiss, his mouth controlling hers, the pressure and passion a prequel to what was to come.

When he pulled away, breathing deeply, he stood, pulling her up too, his gaze raking over her body. 'Strip for me.'

She hesitated but his passion, his long, appreciative gaze on her breasts, on her hips, had her reach around and unclip her bra. She edged the straps over her shoulders, drew the fabric down inch by inch, her nipples hardening at the night air and Ivo's rumbling exhale of approval.

He cupped her breast in his hand, desire throbbing through his body at its firmness. His thumb passed over the tight bud of her nipple, smiling as she gasped.

He wanted to take her now. Push her down onto the sand, whip off her panties, which he hadn't given her the chance to remove, blown away by the sight of her gorgeous breasts. He had never desired someone so wholly.

'Are you okay with all of this?'

She pulled back. 'Why…aren't you?'

'I want to make sure that you are happy to continue.'

She let out a shaky laugh. 'I never thought I'd say this to you, but can we stop talking?'

He lowered his head with a chuckle, drew her breast into his mouth and sucked, the clasp of her hands on his head, her gasps for air confirming that the carnal pulses of pleasure pounding through him in tasting her, in having her nipple pressed against the tip of his tongue, weren't one-sided. He sucked deeper, a ravenous desire that was different to anything he had ever experienced making him lost to everything but the wonder of worshipping her body.

But after a while he reluctantly broke away, wanting her to know him, wanting her to know that all of this was not the norm for him…that this *was* different. Struggling to breathe, he panted out against her skin as he trailed kisses over her collarbone, 'I've always held a fantasy of having sex on this beach, but up until now I hadn't met someone I actually wanted to do it with.'

She gave a soft laugh. 'Should I take that as a compliment?'

'Yes, you should.' He paused, trying to find the right words for what he was trying to express. 'This is different for me…this is not the norm. I want you to know that.'

Dio! Did any of that make sense?

Clearly not, given her puzzled silence. He drew in a breath. 'With you…the need to be with you is different…it's real and raw and essential.' Pausing, he added, 'I hope this is making sense to you.'

Nodding as though it made perfect sense, she whispered, 'It does.'

His heart turned over and he kissed her again, this time with all of the tenderness and care he could muster.

And then he stood and led her into the sea, keeping hold of her hand as they waded through the tepid water until it was at his chest level. Wrapping her legs around his waist, he kissed her, the taste of her mouth and the salty water mingling, her breasts pressed against his chest. He deepened the kiss and she squirmed against his stomach, tightening her legs around his waist.

Still kissing her, he eased her legs down, his hands caressing her bottom, moving between her legs. She bucked hard against his fingers, groaning into his mouth. She pulled away, dragging him to shallower water, and once there she kissed him hard and swiftly before her hands edged down to his briefs.

He kissed her again, needing the warmth of her mouth, the sweet taste of her skin, every inch of him wanting her. His hand went to her hips, pushing down her panties, removing them, before he pulled her back against him, lifting her off her feet so that his arousal pushed into the hard bone of her pelvis, both of them rocking in unison, desperate for release as they exchanged brief, tempestuous kisses, both of them too short of breath, too desperate for anything longer.

'I should take you to the *finca*.'

She shook her head. 'No, I want to be your fan-

tasy. I want to do it here…where it's raw and real…
and beautiful.'

On a groan he left her for a few seconds while
he found protection in his wallet and sheathed himself. Back in the water he carried her out into deeper
water. She gasped when he pushed forward, her head
falling against his shoulder when he eased all his
length into her. Her body countered his movements,
her kisses ever more passionate and desperate. He
clasped her bottom, lost to the push of her nipples
against his skin, their soft femininity, the endless
curves of her entire body.

Her movements grew ever more frantic, driving
him down a narrow tunnel of bittersweet hunger for
fulfilment, but he clung to the desire to stay at this
edge for ever.

She pulled back, her eyes glazed, her lips parting.
She made a tiny noise.

Dio! She was beautiful.

His climax edged ever closer.

She let out another sound. One of pure wonder.
And then, her head tipping backwards, her back
arching, her hair cascading down into the water,
she found release. Her sounds, the rhythm of her
body bringing him to a long and hard climax, his
body convulsed into the sweetest pleasure he had
ever experienced.

CHAPTER EIGHT

SHE WOKE WITH her legs entangled in his. It should seem strange to wake in his bedroom but it just felt right. Just as it felt right to turn and find him staring at her and to return his grin.

He touched the whorl of her ear, his movement as considerate and thoughtful as his lovemaking had been throughout the night…well after what had happened down at the beach. Had they really done that? It had been wild and unpredictable. But in its aftermath they had returned to the *finca*, showered and made love in his bed, time and time again.

'You have sand in your ear.'

His voice was soft and groggy with sleep, his hair tousled.

She was flying too close to the sun. But so what? It would all be over in twenty-four hours. She wasn't going to overthink any of this. Instead she was going to stubbornly remain in this cocoon of pleasure.

She pushed him onto his back, lying on top of him, delight coursing through her at his groan when she nuzzled his neck, inhaling his rich, musky scent that spoke of exertion and freshly laundered cotton.

His hands explored her back with long caresses that instantly turned her to liquid. 'Your hands are incredible.' She lifted her head, her eyes rolling as she gave a tiny, carnal groan. 'If you ever need to give up your day job you'd make a wonderful masseuse.'

Pulling her down so that their mouths touched, he nibbled her lips, muttering, 'Your body is one sensitive point after another... I'll never get enough of you.'

She deepened their kiss, her heart jolting at his words. She knew not to pay too much heed to them—things were said and felt in the heat of lovemaking that bore no relation to life outside of the dream world woven within the confines of a bedroom.

Yes, their lovemaking was more than just physical—even she would admit that there was an emotional joining happening between them—but that didn't alter the fact that neither of them was looking for anything more than a transitory space of simply being together.

She moved down his body, her lips touching the hard landscape of his chest, the ache inside her intensifying as her tongue tasted the saltiness of his skin, his need pressing into her belly.

But before she could go any further he reached down and pulled her upwards, flipping her over in the process. Eyes aflame, he moved on top of her, his head dipping to her breast, his fingers moving between her legs, softly exploring.

'Are you ready?'

She nodded, hot, dizzying desire stripping away her ability to speak. Her hips were moving restlessly, needing him, the heat in his eyes burning her up.

And then he moved into her.

Their gazes holding one another's, they stared and stared into each other's eyes, a silent message of connection, of regard, of care, beating out between them.

And when his movements quickened she lifted her hips higher to meet him, and they fell apart together, the intensity, the intimacy of sharing such a powerful and elemental moment almost breaking her in two.

They sat on the sofa in the living room to record their last interview, the terrace doors open, the warm midday heat flowing in on a breeze.

She was desperately trying not to show it but she was nervous. There was a gentleness, an understanding between them that she didn't want to destroy by some ill-judged question on her part, or Ivo reverting to his usual guarded self.

She adjusted the cuff of her shorts—Ivo had said he would take her hiking to visit the most westerly point of the island after their interview—and asked, 'I want to talk about your rowing career, being royal and family life—is that okay?'

He nodded but the tension lines at the corners of his eyes tightened. She wasn't the only apprehensive one.

'You're uncomfortable with this interview, aren't you?'

He shrugged in answer to her question.

She needed this interview. There wasn't enough material from their other interviews for an hour-long broadcast, and what was there didn't give a real insight into Ivo. But could she really make demands on him because of her professional needs…? Somehow none of this felt right any more. She swallowed, wondering if she had served anyone right this weekend. Meeting his gaze, she admitted, 'I'm struggling with this… I need more content but I don't want to put you in a position you're uncomfortable with. Because of everything that has happened between us on a personal level, I don't have the professional distance I should have.' She stopped trying to figure out exactly what she was trying to say and, taking a deep breath, added, 'I want this interview to serve you well. Of course I want it to be insightful and helpful to listeners, but I also want it to represent who you really are, while respecting your privacy.'

'Why?'

It was such a good question…why, then, was she struggling so much to answer it? She bit her lip trying to put into words the twisting emotion in her heart. 'I've grown to like and respect you… I guess I'm struggling here with balancing how much access you have given me on a personal level to your life and what you want to divulge to the listeners. I don't want to be overly intrusive in my questioning.'

He considered her for the longest time, seriously at first but then a smile lifting the corners of his mouth. 'Thank you.'

She waited for him to say something more, her heart kicking wildly at the quiet pleasure in his expression, the warmth glistening in his eyes. Somehow her inarticulateness had got through to him. He understood this interview was a delicate balancing act in preserving what was between them.

She pushed away the thought that all her words were motivated by more than just doing right by him in the interview...that she was trying to maintain something between them that could last longer than this weekend alone.

Ivo's smile widened even further and once again the fondness between them morphed into heat and desire that danced between them wickedly.

With an exasperated exhale Ivo nodded at the recording equipment. 'Let's get this over and done with before we get sidetracked...again.'

Several times this morning they had attempted to get up, but every time one of them stood, the other would drag them back to bed. And when she had gone for a shower, Ivo had followed her in under the hot spray. And later, when attempting to dress, she had got as far as pulling on her underwear before Ivo had pulled it off again, ignoring her giggles and protests...making love to her against the door of his dressing room.

With a shaky hand she pressed 'record', looking at the questions she had written down over breakfast as Ivo had caught up with his emails. The easy silence between them had made her heart quicken and she had tried to ignore the temptation of daydreaming about long, lazy weekends alone with him in the future.

Now she said, 'You attended two international championships and were favourite to win gold at both. But, while you won gold in your second bid, at the first you famously finished fourth. How did you cope with that, especially the well-publicised media criticism?'

Ivo arched his neck, grimacing before he answered, 'Our performance at the first championships was crushing. As a team we didn't perform to the best of our abilities and we knew we had let all of Monrosa down. We had known that there were special screenings of the race being staged across the island and were inundated with messages of goodwill. Disappointing our supporters was the worst part. For a few weeks after the race I considered quitting the sport. The effort and hours involved in training at that level are gruelling, but I also questioned my ability on the water.'

'But you were considered the lynchpin of the team—what did the rest of them say about you potentially leaving?'

He shrugged. 'We all went our separate ways immediately after the race. None of us was in the mood to talk. The others wanted to be with their wives and partners.'

'Are you saying that you didn't talk to them about how you were feeling?'

'No.'

Taken aback, she paused, shocked but also upset

at the extent to which Ivo had isolated himself. She couldn't imagine being part of a team and not talking openly about something so crucial. 'Didn't you share how you were feeling with them at any point... or with anyone else, for that matter?'

Once again he shrugged. 'What was the point? It wasn't going to change our loss. I soon realised that I was wasting energy focusing on my disappointment and that I needed to concentrate on the end goal— to bring a gold medal back to Monrosa. After the first bid we reviewed every aspect of our training plan, from our nutrition to our race schedule. And it worked. We became a much stronger team. From a defeat you can become stronger, if you focus on what you want to achieve.'

He was shifting the conversation away from the fact that he didn't talk to anyone about how crushed he must have felt after the first bid. No doubt deliberately. Could she push him on it? How would he react if she did? Why did this feel like such a tight-rope of an interview? What did it say about their relationship that she was so worried about driving him back beyond the wall of silence he so favoured, by asking him to explore in greater depth his thoughts and feelings? This was crazy...she had a job to do. 'Can I take you back to the fact that you didn't talk to anyone about how you were feeling during that time...didn't you find that difficult? Didn't it make it worse not being able to talk about it?'

Ivo frowned at her question and for a moment she thought he was going to gloss over it, but then with a minute shake of his head he answered, 'At the time I was of the mind frame that no amount of talking would make a difference—' he paused and smiled '—but thanks to the last few days with you I'm starting to appreciate that sharing experiences can be beneficial.'

She grinned at that, blushed even. 'It's a careful balance between protecting yourself and honesty, isn't it?' Holding his gaze, the intimacy of their love-making so vivid and poignant, she admitted, 'I know you probably won't agree but on balance I think I'd prefer to lead an open life.'

'Actually I do think you're right...it's the braver option, to be open.'

Taken aback by his words, she studied him for a moment and asked, 'Do you really?'

He nodded. 'Yes.'

She had to remember her listeners. Would any of this make any sense to them? She needed to ask him direct and challenging questions that pushed him to be more open, but inside she rebelled at the thought that she might upset the sensitive balance between them. She gritted her teeth, realising that she was scared of giving him a reason to walk away from her. Was what was between them so delicate, so easily broken? 'You were given the nickname the Machine because of your reputation for being impenetrable. Are you saying that you wished you were more open...or that you want to be in the future?'

'I'm private by nature and it has served me in the past...but as my life and career change I'm starting to appreciate the need for openness as well. Whether I can translate that understanding into actual behaviour, time will tell.' He gave her a wry smile. 'As they say, old habits die hard.'

'Who in your life do you want to be more open with?'

Her question earned her another wry smile. 'Thanks to our interviews, I guess I now have the opportunity to be more open with the wider world. I'm talking about aspects of my life that I've never shared before. But it's with those close to me, my family in particular, that I realise that I need a more forthright relationship.'

She nodded encouragingly, wanting him to say more, trying to ignore the thought that she wished he would say that he wanted a closer relationship with her, but hating herself for having such a ridiculous wish when Ivo had never given her any reason to hope for such a thing happening. And mentally she performed an eye roll, frustrated with herself for yet again trying to camouflage her own insecurities by the lure of the distraction and safety of a relationship.

She almost sighed in relief when Ivo spoke again, glad that at least he was moving the interview along and not getting bogged down in rambling inner thoughts as she was. 'Because I attended boarding school as a teenager and then my rowing career dominated my life in the following years, my relationship with my family is somewhat distant, and it's something I know I need to address.'

She was glad. She gave him an encouraging smile,

the tension in his expression lightening. She studied her notes, not wanting to think that from tomorrow, other than what she would glean from conversations with Alice and Kara, she would never know how his attempts to connect with his family would fare. She was in regular contact with her previous interviewees but right now she wasn't certain what type of relationship she would manage to foster with Ivo going forward. 'Given the sacrifices a rowing career demands, what was your motivation for wanting to win a gold medal?'

'I'm incredibly proud to be from Monrosa and I wanted to be able to give something back to the people. I wanted to be able to win a medal for the country.'

'Dedicating your life for the best part of a decade to achieving that for your country takes huge self-discipline and sacrifice. Do you ever regret it, or did you even question it when you were in the middle of it all?'

Ivo shook his head. 'No. I'm deeply conscious and appreciative of the privileges afforded me by my position in the Monrosian royal family. I hope that in my athletic career and now in my advisory role in the Treasury that I can contribute to Monrosa's success and identity.' Pausing, he rubbed his neck. 'I prefer to lead a low-profile life. It's my hope that the public can understand my preference for such a life but know that Monrosa is very important and an integral part of me. Now that I'm living here full-time, I truly appreciate what an incredible country it is. I want to see the country continue to thrive.' He was visibly emotional when he added, 'I'm very proud of all of the changes Edwin is making and want to continue to be part of ensuring the country's continued success.'

For a moment she hesitated in responding, wondering if she was about to destroy just how engaged Ivo was with the interview. And destroy that fragile openness between them. 'The people of Monrosa and external commentators were shocked when your father announced his abdication. Were you? And what do you think his legacy is?'

He frowned at her question, his gaze cooling. She resisted the urge to ask him another question, to smooth away the sudden tension between them, wanting to test how much he was prepared to accept her probing, how much he was prepared to be truly honest with her.

'Yes, I was shocked.' His voice was terse.

'Why?'

Her heart thumped to see his expression tighten. She had lost him. But still she forced herself to hold his gaze, tilting her head upwards, daring him to push her away.

His gaze narrowed but then he answered, 'Being monarch was everything to him. Even more so after the death of my mother. It gave him purpose. I never thought he would be prepared to walk away from that, but he did in order to see Monrosa prosper, believing that the country needed more energy and ideas from a younger monarch. I admire him for taking such a difficult personal decision for the greater good.'

Stopping, he considered her for long moments before adding, 'The following is off the record.'

When she nodded her acceptance, he grimaced and added, 'But that was not the only reason why my father abdicated. He also did so in order to force Edwin to marry and to have children.'

Had she heard right? 'Force him to marry?'

'Edwin and Kara…it was an arranged marriage.'

'No! But they are crazy about one another.' She stopped, realising that she was suddenly close to tears. He had to be making this up. None of this made sense. Kara's marriage couldn't be a sham. If it was…then what hope did anyone else have?

'They were always crazy about one another…but it took my father's interference for them to wake up to that fact.'

'Are you saying that he orchestrated the whole thing?'

'I don't know…perhaps. He definitely wanted heirs to the throne… My father has many faults but he did love my mother greatly. I believe he wanted the same for Edwin.'

'And for you and Luis?'

He gave a brief nod yes. And she swallowed at the thought that Ivo's father wanted him to marry. She pretended to draw a line through some of her questions, trying not to think about sitting and watching Ivo's televised wedding. He might be insistent right now that he didn't want to marry, but, with time and pressure from his father, would he eventually relent?

She needed to ask him another question but, meeting his gaze, she felt her heart lurch, realising that he had just told her something deeply personal and private. Biting her lip, she longed to ask him why he had shared it with her, but, fearing that she would sound needy and that the question would only serve her own vanity and insecurities, she said instead, not stopping to think about the wisdom of doing so, 'You'd be a great dad...if you ever decide to be one.'

He raised a disbelieving eyebrow.

'But you would... I've seen you with Gabriela. You're as soft as putty around her. If I hadn't seen you with my own eyes and got to know you better this weekend I would have said that maybe you would be a distant dad, a little too rigid and strict. But now I know that you would be calm and strong and stable.'

He gave what almost looked like a regretful smile but then shrugged it off, gesturing to her notebook. 'I think we should get back to the main interview.'

She nodded and scanned her list, trying to decide what her next question should be while her mind whirred with a multitude of contemplations.

Did he believe her when she said he'd be a good father? Did he trust and value her opinion enough to listen to what she said? Why was she saying any of this anyway? What was she trying to achieve? What type of mother did he think she would be?

Her brain felt such a mess. This was supposed to

be about her having fun, accepting the joy of a short-term affair. She wasn't supposed to be overthinking it all or placing too much importance on what was only a fleeting, joyous outtake on normal life. She needed to get back to the task at hand—now.

'Going back to what you said earlier about public life—do you feel pressure to lead a more public and open life?'

'I appreciate how important the monarchy is in Monrosian life and I understand why the public and media want to see and have access to the royal family. But I'm a private person by nature and prefer to lead a more low-profile life.'

'Have there been times when you have found public life particularly demanding?'

'Obviously the scrutiny and commentary after our first failed international bid was at times difficult.' He considered her for a moment and her heart missed a beat at the emotion that swirled between them in those few seconds. 'But it was in the aftermath of my mother's death that I struggled most with having to maintain a public presence.'

His heart was hammering in his chest. He couldn't believe he was actually admitting all of this. He was supposed to be stoic and never, ever confess to struggling or personal failures. It would be so easy to blame Toni and her questions that went far beyond anything any other journalist had asked of him before. But in truth he wanted to speak, he wanted to be honest about the strains caused by not being able to be true to himself. He wanted others to understand that they were not alone in needing to find self-acceptance. It was as though Toni had unlocked something in him. Was it how natural and good it felt to have someone else in the *finca*, despite all of his initial reservations about it? Or was it how physically depleted he felt after their endless lovemaking? Or how emotionally calm he felt after looking into her eyes time and time again as their bodies joined, her soft smiles of delight, how eagerly she had accepted his kisses and touches, no barriers, no tension existing between them? Just absolute acceptance of the intimate moments they were sharing.

'Do you want to speak about your mum?'

He closed his eyes, decades-old grief catching him by surprise at her softly spoken question. But he wasn't the only one to lose a parent…people were going through it right now and just maybe he could help them understand that there was no right or wrong way to grieve. 'After she died I was incredibly confused and of course extremely sad. At first I was too shocked to talk, and when I was ready to speak those around me were in different places in their own grieving. I think any parents or carers listening should allow their child to grieve at their own pace and in their own way. At the start I needed time alone to process what was happening…but that was not the case for others in my family who needed to be surrounded by people. There's no one way to grieve and I think there needs to be more awareness and understanding of that fact. Always respect where the person is, but also make them aware that you are there when they are ready to talk.'

'Did you talk to anyone when your mum died?'

He gave a regretful shrug. 'For a long time I wasn't ready...and the people closest to me were struggling too.' He stopped, remembering his father's acceptance yesterday when he said he was going to speak about all of this. He could choose to be angry over his father's impatient fury back then, his insistence on following royal protocol and doing what was right publicly as opposed to what was right for his own sons, but to do so would benefit no one. He *had* to make this new-found openness work for everyone's benefit.

'For a long time I believed that shutting down and denying my feelings was the easiest way to cope. But it comes at a price and for me it was a gulf that developed between me and my family. Because I shut down I couldn't engage with them and it was easier to isolate myself from others because then I didn't have to deal with the regrets and guilt that come from distancing yourself.'

'Why guilt?'

Dio! Did she have all day? What son wanted to be a disappointment to his father? What brother wanted to witness his siblings' concern? To know that they pitied him? And then there was all of the guilt of having abandoned his mother, knowing that there was no one at her side when she died. And worst of all the guilt of knowing that if he hadn't begged his mother to go trekking with him that day, if he hadn't raced ahead, then just maybe she could still have been alive. But he wasn't going to load all that on Toni or her listeners. What would be the point? What good could come from laying out all of his failings for others to pick over?

I needed to withdraw within myself to cope with everything that happened but for various reasons it went on too long—my own inclination to be private, the fact that we were sent away to boarding school at a young age. I used to think that the resilience I learnt in how to deal with life on my own was entirely positive, but increasingly I am appreciating the benefit of connecting with others, of being there for them too. It's something I want to rectify with my family. I don't want past tensions to affect the next generation.'

Toni smiled and his heart tightened at the warm empathy shining in her eyes. She lowered her gaze for a moment, before asking softly, 'What are your hopes for the future?'

Up until a few days ago he could have answered that question easily. To grow Pacolore Investments to ensure that he could employ even more a diverse range of people to careers that truly challenged them, and to support local communities within Monrosa in the rejuvenation of forgotten towns and villages. But after this weekend with Toni, realising just how good it was to have company in the *finca*, the question of personal hopes was suddenly on the agenda, but articulating them when he wasn't certain what it was he actually wanted was not something he wanted to think about right now, never mind talk about. 'I have a very fulfilling life at the moment. There isn't much I want to change other than spending more time with my family.'

Toni nodded. But there was a reticence in the way she smiled at him before asking, 'Will you talk to us again in the future? I'm sure the listeners would like to hear how you are doing.'

Why was he grinning at the prospect of another interview with Toni? After all, he hated interviews. But the idea lightened something in him...bringing a feeling of hope, the sense of a future he hadn't imagined for himself. Inhaling, he knew he needed to hold tight to himself all those crazy thoughts and messy emotions Toni was eliciting in him. He folded his arms. 'Does that mean another four-day interview?'

'We can do it whatever way you want—by phone if you'd prefer it that way.' She shrugged as though to say it was of no consequence to her what way they did it. Was that how she really felt? Didn't she want to see him again? Was catching up with him truly just for the podcast?

Shifting closer to the microphone, she spoke directly into it. 'My time with Prince Ivo is drawing to a close here on Monrosa. Thank you for your hospitality...' Her gaze settling on him, she frowned, her smile wavering before she reached and pressed some buttons on the recording equipment. Standing, she quickly started to pack things away. 'I usually do a summary of my time spent with my podcast guest to round off the interview,' glancing outside, she added, 'but, as it's such a nice day, it'd be a shame not to make the most of it. I can record my summary in London next week.'

He could tell that she didn't want to do the summary for reasons other than making the most of the day. He rolled his neck, suddenly tense. What would she say about him? Would she speak negatively about his way of life? Pass judgement on him personally? 'How are you going to summarise your stay here?'

Closing the zip of her laptop bag, she inhaled a long breath. 'I don't know... I need some time to process the whole weekend.' She rolled her eyes. 'I think the lack of sleep is messing with my ability to think straight.' Lowering her eyelids, she shrugged before adding, 'Everything feels very confused right now.'

The low sadness in her voice felt like a stab to his heart. He got her confusion. His own ability to think straight was long gone. And panic, that he might significantly mess up when it came to Toni, had taken its place. Should he let her go, accept this weekend for what it was, or take the risk of inviting someone into his life? He couldn't believe he was even contemplating doing so.

Toni went and stood by the door out to the terrace, her back to him. Arching her spine, she raised her arms up high, her fingertips touching the top of the doorframe, stretching out. She moved with a slow and graceful fluidity. For a long while she stood there, not moving, content to stare out towards the sea. Had San Jorbo's special magic seeped into her bones too? He smiled at how at peace she seemed...

could she be happy here? Or would she soon long for the noise and chaos of city life?

Turning, she took a hair tie from her shorts, pulling her hair back into a ponytail, and smiled so tenderly and intimately at him that his heart sang with a happiness so deep he knew that he had to find a way to keep her in his life.

Shading her eyes with her hand, Toni looked in the direction Ivo was pointing towards. 'San Amaro Chapel. Princess Isabella funded its construction in the sixteenth century, ordering that it should be built on the most westerly point of the island. She wanted it to be the symbol of welcome to all returning seafarers.'

The small whitewashed chapel had a golden dome that glowed brightly under the relentless sun, and from their vantage point in the hills to its rear Toni could see a group of people milling around outside, their cars parked along the narrow, single-vehicle road that ran beside it.

They followed the track down to join the road, clusters of red rhododendrons flame-like in amongst the otherwise endless dusty green of the open countryside, no other building to be seen for miles. In the distance, the Mediterranean glistened, the vast sapphire sea competing with the endless azure sky. She loved this island. Especially this remote coastline. It soothed something in her, gave her an inner peace, a grounding that had previously eluded her. She got why Ivo loved the solitude of San Jorbo—

being immersed in nature and silence allowed for re-flection and growth and it was something she knew she wanted in her life going forward. But would she ever be able to return to Monrosa again? Would it carry too many bittersweet memories?

Ivo led the way, stopping to help her clamber over a heavy rockfall, asking gently, 'Are you okay? Do you need some water, a break?'

She nodded no, then gave him a grateful smile, pretending, pretending, pretending that all was well.

When he turned away she slowly exhaled, watching his long, agile strides.

Don't think. Don't start hoping and dreaming. Don't confuse the easy connection of a casual hook-up with anything more than that. You spent too many years willing for things to be different with Dan, clinging to your relationship, to go back now into a situation full of uncertainty and doubt and misguided hope.

As they approached the church, the group outside turned in their direction, their expressions moving from surprise to delight on spotting Ivo. The men were dressed in tuxedos, the women in cocktail dresses, rows of potted lemon trees lining the red carpet. A wedding. One of the younger men approached them, his smile infectious. He had to be the groom.

With much excitement he introduced Ivo to his family and then insisted that they accompany him into the chapel, Ivo translating for her that the groom wanted to show them the flowers he had secretly organised for his bride. Toni gasped at the delicate beauty of the pink and cream tea roses that filled every available space of the tiny chapel, their scent exquisite.

And then the rest of the group bustled in, quickly taking their places. The bride had arrived.

Outside, Ivo spoke to the bride and her family and friends, the bride blushing with pleasure at Ivo's good wishes. And Toni's heart cracked open at how deliberately Ivo took his time, speaking not only with the bride but also her parents, who looked ecstatic to have the good fortune to have a member of the beloved royal family give them his good wishes.

Ivo may not enjoy public life in its more intrusive forms, but on a one-to-one level he showed incredible humility and warmth.

And as they stood and watched the bride enter the chapel, a solo guitarist inside heralding her arrival, Toni turned and studied Ivo, and, though she wanted nothing more than to stay one more night with him, she realised it was time that she leave, before she lost her heart and all reason to him.

From the chapel they followed the road down to the coast and then walked along the track that skirted along the coastline and would eventually lead them back to San Jorbo.

'Are you okay? You seem distracted.'

He shrugged at Toni's question, trying not to give way to the panic growing inside of him. 'I'm thinking about the week ahead—the markets were jittery last week because of a disruption in oil production.'

He caught Toni's frown. She didn't believe him. *Dio!* How could he tell her the truth? How could he tell her that earlier he had actually been considering broaching the idea that they meet up again, possibly even date? What they had was good. But now he knew just how nonsensical that idea was. He and Toni had no future together. She deserved something better than a man who could never fully engage in a relationship. He would never be a man so certain, so safe and assured in a relationship that he would beam with happiness on his wedding day. Relationships, permanency, the need to be honest and frank were beyond him. He lived in his own thoughts, he hated being emotionally vulnerable. He wasn't capable of loving a woman the way a man should.

At a fork in the path, they came to a stop and studied the beach below them in silence. He had said that they would have a picnic there and he wanted to go and lie down with her, listen to her chatter and laughter, and lose himself in their kisses and touches. But instead he glanced at his watch. 'This has taken us longer than I thought. I need to get back to the *finca*. The financial markets abroad are open today.'

He hated the disappointment that clouded her eyes. But then with a firm nod of her head she stepped away. 'Of course...actually that suits me, as I've decided that, now that our interview is finished, I'll change my flight home to London to today. It makes sense as you're busy.'

* * *

Toni forced herself to smile through his shocked expression. Pretending, pretending, pretending that going home was exactly what she wanted to do instead of longing for him to ask her to stay. She wanted to stay and watch him shower in the morning, load his toast with honey the way he liked it, hear his serious voice on the phone when he talked business, his sharp intelligence and decisiveness a crazy turn-on. She wanted to spend more evenings playing with Paco and Lore with him, hearing his laughter when one of the dogs easily beat her in the game of catch the four of them played together. She wanted to make love with him time and time again. It was too soon to say goodbye to the ecstasy, the freedom, the rightness they found together. Another few days. That was all she wanted.

'If that's what you want.'

Her heart sank. His tone was distant and cool.

She faked another smile. 'I think it's for the best.'

She backed away and turned in the direction they had been walking. It felt as though a tidal wave of disappointment was pushing against her back, driving her forward.

What did you expect? It was your suggestion that you leave. Don't you want to be in control? You said you wanted to wear relationships lightly, not get emotionally involved.

But I thought we had something special... I thought he felt it too. More than just chemistry... love. I'm in love with him.

There. She had thought it. She was in love with him. How unbelievably stupid.

Oh, come on, Toni. Think about it. Are you really in love with him? How about testing that idea? What would you do if he called to you right now and asked you to stay? You would be thrilled, of course... for about five minutes. And then you'd panic. Panic because you wouldn't know if you could really believe him. Because you couldn't handle being in a relationship again with all the potential hurt and pain that goes with that. Because you know you'd always be waiting for the day he would walk away. Just like Dan. Just like your dad. You love him...but you'd always be scared of what he could do, scared of the pain he could inflict on you. You'd never feel safe with him. Would you really want that life?

On the phone to his Global Emerging Markets team, Ivo tried to concentrate but his head was a jumble of thoughts. She was leaving. He should be glad. It was all too intense and out of control. It had to end, and probably the sooner the better, before he indulged any further in fantasies of waking next to her in the mornings, arriving home to her smiles and chatter, the long hours of lovemaking where the connection between them bound his heart with a sense of peace and belonging and joy.

Her eagerness to leave cut him to the quick. Yes, he knew that he couldn't offer her the love she needed, the openness and absolute conviction that any relationship needed...but her ability to walk away so easily was causing the walls of silence around him to firmly shift back into place.

Twisting in his chair, he saw Toni standing at his office door. Her hair was damp and she had changed into the yellow dress she had worn on her first day in Monrosa. How long had she been standing there? Her eyes held his for the briefest of moments and he swallowed at the confusion in their depths.

But then she gave him a cheerful smile and mouthed if she could speak to him for a few seconds?

Telling his team that he would call them back, he waited for her to speak.

She took a step into the office but then stepped away again, as though she didn't want to be in the same room as him, despite her persistent smile. 'You'll be glad to hear that I've managed to change my flight. I'm packed and ready to go.'

He stood. 'You're leaving now?' He had thought she would leave tonight. Not immediately. Just how keen was she to escape?

'Yeah, my taxi should be here any minute now.' She smiled again, upbeat and positive, as though all of this was a brilliant idea. 'You'll be glad to have me out of your hair, no doubt.' Nodding towards his laptop, she added, 'At least now you'll have some peace to concentrate on work.'

He should be relieved. At least now he wouldn't have to spend the rest of the day resisting the temptation of asking her to stay, of saying that they would figure something out. But to what end? He stared at her, his brain a jumble of messy thoughts, panic closing down any logical thinking.

'I had hoped we could talk later...'

She folded her arms. 'About what?'

He moved towards her, needing somehow to make this all okay. 'The past few days have been special... thank you. I hope you think so too.'

She shrugged, backing away and then, glancing out of the window behind her, she said with obvious relief, 'My taxi is here.'

He watched her dart down the corridor, bewildered by the suddenness of all this. He gathered himself enough to follow her, taking hold of the suitcase on the floor. She opened the front door without looking at him and instinctively he reached out, stopping her from opening it in full. Outside he could hear the low rumble of a car engine.

'Stay. Let's talk.'

She shook her head. 'Thanks but I really want to get back to London.' Meeting his gaze, she winced ever so slightly before she pulled at the door, edging it a little more open, her demeanour and tone still forcibly bright and cheerful. 'Thanks for a lovely weekend.' She lifted the bag that contained all of the recording equipment. 'I'll edit your interview and send you a copy some time this week or next.' Then, holding her hand out, she gave him yet another bright smile. 'Thank you for participating in the interview.' As she paused, heat crept into her cheeks but a defiant glint entered her eyes. 'And thanks for everything else...it was fun.'

'You don't need to leave now.'

Her smile faded. 'Yes, I do.'

'Why?'

She studied him, her expression crumbling. 'Please, Ivo… I'm trying to make this as easy as possible for us both.'

He stepped away, nodding. She was right. It wasn't her problem that he felt totally ill-equipped to deal with the fall-out of growing so extraordinarily close to another human being. For so many years he had deliberately isolated himself and in a matter of days Toni had destroyed the comfort and security that had come with that detachment, leaving him feeling more vulnerable now than he had ever felt in his entire life.

Outside, she got into the waiting taxi.

Stupidly he waved, as though that was appropriate or somehow could convey how he wanted to reach out to her, to say he was sorry, and she responded with a saddened shrug that perfectly summed up her disappointment in him.

Paco and Lore chased after the taxi as it twisted away into the olive groves. Just as he should have done, if he weren't so inhibited by the inability to love without reservation.

CHAPTER NINE

TONI STUMBLED INTO the kitchen and sighed at the breakfast detritus her flatmates had left behind them before they had rushed out to work.

Wincing, she checked the time on her phone charging on the kitchen counter. It was past ten o'clock. She hadn't intended on staying out so late last night, just as she hadn't intended on staying out late every night of the past week, but she had always managed to find some excuse to avoid the awfulness of lying in bed unable to sleep, thinking about Ivo.

Walking into the living room, she eyed the recording equipment sitting on her desk. Two weeks had passed since she'd recorded Ivo's interview. She was scheduled to broadcast it in two days' time but had yet to edit it. She had found every excuse in the book to avoid listening to it—editing prior interviews, creating a new marketing strategy for the podcast with the PR department at Young Adults Together, cleaning the flat, dragging her flatmates out to parties and gallery openings and drinks in the pub.

But now she had no choice but to edit it today.

She had to send it to the palace and Ivo later today to get their approval, and tomorrow she was flying to Amsterdam for another interview. She should be excited. She hadn't visited Amsterdam in years. But, as with everything else in her life right now, no matter how much she tried to deny it, the joy had gone out of everything she did. She felt flattened. Why had she gone and fallen in love with him? Why hadn't she been able to not get entangled with him emotionally? Had she allowed the seclusion, the intimacy of his *finca*, to create a make-believe world that never had a chance of surviving? Had she totally imagined the connection between them? Had it simply been a case of a whole lot of chemistry and very little else for him?

She sighed, remembering the phone calls from Kara and Alice after she had returned to London. Both had wanted to know in great detail how the interview had gone and if she had anything to do with the fact that Ivo was rarely returning to San Jorbo and instead was staying in the palace most evenings. Neither had been subtle in their questioning, Kara eventually admitting that she had hoped that they might get together. Toni had laughed off the suggestion, pointing out the fact that they had so little in common. But Kara had argued that they would balance each other out perfectly. Toni had ended their call at that point, unable to handle Kara's disappointment that her matchmaking had come to nothing. By rights she should be angry with Kara, but who could blame her friend for hoping that those in her life had the same happiness and contentment that her marriage brought her?

Wiping down the kitchen table and counters while she waited for the kettle to boil, Toni knew she couldn't put off editing Ivo's interview any longer.

Coffee cup in hand, she went and sat at her desk. Pulling on her headphones, she selected the first recording in his office, grimacing at the overexcited nervousness in her voice, her heart turning over at his concise replies.

He had stood on his doorstep and waved her goodbye. While she had sat in the taxi, her heart breaking, he had waved her off the way you would a favourite aunt. That had summed up just how easy he had found it when she had left. And he had been right... after all, he had stuck to their deal that there would be no entanglements, just fun. She only had herself to blame. At least she had had the sense to get out of there early. When they had returned to San Jorbo after their trek to San Amaro he had instantly disappeared into his office and she had crazily toyed with the idea of going in and telling him what he meant to her. To what purpose she had no real idea. It was just her usual need to overshare, to wear her heart on her sleeve rearing its idiotic head. Thankfully she had resisted the temptation to emotionally unburden herself to him, realising she would only hurt and humiliate herself in the process. And had poured her nervous energy into changing her flight and packing instead. Needing to take control of the whole situation. Needing to be the one who walked away, rather than being so dangerously close to jumping into yet another relationship which had gaping holes in its very foundations.

Now she closed her eyes at his mention of ice-cream and olive oil in the interview, remembering how he had teased her on the beach. He had never shown her what other uses olive oil could be put to. She pushed away the mental image of him rubbing the golden liquid into her skin…and what would follow as a result.

Her coffee grew cold as she listened to his voice, every sense awake to him, stopping to edit out silences and parts of the interview that didn't flow with the overall structure.

'I needed time alone to process what was happening.'

She pressed 'pause' at the point in the interview when he had talked about the aftermath of his mum's death, closing her eyes, trying to think.

A glimmer of hope had her heart doing a cartwheel. Did he just need time? Maybe he would realise that what they had was special. Ugh! Why was she even thinking this way? Why was she so desperate for him to love her? She had stayed with Dan because it had felt safer to do so. Was that why she'd fallen so hard and fast for Ivo, because she'd simply wanted the security of a relationship? Did she truly love Ivo…or was it the thought of a relationship that she loved even more? But relationships terrified her, so why would she even subconsciously want to be in one? Her head was such a mess. How could she long for something that also terrified her?

She pulled out her headphones and went and stood at the bay window overlooking the street below her. Cars were parked along either side of the tree-lined pavement but there wasn't a soul in sight.

She hated being alone because it reminded her of all the times that her dad had disappeared from her life. The confusion, the wondering of what she had done wrong. She had never felt safe because of it. But in bed with Ivo, when they made love, for the first time ever she *had* felt safe. In their walks, their time on the beach, she had felt safe in his silence, in how he had made no demands of her but simply looked at her as though she was the most wonderful person he had ever encountered. She hadn't imagined that…she was certain of it. She might fool herself over many other things in her life, but Ivo's look of care and fondness wasn't one of them.

But she couldn't force him to love her, to want a life he had never envisioned for himself. And she had to stop being so afraid of being alone. She needed to learn to feel safe in her own life.

Ivo stood on the *finca*'s terrace as Paco and Lore raced down the path to the beach. Palace life didn't suit them. Their movements were too restricted and there were too many people shooing them out of the way. At least they were happy to be back in San Jorbo. His gaze trailed over the beach below, the memories of making love to Toni down there grabbing his heart, and the real reason why he had avoided returning to San Jorbo for the past two weeks. Sure, he had stayed in the palace in order to spend time with his family, but avoiding memories of Toni had been the main reason why time and time again he had delayed his return home. Most evenings he had managed to return to the palace in time to say goodnight to Gabriela, sharing a beer with Edwin afterwards, chatting about the most recent economic news, acting as a sounding board for Edwin's concerns over the Monrosian economy. And after that he would visit Luis and Alice in their villa in the grounds of the palace, more often than not staying for dinner, getting much needed light relief in the constant teasing banter they drew him into, Luis, ever the competitor, challenging him to compete against him in triathlons, insisting he was the fitter of them both. And afterwards he would sometimes drop in to see his father. They had been uncomfortable visits, awkward after so many years of distance. But he was tired of pretending he didn't need a relationship with his father. Because he did. He needed his guidance…his love. He needed to belong to his family.

The sun was fading. He should go for a swim before night fell. But instead he closed his eyes, listened to the cicadas, waiting for the wash of peace that usually came when he returned to San Jorbo after the chaos of a working day.

But the image of Toni, sitting next to him in the studio that first night she arrived, enthusiastically embracing his art, haunted him. He had shown her who he was. Private. Introverted. Damaged. Not an easy person to live with. And she had accepted him. On their last day together, when she had interviewed him for the podcast he had seen with his own eyes how carefully she'd tried to balance his need for privacy with her own need for an in-depth interview. Why, then, had he shut down the moment she announced that she was leaving? Did asking her to stay terrify him that much? Was he so conditioned to a single life that it was intractable now? But he had to face facts—he could never give her his absolute conviction in the truth and rightness of their relationship. Could you really commit to a relationship if you didn't believe in your own capacity to honour the openness and honesty that were fundamental to its survival?

But hadn't her hope and belief in him been what he had been searching for all his life? Someone who believed in him? Someone who had the same hopes and dreams for a shared future?

He threw his head back and studied the darkening sky, Venus shining as brilliantly and defiantly as ever.

He didn't want to be alone. His mother had died so young…she had had so many years of happiness robbed from her. Years of seeing her sons grow up. Years of loving the husband who idolised her. She had been robbed of seeing the birth of her first grandchild.

He may not have been able to save her the day of

her fall, but he could honour her memory a whole lot better than he was doing right now.

He needed to be true to himself. He needed to admit that he wanted love…and to be loved. He closed his eyes. What if she didn't want his love? And didn't love him? When they had made love, when she would touch him whenever she passed him, when he caught her staring at him, when she gave him her absolute attention as though validating everything that was him, all those things had felt like real and meaningful love. He wasn't used to listening to his instincts, preferring logic instead. But deep inside of him, if he discarded his entrenched fears for a moment, he believed that Toni did love him.

He had to tell her what was truly inside him. Every fear and failure, every hope and dream for their future. He needed to speak. But above all else he needed to be fair. And his silence and withdrawal weren't fair on her.

He worked his jaw in frustration. He knew how hurt she was over her relationship with Dan. The damage her father had inflicted on her. He knew how sensitive she was, her need for assurance. To feel safe.

And he had failed to meet every single need she had from a relationship in his silence. He hadn't given her the lifelines, the essential components, which any relationship needed but were even more vital to Toni—true intimacy, security, trust and honesty. He wanted to make amends for how he had messed up…but what if he couldn't? What if she didn't want him to? Worst of all, what if he was the totally wrong person for her? What if she needed a more sensitive, more giving, less complicated person? What if he couldn't make her happy?

With her flight not for another few hours, Toni had planned on visiting the Rijksmuseum, but the long line of queuing tourists had had her turn away.

Her interview with renowned chef Evi Kaag had been stimulating and thought-provoking. Evi's passionate creativeness in the kitchen was matched by her dedication to mentoring her staff to exacting standards whilst also allowing them the space to experiment and fulfil their own creative needs. A mum of three, Evi, together with her husband Christian, had created a home full of love and laughter. But Evi had spoken candidly about how she struggled to balance all of the demands in her life, her regrets over her first marriage failing and her ongoing worry of caring for her elderly parents.

It had been an open and frank interview and had driven home just how tense and awkward her interviews with Ivo had been. Okay, so towards the end he had opened up, but had she really got to know him? Her time with Evi had increased an underlying nagging doubt that she still truly didn't know the man nicknamed the Machine.

And yet, despite all of that, she missed him. She missed his calmness, his warm looks that made every inch of her skin fizzle and her heart dance with joy, his kindness and humanity. She missed his quiet solidness, how he tried to be true to himself, how little ego he had.

Walking over a pedestrian bridge, bicycles whizzing by, she spotted a free bench along the canalside and dragged her suitcase over to it. Sitting down, she heard her phone ping in her handbag. It was yet another message from Kara, wondering if she was still with Evi. She typed no, explaining that earlier Evi and her family had left for their holiday home on the island of Ameland and that she was currently enjoying the views alongside the Herengracht canal, desperate to appear upbeat even if inside she felt numb.

As she popped her phone back into her handbag her attention was drawn to a young couple sitting on a bench on the opposite side of the canal. She could tell by their gentle teasing and tentative touching that their relationship was new. And the sensation that something extremely precious had escaped her came back with a vengeance. Along with the question that if life had been different for them both, could their relationship have been as easy and natural as it was for the couple across the way? Would she and Ivo have glided into a relationship without any reservations? How wonderful it must be to be able to love without hesitation, to be able to accept love with an open heart.

'I was looking for you.'

She leapt off the bench. And stared at Ivo. Her heart lurching in disbelief. 'Did you have to creep up on me like that?'

Her shock evaporated in the face of his sombre

expression. She swallowed hard. The dappled shade of a nearby tree cast shadows over the hard lines of his face. Her heart stumbled and tripped. He looked so foreboding, so tense, so cut off from her.

He gestured to the bench. 'Let's sit down.'

She nodded but dread started to settle in her stomach. Why was he being so formal?

Sitting, she inched away from him when he sat close to her, the distance suddenly of vital importance. The need to protect herself from whatever was to come panicking her.

'Is this about the podcast? Your office said you were happy for it to be broadcast. Was your father unhappy with it? I know it was revealing, but the feedback has been incredible. Ask Kara.'

'I'm not here about the interview... I'm here to apologise.'

Toni's eyes widened. 'For what? And how did you find me in the first place?'

'Kara.'

'So that's what all of her messages were about.' But then, her eyes widening even more, she asked, clearly horrified, 'How did you explain wanting to know where I was? That's all I need right now, Kara suspecting something.'

'I told my family about us.'

'Why on earth did you do that? Ivo...seriously! That's going to complicate my life even further. I told Kara and Alice that nothing happened between us. I'm now going to have them on my case. Just great.'

She flicked her gaze away from him, her mouth pursed.

Great start, Ivo.

He dipped his head, the words he needed to say fading, the instinct to lapse into silence when he felt uncertain flooding back with a vengeance. He gripped his fists tight, fighting the fear that he wasn't deserving of her love. That he could never be open enough to match her need for honest transparency.

Searching for the right words, he looked at her, the hunger of his need to simply watch her stunning him by its ferocity. He had missed her even more than he had admitted to himself. His throat tightened, the true loneliness of her absence intensifying now that he had found her.

The light breeze danced in her hair, sending golden brown strands over her heated cheeks. He had never met someone so beautiful. He prized every tiny detail of her, the ordinary in her a constant source of marvel and worship. The bow in her upper lip. The tight whorl of her ears. The random smattering of dark freckles along her arms. Just how incredible she looked in the simple white T-shirt and jeans she was wearing today.

She turned and gave an exasperated sigh. 'Ivo, are you going to say something or are you just going to sit there and stare at me? For crying out loud, why did you tell your family about me? What was the point?'

'You were the one who said we should be honest.'

'Not about us sleeping together!'

'Well, I obviously didn't tell them that, but I did

tell them that we had grown close but that I had messed up…and I wanted to make amends.'

On a deep sigh, she shook her head. 'You didn't mess up, Ivo. It was never going to work between us. We've both got way too much baggage. Let's face facts. We're not good for one another.'

Did she really mean that? What if she was right? But all of those tender moments when they had made love, the laughter they had shared, the quiet understanding that had marked so many moments of their time together…they all had to count for something, didn't they?

'Maybe I'm not right for you, and I guess only you can decide that. It's something I've been worried about too. But I did mess up. I should have asked you to stay in Monrosa. I should have told you what you meant to me but I didn't because I had convinced myself that I was incapable of truly loving another person.'

Her gaze narrowed. 'Why did you believe that?'

'Our time in Monrosa together was incredible, different from anything I had ever experienced before. I loved being with you and I had been planning on suggesting we see each other again. But when we came across the wedding in San Amaro Chapel, the groom was so confident and certain about marrying, it drove home just how inept I was in loving you the way you deserved. Falling in love, truly falling in love, means being open and honest, being capable of showing the other person how much you love them. And we both know just how terrible I am in showing my emotions. To fall in love you should have the capability to love generously, to make the other person feel content and secure. But I was scared that I was too inarticulate, too closed to do any of that. And when you said that you were leaving early I panicked. I messed up, and since you left I've been miserable. I miss you. For so long I thought that I was content alone and that I accepted who I was. But in truth I was lying to myself about just how lonely and isolated I was. I was too scared to reach out to others. I'm tired of living that life, of pretending that I'm okay on my own. I want us to be together. I want us to have a future.'

She shook her head, her expression one of sad resignation. 'On what basis? What did we really have but lots of attraction? Chemistry is no foundation for a relationship.'

'But doesn't that chemistry tell you a lot?'

'No.'

He winced at the defiant certainty of her answer. He fought the instinctive compulsion to withdraw, to close himself off from potential pain and humiliation, and instead said, 'That chemistry confirms that we're right for one another. Our bodies know it…it's just our minds that need to catch up.'

'And what about our hearts?'

He swallowed, the effort to tell the truth inside of him not getting any easier. 'I lost my heart to you at Luis's wedding. As crazy as this may seem, I fell in love with you that day and each hour that I spend with you I fall deeper and deeper in love.'

Her eyebrows shot up. She stared at him for what felt like an eternity. 'You love me? You fell for me at the wedding…but you spent most of the day dodging out of my way whenever I came close to you.'

'I didn't know how to be around you.' He swallowed again, his throat tight, as though his body was mirroring just how painful he found it to reveal the deepest, most personal sides of himself. 'When my mother died I learnt that the easiest way to survive was to ignore my feelings. For years I have used my indifference, my detachment as a shield to not being hurt. And when we met, your openness, how easily you cried and expressed yourself, totally threw me. I didn't know how to react but deep down I admired you for being so open.'

'You admired the fact that I was a red-eyed, bubbling mess?'

'That's not how I remember you—you were outgoing, enthusiastic, you were alive with energy…and you were very, very beautiful.'

Shifting her gaze across the canal towards the young couple entwined in one another, she said in a voice full of sadness and regret, 'But doesn't it worry you that none of this is easy? We both have so many well-founded reasons not to be in a relationship, can we really overcome them?' Looking at him, her brown eyes forlorn, she murmured, 'I'm terrified that I want to be in a relationship for all of the wrong reasons.'

He heard the fear in her voice. A fear he understood, given her background. He needed to turn this around, help her see the reasons why they should fight for what they had. 'Forget all of the wrong reasons for a moment and tell me what the right reasons to be in a relationship are?'

Her head reeling, Toni stared towards the couple across the water. They were sharing one set of earphones, both heads moving in time to music only they could hear. 'The right reasons? I guess the closeness, the intimacy, knowing that there's someone in your corner. An ally and friend you can trust implicitly—' she paused, realisation hitting her '—and by that I mean not only that I can trust *in* them but also that I allow myself to trust them. After my dad and Dan, I'm not sure that I can fully trust someone again and I know that's not fair.'

Ivo shifted towards her, his eyes holding her captive, his voice a soft whisper. 'I want you to be able to trust me.'

She hesitated for a moment but all of the reasons why she hadn't wanted to fall in love again assailed her and she heard herself say, 'I want to trust you but I'm scared of believing you when you say you love me because one day you might decide to leave me and I couldn't abide the hurt and pain of losing you.'

Moving along the bench, Ivo positioned himself at an angle so that his knee was touching hers, his silver gaze holding hers for what felt like an eternity. 'I will never leave you.' His mouth quirked. 'Do you honestly think that I'd leave you after all this? It has almost broken me to admit everything I have… I may be inarticulate about my feelings and closed to my emotions—I've had to fight internal demons, slay decades-old ways of being, to get to this point—but integrity is everything to me and I will never hurt you again. I want your honesty and openness. I want your laughter, your chatter. I'll even put up with your clutter and untidiness.'

Inhaling deeply, she studied him. She knew just how huge it was for him to tell her all of this. To tell her that he loved her. It would be so easy to accept everything he was saying and fall into a fantasy world, but, rightly or wrongly, she needed more from him. 'Sometimes I feel that I don't truly know you, as though you are holding something back from me. Tell me the deepest parts of you. What's your greatest regret?' The need to test him, to see if he would be brutally honest, drove her on to ask, 'Tell me what you want from our relationship and what you are willing to sacrifice for it? What if I want to continue living in London for instance?'

He held up his hand as though to stop her flow of questions. 'I'll answer every question you have... but you need to slow down. Ask me them individually. I want to make sure that I answer every question in detail.'

'Tell me about the deepest regret?'

'Letting you go...but there are many others.' She could see that it was an effort for him to continue as he ran his hand against his neck. Seconds passed and her heart sank. He was avoiding looking at her. Was he already clamming up?

On a heavy exhale his eyes met hers and she flinched at the strain in his expression. 'I regret insisting that my mother take me trekking on the day she died. She had told us that she had a headache. Even knowing that, when we did go I didn't stay with her but rushed ahead. And then when I found her on the ground I ran away, to get help but also because I was so scared. I shouldn't have left her alone to die. And on top of all of that, what I regret most is that she was stolen from my father's and brothers' lives and the guilt of that eats me up. I could see their pain after she died and I couldn't face it, so it was easier to stay in my room and detach myself from them.'

It would be so easy to give a glib response, to try to convince him that he was wrong to feel any responsibility or guilt. And that it was understandable that he struggled with witnessing his family's grief. But to do so would be to disregard and diminish what were clearly very painful feelings for him. 'It's no wonder that you withdrew. What you went through was horrible. I so dearly wish life had been different for you and I'm sorry that you had to carry that responsibility on your own all these years.' Her throat felt too tight to continue as she thought of all the years Ivo had kept his guilt to himself, his natural need for privacy becoming extreme in his grief, and her heart tumbled as she realised what it must have taken him to admit all of this to her. 'Thanks for telling me.'

He nodded and then looked away. Before she would have thought that that act of looking away was him somehow distancing himself from her, but now she recognised that it was a combination of his reserved nature but also his pride and composure. Moving her hand to rest on his, she quietly said, 'Sometimes I've mistaken your quietness for a personal rejection.'

He turned and regarded her. 'It's not intentional… please tell me when you feel that way.'

'Sometimes I don't even understand why I even think you are pushing me away, given just how kind you were to me when we first met.' Closing her eyes, she grimaced and then, looking back at him, she gave a long exhale. 'I should explain why I was so emotional at Alice's wedding. When we danced, the way you held me, the understanding in your voice when we spoke, broke me. I realised just how desperately I wanted to be looked at with that kindness and care. I wanted to truly matter to someone. I wanted to be the centre of someone's life.'

He shifted on the seat towards her and her heart swelled at the tenderness in his eyes. 'You matter to me…and you are already the centre of my life. I love you.'

She blinked back tears, the sincerity in his eyes, the passion in his voice freeing her of all the doubts and misgivings she had been harbouring over entering a relationship again. 'I used to think that love is unreliable, but it's only people that are unreliable, not love. And in our time together you have always been consistent and true, you've always shown me huge respect and integrity. You believed in me. I didn't want to trust you, I was so scared of being hurt again, but not once have you done anything to cause me to doubt your loyalty. Instead you've helped me to learn to appreciate my strengths, and what better way can I prove to myself that I believe in myself than by trusting my judgement and allowing myself to completely trust you?' She paused and with a certainty that brought fresh tears to her eyes she said, 'I love you, Ivo, and want to be with you.'

A look of relief and then joy passed over his features. With a grin he said, 'I can't tell you how good that sounds. Say it again.'

She laughed. 'I love you.'

'And again.'

'I love you.'

He gathered her to him, his kiss quick, reflecting his delight. He was still grinning when he pulled away.

Thinking about how far they had come in truly knowing each other, she said, 'We still have so much to learn and understand about each other...doesn't that worry you?'

He looked out to a passing boat on the canal as he considered her question. 'In truth, I'm only learning about myself now because of you.' Then with a determined expression he added, 'But we *will* be okay. This openness and honesty we have with each other will see us through.'

He was right. This candidness and truth would be the bedrock of their relationship. But even knowing that didn't stop the fluttering of dread that came with her next question. 'What future do you want for us?'

His expression grew tense. For a moment she panicked, thinking he was perhaps about to tell her something she didn't want to hear, but then she realised it was because he was nervous. 'I'd like you to come and live with me in San Jorbo. The land there feels as though it's part of me. I hope that in time you might grow to love it as much as I do. But if you want to live in the palace or stay in London we can make that work too. We would need to travel to Monrosa for my royal duties.'

'I've grown to love Monrosa, and being close to Kara and Alice would be wonderful. I've missed San Jorbo too, but I will need a studio and easy access to the airport for when I travel for my podcast interviews.'

He nodded. 'We can set up a studio in San Jorbo, and when you need to fly anywhere we can base ourselves at the palace so that you'll be closer to the airport. And Kara has her offices there too, so you'll be able to work even closer with her.'

'A studio in San Jorbo sounds perfect,' she admitted with a wide smile, 'but be warned I'll drag you to parties every now and again.'

The laughter lines at the corners of his eyes crinkled. 'With you at my side I might even tolerate them, but be warned, I will drag you home from them early…' Heat formed in his eyes and, leaning into her ear, he whispered, 'You're irresistible when you wear lipstick and high heels.'

A thrill torpedoed through her body and another had her physically tremble when his mouth playfully nuzzled against her throat. Her head swimming, she edged closer to him, sighing when his mouth found hers, his gentle kiss electrifying. Pulling back, he held her eyes for long, tender moments before he softly whispered, 'I hope in time that we'll want to leave parties early to get home to our children.'

She gave a cry of surprise that was half shock and half absolute joy. For a moment she wanted to tell him that he was jumping ahead, not wanting to dare to dream of such a future with him, but then she stopped herself, needing to voice the truth of her hopes. 'I can't think of anything more wonderful.'

Looking across the canal again towards the young couple, who were busy taking selfies, Ivo's arm around her shoulders anchoring her to him, she asked, 'Doesn't it scare you that this could so easily not have happened?'

Placing a hand beneath her chin, turning her gaze towards him, he nodded. 'Yes...' his thumb gently moved along her jawline '...and that's why I will never take you or our love for granted.'

Later that night the silver moon guided them through the olive groves and on through the mountain forest, Paco and Lore leading the way, excited to have another companion on their nightly walk.

Wrapped up in one of his fleece jackets against the chill in the mountain air, her hand in his as they walked side by side, Toni muttered, 'I didn't realise that you walked so far every night… I had thought it would be nothing but a quick leg-stretch.'

He knew that he was probably rushing things, but it felt so right and good and amazing to have her back in his life that he couldn't hold back on sharing the future he wanted them to have. 'There's something I want to show you.'

'Please don't tell me that it's a Monrosian Hairy-Back Spider.'

He laughed at her pretend horror, his heart squeezing at the sheer joy of having her here. And when they reached their destination, a clearing on the edge of the mountain, he pointed across the bay to San Amaro Chapel. All the way here he had waited for his nerves to kick in, for all the old worries about sharing his life with anyone to take over again. But they didn't come. The rightness and the power of their love, the truth and honest connection between them had banished all those fears. 'I'd like us to marry in San Amaro…if you are happy with a small wedding, of course.'

Open-mouthed, Toni stared at him, then towards the chapel, before staring at him again. 'Marry…in San Amaro?'

'I'd like the wedding to be private…and intimate. We can marry in the cathedral if you prefer, but I want to be able to focus just on you on our wedding day, and that's difficult when you have hundreds of guests.'

'You want to marry me? Is this a proposal?'

He laughed at her astonishment. But then, sobering, he realised that perhaps this wasn't the most romantic of ways to propose. He started to backtrack. 'I can do it properly…take you somewhere more romantic, Paris or Venice. And, of course, there's the engagement ring…'

Stepping forward, she placed her hands on his arms, laughter in her eyes. 'I didn't mean it that way. I can't think of a more special place than here, where we will spend our life together. I'm just taken aback that you are proposing now…it's all so sudden.'

Disappointment kicked him in the stomach. 'We can talk about it some other time if you prefer.'

She shook her head firmly, a smile lifting her lips. 'No, no, I don't mean sudden in a bad way, just in an *I didn't expect this from you* sort of way. I'm supposed to be the emotional and impetuous one in this relationship.' Her smile widening even more, those brown eyes of hers gleaming with love and dreams, she said, 'San Amaro would be perfect.'

EPILOGUE

WHEN DESIGNING HER wedding gown, Toni had asked for pockets in the vintage silk and lace gown, so that she could carry a handkerchief. She had been convinced that she would cry endlessly.

Admittedly, she had shed a tear when Alice and Kara had joined her this morning, both of them looking radiant in their blush-pink bridesmaid gowns, Alice in particular, her eight-month pregnancy bump swathed beneath the soft silk folds of her gown. And a lump had formed in her throat when she had stood at the end of the short aisle of San Amaro and taken her mother's arm, seeing the natural beauty of the chapel enhanced with the white rose and olive branch floral displays.

The wide smiles of their small group of wedding guests—her friends from London, Ivo's rowing team and university friends he was in regular contact with—had also threatened her composure. But now, taking the light cotton and lace handkerchief from her pocket wasn't for her tears but for Ivo's.

Reluctantly taking the handkerchief from her, Ivo

quickly wiped his eyes, ignoring the amused looks of his brothers and best men, Edwin and Luis, both dressed in tuxedos, as were the rest of their male guests. In her father's arms, Gabriela, wearing the same simple floral crown of white roses as Toni's in her dark hair, gave a chortle, and the rest of the guests chuckled. Ivo shook his head, his watery eyes filled with amusement, and then he softly whispered, 'I love you.'

From the altar the priest cleared his throat. 'Shall we start again?'

They both nodded, but in truth she was in no rush. She wanted to enjoy every second of this ceremony, savour every minute of this extraordinary day.

Looking down at the vows he had written himself, Ivo cleared his throat and this time managed to say the words without his voice cracking. 'You are the centre of my world. You bring me joy, acceptance and contentment. Every day throughout our marriage I promise to hear and react to your feelings and thoughts. I vow to love, respect, and cherish you. I pledge myself only to you, as long as we both shall live.'

Her heart filled with love, Toni repeated her own vows, her voice steady, not even a single tear in her eye, her safety and security in their relationship, Ivo time and time again proving over the past year of their life together in San Jorbo that she was the centre of his world, his constant gentle kindness, their intimate lovemaking, freeing her of any doubts as to his love.

And after her vows, Ivo's father stepped forward to recite the reflection he had written. When he had asked them if he could read the reflection they had both been taken aback. After all, he wasn't known for taking part in any ceremony outside the set royal protocols. But they had immediately agreed, touched by the gesture, if not a little apprehensive as to what he might say.

Lifting his gaze from where he stood at the lectern, he studied each of his sons in turn before saying, 'I have written a reflection on love that I would like to share with you all. "Love is found in the quiet moments. In the touch of a hand. A soothing whisper. In the acceptance of who you are. Love is holding tight in the storms of life, the willingness to change. Love is being able to say goodbye and honouring what you had. Love is generosity and forgiveness, the embracing of life. Love well, my sons and daughters. Love with joy and open hearts.'"

* * * * *

THEIR SECOND-TIME VALENTINE

HELEN LACEY

For my dear friend Jenny
Time doesn't dictate the strength of a friendship…
it's all in the heart.

Chapter One

Kane Fortune knew he was considered the go-to guy by his family and friends. Perhaps because he was single and generally accommodating of others without being a pushover.

Today was no exception. Picking up his nephew from day care hadn't been on his agenda for the afternoon. But his sister-in-law had called, saying she was held up at a doctor's appointment, and since his brother Adam was out of town, Kane was next on the list.

Besides, he adored his nephew, Larkin. The kid was cute and Kane really enjoyed his uncle duties. He eased his Ranger pickup into a space outside the day care center, got out and ignored the pain in his knee. The old football injury still gave him grief occasionally, but he pushed himself forward and headed through the gate and up the pathway and entered the building.

The center was typical of its kind, he figured, with its brightly painted walls and blue linoleum floor. Paintings dotted the hallway walls, many of them collages of dozens of tiny handprints, others of family scenes and an assortment of animals. The pictures made him smile as he made his way to the reception desk. A fiftysomething woman he didn't recognize stood behind the desk and greeted him as he approached. He quickly explained who he was and that he was there to collect Larkin, and the woman gave him a curious look before clicking keys on the computer in front of her.

"Fortune, you said?" she queried, concentrating on the computer screen.

"Yes, Kane Fortune. I'm Larkin Fortune's uncle."

"I'll just need to see some identification."

Kane quickly took out his driver's license and passed it over the countertop. The receptionist, obviously a temp, perused his license, still clicking keys on the computer, taking her time to confirm his place on the list of family members approved to pick up his nephew.

"Is there a problem?" he asked.

"This will just take a moment," she replied. "It's for safety. I'm sure you understand."

Kane tapped fingers on the counter and heard the swoosh of the automatic doors and heels hurriedly tapping over the linoleum. A woman rushed toward the counter, a handbag over one shoulder, a diaper bag flung over the other. Late twenties, he figured, with long blond hair and brown eyes. He looked at her, trying to be discreet, noticing her curves and flawless skin. She was incredibly pretty, and the scent of her fragrance was quite distracting. He shook off the feeling and turned his attention back to the receptionist, who was still concentrating on the computer screen.

"I'm here to pick up my daughter, Erin. I got a call to say she was having separation issues again today," the woman said hurriedly, and then stepped back a little to look at him, clearly realizing she'd cut in on his interaction with the woman behind the counter. "Oh, I'm so sorry… I didn't mean to interrupt."

"No problem," he said easily. "You look like you're in a hurry."

She nodded, obviously frazzled. "I had to leave work early. You know how it is with kids. Never enough time to get things done."

Actually, he didn't know, but he wasn't about to correct her. He wasn't about to admit that he mostly liked his single, commitment-free life. A life he wasn't planning on changing any time soon. Kane didn't do commitment. In fact, he really didn't do relationships. He hadn't had a serious girlfriend for over five years. Truth be told, he couldn't remember the last time he'd been on a date. Months. Maybe six or seven. Or the last time he'd met someone who piqued his interest.

But there was something about the woman in front of him that made him want to prolong their conversation. He glanced at her left hand. A platinum wedding band.

Of *course* she was married. He experienced a foolish rush of relief. Married meant off the market.

"No problem," he said, and ushered her toward the counter. "Go ahead."

Relief flooded her expression. "Thank you," she said on a rush of breath. "That's very kind of you."

She quickly turned her attention to the woman behind the desk and spoke for several seconds about collecting her child. The temp asked for identification and she complied, pulling out a wallet from her handbag. Other things spilled out onto the floor—a hairbrush, a makeup compact, a small calendar with a pen attached by a string.

He bent down to pick them up and she followed quickly. Their heads collided and they pulled back, both rubbing their temples, laughing a little. His hand touched hers and he quickly snatched it back as a jolt of something that felt a lot like electricity coursed up his arm. Stupid, he thought, and gathered up her belongings, passing them to her. She struggled to hold the items in her small hands and fumbled as she stood.

"Oh, gosh, I'm so sorry. I've been dropping things all day," she said, and pushed the belongings back into her bag. She stood up straight and turned her attention back to the receptionist, passing over her identification. "Ah… I'd like to get my daughter now, if that's okay."

"Just a moment," the older woman said.

Kane tapped his fingers on the counter again, his impatience growing. Another staff member came out through a door to the left and moved behind the counter, a cell phone at her ear. After a brief conference, another worker finally brought Larkin out to him, and Kane was delighted that the little boy waved his arms frantically when he spotted him.

Kane took his nephew into his arms and a strong wave of affection washed over him as the little boy clung to his shoulder.

"He's so adorable," the blonde woman at his side said with a smile. "And he looks so much like you."

Larkin actually looked like Adam—but since he and Adam were brothers, Kane could easily see why she'd pick up on the family resemblance. "I guess he does."

A tiny frown suddenly marred her forehead, as if she was trying to figure out Larkin's parentage, and then realized. "But you're not his father?"

"No," he said, and smiled. "Uncle. He's my brother's son."

She nodded and dropped her gaze. The whole town knew the complicated story of Larkin's paternity. He was about to make a casual comment when another child was brought out to the reception area. But this one wasn't chuckling like Larkin—this child looked very unhappy, with tearstained cheeks and red-rimmed eyes. She was cute, though, and looked to be around two years old. Once she was in her mother's arms, the crying stopped, and she hiccupped and buried her face in her mom's shoulder.

"Thank you again," she said to him as she carried her daughter past him. "Bye."

Kane watched her leave the building and then grabbed Larkin's backpack before heading off. He had a car seat in the back of his Ranger, compliments of Adam, who had also provided him with a crib and high chair for his home for those occasions when he watched his nephew. Adam was one of those over-organized parents and although Kane sometimes laughed at Adam's compulsion to do the right thing, he also admired the way his brother had stepped up to fatherhood since finding out about Larkin.

It had been a hard road—since Adam had only found out that Larkin was his son after the child was left on the doorstep of the local pediatric center. When the presumed orphan needed a bone marrow transplant, the whole town had rallied and begun searching for a suitable donor. When Adam turned out to be a perfect match, it wasn't long before the truth of Larkin's paternity came out. The child was the result of his brother's relationship with Laurel Hudson, his college girlfriend. Years after she'd ended it, they'd had one night together, a night that had resulted in Larkin. Unfortunately, Laurel had suffered an episode of postpartum panic and left her baby in Rambling Rose and had then been involved in a car wreck that left her comatose for months and, when she awoke, without memory of her life, Adam or their son. Thankfully, her memory had returned and they'd worked it out, and Kane was pleased his brother had found his happily-ever-after.

Once he'd settled Larkin in the back of the vehicle, Kane headed for Adam and Laurel's home. His own place was in town, in the center of Rambling Rose, a small two-bedroom bungalow he'd shared with Adam until his brother had married Laurel and moved into the guesthouse on the Fame and Fortune Ranch, which was owned by their cousin Callum Fortune.

Sitting in between Houston and Austin, Rambling Rose had grown a lot in the last couple of years—new restaurants, a luxurious day spa, stores—businesses were popping up regularly, some courtesy of the Fortunes' construction company. Their newest contribution was the Hotel Fortune, which was due to open on Valentine's Day. Kane had been working at the hotel for the past six months, heading the construction team, a job he'd secured thanks to Callum and his other cousins who in their individual ways were turning Rambling Rose into a thriving township.

He liked his job and the people he worked with, even with the drama of the past month. A balcony collapse had nearly pushed back the opening, and the ensuing investigation into the incident was ongoing—because the authorities hadn't exactly determined it to be an accident. Kane didn't want to believe it was a deliberate act of sabotage, although like most of the Fortunes, Kane had his suspicions. After all, there were a lot of people who resented the name Fortune.

He knew where the spare key for the guesthouse was hidden and quickly got the baby inside. It was a quarter to four by the time he'd fed and changed Larkin and then put him down for a nap, and half past four when Laurel, who managed the art gallery in town, arrived home.

She looked frazzled and gave him a quick hug. "Thank you for saving the day," she said when she returned from checking on her son and met him in the kitchen. "You know, you'll make a good dad one day."

Kane grinned. "I'm happy enough being a good uncle for the moment."

Her brows came up. "Good enough to pick him up again on Thursday afternoon?" she asked sweetly. "I have a meeting at the main gallery in Austin and I'm not sure I'll get back in time, and Adam's flight doesn't get in until after five. I could ask Brady," she said, referring to his and Adam's younger brother, "but he's got his hands full with the twins and getting settled in to the new house. If it's too much to ask, I can work something else out. I know the hotel opening is only a few days away, so you probably need to concentrate on that."

Kane considered his plan for Thursday afternoon—which was just hitting the gym for an hour after work—and replied. "Of course, no problem. The plans for the opening are all set—nothing to worry about."

She sighed with relief. "I don't know what we'd do without you."

His cheeks warmed. "I'm sure you'd manage."

"It's amazing how everything has come together, particularly since the balcony collapse. Adam insists you're the voice of reason among all the chaos."

"Someone needs to be," he said, and grinned. "All those Fortune egos together can be dangerous."

"I think it's great that they listen, though," Laurel said with a smile. "And it's good to see you all getting along, like a real family."

Family. Yeah. For most of his life, Kane's family had been settled in upstate New York. His parents were still there, and most of his siblings, but since he and Adam and Brady had moved to Rambling Rose, they'd been welcomed by their cousins and created a strong family connection. And now that Adam was married to Laurel and had a family, and Brady was now legal guardian to orphaned twin boys, they all felt a deeper connection to one another and to Texas than any of them had originally imagined. Rambling Rose was a good town with good people. And he intended to stick around for a while.

He left a short while later, pleased he was able to pick Larkin up from day care on Thursday. Maybe, he thought as he got into his truck and headed back to the hotel for his meeting, he'd see the pretty blonde with the nice smile while he was there.

Layla McCarthy was having the week from hell. Admittedly, most of her weeks felt like that lately. The truth was, she couldn't remember a time in the last year or so when she hadn't felt as though her whole life was like some kind of ongoing improvisation. With work, studying, her aging grandparents and her two-year-old daughter, Erin, all she seemed to do was think about everyone else and give little heed to her own needs. She loved being Erin's mom and adored her grandparents, but occasionally she wondered what it might be like to have a moment for herself.

But not tonight, she thought as she dished out

pasta into containers and popped them into the freezer. Being organized was her salvation. She cooked up a storm every Wednesday night and filled the freezer with meals for the remainder of the week. And this week she needed to save as much time as she could so she could pick up more hours at Paz Spa, where she worked at reception. She'd been there for over four months and enjoyed the job. Her boss was great to work with and she genuinely liked all of her colleagues. While she didn't have time to socialize with any of them outside of work, she did get the opportunity to share coffee and a chat in the lunchroom some days.

Once she'd cleaned up, Layla checked on Erin, saw that she was sleeping soundly, and grabbed the baby monitor and headed to the bathroom for a shower. Once she was in her pajamas, she sat on the edge of the bed and glanced at the small framed photograph on the bedside table. Frank's smiling face beamed up at her and a familiar surge of sadness enveloped her like a cloak. Over eighteen months had passed since his death and she still felt his loss with the same intensity as she had from the moment he'd left her. Heartbreak didn't ease. When love was as strong as theirs had been, it lingered in the mind like the lyrics of an old song.

They'd been married for four years, dated for seven months, been friends for a year before that. Marrying Frank had been a no-brainer. He was the best man she'd ever known—kind, considerate and gentle. Their relationship had been a happy one and she missed him down to the depths of her soul. She missed his friendship and his company. She missed sharing that first cup of coffee and conversation over breakfast. She missed lingering in bed on Sunday morning and then making love for a few hours. She missed the intimacy they'd shared every day. She missed his arms around her. And she mourned that he didn't have the chance to watch his daughter grow up. Of course Erin didn't really remember him. And now, all Layla had were photographs and the memories in her heart.

She let out a weary sigh, grabbed her laptop and slipped into bed. She opened the document of her current assignment and reread the passages she'd written early that morning. Taking online college courses had seemed like a good idea six months ago, but with the workload increasing and two assignments due, Layla wondered if she'd overcommitted herself. Getting her degree in marketing had been a goal since high school. College hadn't been in her future then, since she had no father and her mother had left years earlier, and her grandparents weren't in any kind of financial position to fund her education. Instead, Layla had started working full time at eighteen. Without a college degree her options were limited, so she worked mostly as a receptionist, changing jobs every twelve months or so.

She met Frank when she was working the front desk at a car dealership. He'd come in looking for a new car, and she'd supplied him with coffee while the paperwork was being done. By the end of the afternoon, he'd bought the car and she'd agreed to go out with him. As friends at first, because he'd just come out of a serious relationship and she wasn't prepared to be anyone's rebound girl. So they got to know each other as friends and when she finally agreed to a real date, Layla was already half in love with him.

Since his death, she'd remained resolutely single. She didn't date. And no one had been so much as a blip on her radar.

Until yesterday.

Layla couldn't stop herself from remembering the tall, broad-shouldered, green-eyed, über-good-looking man she'd met at the day care center. *Larkin Fortune's uncle.* He wasn't wearing a wedding ring, she'd noticed. Which didn't mean he wasn't married or involved with someone. A man who looked like that was hardly going to be on the market. Still, it didn't hurt to fantasize a little. It was a huge leap from believing she'd never feel anything again. Not that she was looking for a relationship. The idea of getting involved with someone else didn't seem possible when her heart was still filled with the memory of Frank. But the thought lingered as she worked on her assignment. By ten o'clock the light was out and she spent an hour listening to relaxation music on her phone. It helped her drift off to sleep, until she woke up to the sound of Erin's happy babbling through the baby monitor around six.

Layla headed for her daughter's room. As always, her heart rolled over when she saw Erin standing in her crib, her blond curls bouncing, her big brown eyes wide and full of wonder.

"Momma."

Layla still felt a thrill every time she heard the word. Erin didn't talk much, but the few words she did say usually included the word *momma*. She was mostly a happy child, but the last few weeks she'd been unusually unsettled. She'd run a fever for a couple of days and, after a visit to the pediatrician, was diagnosed with a cold. Layla had taken a week off work and was still trying to make up the time by starting earlier. Of course, that meant leaving Erin longer in day care. But what choice did she have? Frank's life insurance had covered their mortgage, but she still had a house to run and utilities to pay.

She hauled Erin into her arms and gave her a hug, then quickly changed her diaper before heading to the kitchen. She made breakfast and switched on the small television in the corner to keep her daughter entertained while she packed lunches for the day. With her routine set, she had everything organized and was out the door by eight. Forty-five minutes later Erin was in day care and Layla was at her desk at Paz Spa.

The appointment book was full for the day and clients began arriving just before nine. Several people were waiting in the reception area when Hailey Miller, the spa's assistant manager, came out of her office and joined her behind the counter.

"Good morning," Hailey said cheerfully. "How's Erin doing? Over her cold?"

"Mostly," Layla replied. "Looks like we've got a full day today."

"Business is good. The Fortunes certainly know how to turn straw into gold," Hailey said, and grinned. "And I say that with absolutely no agenda, since I'm engaged to one of them," she added, and wriggled her left hand, showing off a perfectly beautiful diamond ring.

Hailey was engaged to Dillon, the younger brother of Callum Fortune who was the brains behind Paz Spa. Since its opening, business was booming, as it was in most of the Fortune-run enterprises. After the news reports about baby Larkin needing a bone marrow transplant last year, the town had not only become something of a tourist attraction but was now recognized as a great place to settle down. Of course, Layla had always known it. Her grandparents had settled in Rambling Rose years earlier, when it was a small blue-collar community. She'd gone to the local high school, moving in with her grandparents when she was fifteen after years bouncing around from one place to the next with her mother.

Rambling Rose was her home and she had no plans to live anywhere else. Even though there were times when the loneliness was acute and made her long for a simpler time—when Frank was alive and she had someone to share her life with.

By three o'clock on Thursday afternoon, after a day of answering phone calls and scheduling appointments, she was happy to hand over the reins to Hailey for the last two hours. She headed directly to the day care center and pulled up outside. There was a large, hulking Ranger pulling in the space next to her and she waited until its engine turned off before she stepped out onto the sidewalk. And stopped in her tracks.

The handsome, incredibly broad-shouldered man—her first "blip" since losing her husband—was getting out of the Ranger. He smiled when he spotted her and she colored down to the soles of her feet, resisting the urge to straighten out her ponytail.

"Hey there," he said, his deep voice quickly running riot over her burgeoning awareness. He was so darn hot. Maybe the hottest man she'd ever seen up close. Ruggedly handsome with enough charm to raise her temperature a zillion degrees.

"Oh, hello, it's nice to see you," she managed to say without stuttering. "You're picking up your nephew again?"

"Yeah," he replied. "My brother's out of town and my sister-in-law has an appointment. So I'm it."

Layla's hasn't-been-used-for-anything-other-than-talking tongue almost stuck to the roof of her mouth as she looked at him. "That's so good of you," she somehow managed to say. "It's nice to have a big family you can rely on." Then she sighed a little as she shrugged. "Well, I imagine it would be."

He looked at her, his mouth curling at the edges. "You don't have family?" he asked, glancing at her left hand, and she followed the path of his gaze. "Husband?"

"I'm a widow," she said quietly, the words making her heart ache as it always did. "I do have grandparents, but they're elderly."

He took a second to reply. "I'm sorry. I didn't mean to pry."

"You weren't," she assured him, feeling the mood become awkward.

"After you," he said, and motioned toward the pathway as a couple of other parents walked by them.

She clutched her tote and walked on ahead, through the doors and into the reception area. There was a line of people at the desk and she stood in turn, conscious that he was beside her.

"I'm Layla, by the way," she said, and held out her hand. "Layla McCarthy."

He took her hand and she felt the burn of his touch like it was poker hot. It was unexpected. And on some base level, unwanted. It was silly, of course. She didn't know him. She'd *never* know him. He was just some random hot guy who had turned her head for a few minutes.

"Kane Fortune," he said. "Nice to meet you."

She smiled. "Of course, one of *the* Fortunes."

His mouth twisted a fraction. "One of the lesser ones," he replied.

His words made her laugh softly. "I'm sure that's not true. I work with Hailey Miller at Paz Spa—she's engaged to Dillon. And I've met Callum a number of times."

"Cousins," he supplied. "My brother Adam and I moved to Rambling Rose from New York last year. And one of my younger brothers just moved here, too."

"Adam is your nephew's father, correct?" she asked, conscious that they were next in line. "He's the baby who needed a transplant?"

He nodded. "Yes," he said as they approached the counter. "Larkin."

Layla nodded, but she didn't comment. Instead, she greeted the regular receptionist behind the counter who was back and clearly recognized them both. The children were brought out a couple of minutes later and Erin's arms were outstretched the moment she saw her mother.

"She had a much better day today," the aide said as she passed Erin's backpack to her.

Layla grabbed the bag and her child and hugged Erin close. "Oh, great. Thank you."

She turned on her heel and saw Kane was holding his nephew. It was a good look on him, she thought, and then figured he probably had a girlfriend or significant other waiting for him at home. He might even have kids. Sure, he'd said he was an uncle, but maybe he was one of those all-around great guys who were great dads and uncles. And he hadn't said anything about being single. Not that she cared, Layla reminded herself.

With Erin's backpack in one hand, she pushed her tote over one shoulder and walked outside. He was close behind and they reached their vehicles at the same time. Once she secured Erin in the car seat, she turned and saw that Kane was behind her, strapping his nephew into his Ranger. The boy was chuckling delightedly and it made Layla smile.

"He's such a happy child," she remarked. "And he obviously adores you."

"Who wouldn't?" Kane replied, and grinned. "Your daughter's cute."

Layla nodded. "Yes, I know. Takes after her mom."

His grin turned into a soft chuckle. "Obviously. Do you have any more children?"

"Just Erin," she replied. "Do you have kids?"

"No," he said, and hooked a thumb backward. "I'm just an uncle to Larkin. I'm not married," he added, and smiled again.

Layla realized she had a serious case of Captain

Obvious. Gawd...she needed to get a grip. "Oh...well..."

"I was wondering, are you busy on Saturday?" he asked unexpectedly.

She sucked in a sharp breath. "Saturday?"

He nodded. "There's a grand opening celebration at the Hotel Fortune on Saturday afternoon. It's going to be like a big party—kids are welcome, so you can bring your daughter. I'm pretty sure Hailey will be there, and it should be a fun afternoon."

Was he asking her on a date? She wasn't sure. She'd had so little interaction with men in the last year or so, she was inept at reading signals.

"It's Valentine's Day on Saturday," she reminded him.

"I know," he said and met her gaze straight on. "So...is that a yes?"

Layla's first thought was to refuse. She didn't need anything derailing her at the moment. And the man in front of her was pure distraction. But still...he hadn't indicated it was anything other than an afternoon at a party and Erin might enjoy it. And she had no real reason to refuse. In fact, getting out and socializing would probably be good for herself and her daughter.

"Ah...okay. What time?"

He ducked into the Ranger for a second and returned holding a small business card. "My cell number is on there. Send me a text message and I'll let you know the time and address."

"I know where the hotel is," she said. "But I'll send you a text anyway."

He grinned. "Great. See you Saturday."

Layla got into her car and waited until he pulled out of the parking space before she started the ignition. Somehow, she thought as she drove home, she'd agreed to a pseudo date with Kane Fortune.

Now all she had to do was decide if she had the courage to actually go.

Chapter Two

"So, everything is going to go smoothly tomorrow, correct?"

Kane looked up from his desk in the corner of his cousin's office and spotted Callum in the doorway. It was Friday afternoon and the hotel's grand opening was less than twenty-four hours away. He knew Callum had concerns, and rightly so, considering what had happened over a month ago.

"It'll be fine. The place looks amazing. Everything is on track. There won't be any surprises," he assured his cousin.

"There might be if the authorities don't determine if we were sabotaged, or if the balcony collapse was an accident."

"I'm sure they're doing their best," he said, once again trying to be the voice of reason. It occurred to him that he did that a lot.

"I wish I had your confidence," Callum said, and frowned. "Perhaps we should hire more security?"

"We could," Kane said, and got to his feet. "But remember that tomorrow is meant to be a family-friendly event," he asked. "Besides, the hotel security system is the best money can buy and the regular security staff have been briefed and I'll be there. So will you, Steven, Wiley and Dillon. And Adam and Brady, too. Plus, Grace is in full charge of the hotel, so it'll be fine."

"Okay," Callum breathed on a sigh. "I'll trust your instincts. Let's face it, without them we probably wouldn't be having the opening tomorrow."

Kane stayed silent, but figured his cousin was right. Callum and his siblings had money, ambition and great ideas—but what his Fortune cousins occasionally lacked was a little dose of the "real world." They'd been raised without the burden of any financial hardship. Their father had made millions in the computer gaming industry and although Kane didn't envy their background, he certainly understood what it meant to grow up without wealth. His own father, Gary, was a hardworking man who raised his family to have a strong work ethic and Kane was grateful for that. It kept him grounded, a quality that came in handy when he was dealing with all the Fortune egos.

As much as he enjoyed being part of the Fortune legacy, there were times when he missed his old life and his family in upstate New York. Sure, having Adam and Brady in town was great, but he had always been close to the rest of his siblings and his parents. His father had made it clear that he didn't agree with his and Adam's decision to move to Texas and take up their roles as part of the Texas Fortune arm of the family.

When his father had discovered he was the illegitimate son of Julius Fortune he didn't exactly embrace the idea. In fact, he wasn't interested in connecting with any of his half brothers—all of whom had created their own legacy in one form or another. His half brothers Gerald and David had both found riches in computer technology, and Kenneth in real estate. Gary's background was more blue-collar, and the recession had hit the family hard. Still, Kane was grateful for the happy childhood he and his siblings had shared together. There might not have been much money, but there was always a lot of love.

Kane left the office with Callum and they took a quick tour of the hotel. The first reservations were booked from Saturday and so far, business looked promising. The place was built exactly how Kane had envisioned. Its mission-style architecture paid respect to the town's Spanish roots, and it was smaller and more intimate than Callum's original plans. Plans that had originally created dissent and disagreement in the town, because the Fortunes had wanted to build a monster-sized hotel that rivaled ones in cities like Houston and Austin. Kane had urged them to scale back once the locals had gotten wind of the proposal and began campaigning against the venture. He came up with an alternate plan for a smaller but equally luxurious boutique-style hotel—and one that was also about inclusion, staying loyal to the town's heritage, using local contractors to complete as much of the construction work as possible, and hiring and training local staff. Thankfully, his cousins listened, and now the hotel was only a day away from opening.

Kane spent another half an hour convincing Callum the opening would go off without a hitch before the other man headed back to his office, and then Kane did a final sweep of the hotel, floor by floor, checking rooms, inspecting the kitchen, restaurant and reception area. He spent ten minutes with Grace Williams, the hotel manager, who'd been injured in the balcony collapse and still wore a boot on her injured leg. Afterward, he had another quick meeting with the security team and then spotted his younger brother Brady striding across the foyer.

"What are you doing here?" he asked, happy to see his sibling.

His brother looked around. "Just checking things out. Callum's nuts today," he added, and laughed.

"Well," Kane said, and shrugged lightly. "At the

end of the day it's his wallet *and* his reputation as a developer on the line, so that's not surprising. But everything is organized and I'm sure it will be a successful opening tomorrow."

Brady nodded. "I guess. Have you talked to Mom or Dad this week?"

"Mom," Kane replied. "I think Dad's avoiding me. He doesn't want to talk about the hotel or what we're all doing here in Rambling Rose. And I'm pretty sure he hasn't forgiven Adam for getting married and settling down here. And now that you've moved here, too..." Kane's words trailed off for a moment. "Dad's had a lot of changes to get used to lately."

"He's not the only one," Brady said. "I don't think I've slept the night through in the last six months."

"Well, being a parent to a pair of four-year-olds can't be easy."

When Brady's best friend and his wife had died in an accident six months earlier, his brother had become legal guardian to the couple's four-year-old twin boys. Kane had to admit that Brady had certainly stepped up to the plate in the parenting department. Recently, Brady realized it would make sense for him to be closer to his extended family, so that the boys would be able to grow up around more family—just as he and Kane had—and he had relocated with the twins to Rambling Rose. Of course, Kane and Adam were delighted their brother was in town and gave him as much support with his kids as they could.

"Where are the boys, by the way?" he asked.

"With Adam for a couple of hours. I haven't quite mastered grocery shopping with both boys yet," Brady said and grinned.

"Maybe you should think about getting a nanny," Kane suggested.

Brady shrugged. "Yeah, eventually. I need a job, too. The boys can be a handful so I'll have to figure something out soon. Right now we're just working on getting settled. They've had so much change lately I want them to feel some stability. Thanks for helping me out with them last weekend, by the way. I know you've got a lot going on with the hotel at the moment, so I appreciate you watching the boys on Saturday."

Kane nodded. "Family first, remember."

Brady slapped his shoulder affectionately and then Kane noticed another man standing by the reception desk. Jay Cross worked at the hotel as part of the Fortune management training program. Kane had befriended the other man, but Jay was a quiet, private sort of guy, who seemed to keep his reasons for being in Rambling Rose pretty close to the vest. Still, he worked hard and had so far proven himself to be an asset to the hotel.

Kane spoke to both men for a few minutes and

was interrupted when his cell pinged. He pulled his phone from his pocket and swiped the screen.

Hi. I owed you a message. What time tomorrow? Layla.

His gut rolled over as he slowly worked through the words and a familiar dread rattled through him for a moment. Kane took a breath and didn't give the uneasiness too much traction. It was only a short message and he had an app that turned text to speech and used it when he was in a hurry or on a deadline, although he usually avoided the app when he was in company. Even nearly twenty years after his diagnosis with dyslexia, he still sometimes felt the stigma associated with the disorder. Not from his family and friends, since those closest to him were well aware of his issues, but the struggle he'd endured through his school years sometimes lingered when he was in social situations. And he wasn't familiar enough with Jay to reveal something so personal.

He excused himself and stepped away, checking the message again. *Layla.* It had been a long time since he'd any inclination to hang out with someone and he was very pleased she'd texted—since he wasn't sure she would. In fact, early that morning, since he hadn't heard from her, he'd convinced himself she wasn't going to accept his invitation.

Kane took his time and texted back, adding the

formal invitation to the opening in an attachment. A few seconds later she responded with a thumbs-up emoji and he was foolishly pleased.

He quickly rejoined the two men. "Sorry about that."

Brady raised a brow. "You're grinning," his brother remarked. "Any reason for that?"

Heat crawled up Kane's neck. He was? Kane didn't want to admit that Layla's friendly text was behind his expression. "Nope."

Brady laughed. "I gotta go, catch you later."

Once Brady left, Kane discussed a few minor issues that needed to be addressed before the following day with Jay. The other man agreed to see to a lingering problem with the door in the restaurant kitchen before he clocked out for the day. Kane left the hotel around four thirty and, instead of going to the gym as he usually did, headed for his brother's place.

Adam was home and greeted him with a smile and one of his famous home-brewed craft beers. Kane was close to all his siblings, but he had a particularly good relationship with Adam.

"Didn't expect to see you today," his brother said as they sat in the kitchen, and Larkin chuckled happily from his spot in his high chair. "I thought it would be all hands on deck at the hotel this afternoon, since the big opening is tomorrow."

"Everything's on track to go smoothly," Kane replied. "I bumped into Brady at the hotel—he said the boys were here?"

"Laurel settled them in the living room with a DVD," Adam said.

Kane nodded and took a sip of the beer. "This is good," he remarked, and shook the bottle a little. "A new blend?"

Adam had a keen interest in craft beer and was working toward setting up his own brewing company. "Yeah, it's the best yet I think."

"Agreed."

"So, how do you think tomorrow will go?" Adam asked. "Is Callum ready for the big reveal?"

"He's concerned," Kane said, and shrugged a fraction. "Natural, I guess, considering what happened last month. The last thing we want is another thing to go wrong at the hotel, particularly on opening day. But every precaution has been taken and I think it will be a good day tomorrow."

"Valentine's Day," Adam said, and grinned. "A nice touch. Your idea?"

He laughed. "You know me. Mr. Romantic."

"It wouldn't hurt, you know," Adam said a little more seriously. "Might make you less of a workaholic."

"You mean romance?" he said, and laughed again. "Actually, I…" He paused and shrugged again. "Nothing."

Adam's gaze sharpened. "What?"

"I met someone," he said quickly before he lost his nerve. "Or at least, I think I *might* have."

"You think?"

"She's a parent at Larkin's day care," he admitted, heat rising up his collar. "A single parent," he clarified quickly. "I met her when I picked him up the other day."

"A single mom?" Adam chuckled. "I'm impressed. Sounds very grown up."

Kane raised a brow. "Thanks for the vote of confidence."

"Well, you gotta admit, you usually date women who aren't any more interested in settling down than you are."

Kane scowled. "Neither did you until you married Laurel."

"That's because I've been in love with Laurel since college," his brother remarked. "What's your excuse?"

"Okay," he said, and drank some beer. "You got me. I'm obviously afraid of commitment."

"Not surprising after you got your heart busted up by that Swedish girl."

"That was high school," he said, and frowned, recalling the exchange student who'd captured his heart in senior year and then summarily broke it when she said she had no intention of settling for a dumb jock. Her criticism had stung and although his heart had recovered quickly, he'd never quite gotten over being labeled that way. "It was just kid's stuff and a long time ago."

"To prove my point, though, just how long has it been since you've had a serious relationship?" Adam inquired. "Since Jane, right?"

"Janine," Kane corrected.

How long had it been since he'd thought about Janine? A long time. After high school and throughout college he'd avoided anything serious, and then he met Janine and they'd dated for a while. But it didn't last. With Kane, it never lasted. He sidestepped commitment like it was the plague. The moment Janine had pressured him for more, he'd pulled back. He knew it was illogical—Janine was a nice woman and they'd had a lot in common. But something held him back. His inability to commit had waved like a red flag between them. Something was missing from their relationship. He didn't know what…but he knew enough to get out before things got too serious.

"Kane, is my husband hounding you about your singledom again?" Laurel asked as she appeared in the doorway.

He looked up and grinned. "Yes. Save me, will you?"

She came into the room and outstretched her arms toward her son. "Ignore him, he always gets sentimental around Valentine's Day."

"That's true," Adam agreed. "So, tell us about this mystery woman."

Kane finished his beer and got to his feet. "See for yourself tomorrow," he said. "I invited her to the hotel opening. Right now, though, I have to bail. See you at the party." He said his goodbyes and headed home.

His bungalow was small and neat, not far from the center of Rambling Rose and Provisions restaurant, where Adam was the manager. Since his brother had moved out and into the guesthouse on Fame and Fortune Ranch with Laurel and Larkin, Kane had bought some new furniture and painted the kitchen.

After he showered and zapped a frozen dinner in the microwave, he sat down with a root beer in front of the television. Not exactly a wild Friday night, he thought as he ate. Truthfully, his isolation had become a regular thing since he'd relocated to Rambling Rose and Adam had moved out. The notion made him think of Layla McCarthy and Kane realized she was the first woman he'd been attracted to in longer than he could remember. He looked forward to seeing her again, and the thought quickly made his Friday night seem a little less lonely than usual.

"Ah… Hailey," Layla said Friday afternoon after she hit the send button on a text she'd written to the man she'd come to think of as Hot Uncle. "Do you know Kane Fortune?"

Hailey swung around the side of the spa's reception desk. "Of course, he's Dillon's cousin. Why?" she asked, one steep brow up.

Layla shuffled a few things on the desk. "No reason…but I met him the other day and he seemed…" Her words trailed off as she was reluctant to incriminate herself.

"Nice?" Hailey finished for her. "He is nice. He's a good guy. In fact, Dillon reckons that if it wasn't for Kane, the new hotel wouldn't have really gotten off the ground. Even though Callum is generally considered the checkbook, the whole family is working on or at the hotel and Kane has been helping get the place ready and the big opening is tomorrow," she added,

"I know," Layla admitted. "He invited me."

"Really? A date?"

She shrugged. "I'm not sure it's a real date. He invited Erin, too."

"That's sweet," Hailey said. "How did you meet?"

Layla quickly explained the circumstances and then sighed. "I thought Erin might enjoy the party."

"Just Erin?" Hailey queried.

She colored hotly. "Me, too, I guess. The truth is, I haven't been on anything resembling a date since Frank died. I'm not sure I even remember how to act on a date—if that's what this is—or if I'm even ready to start thinking about dating again."

"Well, there's only one way to find out," Hailey

said, and smiled. "And Kane is a great guy. I think you should go for it."

Layla glanced at her phone, waiting for a reply. She knew it *was* time she came out of her self-imposed hibernation. Even if it was simply to get out of the house and enjoy herself with some male company. It's not like she *had* to see him again after the party. What harm would it do? When the reply came, she ignored the way her nerves tingled a little at the thought of seeing him again.

Later that evening she was sorting through her wardrobe, looking for something suitable to wear to the event. She had a cute red-and-white outfit picked out for Erin, and flicked through her own clothes, smiling when she came upon a dress she hadn't worn in years. It had been Frank's favorite, she recalled as she pulled it from the wardrobe and held it against herself. But no, she thought as she placed the dress back into the wardrobe. Living in the past wasn't healthy. She pulled out another dress, one she hadn't worn before and had purchased on a whim a couple of months earlier. Perfect, she thought, and hung the hanger on the top of the door to let any creases fall out.

Erin woke up early Saturday morning and Layla dragged herself out of bed to attend to her daughter. After breakfast, she did a load of washing and once the supermarket trip was done, Layla headed home, got ready for the event at the hotel and drove into town.

The multistory hotel was certainly a welcome addition to Rambling Rose. Like Paz Spa and the restaurants and cafés that had popped up in the last year, the hotel would obviously bring jobs and more dollars into the local economy. The scaled-back construction was an architectural beauty that seemed to fit in perfectly with the town. Even the gardens were breathtaking, and she slowed down to get a better look. The building loomed ahead, a row of adobe brick archways greeting her as she drove past the front entrance and followed several signs indicating guest parking. There were dozens of cars already there and people were walking toward the rear of the hotel. She parked the car, pulled the stroller from the back and quickly got Erin settled before she followed the throngs of guests.

The gardens at the rear of the building were equally lovely and she spotted a huge white rotunda and several large tents set out on the grassy area behind the swimming pool. She checked her watch, noticed that she was on time and looked around for someone she might know.

I should text Hot Uncle and tell him I'm here.

She didn't, though. She wandered around a little, smiling at a few people she recognized but didn't know by name. She considered messaging Hailey to see if she'd arrived yet, but quickly changed her mind. Instead, she pushed Erin past the rotunda where a lectern and microphone were set up, along with a few chairs that were clearly for VIPs. Then she headed for the tents with gourmet food stalls and several small carnival-style rides. She noticed one of the tents housed a collection of little tables and chairs where children were seated, coloring pictures with crayons. She pushed the stroller into the tent and quickly sat Erin at one of the tables.

"Hey there."

At the sound of the deep male voice, Layla straightened and turned, finding Kane Fortune standing behind her. The breath rushed from her lungs and she managed a smile. "Hi."

"You came?"

She nodded. "I said I would."

His gaze traveled over her. "You look lovely."

Foolishly pleased he liked her dress, Layla tried to ignore the heat wrapping itself around her limbs. Because in navy cargos and a white shirt and dark jacket, he looked so darn hot she felt like someone had lit a fire under her dormant libido.

"Thank you," she managed to say. "And thank you for the invitation. It's nice to get out and celebrate something. The hotel looks amazing. Like, boutique style, but bigger, if that makes sense."

"It does," he replied, and nodded. "That was the idea. I'll give you a tour later, if you like?"

She nodded. "I remember reading in the local

newspaper how much resistance there was to the hotel being built, but by the look of everyone here today, there's no more of that."

"Not like there was," he said, and looked relieved. "It was definitely a tough sell in the beginning. But I think that something new and different always gets people's attention. And you may have read about the accident last month."

She nodded again. "An employee was injured, right?"

"That's right, Grace Williams. Thankfully she's okay. In fact, Grace is now the general manager and she's dating my cousin Wiley, so she's obviously not holding a grudge." He smiled and the action made her belly somersault because he had one hell of a sexy smile. "Your daughter looks like she's enjoying herself."

Layla glanced down at Erin and saw she was content with her drawing and ignoring the other two children now sitting at the small table. "She's something of a loner," Layla said, and sighed. "At day care she'll take herself off into a corner with a book or a toy and stay there for an hour or so. Well, I'm not that great at making friends, so maybe the apple doesn't fall far from the tree."

"Oh, I don't know about that," he said quietly. "You're doing pretty well so far."

Layla laughed and it felt good. She didn't laugh anywhere near enough. "You make it easy." Surprisingly, she held his gaze. "I asked Hailey about you," she admitted.

"My soon-to-be cousin-in-law," he said, and grinned. "There are a lot of cousins in this town. So, what did Hailey say?"

"That you were nice," she replied. "A good guy."

"I always did like Hailey," he said, and grinned again. "Can I get you a drink?" he asked, and gestured to the food and beverage vendors.

"That would be great, but I don't want to monopolize you," she said, and glanced at the lanyard around his neck. "I'm guessing you're on duty today."

His gaze narrowed. "What is it you think I do here?"

"With those shoulders, I guess I figured you were in security or something," she said, and quickly realized how provocative she must sound. *God, I'm so out of practice at this.* "Sorry...that sounds like I've been ogling you or something."

He chuckled. "Now you're blushing," he said, still grinning. "I'll be back in a minute."

Layla watched him walk away, noticing the confident way he walked, like he was a man who knew exactly who and what he was. And those shoulders... phew...they were the stuff of fantasies. She shook off the notion and turned her attention back to Erin, who was still happily drawing. When Kane returned a few minutes later, he carried two sodas and a mini juice box.

"Thank you," she said, and took the drink for Erin.

Her daughter surprised her by getting up from the small seat, grabbing the paper she'd been drawing on and promptly holding the drawing out to Kane.

He looked down. "Is that for me?"

Erin thrust the paper higher. He took it and regarded the artwork. "Hey, that's awesome. Thank you, sweetheart."

Layla stared at the interaction. Erin never willingly approached people she didn't know. She was a quiet, solitary child. Layla had her concerns, but her pediatrician said there was nothing to worry about, and said it was most likely just the trauma of losing her father, even if she couldn't compartmentalize the loss at such a young age.

Erin popped back to the table and Layla met his gaze. "She's never done that before. Other than my grandfather, she doesn't have much interaction with men."

"How old was she when your husband passed away?"

"Six months," she replied, a familiar ache forming behind her ribs. "And she just turned two."

"Natural then," he said softly, "that she'd be reserved around strangers."

"But not you," Layla remarked, and noticed that her daughter was off her chair again and passing Kane another drawing. "Like a bee to a flower."

His mouth curled at the edges as he took the drawing and Erin returned to her chair. "I'm very charming."

"I'm starting to notice," she said, oddly not the least bit embarrassed by their mild flirting. She might be out of practice, but there was something quintessentially *good* about Kane Fortune. She felt foolish thinking it, since she hardly knew him. But Hailey's endorsement was enough to make her feel safe around him. "Isn't that our mayor?" she asked when she noticed a well-dressed woman walking toward the gazebo, with a tall man on one side and a baby in her arms. She was also flanked by several other people who chatted as she walked.

"Yep," he replied. "Ellie Fortune Hernandez. She's married to my cousin. A complicated family tree," he added, and smiled. "But you probably know that from all the social media hype."

Her brows came up. "Would it shock you to discover I'm something of a purist? I read the paper every Sunday and I don't have any social media accounts, other than Facebook, and that's really only to connect with work and Erin's day care."

He looked surprised. "Really? No Instagram? Pinterest? Twitter?" He laughed softly when she shook her head. "How on earth have you coped?"

Layla smiled. "I guess I prefer a good book to a gossip column. So, tell me about this complicated family tree of yours."

"I will," he assured her. "I promise. But only once

I'm sure you like me enough to not get scared off by the craziness."

"I do like you," she admitted, and dropped her gaze.

When she looked up, she saw he was watching her with blistering intensity—as though her admission had somehow shifted the dynamic between them. Layla didn't quite know what to think. Or say. And thankfully, he spoke next.

"I need to bail for about half an hour while speeches are being made and the opening gets its official sign-off." He dipped into his pocket and extracted a lanyard and passed it to her. "Wear this. It's a VIP pass for your seating near the rotunda when the speeches start. I'll find you when I'm done."

She took the lanyard and nodded. "You know, you never did say what you actually do here."

He looked at her. "I guess you could say I'm the jack-of-all-trades around here. See you soon," he said, and then turned and walked off.

Layla stared after him. He really was unfairly attractive. And charming to boot!

She stayed in the kids' tent for another ten minutes and then put Erin back into the stroller and walked around the grounds. There were hundreds of people at the event now, and she weaved through them with the stroller, spotting a few people she knew as clients of Paz Spa, and then saw Hailey walking toward her.

"You made it," her boss and friend said, and then added teasingly, "Where's your date?"

"Working, I think," Layla replied. "He'll be back."

Hailey smiled. "The speeches are about to start so we should sit down."

They found their seats and Layla was touched to discover she was seated next to Hailey. Kane's doing, she figured. He really was incredibly thoughtful.

The speeches began and they listened as Ellie Fortune Hernandez took to the microphone and welcomed everyone to the party. She talked briefly about the town, about the people, and thanked several members of the Fortune family by name before officially opening the hotel. Then there was a long and hearty applause. Callum Fortune spoke next and once the officiating was over, the crowd dispersed and Dillon approached, quickly draping an arm over Hailey's shoulder and bringing her close.

Layla experienced a spike of envy. Normally, she wasn't the jealous type. But the intimacy between the pair was obvious and it made her ache deep in her chest. She'd had that once, long ago.

And then, just as she was wondering if she'd ever feel that kind of love again, Layla spotted Kane standing by the gazebo, and suddenly the ache in her heart eased a little.

It was crazy. She hardly knew him.

Still, the sensation lingered. He was nice. He was attractive. And she liked him. Which she figured was a good place to start.

Chapter Three

Kane had never been a big believer in love at first sight. Or second sight. Or even third.

Lust at first sight? Well, yeah.

He'd been there a few times, but it had never morphed into anything more. A few dates. And other than his relationship with Janine, usually lasted a couple of months, at the most.

Then there was Layla.

Seeing her in her red dress and black heels, her hair floating around her shoulders, had almost knocked him to his knees. There was no doubt he was attracted to her, and he was pretty sure the feeling was mutual.

"Where you heading in such a hurry?" Adam

asked once the speeches were done and they'd taken a moment to thank the VIPs for attending. "Is your mystery woman here?"

"She's not a mystery," Kane replied as he stepped away from the gazebo, scanning the crowds for Layla. "Her name is Layla McCarthy. I'll introduce you."

"Introduce him to who?" Brady asked as he stepped into their circle, a twin holding on to each hand.

"He brought a date today," Adam supplied. "A single mother he met at Larkin's day care."

"Really?" Brady queried, brows up. "An instant family."

Kane couldn't ignore the gibe. "We just met the other day, so hold up on any *instant family* jokes, will you. She lost her husband a year or so ago, so I don't think she's in any frame of mind to get serious. And neither am I," he added; however, his brothers didn't look convinced. "Don't interfere, okay?"

"Who? Us?" Adam suggested innocently. "It's not like we're gonna tell Mom or anything," he said, and winked toward Brady.

Kane shook his head, excused himself and headed across the grass, quickly spotting Layla. He experienced a tight knot in his gut as he walked toward her, which increased when he also noticed Hailey and his cousin at her side. *Great, more relatives.* Sometimes he wished for the days when he had a much simpler family tree.

Layla smiled as he approached and the knot quickly subsided. He shook Dillon's and Hailey's hands and turned toward Layla. "Everything okay?"

She nodded. "Great. The speeches were good. And this is a fabulous venue. You should all be really proud of this place."

"It wouldn't be here if it wasn't for Kane," Dillon said.

"Well, I come from humbler beginnings," Kane said, and half shrugged. "So, figuring out what a small town like Rambling Rose needed was easier." He turned his full attention to Layla. "Would you like to take a walk?"

"Sure," she replied, and quickly secured a small blanket around Erin's legs.

He excused them and ushered her forward, giving her a moment to get some traction with the stroller. "She seems settled," he said as he gestured to her daughter, who was quietly playing with a soft stuffed toy.

"I'm sure she's happy that our usual Saturday routine is shaken up," she said, and smiled. "We don't get out much."

Kane led them around the rotunda and into the pathed garden area. "You know what they say about all work and no play, right?"

She nodded. "They would be correct," she said,

and laughed a little. "The truth is, with work and Erin, sometimes I feel like I don't even have time to catch my breath."

"I don't imagine it's easy being a single parent," he said as they veered to the left of the path.

"It's not," she replied, and sighed. "But I love Erin more than life, so even when it's hard, it's worth it. What about you? Do you want kids?"

"One day. I guess I don't think about it much. If I met the right person," he said, and shrugged. "Then...yeah, sign me up."

He was sure he saw a tiny smile play around at the corners of her mouth. "And in the meantime, you are getting plenty of practice with your nephew."

"Nephews," he corrected, and briefly explained about his brother taking over guardianship of the twins. "Brady's the last person I would ever have imagined taking on two kids, but he's doing a good job."

"Wow, that's admirable," she said. "It takes a big heart to raise someone else's children. I know that if I ever..." She stopped, her words trailing off.

"If you ever...what?"

She shrugged one shoulder. "Let's just say that if I ever...you know...found someone again, I'd have to be sure he'd care about Erin first and foremost," she said, and then shivered as a gust of wind ripped down the pathway and between the hedges.

Kane took a quick look at the thin sweater she

wore over her dress and immediately pulled off his jacket and offered it to her.

"Oh, I couldn't," she protested. "You'll get cold."

"It's okay," he assured. "Take it."

She hesitated for a second before finally taking the jacket and draping it over her shoulders. "Thank you. I didn't exactly dress for the weather."

"You look pretty. Very Valentine's Day-ish."

"Thanks. I like red," she said as she stopped the stroller for a moment and checked her daughter, who was now fast asleep. "I think she wore herself out with all the coloring."

"Well, she did create a couple of masterpieces and that's tiring work. Would you like to head to the hotel? If you're hungry I could ask the chef at Roja to make something for you."

"Roja?"

"The restaurant in the hotel. My cousin Nicole is the chef there. I think she gave the opening celebrations a pass because she is still working on the menu for this evening, which is when the first guests arrive."

Her expression narrowed a little. "Wasn't it the restaurant that got damaged last month?"

He shook his head. "The balcony collapsed, but the inside of the restaurant wasn't affected."

"It must have been a difficult time for you all," she said. "I only know what I read in the paper. Has the cause of the accident been determined?"

"Well, that's the thing," he replied as they turned and headed toward the main building. "We're not entirely convinced it was an accident. The Fortune family have made a few enemies over the years— and not everyone in this town supported the hotel being built. It only takes one person with a grudge to do harm."

"I guess," she agreed. "But seeing the hotel now, it's hard to imagine anyone thinking it wouldn't be good for the town. I've lived in Rambling Rose all of my adult life and I've never experienced it being so vibrant and so alive. For a long time it was forgotten…just another blue-collar town that was little more than an accidental veer off the highway for most people. But not anymore. We have restaurants, a pediatric center, Paz Spa and now this hotel. Your family did that…and that's quite a legacy."

"Callum had a vision," Kane said as they walked through the main doors, passing two security officers who were stationed in the foyer. "His brothers Dillon and Steven supported that vision."

"And you?" she queried as he led her past reception and into the restaurant.

"I think I'm here by default," he replied, and grinned. "And I mean that in the best possible way. When Callum asked me to manage the construction of the hotel, I think I was still a little shell-shocked from discovering we were related to the Texas Fortunes."

She looked around, wide-eyed. "You did this?"

"It was a joint effort."

"Now you're being modest."

He laughed and then spotted his cousin Nicole by the bar. "I'm glad to be a part of it."

"But Rambling Rose is a long way from New York," she said, with way more intuition than he expected. Or frankly, wanted. Kane had never considered himself that easy to read. "Right?"

"I guess," he replied. "But my family's from upstate, not New York City. We lived a fairly ordinary life. When I think about it, I don't see a lot of change in how I live my day-to-day life in Rambling Rose. Tell me about your family," he said, shifting the topic back to her as she parked the stroller beside a table, and then he offered her a seat.

"You mean the whole sad story?" she queried.

"It's a sad story?"

She nodded. "It could take a while."

He glanced at the sleeping child in the stroller. "We have time."

Nicole took that moment to approach and say hello, and Kane quickly made the introductions. "Did you bail on the party outside?" his cousin asked with a chuckle.

"Just taking a break while the baby's asleep. Any chance of coffee?"

"Well, my barista has left for the day, but I think I can manage the task. And if you're here for coffee then you must try some cake." Nicole looked at Erin in the stroller. "Your daughter is adorable," she said before she walked off.

"She seems nice," Layla remarked as she slipped off his jacket and hung it over the back of a chair. "But then, all your family is nice."

He didn't disagree. "What about you? Ready to tell me your sad family story?"

She sighed as she tucked her legs underneath the table and faced him. "Erin is my family. I'm an only child. So was my husband. I have grandparents who I'm very close to. They live in town at a retirement center and I visit them once a week."

"And your parents?"

She sucked in a breath. "I never knew my father. My mom... Well, she had me when she was very young. I'm not sure where she is right now. She travels a lot for her work." She paused for a moment, taking another breath. "She's a dancer. But I haven't seen her for a number of years. When I was fifteen I moved in with my grandparents and I lived with them until I got married when I was twenty-two."

"College?"

"No," she replied. "I've worked in a few different admin positions since I left high school."

"And now you work at Paz Spa."

"Yes," she replied. "You know, I've never seen you there."

Kane grinned. "Yoga and pedicures aren't really my thing."

"Mine either, if I'm being honest," she admitted. "But it's a good place to work and Hailey is really understanding of the time I need to be with Erin."

Nicole returned with coffee and two slices of carrot cake and they chatted for a while before she returned to her spot at the bar. Kane turned his attention back to the woman sitting opposite him and he realized the more time he spent with Layla, the more he relaxed. He liked her company. She was good-humored and self-effacing and good to be around. And as pretty as hell. Yeah…he liked her. A lot.

"I'd like to see you again," he said candidly.

Her fork stalled midway to her mouth. "As opposed to seeing me right now?"

Kane bit back a grin. "How about I take you and Erin out for breakfast tomorrow?"

She put down her fork, placed her elbow on the table and rested her chin in her hand. "I'm not sure I can."

Kane's gut rolled. "You're not sure about me, you mean?"

She sighed softly. "Actually, it's more like not being sure about myself."

He could see the hesitation and concern in her expression and wasn't about to push the issue or the invitation. "Fair enough."

She smiled, took a breath, and then spoke. "I'm

seeing my grandparents in the morning. How about we have a late lunch instead? I'll cook."

Kane stilled in his seat. "At your place?"

She nodded. "It's easier than handling a two-year-old in a restaurant. Unless she's sleeping," she added and gazed at the stroller. "So…yes?"

"Yes," he replied.

"I'll text you my address."

And that, Kane thought as he sipped his coffee and looked at the remarkably beautiful woman sitting opposite him, meant that he had a date.

Layla visited her grandparents early Sunday morning at their retirement home villa. Maude, her grandmother, was always welcoming and Grandpa Joe adored Erin to pieces. Layla sat with Maude at the kitchen counter while Erin played in the living room with her grandfather. She gave her grandmother a quick rundown on the hotel opening party, mentioning that she and Erin were invited.

"By a man, you said?" Maude queried.

Layla tried to look casual. "He's nice."

"It's good that you're getting out. Frank wouldn't want you to—"

"It's just a new thing, Nan," she insisted. "We'll see how it goes."

As she said the words, Layla realized that despite only knowing Kane for a few days, there was something achingly *familiar* about him that gave her a sense of comfort. She knew it was silly, since they'd only met five days earlier, but she couldn't dismiss the feeling. Still, she didn't want to verbalize it—not even to her grandmother.

"He's just a friend," she said instead.

Maude's eyes twinkled. "Well, that's how it starts."

Thinking about Kane made her insides quiver. A normal reaction, she thought, after spending time with a man who was so attractive and clearly interested in her. They'd parted companionably the day before, after finishing their coffee. Layla had been disappointed that the afternoon had come to an end, but he had things to attend to at the hotel. He'd walked her to her car and gently taken her hand. She hadn't expected a kiss goodbye and didn't want one. It was too soon for her and she suspected he knew it. Kane Fortune was a smart guy and clearly adept at reading signals. He'd lingered holding her hand, though, and had rubbed his thumb over her knuckles before releasing her with the promise of seeing her again the following day.

Slow is best, she told herself. She wasn't anywhere near prepared for anything else.

"Maybe," she said, and shrugged. "But I don't think I'm ready for anything more. Frank is still in my heart."

"Of course he is. But that doesn't mean there isn't room for someone else."

"If there was only myself to think about, then yeah, I probably wouldn't want to play it so safe. But I have to think of Erin. I have to put her first, Nan. You know why," she said, and sighed heavily.

Maude regarded her over her teacup. "I know how it was for you and your mother. Iliana is my daughter and I love her, but I'm not blind to her behavior over the years. I know how disruptive it was for you moving around so much when you were a child."

Layla nodded as old feelings quickly surfaced. "I made a promise to Erin when she was born that I would make sure she had a stable home and felt safe. It was easier to promise that when Frank was here, because he was so reliable and sensible. But I don't have that now…there's just me. And I have to put her needs above my own and protect her from disappointment and hurt. Even if that means I'm alone."

Maude regarded her gently. "Not every relationship with a man is destined to work out like your mother's did."

"Relationships," Layla corrected. "I was there, Nan, remember? I went through every breakup when she did. I heard the crying, the arguing, the despair and then the anger, and I don't want that for Erin. I won't do it."

Her grandmother's eyes glistened. "I understand. But you have a great capacity for love and I'm sure there's someone special out there for you, Layla."

Layla's chest tightened. "I've had my someone

special," she said softly. "I don't expect to get that lucky again."

She stayed with her grandparents for another hour, then got home at eleven and put Erin down for a nap. And the whole time she was making a lasagna and then baking a cake, she figured she should probably text Kane and cancel their lunch date. Because what she'd said to her grandmother lingered in her thoughts. She *wasn't* in the market for a relationship. She was nowhere near ready. Yes, he was nice. He was smart and incredibly attractive and made her smile. But experience warned her that all those qualities were sometimes a recipe for disaster. She'd witnessed it firsthand with her mother.

But she didn't cancel. Instead, she straightened her spine, changed into jeans and a light green sweater, brushed her hair and added a little makeup, and waited for him to arrive. Thankfully, Erin was in a happy mood and when his truck pulled up outside her house at three minutes to two, her daughter was laughing and waving her hands. Layla watched as Kane walked up to the house. In jeans, blue checkered shirt and leather jacket, he looked like the perfect picture of masculinity and her insides crunched up instantly.

And he had flowers.

Flowers.

A bunch of tiny pale lavender roses mixed with greenery and wrapped in bright pink cellophane. Her crunching morphed into something that resembled swooning and she forgot all about her previous inclination to cancel their date.

"Hi," she said, shifting Erin onto her hip.

"Hello," he said when he reached the bottom step. "Happy Day-after-Valentine's-Day," he said, and held out the bouquet.

Layla turned hot all over. Boy, he oozed sexy from every pore. "Thank you," she said, and stepped back to open the door. "Please come in."

She took the flowers and he followed her through the door and into the long hallway. Once the door was closed, she made her way through the house and into the kitchen. Erin chatted as they walked and tried to pull a bud from the bouquet. Layla placed the flowers on the countertop and grabbed a vase.

"Want some help with that?" he asked.

"Sure." She shifted Erin on her hip again and held out the vase.

He moved around the counter and filled it with water, quickly placing the flowers inside. "You have a nice home. How long have you lived here?"

"Five years," she replied. "It's really too big for the two of us. And the upkeep alone is difficult on the purse strings. I'm not good at fixing things, either. But we're settled here. What about you? Where do you live?"

He grinned. "I rent a tiny two-bedroom place in town. It's temporary," he added. "I shared it with my brother until he got married. It's okay, but it's really just a place to sleep. Not a home," he added, and looked around. "Like this."

Layla watched as he placed the vase on the counter and then took off his jacket, quickly hanging it over the back of a chair. He filled the room with his broad shoulders and strong-looking arms. "Do you work out?" she asked bluntly. Instantly she wished she could take back the question. Especially when his gaze intensified.

"I hit the gym most days. Why?"

She swallowed hard as heat crawled up her neck. "You look very...fit."

He chuckled. "I try to keep in shape. But I'm not a gym rat. I don't drink alcohol much, don't smoke, don't have too many vices and try to eat healthily. Speaking of which, something smells good," he said, and gestured to the oven.

"Lasagna," she said, and laughed. "Erin's favorite."

"Mine, too," he said.

"I'll put her in her high chair while I get things ready."

"Want me to take her?" he asked, his hands outstretched a little.

"Oh, she probably won't go to you so—" Her words cut off when she felt Erin lean toward him eagerly, her little arms moving. "Well, forget what I said. It looks like she will."

Within seconds her daughter was in his arms and digging her fingers into his face. Layla had to admit, he really did know how to handle a young child. She relaxed when it was clear he had it under control and moved around the counter. Despite how casual and easy he was to be around, there was an intense undercurrent floating around the room. She wondered if he felt it, and then figured it was all in her imagination.

She busied herself with the food and took the jug of iced tea she'd prepared earlier from the refrigerator, keeping a watchful eye on her daughter and the man she seemed so enamored with. Other than her grandfather, he was the first man Erin had spent any real time with since Frank's death and Layla was amazed at how easily she had taken to him.

"She likes you," she said, and smiled.

"Kid has impeccable taste," he said with a grin. "So, how long have you been at Paz Spa?" he asked.

"A few months," she replied as she prepared her daughter's food. "I leave early most afternoons, so I can pick up Erin in plenty of time. But if I need to be at work for an afternoon shift, my grandmother picks her up and then I get her from their place on the way home. It would be great if I had a sibling or two," she said on a sigh. Then she remembered his huge collection of relatives. "I'll bet it was noisy growing up in your family, huh?"

He nodded. "Six kids, so yeah. But my parents handled it well."

"You're close to your folks?"

"Yes," he said, and then exhaled heavily. "It's been a little strained in the last year, since my father found out he was Julius Fortune's son. I think when Adam and I moved here, my father felt a little betrayed—like we'd chosen a side. But that wasn't it. We just wanted to find out where we fit. But Dad…" He paused for a moment, his words trailing off. "He's taken it hard."

"The Fortune family is famous in this state," she remarked, seeing his shoulders drop a little. "And I understand why you'd want to spend some time developing a relationship with your extended family. It would be great having so many cousins."

"It's never dull," he said, and grinned. "Do you want more kids?"

Layla's hand paused midair. She couldn't tell him that she and Frank had planned to have four kids. It was too personal. "Ah… I guess I don't think about it. I mean, I'm very grateful for Erin. But more? I'd have to be, you know, sure that it was the right thing for everyone."

"Assurances?" he queried. "Makes sense, after everything you've been through. Can I ask how your husband died?"

"In a car accident," she replied, saying the words

she said so many times. "He was on his way home from work and a truck hit him on the highway."

"I'm sorry."

"Me, too," she said sadly, and blinked away the heat in her eyes.

"Was he a good man?"

She nodded. "Very good. He adored Erin."

"Well," he said, and looked at her daughter, who seemed very content to be in his arms, "she is pretty adorable."

Layla smiled. "So, I know you've never been married, but what about engaged?"

"Nope."

"Close?"

He shook his head. "Nope."

"Longest serious relationship?"

He held up the fingers on one hand.

"Five years?"

He shook his head, clearly okay with her questions. "Shocking, I know."

"Five months?" she queried, reading his hand signal correctly. "And you're what…thirtyish?"

"Thirty-one."

She raised a brow. "Are you…afraid of commitment?"

He inhaled, looking at Erin for a moment, then back to Layla. "Afraid of screwing up," he said quietly. "Particularly if there are one or two of these involved. If I do it, I want to get it right, like my parents did."

She laughed humorlessly. "Whereas I want to do the exact opposite of my parents. That's why I'll always put my daughter first."

"Book!" Erin said, and grabbed a handful of Kane's hair. "More!"

Layla watched as he untangled Erin's fingers from his hair without so much as a grimace. "You want to read a book?"

Erin nodded her head. "Book!"

"She has a favorite book at the moment that I've been reading to her," Layla explained. "It's one with a talking yellow hippo and a purple giraffe that wears ballet shoes. A classic," she added, and grinned, and she began bringing the food to the table. "Actually, she's good at keeping herself entertained with a book. Like me, I suppose."

"What else do you like to do?" he asked, and adeptly settled Erin in her high chair.

"I like music," she said, and placed a second round of dishes on the table.

"Let me guess...country music?"

Layla smiled. "Of course, I'm from Texas. And you? Let *me* guess...jazz?"

"Show tunes," he said, deadpan.

Layla laughed. "I don't believe you. I'm thinking classic rock?"

"You got me," he replied, and sat down, positioning the high chair near the dining chair Layla had pulled out for herself.

"What about you?" she asked as she sat. "What do you do in your spare time?"

"The last few months I haven't had a whole lot of spare time, but now that the hotel is operating, I can probably relax a little and take some time to do the things I like. I'd like to get a marine fish tank," he said, and grinned. "You know, for relaxation purposes."

"Are fish relaxing?"

"Sure," he replied. "They swim around without a care in the world."

"I wonder what that's like," she mused. "Not having a care in the world."

"I'm not sure. If you find out, let me know."

Layla laughed softly and realized she did that a lot around Kane. He had a calm, steady way about him. And she liked it. She liked him.

A lot.

More than she'd expected.

Which scared her. Because liking Kane meant opening up her heart. And Layla didn't know if she'd have room in her heart for anyone, ever again.

Chapter Four

At work on Monday morning, around eleven, Layla signed for a package addressed to her. While there was nothing unusual about that, the return address warranted another look. It was from a local bakery. She opened it to find a selection of four cupcakes, decorated with red and white hearts. There was a note inside the box and when she read the words her heart skipped a couple of beats.

Happy Second-Day-after-Valentine's-Day. Thanks for lunch yesterday. Kane

Layla was rereading the note when Hailey stopped by her desk.

"What's this?" her boss queried, and peered into the box. "Cupcakes?"

She looked up and smiled. "From Kane," she explained, experiencing a silly fluttering in her belly, and showed her the note.

Hailey's expressive brows shot up. "I see. It's romantic, don't you think?"

"Er... I'm not sure either of us is in the market for romance."

"Are you sure about that?" Hailey queried and grinned. "I mean, little cakes with hearts on them is a pretty romantic gesture, don't you think?"

Yes, she did think.

"I couldn't, you know, say," she muttered and avoided the other woman's gaze.

"He's a nice guy," Hailey said, like she was trying to reassure her. "We should all go out sometime. The four of us, I mean. It would be fun."

Layla didn't comment and quickly got back to work, trying to put the gift—and the giver—out of her mind. The afternoon went by quickly, as they were fully booked, and she maneuvered appointments around to accommodate a couple of walk-ins. She left on time and realized she'd failed in her objective to not think about Kane. Because she was on edge as she pulled up at the day care and hoped she might bump into him. But his truck wasn't in the parking lot and disappointment set in. It was foolish, she knew, to be so conflicted. But the mind and heart couldn't be told how to feel. Instead of Kane, she spotted Larkin's mother coming out of the building as she was walking up the path. The little boy was cooing cheerfully in his mom's arms and it made Layla smile.

"Hi," the other woman said, and stopped walking. "I saw you on Saturday, didn't I? With Kane. I'm Laurel Fortune, Kane's sister-in-law. I'm sorry we didn't get to officially catch up at the party. Larkin had a little sniffle and I didn't want to keep him out for too long, so we left early. It's nice to meet you."

"You, too," she said. "Layla McCarthy."

"We should set up a playdate," she suggested. "I know my son would love it."

From playdates to double dates, she had Fortunes coming out of the woodwork trying to mesh into her life. Her usual modus operandi was to put up a wall and come up with one of many excuses. But oddly, she didn't. Instead, she smiled and replied that it was a great idea before she said goodbye and headed inside.

Layla had never been very good at making friends and knew it was a hang-up from her childhood. She'd moved around so much, so often, and sometimes so quickly, she was continually dragged from school after one semester and placed in another. It made making real friendships impossible. And the behavior stuck as she entered her teenage years. She'd never had a best friend—other than Frank. And certainly never had the experience of a close female friend. She often saw friends come into Paz Spa together, laughing and enjoying each other's company, and at times it made her envious. Silly, she supposed, to be jealous of something she'd never had. Perhaps she should take Hailey up on her offer and arrange for the four of them to go out.

Except that Kane hadn't actually said he wanted to see her again.

And that was what confused her.

Take care, he'd said. *Thanks for lunch*, he'd said. *It was fun*, he'd said.

And then he sent her a box of cupcakes as a thank-you.

It was sweet, she supposed. Not romantic, as Hailey had suggested. It was silly thinking along those lines when they'd only just met. But he was clearly a nice guy…easy to like, easy to talk to, easy to be around.

Except I'm not looking for romance.

That thought planted firmly in her mind, Layla picked up her daughter and headed home.

It was past eight o'clock when, with Erin fed, bathed and tucked in bed, Layla settled herself at the kitchen table with her laptop to study for an hour or so. She'd been at it for about twenty minutes when she grabbed her cell phone and sent Kane a quick message.

Thank you for the cupcakes.

She added a smiley emoji and waited a minute for a response. She was being polite, that's all. Saying thank you didn't mean anything. Five minutes later, her cell pinged.

My pleasure.

Layla considered replying with a thumbs-up or something humorous, but her fingers hesitated over the keys. She was just about to place the phone back onto the table when it pinged again.

Would you like to go out one night this week?

Layla sucked in a breath. A date. On a school night. She quickly replied.

I don't really have a sitter available.

A couple of minutes later, he replied.

Of course I meant for you to bring Erin. An early dinner on Wednesday? I could pick you up around 5 and have you both home by 7 so she's not out too late.

He was thoughtful, that was for sure. Layla hesitated a little more, trying to think of as many reasons as she could to decline his invitation. And failed to come up with any that stuck.

Great. See you then.

She placed the phone back onto the table like it was a hot poker and took a long breath. Okay…it was done. She had a date with Kane.

Oddly, she slept well that night. And since she hadn't had many full nights' sleep since Frank died, she woke up chirpier than usual. She got up early and even managed half an hour on the treadmill before Erin woke up. It was a cold morning, so she dressed Erin in a pink turtleneck and denim overalls and her favorite sneakers. She was at the day care center by eight thirty and bumped into Laurel Fortune once again.

"Hello," the other woman said as Layla handed Erin to one of the teachers.

"Hi," she said, and tried to disguise her anxiety at Erin's whimpering as she was taken into the play area. "Beautiful day."

Laurel nodded. "Yes, and a busy one ahead. I was wondering if you and your daughter would like to come over Saturday morning. We live in the guest-house on the Fame and Fortune Ranch. Do you know the place?"

Layla nodded. Everyone knew the sprawling ranch on the outskirts of town. She thought about her usual Saturday ahead, which was just her and Erin hanging out together. The idea of a playdate for her daughter sounded good. She needed to start thinking about increasing her social circle, and this was Kane's family, so she felt safe agreeing. "Sure, that would be great."

Laurel smiled and they quickly exchanged numbers and settled on a time.

"See you then," the other woman said before she left. "If not before."

When Layla arrived at work there were already clients waiting to enter the spa. She quickly got to her desk and checked through the day's appointments and made several confirmation calls for later that afternoon. It was a busy day, with a couple of clients turning up late, which threw everything else behind schedule. After one of the tanning booths broke down she spent almost an hour on the phone trying to get someone out to look at it. And since she didn't manage to grab even a short lunch break, it was after one o'clock when Hailey dropped by her desk with a cola can and a protein bar from the vending machine in the staff room.

"Caffeine," the other woman said, and raised her brows. "You look like you need it. It's been a busy morning and the rest of the week is pretty well booked, too. At this rate we're going to have to hire another beauty therapist and extra help for you at reception over the lunchtimes."

"But busy is good, though," Layla said, and then turned more serious. "I wish I could do more hours for you, but with having Erin in day care I simply can't commit to more than—"

"I understand," Hailey said, gently cutting her off. "And you always give one hundred percent when you're here. Family has to come first, Layla. We'll look at hiring someone to cover the lunch hours in the next week or so. The agency that found you for us might be able to help. Just don't run yourself ragged, okay?"

When she picked up Erin from day care that afternoon, she was surprised to see Kane's truck parked outside. And then more surprised, plus a little disappointed, to see another man coming out of the day care center, carrying Larkin. His brother Adam.

"Hi there," he said pleasantly. "Layla, isn't it?"

She nodded, registering that he was a little taller than his brother, but not as broad in the shoulders or as muscular. "Yes. Hello, Adam, it's nice to officially meet you."

"Likewise."

"That's your brother's truck."

His brows shot up with surprise and his mouth curled at the edges. "Yes, it is. Disappointed?"

Heat crawled up her neck. "Ah...no, of course not."

"My car's in the shop so I borrowed Kane's rig to pick up my son. My wife tells me that you and your daughter are coming over on Saturday," he remarked, smiling as he shifted his son's backpack onto his shoulder. "She's looking forward to it."

She responded in kind and headed inside, waving vaguely to him as he drove off.

And for the first time since Frank died, Layla experienced a real sense of belonging.

"I met your girlfriend yesterday."

Kane had met Adam and Brady for lunch at Roja on Wednesday, before his scheduled meeting with Grace Williams and Callum at three.

He looked at Adam and frowned. "My what?"

"The pretty single mom," Adam reminded him, and winked. "You know exactly who I mean. She seemed pretty disappointed when I pulled up in your truck. I think she likes you."

"Shut up."

"She's coming over on Saturday for a playdate with Larkin and Laurel," Adam stated.

Kane held his fork midair. "Huh?"

"Yep," Adam said, and grinned. "She seems nice."

She is nice. So nice he hadn't been able to think about much else. "Stop meddling."

"You were going to introduce her to us at the grand opening party," Brady said, also grinning. "I must have missed that."

"I didn't realize my personal life was so interesting for you all," he replied, stone-faced.

Brady laughed. "Well, he's boring and married," he said, jerking a thumb in Adam's direction, "and I'm now a single parent with two kids so I have no chance of getting laid in the near future. We have to live vicariously through you."

"Believe me," Kane said, "I'm as boring as he is."

"Which is code for *he really likes this girl*," Adam said, and chuckled. "You should drop by on Saturday. It'll be cute watching you together."

Kane called his brother an idiot in more colorful language and Brady laughed. He really wasn't in the mood for his brothers' teasing.

He hung around the restaurant for another half an hour, and by three o'clock he was in Grace's office. He admired the way she had handled herself since the accident, and the fortitude she'd displayed in getting back to work so quickly. She was calm and organized in the manager's role and Kane knew the hotel was in good hands.

"So," Callum said when he arrived, "I spoke to the lead detective on the case earlier today. There's still nothing substantial to go on. We may have to accept that we'll never really know what happened."

"What will they do now?" Grace asked, her brows almost fused together.

"Continue the investigation," Callum said, and sighed heavily. "I know this must be frustrating for you, Grace, considering what you went through. Be assured that we'll get to the bottom of this, no matter how long it takes. Does anyone seem like a red flag?" Callum asked, directing the question toward Kane.

"I think it's safe to assume that everyone is a potential suspect," Kane replied. "However, the most obvious person isn't necessarily the most guilty. Let's face it, there was some backlash from the community when the hotel proposal was cleared through council. Could be there's someone out there holding a major grudge. Thankfully, nothing else has happened since the balcony collapse, so I think we need to let the authorities do their job."

His colleagues looked solemn and quickly agreed.

The meeting lasted another fifteen minutes and then Kane headed home to shower and change. He'd made a reservation at a small family-owned restaurant in Rambling Rose that Brady assured him was child-friendly and drove to Layla's by five o'clock.

She greeted him at the door and looked effortlessly beautiful in dark jeans, a floral shirt and a denim jacket. Her hair was down, touching her shoulders, and she smiled when she greeted him.

"Hi," she said, and opened the screen wider. "I'll just get Erin."

Kane waited by the door and she returned less than a minute later, holding Erin in one arm, the other carrying a tote and diaper bag. "I can take that," he said and gestured to the bags.

She handed them over, turned on the porch light and locked the door. "You have a car seat in your truck, right?"

He nodded. "Sure do."

Minutes later, the baby was strapped into the car seat and Kane strode around the truck and opened the passenger door for Layla. She seemed surprised by the gesture and he smiled.

"A bit too last century for you?" he asked as she got into the Ranger.

"Chivalry? Not at all. I think you're very sweet."

Kane groaned. "Promise me you won't say that in front of either of my brothers, okay?"

She smiled again. "I promise."

He got into the car and pulled away from the sidewalk. "I hear you're hanging out with Laurel and Larkin on Saturday."

"We were invited for a playdate," she replied. "I thought it would be good for Erin." She shrugged lightly. "My grandmother thinks I need to get out more, too. She was very impressed when I told her we were going out tonight."

"I think I like your grandmother," he said, and grinned.

Layla chuckled and the sound echoed through his chest. "I'm sure she'd like you, too. She's got a soft spot for broad shoulders and a nice smile. My grandfather was a carpenter, and Nan always says that a strong man who can fix things is definitely the type of guy to have around."

"Smart woman."

"I guess you can fix things, right?"

Kane grinned. "Absolutely."

She laughed a little nervously, as if she'd said too much, admitted too much. Kane didn't push the conversation because he didn't want to scare her off. She seemed to scare easily, and he suspected she'd had her heart well and truly broken when her husband died and wasn't quite recovered from the loss. And for the moment, he wanted to go slow, too. He liked Layla, but she wasn't a one-night-stand sort of woman.

"Where are we going?" she asked.

He named the restaurant. "Brady said they have a good kids' menu. He said he's brought the twins here a couple of times since he arrived in town and they like the food."

"You're very considerate," she remarked, and glanced at her child in the back. "Have you done this before?"

"Done what before?"

"Dated a single parent?" she asked, and then waved a hand. "I mean, not that we're really dating or anything, but I was curious."

"No," he replied honestly. "But I haven't been on a date for a while."

She didn't respond for a moment, seeming to absorb his words, then she sighed, her hands twisting in her lap as she spoke. "I've only ever had one serious relationship, and that was with my husband."

"No high school boyfriend?" he asked, eager to know more about her.

She shook her head. "I told you my mother was a dancer. We spent a lot of time on the road and when I finally moved in with my grandparents, I wanted stability. I'd witnessed too many people coming and going through my mother's life to want that for myself. I guess what I'm trying to say is that I'm relatively new to all this…whatever *this* is," she added for clarity. "And out of practice. So I apologize if I'm assuming anything."

"I understand," he said, and meant it.

Kane wasn't a *jump in quick* kind of guy. His decisions were generally measured and controlled. He didn't fall often and never hard enough to leave any real battle scars. But he liked Layla, and suspected the feeling was mutual.

The drive into town didn't take long and he figured she'd admitted enough that she needed some quiet time, so he stayed silent for a while and listened to Erin's soft baby talk and Layla's encouraging responses.

"She seems happy tonight," he remarked.

"As opposed to how grumpy she's been lately? She must be going through a growth spurt," she said, and then sighed.

Once they reached the restaurant, he secured a parking space and soon they were inside and being shown to their seats.

"You know," Layla said as she tucked Erin into

the high chair, "I've lived in Rambling Rose for years and never been here. It's really quite lovely."

The restaurant was small, with only about ten tables, and styled like an old-fashioned saloon, with polished timbers and dark gingham tablecloths. He nodded in agreement and waited until she was seated before he sat down. Half the tables were full, and another group entered the restaurant just as the waitress handed them menus. He ordered his favorite craft beer and waited while Layla perused the drinks menu for a moment before selecting a wine spritzer. Erin was tapping her hands on the high chair and Kane drummed his fingertips on the table to keep her amused.

"She's so relaxed around you," Layla said after a few minutes and dipped into the diaper bag for a plastic spoon and Erin's sippy cup. "I think it's what you do…make people feel at ease."

He figured it was a compliment and heat crawled up his neck. "It's not deliberate."

"That's why it works," she said, and smiled. "You shouldn't be embarrassed because you're a nice person."

Kane grinned. "I have plenty of flaws, believe me."

The waitress arrived with their drinks and took their dinner orders. Kane ordered the fillet steak and seasoned fries, while Layla spent another few moments glancing at the menu again before selecting veal parmigiana for herself and a kid's chicken meal for Erin.

"Sorry," she said, and grinned once the waitress disappeared. "I have been known to labor over a menu for half an hour. Procrastination is my middle name. Not you, though. You didn't even touch the menu," she said. "Do you always know what you want?"

There was a flirtatious edge to her words and Kane concentrated on that, and not on her remark about his untouched menu. He wasn't about to admit that he checked out the menu the night before on the restaurant's website, determined not to be seen fumbling through the selections when put on the spot to make a quick decision. It was something he'd done for years, and a fail-safe to avoid looking foolish and highlighting his condition in front of strangers. Not that Layla was a stranger. But he didn't know her well enough to admit such a personal thing about himself.

"Usually," he replied, and drank some beer. "I guess I'm predictably a meat-and-potatoes kind of guy."

"Nothing wrong with knowing who you are and what you want," she said, and sighed. "So, these flaws you mentioned earlier—anything specific?"

"Sure," he replied. "I've never watched *Star Wars*. I don't like snakes. When I was sixteen, I hid my first tattoo from my parents for nearly a year. I'll watch any kind of sport on television, even two ants racing up a wall. Oh, and I will never sing karaoke."

She laughed and the sound hit him deep down. "I like watching sports, too, particularly football."

"I'm guessing you're a Houston Texans fan?"

She laughed again. "Of course. And you, the Giants?"

"See?" He grinned. "Predictable."

"Did you ever play?"

"Yeah, I played ball in high school and college."

"I sense there's a 'but' in there somewhere," she said astutely.

"I injured my knee and that was the end of my football career," he replied. "I got an engineering degree instead from Columbia."

Her eyes widened. "That's a good school. Your parents must have—"

"Scholarship," he said quickly, before her next question. "I was good at sports and okay at math."

He wasn't about to tell her how hard he had to study, about tutors and strategies employed to help him through the dyslexia to maintain a B-minus average. Or about how close he came to quitting school when the scholarship ended in the second year after his injury, and he had to work two jobs to help with the tuition.

"I envy you," she said quietly, her hand resting on the table. "I'm terrible at math."

"I'm sure you're good at a lot of other things," he

said and covered her hand with his. Her skin was warm to the touch and for a moment he thought she might pull away. But she didn't. "I mean, you're clearly a wonderful mom, and you're smart and funny. And of course, you're really quite beautiful. I imagine you're good at your job, too."

She smiled again, and he wondered if she knew how the gesture added even more warmth to her brown eyes. "I like the work, and Hailey is a great boss, but of course I want to do more with my life."

"Such as?" he asked and removed his hand.

"I'm taking an online course in marketing at the moment," she explained, her gaze darting to her daughter. "In between working and raising Erin. But I'm enjoying it and hopefully it will lead to a career one day."

His admiration spiked and he smiled. "I'm sure you'd be successful at anything you do."

She looked embarrassed for a moment, and then shrugged. "Thank you. What about you?" she asked. "What do you do now that the hotel is built and operating?"

"Good question," he replied.

"Are you staying in Rambling Rose? In Texas?"

"Do you mean am I homesick for New York? A little," he admitted. "Actually, I got a job offer to manage the construction of a new shopping mall in Houston."

"But?" she queried intuitively.

"I'm undecided about the offer. Callum has other plans for Rambling Rose and I'm committed to staying close and on hand for the moment. Family first," he added, and sighed. "And the Fortunes are good to work for."

"You talk about them as though you're not one of them," she remarked. "But you are."

"It's complicated. As I told you before, my father didn't know he was Julius Fortune's son until last year," he explained. "And he hasn't exactly embraced the idea."

"Why not?"

Kane sipped his drink. "I guess because the upstate New York Fortunes are a world away from the Texas Fortunes."

"They are?" she queried.

"Humbler beginnings," he explained. "My dad has a lot of resentment directed toward his father and his half brothers. Adam and I have tried to make him see that they're not the enemy. But Dad can be stubborn and hard-nosed about some things. He never approved of our decision to move here and I can't see that changing…particularly now that Brady is here, too."

"What about the rest of your family?" she inquired. "How do they feel?"

"Well, Brian is Brady's twin, so he'll always support the decision. I don't think my siblings Joshua and Arabella have quite made up their minds yet.

And Mom..." His voice trailed off and he sighed, re-alizing it was the most he'd ever said about his family to anyone outside the Fortune circle. "She loves Dad and will stand by his side no matter what."

"I can understand that," she said softly.

"True love, you mean?" he queried, noticing that her eyes glittered brilliantly. "That's how you felt about your husband?"

She nodded. "Very much so."

"I've never..." His words trailed off and Kane was thankful that their meals arrived and Layla was distracted with attending to Erin. He'd been close to admitting he'd never been in love...never felt that intense connection to another person. Not like his parents had. Or Adam and Laurel. For a long time, he'd wondered if he simply wasn't someone who felt things deeply, but the reality was, he just hadn't met the right someone.

Until now...

The notion pushed him back in his seat and he stared at her, confused by the quiet intensity of his feelings. Was this how it happened? Without drama? Without so much as a kiss? No, he told himself. Of course, he was imagining it. It was desire, plain and simple. Just sex. Physical attraction. The kind that could be sated by a brief hookup. Right?

Only, Kane knew he was kidding himself. For one, Layla wasn't a hookup kind of woman. She was a single mom with responsibilities. And secondly, he wasn't really that guy, either.

"You've never...what?" she asked, surprising him by referring back to the comment after a couple of minutes.

Kane shrugged. "Nothing," he replied, and picked up the spoon Erin had tossed onto the floor. "Hey, kid, that's quite a pitching arm you got there."

Erin laughed and squished her fingers into her food before offering him a piece of chicken nugget. Kane glanced toward Layla and saw she was watching the interaction with a tiny sort of smile.

"I love seeing her smile," Layla said. "She does that a lot around you. So do I," she admitted.

"I'm thrilled to hear it," he replied.

The conversation lightened over dinner and by quarter to seven they were finished and Kane had paid the check. He offered to carry a weary Erin to the Ranger and Layla agreed, watching as her daughter laid her head against his shoulder as they left the restaurant. He gently placed the child into the car seat and waited until Layla was in the vehicle before he climbed into the driver's seat.

She was mostly silent on the trip back to her home and Kane was content to drive and hear Erin murmuring in the back. The township quickly turned into suburban streets and within minutes he pulled up outside her house.

"Thank you for a lovely evening," she said as he switched off the ignition.

He nodded and glanced backward. "She's asleep."

"She's relaxed," Layla said. "I wish she fell asleep this easily every night."

"Does she have trouble sleeping?"

"Sometimes," she replied. "She likes me to read to her at night. It seems to settle her down. You probably noticed the other day when you were picking up your nephew that she gets separation anxiety. Her pediatrician has assured me it's nothing to worry about and she'll grow out of it, but of course I'm still concerned."

"Naturally," he agreed. "But she's been great tonight and perhaps all you can do is take things one day at a time."

"You're probably right," she said and sighed. "I think I worry too much."

"You're her mom, of course you worry. My mom still worries about her kids. Goes with the territory. Maybe you need to be a little kinder to yourself, hmm?"

"I'm not good at thinking about…me…you know," she admitted and he felt the rawness in her words. "I guess you've figured that out already?"

Kane reached out and grasped her hand, holding it gently within his own. Her skin was warm, her fingertips soft as they instinctively linked with his. In the darkened space the intimacy between them heightened, their combined touch amplifying the connection. Had a simple touch ever reached him with such intensity before? He couldn't recall. Couldn't think of a time when he'd been so drawn to someone.

"Layla." He said her name quietly and she met his gaze. "Would you like to—"

"Good night, Kane."

Was that a shutdown? He wasn't sure. He noticed she looked tense and tired, and of course she had her sleeping toddler in the back seat. Somehow, in a matter of seconds, the mood between them was suddenly strained. And he quickly realized the reason—she thought he was going to make a move.

"Layla," he said her name again, brushing his thumb across her knuckles before releasing her hand. "I'm not going to pressure you for anything. I mean, I don't think we're…" His words trailed off and he gestured to the sleeping child in the back. "This isn't the time. Let's get her inside."

He was out of the truck within seconds and soon she had her daughter in her arms and they were walking to her door. Kane passed her the diaper bag as they crossed the threshold and she dropped it by the hall stand.

"Thank you, Kane," she said as she turned to face him.

"Get some sleep." He reached out and cupped her cheek with his palm. "I'll talk to you soon."

She nodded and Erin stirred in her arms. "Good night."

"Sweet dreams, Layla. Lock the door behind me."

Feeling like he'd been punched in the gut, Kane walked out the door and headed home.

Chapter Five

Coward.

Layla was still thinking that on Friday. And about why she'd frozen like a Popsicle at the end of her date with Kane. Because of course she knew. She was scared witless about the idea of kissing him good-night. And of real intimacy. It had been so long since she'd felt the strength and comfort of a man's arms around her that she'd put a wall up the moment the evening was near the end.

Because that was what she did. She put walls up. She protected herself.

"Everything okay, Layla?"

She turned in her chair and saw Hailey standing

by her desk. "Yeah," she lied, "all good. Just finishing up the reminder texts for Monday's bookings."

The other woman nodded. "So, Dillon and I were thinking of having a small dinner party in a few weeks. You should get Kane to bring you," she said, and raised a brow. "I mean, if you two are still... you know..."

Layla's skin heated instantly and she managed a tight smile. "We'll see."

It was all she could offer, since she hadn't heard from him since their last date and it was now two thirty on Friday afternoon. Sure, it was barely a couple of days, but still, she suspected their brief dalliance might have run its course. She hadn't given him any real encouragement, after all. By now he probably thought she was hard work and not worth the effort.

Snap out of it!

Layla shook herself off and berated her foolishness. She wasn't that girl...the one who pined and mooned over a man. She was a got-it-together single mom who didn't have time to waste on romantic drama.

With that thought, she grabbed her cell and sent him a quick text.

Thank you for dinner the other night. We had a lovely time. L & E.

She tidied up her desk and wrote a few things in the planner for the following week, glancing at her phone every few seconds to see if he'd replied. But he didn't. When three o'clock came and it was time to leave, she snatched up her cell and clocked out, still wondering why he hadn't responded when she arrived at the day care center to get Erin about half an hour later, and then again after four when she got home.

And she might have dwelled on it some more if it weren't for the fact her kitchen floor was flooded with water. Layla sucked in a long breath, muttered a few curse words to herself, and sat a now-crying Erin into her crib and investigated the situation. She tried cleaning up the mess, but water kept flowing from the pipes beneath the sink, so she rolled up several thick towels and laid them in the doorway to stop the flood heading into the living room. She grabbed her cell and googled local plumbers and started calling the numbers. Two didn't answer, the third couldn't possibly come out until the following afternoon. She was just about to call her grandfather when her cell pealed. Thinking it was one of the plumbers returning her call, she didn't look at the screen.

"Hello," she said on a rushed breath.

"Hey there, sorry I missed your text earlier. I was in a meeting."

Kane.

Layla's chest tightened and she couldn't stop the heat from burning her eyes. Standing in the kitchen with water running over her shoes, she experienced such an acute sense of hopelessness she could barely breathe. And hearing Kane's voice somehow amplified that, making her feel more alone than she believed possible.

"I can't talk right now," she said as she shuddered out a breath, and then quickly explained about the leak. "I have to try to find a plumber to come out right away and—"

"I'll be there in fifteen minutes," he said quickly, cutting her off, and then the call ended.

Layla tucked the phone in her pocket and tiptoed across the floor, swiftly removed her shoes and wiped her feet on a towel. Erin was still crying so she headed for the crib and picked her up.

"It's okay, sweetie, Mommy's here," she said as her daughter snuggled into her neck.

She rocked her gently and walked around the house, singing her daughter's favorite song to settle her down, and then lingered by the front door. Thirteen minutes later, Kane's SUV pulled up outside her house and relief coursed through her veins. She watched as he strode up the path, looking innately masculine in jeans, boots and a light blue flannel over a white tank shirt.

Layla opened the door to greet him and he lingered by the step for a moment, looking up.

"Are you okay?" he asked.

She nodded. "Just a bit frazzled, as much as I hate to admit it."

He climbed the porch steps and touched her shoulder. "We'll sort it out."

Layla was amazed when Erin wriggled and turned and held out her arms to him. "No, honey, stay with Mommy for the moment."

He grinned. "It's fine," he said, and took her without hesitation, and Erin was quickly settled against his shoulder. "Lead the way."

He looked so relaxed holding Erin she almost envied him. Layla nodded and closed the door, walking directly to the kitchen.

"So, yeah," she said, and pointed to the floor. "As you can see, I have a problem."

He gently handed Erin back to her and walked into the kitchen, crouching down and quickly checking underneath the sink. "I've got some tools in the truck. Be back in a minute," he said, and moved past her, lingering for a moment in the doorway. "Get Erin settled, and I'll see to this."

Half an hour later, Erin was drinking juice from her sippy cup and playing with some toys, Kane had done a temporary fix on the leaking pipe and Layla was mopping up the floor. Once the floor was dry, she dropped a pile of sopping towels into the hamper and returned to the kitchen just as he was packing away his tools.

"Looks like the seals have split and there's a small crack in the pipe," he explained. "I'm sure the repair will hold it until tomorrow. I've arranged for a plumber to be here at eight in the morning," he said, and then paused. "Is that okay? Not too early?"

"Not at all... I couldn't get anyone to call me back."

"I know a guy who owes me a favor," he said, and grinned. "It should be fine now."

"Thank you," she said, and blinked back tears of gratitude. "I can't tell you how much I appreciate your help."

"No problem," he said easily. "Well, I'll head off."

"You could stay," she suggested quickly. "I mean, it's nearly five thirty and I was planning on cooking dinner for Erin and myself. Nothing too exotic, just chicken casserole. You're welcome to join us... as a thank-you," she added, and then realized she was making all kinds of presumptions because he probably already had plans. Perhaps even a date. He was a single guy—and a hot one—and women were probably lining up for him. "Although you probably already have plans for tonight."

"No plans," he said with a wry grin, and held out his hands and nodded. "And I'd like to stay, but on the condition that we order pizza to save you the trouble of cooking. But I need to wash up first," he said, and then looked down to his feet and the jeans that were soaked at the hems. "And change. I have my gym bag in the truck, so I'll be back in a minute."

He grabbed his tool bag and headed outside, returning a few minutes later with a gym bag.

"The bathroom is down the hall, third door on the left," she said when he hovered in the hallway. "I need to give Erin her bath, so I'll do that when you're done."

When he emerged five minutes later he was dressed in dark gray sweatpants, a white T-shirt and sneakers. Layla almost swallowed her tongue when she caught sight of the hard muscles peeking out from beneath the sleeves, and a Celtic braid tattoo circling his biceps on one arm. He really did have the most divine shoulders, and her long-dormant, starved libido came back to life. And something else—the loneliness that had become her constant companion over the last eighteen months, that often clung to her limbs like a second skin, didn't feel quite so intense in that moment.

Layla didn't want to feel needy and hopeless—that wasn't her style. She hid those feelings deep down, because she was too proud to admit she wasn't capable of managing things—of managing life—on her own. To admit it would be like admitting failure and defeat. She was an independent woman with a child to raise and didn't have the time to waste on what-ifs or the memory of how her life had once been. She'd had to learn to embrace her solitude—to accept she was navigating life without someone at her side. But in the last hour she hadn't felt alone. Instead, she felt as though suddenly she had someone to lean on, to rely on, and wasn't sure how to compartmentalize the feeling.

It was crazy, of course, since she'd known Kane a little over a week. A connection so strong didn't happen that quickly. It took time and patience. It didn't simply *happen* with a life force of its own. If she allowed herself to believe that, Layla knew she was setting herself up for one almighty fall—which she couldn't do because she had to protect Erin first and foremost.

Only, for one wild moment, she wondered if she was allowed to have something for herself.

And that something was the man standing in front of her.

"Are you okay, Layla?" Kane asked, noticing her expression.

She met his gaze, her eyes darker than usual, and then nodded a little too quickly to convince him that she was really okay. "Yes, all good. I'm going to get Erin bathed and changed. Make yourself at home."

"I'll order dinner," he said. "Any pizza toppings I should avoid?"

"Anchovies," she said, and screwed up her nose. "And red peppers."

"Got it." He watched her walk down the hall with Erin in her arms, trying to avoid admiring the natural sway of her hips—and failing. He figured it made him predictable but he didn't care. He enjoyed the sight too much.

Bath time took about half an hour and when she returned to the living room Kane was on the sofa. Erin pulled away from her mother's hand and walked toward him, her arms outstretched.

"I really can't believe how relaxed she is around you," Layla said as she came around the couch.

Kane noticed she'd changed into jeans and a red sweater that was scooped at the front and exposed more skin than usual. But he averted his gaze immediately and smiled as Erin grabbed hold of his knee and began climbing up. He gently helped her onto the couch and she was soon happily settled beside him.

"Just call me the baby whisperer," he said, and smiled.

"It gives me hope that she might actually grow out of her separation issues sooner rather than later," Layla said, and sat on the ottoman opposite the couch. "But the truth is, I feel guilty every time I leave her at day care and hear her crying when I walk away."

"I'm sure you shouldn't be so hard on yourself," Kane said, and grinned as Erin linked her hand around one of his fingers. "I'm also sure you do the very best for her."

"I try to keep it all together," she replied. "Some days it isn't easy. Like today," she added, and sighed. "I'm not usually so helpless in a crisis. But when I saw the water on the floor and couldn't contact a plumber…it all seemed so darn overwhelming. And then you came to my rescue like a white knight," she said, her brown eyes darkening. "Thank you."

"That's what friends are for, right?" he queried, watching her gaze dart down and then back up. "That's what we are, yes?"

She shrugged, as though she didn't know what to do with the words. She was biting her lip a little and he realized she was nervous, and it also occurred to him that maybe she was nervous around all men. Had something happened to her? The very idea cut him deep down in his gut and made his protective instincts surge into overdrive.

"Layla, do all men make you nervous?" he asked quietly. "Or just me?"

Her gaze jerked up and she clutched her hands in her lap. "Actually, I think this is the least nervous I've ever been around a man."

That surprised him. And pleased him. "Really?"

She nodded. "Well, except for Frank...and he was older and not as..." Her words trailed off and she waved her hands expressively, her cheeks burning scarlet. "Not as...you know...hot."

Kane bit back the grin hovering on his lips. "Well, my unbelievable hotness aside," he said with a good dose of self-deprecating humor, "I'm not any kind of threat to you. Or Erin," he added.

"I know that," she said. "I think that's what terrifies me the most."

Her candor startled him. "I do get it, Layla. You're

unsure about getting involved. You're not alone on that score. But I think it's obvious that I like you. I'd kinda hoped that you liked me, too."

She looked at him, then at Erin, who was happily pulling at his shirt with chubby fingers and chatting indecipherable words, and then took a long and steadying breath. "I do like you. And you're right, I'm unsure. I haven't been on a date since my husband died. The truth is, I haven't been on anything even resembling a date until last Saturday. I don't have a large circle of friends. I don't have much family. I have Erin," she said, and swallowed hard. "She has to come first and I'm not sure I have room *within* myself for anything else or anyone else."

He pushed back a little in his seat, his gaze unwavering. "I understand."

"And it doesn't make you want to run a mile?"

"Not at all," he said honestly, surprising himself a little. "You want the truth? I haven't been this attracted to someone for a long time. Maybe never. I'd like to see where it goes."

"And what if it doesn't go anywhere?" she asked.

"Then I guess we'll just be friends."

The doorbell rang, jerking them both out of the intensity of the moment, and Kane was relieved. The words between them were getting heavy—too heavy, he suspected—because clearly neither of them was really ready for serious.

"Our dinner," he said, and got to his feet, hauling

Erin into his arms. She said a few words, something about *bow-wows*, he thought, and they both laughed as he passed her to her mom. "Be back in a minute."

"Meet you in the kitchen," she said.

Five minutes later they were settled at the kitchen table, with Erin in her high chair, watching the toddler pull the cheese off the pieces of pizza her mother had cut up for her. They ate and chatted about ordinary, mundane things in between taking turns picking up pizza bits that Erin tossed onto the floor. The domesticity of the scene wasn't lost on Kane. Somehow, the pull of both Layla and Erin was so powerful he knew he was getting sucked deeper into their vortex the more time they spent together.

And oddly, it didn't make him want to bail.

It made him want to stay.

"What time's your playdate tomorrow?" he asked.

"Ten thirty," she replied. "But I may have to cancel if the plumber takes a long time to fix the pipe."

"I'm sure Laurel won't mind if you're a little late."

Layla nodded fractionally. "Will you be there?"

Kane's hands stilled. "Would you like me to be?"

She nodded again. "If you could. You seem to have quite the calming effect on my daughter," she remarked, and met his gaze. "And me."

"Then of course I'll be there."

"Thank you," she said, and sighed. "You know, I'm not always this needy. I'm usually quite self-sufficient and in control."

"So you said. But, Layla, needing support isn't a weakness, you know," he said quietly.

"Says a man who's clearly a tower of strength," she remarked, her brows rising.

It was a nice compliment, and mostly true. *Mostly.* "Maybe, but I come from a large and loving family and I only have myself to be concerned about," he said, his gaze darting to Erin. "I imagine that if I ever have kids I'll be as neurotic as everyone else. Not that you're neurotic or anything."

She chuckled. "You're right, though. Having Erin changed the way I think about things. Suddenly I had this little person who relied on me and I had to be the best version of myself to make sure she was cared for."

"And then you lost your husband?"

She nodded. "Yeah…and it was like, *wham*, now it's just me doing everything. I don't think I've taken a breath since."

"You know, you can talk about him if you want."

She sighed heavily. "Thank you," she said, and then looked at him. "I seem to say that to you a lot. Okay… Frank was a wonderful man. He was kind and considerate and loving and my best friend. I miss that. I miss him. It's hard, though, because the more time goes by, the more I get used to him not being here…and that feels disloyal." She shrugged and shook her head. "That probably doesn't make any sense."

"It does," he assured her. "But you're lucky. A lot of people never find what you had."

"You mean, being in love?"

He nodded, heat suddenly clawing at his neck. "Yeah."

"So, what you're saying is you've never felt that for anyone?"

"Not even close," he replied.

"Neither had I, until I met my husband," she said, absently picking at her food. "I was twenty years old when we met and had never had a boyfriend. Never had...*anything.* Because I moved around so much when I was young, and went to different schools every year, sometimes every semester, I always felt like I didn't belong. I guess I just wasn't good at connecting with people."

Kane heard the hollowness in her voice. "Now you are."

She shrugged. "I still have my training wheels on. You make it look easy."

He smiled. "Don't underestimate yourself."

She laughed humorlessly. "Funny, that's what Frank used to say. You know, he would have liked you. You have the same kind of calm demeanor."

Kane was pretty sure the other man wouldn't have liked him one iota if he knew what he'd been thinking for the past half hour. Hell, for the past week. She was so beautiful, but Kane suspected she didn't know it. He'd never been at the mercy of his libido, but over the past week, his initial attraction for her had steadily morphed into a deep, intense desire. And yet it was more than that, too. He liked her— he liked her laugh and her smile and the way they could talk about things. Or not talk, he realized, because sometimes there were long silences between them that weren't awkward or uncomfortable. As though they'd been acquainted a long time...*friends* a long time.

But he wanted more than to be her friend. Kane wanted to kiss her. He wanted to know if her mouth was as sweet as it looked, or if her warm brown eyes darkened when she was overcome with desire. He wanted to know a whole lot of things about her, but he already knew one indisputable fact—Layla McCarthy wasn't a woman to be rushed. And truthfully, he wasn't that guy, either.

Erin tossed a piece of cheese at him and he laughed. "Sweetheart, you're supposed to eat the pizza, not throw it."

"Dada."

The word hung in the air like a balloon and Kane quickly darted his gaze toward Layla, who was staring at him with a stunned expression. Neither of them corrected her. Neither of them, he suspected, had the right words.

"I'm sorry," Layla said on a rush of breath. "She's never said that before. I mean, she's never had anyone to—"

"It's okay," Kane assured her, and picked the cheese off his arm.

"I think she must have heard the word at day care," Layla said, and cleaned up her daughter's hands. "And of course I talk to her about Frank, but I've never had a man here and I—"

"Layla," Kane said gently, and grasped her hand. "Relax. It's fine. She's just a kid."

She looked down at their linked hands and he felt her grip tighten, as though his assurance gave her comfort. "Remember how I said the other day that you were sweet? I'm convinced now...you *are* sweet."

He turned her hand over and stroked the inside of her palm. "And you promised me you wouldn't ever say that in front of my brothers," he said, and grinned. "Or I'll be paying for it for the rest of my life."

She chuckled and the mood instantly lightened. "I promise. It must be wonderful to have siblings. Frank and I always said we wanted four kids, since we were both only children and had a fairly lonely time growing up. I'll bet you've never had a lonely moment in your life."

He shrugged, still holding her hand. "There's a difference between being alone and being lonely, though. I guess I've felt it a little since Adam got married and moved out. And leaving behind my friends and family in New York was hard going at first. Things feel more normal now that Brady's here, too. So, four kids, huh?"

She shifted and moved her hand, meeting his gaze in a way that indicated they both felt the loss of touch the moment she withdrew. "That was the plan. Plans change, I guess."

"You're young. You could still have the large family you planned on."

"I know," she responded agreeably, but Kane sensed her uncertainty. "I guess I can't predict the future."

"What about tomorrow night?" he asked. "Would you be free for dinner at Roja?"

Her gaze darted to her daughter and she hesitated for a moment before responding. "I could ask my grandparents to watch Erin for the night. They have a room set up for her at their place."

"So, yes?"

She nodded. "Yes. I could meet you there after I've dropped Erin off."

"How about I pick you up here and drive you and Erin to your grandparents' home?" Kane suggested. "That way they can meet me and be assured that I'm perfectly respectable," he said as he grinned.

She laughed. "Do I come across as someone needing approval from my elders?"

"Not at all," he replied. "But you're obviously close to them and I think it's important to respect that and do the right thing."

"See," she teased. "Sweet."

Laughter rumbled in his chest. "Let's bet you won't think that once you know me better."

"Let's bet I do," she countered, still smiling as she got to her feet and stood beside Erin. "I should get her ready for bed."

"That's my cue, then," he said, and stood. "Thanks for dinner."

Her brow rose. "You paid for the pizza."

"Thanks for the company, then."

They walked to the door together, with Erin dozing in her mother's arms. Kane touched the baby's cheek and then met Layla's gaze. "I'll see you soon, okay?"

She nodded. "That would be great."

Kane stared at her mouth for a moment, thinking about how much he wanted to kiss her and knowing he couldn't. "Good night."

"Night, Kane."

He left quickly, stopping by the hotel to collect the laptop he'd left in Callum's office in his urgency to get to Layla's earlier that afternoon. He was walking through the back office when he bumped into Jay Cross. "What are you still doing here? Anything wrong?"

"No, everything seems to be going well so far," Jay said. "Grace just has me double-checking everything."

"That's her job," Kane replied.

"Yeah, I know," Jay said. "Considering what happened, I imagine she has every right to be cautious. And I don't mind. I like being kept busy."

"Do you think you'll stay on once your training program is over?" Kane asked.

Jay shrugged. "Maybe. I guess Rambling Rose is as good a place as any to make a fresh start."

"And you're looking for one?" Kane asked. He wasn't usually so interested in other people's business, but Jay Cross had been particularly closed off about his past and his reasons for coming to Rambling Rose—and Kane had a duty to his extended Fortune family. No one was beyond suspicion, or at least, a few questions.

Jay shrugged again. "I guess you could say I'm in between gigs. So, any news on finding out who was responsible for tampering with the balcony?" Jay asked as they walked from the office and toward the foyer.

"Last I heard, there's no new information," Kane replied. "Callum said the authorities are still looking into anyone who might hold a grudge against the hotel or the Fortune family."

"That could be a long list," Jay said as they moved past the concierge desk. "Although I wouldn't be surprised if the culprit is closer than people think."

Kane almost skipped a stride. He liked Jay well enough, but the other man was still a relative stranger in Rambling Rose—and that made him just as much a suspect as anyone else.

"Do you think?" Kane remarked.

"I've learned over the years that people can do surprising things," Jay replied. "Like enemies staying close, or bad guys hiding in plain sight."

Oddly, Jay's insight sounded completely logical. Perhaps because Kane had thought the same thing himself. If the balcony had been sabotaged, it wasn't random. It meant someone had it in for the hotel and the Fortunes.

That thought stayed with him all the way home. It was only when he was getting ready for a shower that his mind took him elsewhere. To Layla. He sent her a text before he headed to the bathroom.

Everything okay?

She responded seconds later.

Perfect. Thanks to you.

He tried not to overthink her words. The truth was, Kane was confused by what was going on between them—or, rather, what wasn't going on. There was something so companionable about the time they spent together, he was struggling to figure out what it meant. Or didn't mean. Were they destined to be just friends? If so, why did he have the continued de-

bate in his mind about when would be the right time
to kiss her? With any other woman he'd dated over
the years he'd certainly gotten to first or second base
within the week. With Layla, they were definitely
just sitting on the bleachers holding hands.

The dreaded friend zone...

Yeah…it wasn't a place he was used to.

And he didn't know for sure if he'd ever get out
of it.

Chapter Six

Layla couldn't quite believe her luck. The plumber arrived at quarter to eight and had the problem fixed within half an hour, and then said he'd send her the bill for parts only because she was a friend of Kane's and that was all the assurance he needed. She'd woken up early to get some studying done and managed to finish her assignment. She received a text message from a store in Austin informing her that the playhouse she'd ordered for Erin had arrived and would be delivered that afternoon. Plus, Erin was in such a happy mood that it was infectious.

She hoped that would carry over to the playdate at the Fame and Fortune Ranch.

Laurel Fortune greeted her by the door of the

guesthouse with a wide smile and Larkin in her arms. She ushered them inside and it wasn't long before the kids were playing in the living room and she and Laurel were sitting close by. Layla had packed some of Erin's favorite toys, but her daughter seemed content amusing herself with the array of stuffed animals, books and blocks spread out around her. Even though Larkin was younger than Erin, the kids seemed to get along and interacted well, even if they weren't exactly 'playing' together. Plus, Laurel was warm and friendly and Layla was immediately put at ease.

Adam dropped by to chat, and Layla couldn't help wondering if Kane would make an appearance. Finally, he turned up around eleven. With the brothers together, it was easy to see their camaraderie and their physical similarities. Adam was a little taller, but Kane was broader through the shoulders and more muscular. He hovered in the doorway, smiling at her, and she felt a rush of attraction. Erin, too, seemed happy to see him. Her little arms were quickly waving around for his attention. He walked into the room and plunked down on a nearby chair, his legs stretched out, and both Erin and Larkin came over and brought him toys.

"I know," Laurel said, and laughed as they watched the interaction. "Adam and I often think that our son prefers his uncle Kane to us. Don't feel bad."

Layla nodded and watched with a smile as Kane

grabbed a stuffed green dinosaur and played a game with the kids for a few minutes. Layla couldn't take her eyes off him the whole time. His easygoing nature, the calm and even tone of his voice, were hypnotic and she listened as he talked Erin through counting to ten using her fingers. She noticed that Laurel and Adam were watching her and Kane, and sharing a private look between them as couples often did.

Layla wasn't usually so relaxed around strangers—most likely from not having real friendships as a child—and then, not being able to trust anyone. Frank had changed all that. He'd shown her it was good to trust, to give your whole heart, to believe in someone and know that they believed in you.

Kane looked up and met her gaze and Layla's heart rolled over. There was something deep and penetrating in his eyes, a connection that went beyond words. Last night she'd realized that Kane and her husband were a lot alike—they had the same calm demeanor, the same innate integrity, the same ability to make people feel a part of things. No doubt Erin, too, had recognized that quality immediately. And Larkin, who was now also climbing over Kane's legs, knew it, too.

"Let's make coffee," Laurel said to her husband, and within seconds the couple had left the room.

Layla watched Kane effortlessly interacting with

both children. "You'll make a good father one day," she said quietly.

He looked up, his expression a little startled. And Layla realized how her words must sound. Like she was probing, insinuating, almost lining him up for the job.

"I didn't mean…" Her words trailed off as color smacked her cheeks. "I wasn't implying anything… it was only an observation."

He smiled and it kicked at something inside her, the spot where she let her dreams lie, dreams long forgotten, dreams she'd thought lost to her since Frank had passed. Dreams that offered both pleasure and panic. Because as much as she longed to believe it, Layla wondered if she'd ever be ready to risk again, to love again, to offer her heart and body to someone.

And particularly if that someone was Kane Fortune—a man who had admitted to having a history of brief and casual relationships. Because the reality pulled at all her insecurities. At all of the uncertainty she felt growing up and watching her mother fall in and out of love with men who had no staying power. Men who didn't believe in commitment. Men who left. Like Paul, and Linc, and Stuart…names that were now little more than a shadow of a memory. Lovers, boyfriends, fiancés—her mother had had them all over the years. Some, Layla couldn't remember. They were all kind, all had treated Layla decently. A few she had even grown fond of in her longing for a father to call her own. But none had stayed. Iliana had clung to them and they'd bailed, one after the other, leaving broken hearts in their wake. And leaving Layla feeling as though she didn't deserve the happiness she craved.

It wasn't a cycle she intended repeating with Erin. She wasn't about to sit back and watch her daughter get attached to someone, only to have that someone walk out of her life—their lives—a few months down the road. So it was better that she and Kane stay friends and nothing more. If she allowed more, if she let herself act on the attraction that was growing more each time they were together, she knew where it would end. He'd pretty much admitted he wasn't the settle-down type, and Layla wasn't prepared to accept anything less.

When Laurel and Adam returned to the living room, the latter was carrying a tray and soon Layla had coffee in her hand. Kane declined and she suspected he didn't want to be holding a hot beverage while the kids were climbing on him. Both kids, in fact, were sitting on his lap now, and Erin was waving a book at him.

"She wants you to read her a story," Layla said.

She noticed that his expression tightened for a moment, but it was Adam who spoke next.

"Here," his brother said, and walked across the

room, quickly taking the book from Erin's waving hands, "I'll do it."

"Ah, Layla," Laurel said, and stood, "why don't we take our coffee outside. I would love to show you the start of what is going to be my vegetable garden when spring gets here."

Layla looked at Kane and saw him nod, and since Erin was now entranced by Adam's storytelling about a tiny pink dragon, she didn't have any real reason to linger. She left the room, expecting Erin's separation anxiety to kick in—but all she heard was her daughter's delighted laughter.

"Thanks," Kane said to his brother once both women were gone and the story was finished.

Adam cocked one brow. "I take it you haven't told her?"

Kane sat both kids on the sofa and maintained a watchful eye as they played together.

"No," he replied. "I don't usually lead with that information."

He was smiling as he spoke, but he wasn't amused. Talking about his dyslexia was deeply personal. And yeah, he was sensitive about it. He didn't enjoy the inevitable sympathy or, worse, judgment that came from disclosing his condition. He suspected Layla would be in the sympathy group, but that didn't mean he wanted to spill his guts about his condition just yet.

"I know that," Adam said. "But you like her, right?"

"We're friends," he reiterated. "That's all."

"For now," Adam remarked.

Kane shrugged. "Maybe that's all it is. It's new territory, this having a woman friend thing. Although we do have a date tonight."

Adam smiled. "Laurel and I were friends before anything else. I think it made everything else stronger."

Kane heard the affection in his brother's voice. He knew how much Adam adored Laurel and how much they'd gone through to be together. He admired and respected them both for not giving up on each other, even when it seemed hopeless. Kane had never experienced that kind of deep, all-consuming love. Not even close.

"We'll see what happens," he offered casually, and didn't get a response because Layla and Laurel returned and they all chatted for a while about the garden and the kids, and Adam got into a long conversation with Layla about his plans to brew his own beer. She was relaxed and looked so effortlessly beautiful it was difficult thinking of her as just a friend.

It was after twelve when he walked her to her car, a sleepy Erin in her arms.

"That was so much fun," she said as he placed the diaper bag in the back seat. "Your family's so nice."

He nodded. "So, I'll pick you up this evening, about six?"

"Sure, bye now."

Kane watched her drive off and felt disappointment settle in his chest. When he went back inside, Laurel and Adam were smiling broadly, their approval obvious.

"We think she's perfect for you," Laurel said. "And her daughter adores you already. I'm so happy for you both."

Kane held up his hand. "Ah, you're getting a little ahead of yourselves here. We've only known each other for a just over a week."

"Sometimes that's all it takes," Laurel assured him. "She likes you, too, I can tell."

"She's still in love with her husband," Kane said, and then wanted to snatch the words back immediately. He didn't want Laurel or Adam speculating; he didn't want anyone thinking he was mooning around like a lovesick idiot.

If that was what he was doing.

"I gotta go," he said, and grabbed his keys from the hall table. "Catch you later."

Kane went to the gym and worked out for an hour, then headed home. He grabbed a snack and tried to watch television but he couldn't stay still. After some cleaning up, he hit the shower, changed into dark trousers and a pale gray shirt, and was back at Layla's a little before six o'clock.

When she came to the door she looked so beautiful he almost buckled at the knees. She wore a blue dress and matching shoes and a thin gold watch on her left wrist, and her hair was pinned up.

"You look beautiful," he said when he reached the top step.

"Thank you," she said with a tiny smile. "You look pretty good yourself. I'll just get Erin and her things. I might need a hand with her toy bag."

Kane followed her inside and spotted a large cardboard box in the middle of the living room. "What's that?"

She turned her head as she walked down the hall. "A playhouse for Erin. My grandfather is coming over Monday to put it together."

When they reached Erin's room, the toddler immediately came to Kane and stretched her arms out to him.

"Hey there, kiddo," he said.

Layla laughed softly. "I really do think she now prefers you to me."

He grinned. "Want me to carry her?"

"Sure," she replied, and grabbed the diaper bag and a bigger tote with a selection of toys. "Traitorous child."

Kane hauled Erin into his arms and settled her on his hip and she immediately pulled his hair. "Ouch."

"That's a small price to pay for being her favorite," Layla said jokingly.

They drove to her grandparents' retirement community on the outskirts of town. Her grandmother, Maude, greeted them at the door and Joe shook his hand as Kane crossed the threshold with a chattering Erin in his arms. Layla quickly made the introductions and he was instantly put at ease by the elderly couple. They clearly adored both Layla and Erin and reassured their granddaughter several times that the child would be fine on her overnight stay. They lingered for about ten minutes, chatting about the hotel and the town and her grandfather's '57 Chevrolet Bel Air that he'd lovingly restored and kept under cover in the garage.

"Are you okay?" Kane asked once they were in the car and heading into Rambling Rose. "You seem tense."

"I don't like leaving her," she admitted with a long sigh. "Is it that obvious?"

"Yeah," he replied. "And perfectly natural."

"I worry," she said. "You've seen how upset she gets at day care. I can't bear seeing her cry—it breaks me inside."

"I'm sure your grandparents will take good care of her," he assured her. "But if you don't want to leave her, I'll understand."

She shook her head. "No, I'm being silly. I know she's safe. She loves my grandparents and usually has no trouble spending time with them."

He talked about the hotel on the trip into town

to deflect her concerns. And it worked, because by the time they reached the restaurant, she was much more relaxed. The restaurant was busy, but they were quickly shown to their table. They were being seated when she spoke again.

"A lavender rose?"

Kane glanced at the single flower wrapped in cellophane that he'd arranged to have waiting for her. "Think of it as a belated Valentine."

"It's beautiful," she said, and raised the flower to her face, inhaling deeply. "I love the color."

"It's the symbol of enchantment," he explained, and then shrugged, feeling faintly embarrassed, hoping she didn't ask for any more details—like the fact that a lavender rose also meant love at first sight. "My mother grows roses, so we were all taught the meaning of each color when we were kids."

"Really?" she queried. "So you're really a romantic underneath the workingman facade?"

"Now you're making fun of me."

Layla chuckled softly. "A little. But thank you. I love flowers."

The waitress arrived, one he knew by name, and they chatted for a few seconds before he ordered a bottle of wine once he'd established Layla's preference.

"How do you order without looking at the wine list?" she asked once the waitress disappeared. "I'm terrible at making decisions."

"I guess I just know what I like."

She met his gaze, like his words rattled her. "Kane... I..."

He rested his elbows on the table and leaned in closer. "I'd like to ask you something."

"Go ahead."

"We've been out a few times now," he reminded her. "But I'm curious about something—have I been parked in the friend zone?"

She inhaled sharply. "Yes," she replied. "And no."

He laughed softly. "Okay..."

"What I mean to say is that in here," she said and tapped her temple, "I'm not ready for a romantic relationship. However, the rest of me," she added and gestured down the side of her body, "hasn't quite caught up with that idea yet."

Awareness swirled through the space between them. Whatever was happening, she was fighting it. And from the sound of it, failing. "I'm really attracted to you," he said bluntly.

She didn't flinch. "Me, too. The thing is, I'm not sure what to do about it. I've never been with anyone except my husband," she said softly, her voice lowering an octave. "And by that, I mean I've never so much as kissed anyone else...let alone, anything more."

It was quite the admission and one he was pretty sure she hadn't intended on sharing. But there was a rawness to the mood that amplified the attraction dancing over his skin. "I see."

"Does that make you want to run away?"

"Not at all," he replied. "It helps me understand you, though."

"You mean, why I seem so clumsy and naive?"

The waitress returned and they stayed silent while the wine was poured and menus were placed on the table. Once they were alone again, Kane replied.

"You're not clumsy. And being naive isn't a flaw. Frankly, there's something about you that makes me feel almost…protective—and that hasn't happened to me before. So, if all you want is for us to be friends, then we'll be friends. If you want more than that, then we'll take it as slow as you need to take it."

"Honestly," she said and sighed, "I'm not sure what I want." She reached across the table and grabbed his hand, holding his fingers firm. "But, Kane, I do know that I don't want to do anything that will hurt my daughter."

Kane glanced at the wedding band and rubbed the ring with his thumb. "I don't want to confuse anyone, either, Layla. I don't want to make you question whether you're doing the right thing or rush you into making a decision that's not the right one for you. I realize there's a lot at stake."

"Erin," she added quietly.

He nodded. "I would never intentionally hurt either of you. That doesn't mean I won't do or say something stupid and thoughtless at some point. I'm a guy, and guys do stupid things when they're distracted by a beautiful woman. Or when we're thinking with the lower half of our anatomy. And that's not an excuse," he added. "Just a reason."

She was smiling and the brown eyes were darker than he'd ever seen them. "I appreciate your honesty, Kane."

She might, but he still didn't feel particularly honest. If he were, he'd tell her he felt like he was sinking in quicksand when he was around her. And how much the knowledge stunned him. He'd never felt deeply in any relationship he'd had in the past. He'd never wanted to spend time with someone with the intensity that he felt when he was with Layla. He'd never wanted to kiss someone as much. Or make love as much. He was confused by those new feelings. Part of him wanted to harness them tightly inside, while the other part—the one that was fueled by his increasing desire—wanted to see where the feelings would go.

Either way, Kane knew he was utterly screwed.

Layla busied herself by looking over the menu, trying not to think about how she'd admitted way too much about herself. Weirdly, she found Kane easy to talk to, easy to confide in…and as it turned out, easy to trust. She didn't know why since they barely knew each other, but she couldn't deny it.

Other than the day the hotel opened and Kane had brought her into the restaurant for coffee, it was her first time at Roja. The last time she'd been to dinner alone with a man was with her husband a few weeks before Erin was born, and that had been at Frank's favorite Thai place in Houston. But Roja was much more upscale than the places she'd gone with Frank. Most of the tables were filled and the waitstaff was busily attending to patrons.

She looked up and saw Kane was watching her, his menu face down on the table.

"I'm guessing you already know what you want?" she asked.

He nodded. "Predictable, remember?"

The waitress approached and she ordered a small appetizer and mushroom risotto, then waited while Kane ordered herb bread and a veal pasta dish. Once the waitress left, she grabbed the rose and inhaled the scent from the petals.

"Tell me more about your mom. You said she grew flowers."

"Yeah," he said, and shrugged. "She's a typical mom, I guess."

Layla had no idea what that meant. "What's a 'typical' mom like?"

"Caring," he replied, his gaze narrowing a little. "Kind. She always puts us first—even now that we're all adults and living our own lives. She bakes and grows roses."

"She sounds perfect."

He smiled. "Well, I guess she is. She loves us a lot. And she loves my dad. I suppose you could say that's what she does best—she loves."

"Wow," she said. "It's no wonder you're so...you know...nice and normal. And since Adam seems the same, I'll bet all your siblings are good people."

He nodded. "That they are. You've told me about your mom, but what about your father?"

She shrugged. "He ran out when he found out my mom was pregnant. He was young and not ready to be a dad, I guess. Mom's never talked much about him. I know he lives in Minnesota and that he's married with a couple of stepchildren." When his brows shot upward she explained. "I tracked him down when I was seventeen. I was curious about him. But as it turned out, he wasn't so curious about me. So I forgot I actually had a father and got on with the rest of my life."

She saw sympathy in his expression and experienced a familiar heat over her skin. She'd seen that look before—on Frank when they'd first met and she'd explained the story over cake and coffee one rainy afternoon. Although his parents had passed away, he had also come from a loving and close family.

"Don't feel sorry for me," she said quietly. "I'm a grown-up now and I don't have any abandonment issues. My grandparents and Erin are all the family I need."

"I think you're remarkable."

It might have been the nicest thing anyone had ever said to her. But she didn't respond because their food arrived and she had an excuse to retreat back into her shell. She relaxed, drank some wine, and settled into some light conversation about the hotel and the job he'd been offered in Houston but still hadn't decided upon. Once their meals were over, they lingered over coffee and Layla sent a quick text to her grandmother to check on Erin.

"I take it she's okay?" he asked as the waitress approached with the check and he passed over his credit card.

Layla nodded with relief as the reply text came through. "Fine. She went to bed like an angel and is sound asleep."

It was after nine thirty when they left, and nearly ten when they arrived back at her house. Layla grabbed her bag and was out of the Ranger before he'd come around to the passenger side, her nerves suddenly rattling around like a tack in a tin cup.

"Thank you for a lovely evening," she said, clutching the wrapped rose in one hand. "I forgot how nice it is to eat out and be a grown-up."

He nodded and opened the gate. Layla walked up the path and rummaged in her bag for the house keys with her free hand. The porch sensor light came on and she immediately felt conspicuous, like they were on display for the whole world. Silly, she supposed. She lived on a quiet street and had elderly neighbors who retired most nights by nine o'clock.

"Well, good night," he said.

Layla inhaled. "Would you like to come inside? I think I have a bottle of wine in the pantry. Or coffee. Or soda if you'd prefer."

He took a second, then nodded. "Soda sounds great."

He was close as she opened the door and Layla picked up the scent of his cologne. It was warm and woodsy and masculine and a heady mix for her senses. Once they were in the kitchen, Layla quickly grabbed two sodas from the refrigerator and came around the counter and passed him a bottle.

"Cheers," she said as they clinked. "To new friends."

"To good friends," he corrected softly.

They stood by the counter for what felt like endless seconds, one hip pressed against the granite, and Layla couldn't drag her eyes away from his gaze. His green eyes were blisteringly intense and their connection didn't waver. Layla knew what was coming. She could feel the inevitability in every pore, every nerve, every inch of her skin. She also knew, somehow, that he wouldn't make the first move. That wasn't his way.

It was up to her. And Layla knew she had a decision to make. Over dinner he'd asked if she'd put him in the friend zone and she had given him an ambiguous reply. Yes and no. Which didn't make sense to her now. Because of course her feelings were not platonic. She might want them to be—in fact, she might long for them to be—but she couldn't fight the traitor tormenting her since she'd first laid eyes on him. Her long-starved libido.

And her lonely, aching heart.

Strangely, she didn't think of Frank, and the memory of his kiss, which was usually so strong to her senses. Her memories were overshadowed by the desire running riot through her system.

She placed her bottle on the counter and waited a couple of agonizing seconds until he did the same. Then she stepped closer, and almost in slow motion, rested one hand on his shoulder. The muscles beneath her palm bunched instantly, as though her touch was poker hot. She looked up, noticing everything about his handsome face—the strong jaw, the tiny scar above his left eye, the way his dark hair flipped over his forehead, and the mouth she knew she was about to kiss.

Layla rose onto her toes and leaned into him. He didn't speak, didn't move, didn't flinch as she pressed her lips to his, the sensation almost fleeting and whispery, as though she was taking her first step into the unknown. She pressed further, the pressure increasing, her lips asking for a little more, her fingers curling around his shoulder, her sigh soft against his mouth. And still, he didn't respond. For a moment, she wondered if she'd imagined his interest, if *he* was the one thinking they were nothing more than friends. But then he reached up and cupped her nape, his fingers resting softly at her neck for a second before his mouth slowly moved against hers. She inhaled, feeling the tempo of the kiss shift on some invisible, seductive axis. And she was lost.

He anchored her head and her lips parted, allowing the gentle slide of his tongue into her mouth. Layla gripped him harder, stunned by the sensations quickly racing through her. The kiss deepened a little more and she let the pleasure of it roll over her like a wave. She'd always enjoyed kissing, and this one was gentle and slow and exactly what she needed. He knew that, of course. Kane wasn't the kind of man who would rush a first kiss, and probably a second. He was controlled and measured and the quintessential nice guy. Someone she could trust. And more. She had no doubt that he would be a wonderfully generous lover.

When he raised his head she was breathing hard, her hands both clinging to his shoulders. Layla met his gaze and shuddered out a sigh as he spoke. "I should probably get going."

He should, but she didn't want him to. For the first time in forever she wanted to feel something.

She wanted to feel his arms around her just a little longer. Kane's arms.

And it tormented her. She tried to think about Frank...tried to conjure up his image. But somehow, because a flesh-and-blood man was standing in front of her, a man who was all strength and temptation, she struggled recalling the man she'd loved for so many years. In that moment, it was Kane she wanted, Kane she longed for.

But she didn't say it. Instead, she let go of his shoulders and stepped back. "Okay...good night."

He moved back. "Yeah, good night. So, there's a Creedence Clearwater Revival tribute band playing in Houston at the end of next month, and I'd really like to take you to see the show."

Layla stared at him. He was talking about something that was weeks away. Another date. Just the two of them. It would mean she'd need to find a sitter for Erin again. Of course her grandparents would take care of her. She would be free for the night. To see a band. To stay up late. It sounded like the perfect plan. They could go out. Hang out. Spend time together. Hold hands. Probably kiss. Become a couple. And then maybe they'd have sex. And more—fall in love. All the things people did every day.

In that moment Layla had fear in one hand, and curiosity in the other.

She just wasn't sure which hand she could offer.

Chapter Seven

"He seems very nice."

The following morning, at her grandparents' home, Layla regarded her grandmother over a hot cup of tea. "Kane *is* nice."

"When are you seeing him again?"

She shrugged. "We haven't made any firm plans."

Layla wasn't about to admit to her grandmother that she hadn't committed to Kane's offer to go out and see the band. Nor did she make any more plans with him. He'd left quickly after their kiss and she'd spent the following hour walking around the house in a daze, wondering why she'd acted so out of character and initiated the kiss. And why she was spending time thinking about more than simply kissing him.

"Lovely shoulders," her grandmother said, and winked.

"Nan," Layla implored. "Really."

Maude laughed softly. "I'm old, not blind. However, I do remember how good your grandfather used to look in a tool belt when he was young."

Layla covered her ears with a chagrin. "Nan... please stop."

Maude laughed again. "I like that workingman type—so do you, it seems."

Layla felt heat crawl up her chest. "Well, he's obviously attractive."

"Mmm," Maude said agreeably. "Different from Frank."

Layla glanced at her grandmother and shrugged. Frank was tall and lean, with light brown hair that had begun to recede a little, and neat Clark Kent glasses. He'd worked in the finance department at a company in Houston and was more white-collar than blue, more of a thinker than a doer. "I'm not looking to replace my husband with an exact copy, if that's what you're getting at."

"Of course you're not," Maude said gently. "Frank was a lovely man. And he adored you and Erin. All I'm saying is that's it's okay to think about the possibility of someone else."

"Is it?" Layla shot back quickly, and then wanted to snatch the words back. "Sometimes I..." She stopped, looking deep into the teacup. "I feel guilty for thinking I could be happy again. That I could…"

"Love someone else?"

She stilled, meeting her grandmother's gaze. "Yes."

"That doesn't mean you love Frank less, you know."

She knew that logically. She also knew that since Frank was the only man she'd ever had feelings for, she had no other comparison. She'd never crushed on anyone in high school. She'd never pined after the boy next door. She'd never dreamed of falling in love with a rock star or prince from a fairy tale. There was only ever Frank—rock solid, trustworthy, honest. The kind of man she'd sworn to find after watching her mother flit from one unreliable hookup to the next. Layla had promised herself that she wouldn't walk in her mom's shoes. She'd never cry or plead or beg someone to stay through tears of rage or resentment. She'd find someone who had staying power—who had integrity and consideration. A man who was worthy of loving. And a man who was never going to break her heart.

Until he died and left me alone…

The words rattled around inside her mind. She didn't like herself when the demons pressed down on her shoulders. But they did. And they hurt. Blaming Frank for leaving didn't make sense—she knew that logically. Unfortunately, logic rarely found a place in a broken heart.

"I don't want to be one of those women who *have* to have a man to be happy," she said, and grimaced a little.

"You mean, you don't want to be like your mother?" Maude asked.

"Exactly," she replied. "I saw too much, Nan. I watched her move from one failed relationship to the next and she was never truly happy, never content with who she was or what she had. I made a promise to myself when I was young that I'd never be like that."

"Perhaps if your mother had met someone like Frank, she would have found what she was looking for," Maude said quietly.

"I'm sorry, Nan," Layla said. "I don't mean to upset you by talking about her. She's still your daughter and despite how she is, she's also still my mother. And I hope she does find happiness in her life."

Maude placed her cup in the saucer and rested her elbows on the table. "And you?"

"I have Erin," Layla said, and glanced at her daughter, sitting on the carpet flipping through pages of a picture book. "She's what matters most. You, Grandpa and Erin are all I need to make me happy."

But as she spoke, a weird hollowness prevailed, sitting deep in her chest. For eighteen months she'd been in a kind of limbo—quietly grieving Frank and not having to think about anything else. She had her daughter, her grandparents, her work and her studies. It was an easy out—a simple way of staying sane and being able to get on with things. No pressure. No expectation. And no need to feel anything else.

Until ten days ago.

Meeting Kane Fortune had changed things.

Because now she had cracks in her armor.

They were small cracks, of course, because that's how she did things, little by little, step by step. But the tiny cracks did something she hadn't expected— they made her vulnerable.

Of course, she *could* never see him again and get on with her life as she had been doing. She could forget about the intense connection they seemed to have. She could dismiss all the quiet conversations. The laughter. The sense of easy companionship that had quickly come to define their interactions. She could forget the way he touched her hand. Her cheek. And the incredible kiss they'd shared.

It would be easy. Neither of them was invested too deeply.

It wasn't like they were falling in love with each other.

At least, not yet.

But they would—she was sure of it. And once she waded through the internal monologue in her head, Layla knew she wasn't really thinking about the *they*.

It was the *she*. The *me*. Because she couldn't possibly know what was going on in Kane's mind. However, she knew herself. She knew she was risking herself big-time if she continued to see him.

Which meant one thing.

She had to end it before it really began.

Kane was at the hotel in the concierge's office on Tuesday morning, talking to Jay about a niggling issue with a couple of storage rooms on the second floor, when he received a text message from Callum asking if he could meet him at Paz Spa by eleven thirty. He texted back with a thumbs-up emoji, ended the meeting and headed into town by eleven fifteen. The spa was busy and there were about half a dozen people sitting in the reception area, plus Callum and Hailey standing to one side and deep in conversation—but the only person he really saw was Layla.

She was standing behind the long counter, her fingers tapping on a keyboard, a small earbud in her ear. Kane lingered by the door for a moment, watching her as she worked, noticing the tiny furrow of concentration between her brows. She looked up and her eyes widened. He spotted a tiny smile, but it quickly disappeared and he nodded in greeting. They hadn't spoken since the weekend. Not that he was avoiding her—but he was giving her the space he sensed she needed. But that didn't stop him from remembering the incredible kiss they shared.

Hailey gave him a wave as she headed for the reception desk and Callum met him with a handshake. They talked for several minutes about Fortune Brothers Construction's tentative plans to expand the spa into the adjoining tenancy.

"I don't think we expected the place to take off like it has," Callum said as they headed for the staff lunchroom. They sat down and Callum continued the conversation. "But each month the business is increasing significantly over the last, so the projections for the next year look really encouraging." He handed Kane a folder. "This is a rough draft of what I was thinking, so check this out when you get a chance and I'll email you the building specs this afternoon."

They talked for close to ten more minutes before Callum's cell rang and he excused himself. Kane remained in the office for a while and flicked through the file he'd been given. The drafted layout was simple enough, and he was checking over the dimensions when he heard someone enter the room.

Layla.

"Oh...hi," she said, looking flustered. "You're still here? I saw Callum leave and thought you'd also—"

"I'm still here," he said. "Clearly."

"I was about to have lunch."

"Don't let me stop you," he said, and closed the folder.

She nodded and walked to the refrigerator, extracting a flat plastic container and a juice bottle. "Would you like a drink or something?"

"No thanks."

She exhaled and sat at the other end of the table, looking as though she was filled with a kind of nervous energy.

"Everything all right?" he asked.

She looked up. "Yes, fine."

"How's Erin?"

"Great."

"Enjoying her new playhouse, I bet," he remarked.

"Not quite," she replied. "Grandpa has had a bout of sciatica and hasn't been over to put it together yet. Erin's been tapping on the box for days. I didn't want to start it in case I messed it up and put screws in the wrong place," she added with a soft but shrill laugh.

Kane stared at her, watching as she fiddled with the lid on the plastic container. "Would you like me to come over tomorrow afternoon and put it together for her?"

Layla's gaze dropped. "Oh, I wouldn't want to bother you and take up too much of your time."

"It's no bother."

She glanced up. "Well, actually, I have an assignment due this week and I should probably spend my—"

"It was just a kiss, Layla."

Crickets. Or a deafening silence that was as uncomfortable as hearing nails down a chalkboard. But it needed to be said. And he needed to say it—because he figured she wouldn't.

Kane got to his feet and moved around the table, sitting down beside her. He watched for a moment as her fingers tapped the top of the container and then he spoke again. "All I'm saying is that it doesn't have to mean anything or everything. I know you're not ready for anything serious and honestly, I'm not sure I'm ready, either. I don't know, it's all happened very fast. But I can't deny there's some connection here. Can you?"

"No," she replied quietly. "But you're right. I'm not ready for…whatever this is."

"Friends then," he suggested, and saw her palpable sigh of relief. He felt relief, too, because he'd told her the truth—they barely knew each other and Kane wasn't in any kind of headspace to have a serious relationship. He was still settling into his place among the Fortunes, still working out his role as part of the family, still finding out if he wanted to stay in Rambling Rose long term—and wasn't sure if New York would call him back. Getting involved with anyone seriously would be unfair to both parties. Particularly a woman who had a child. It could turn into a train wreck. Or it could turn into the best thing that had ever happened to him.

"Friends," she echoed. "Okay…we can do that."

"So I'll come over tomorrow afternoon and put the playhouse together?"

She nodded, still looking a little pensive. "I'm sorry, Kane."

"For what?"

She shrugged, sighing deeply. "I don't know... well, I *do* know. For giving mixed signals. For confusing you. For maybe acting as though I was ready for something when I'm not."

"I'm not confused," he said quietly, fibbing a little to make her feel better. "The truth is, I like hanging out with you."

"I like that, too."

He grinned and cleared his throat, eager to lighten the mood between them. "So, I'll see you tomorrow. Around four?"

He didn't wait for a reply. Instead, he quickly got to his feet and left, heading back to his office at the hotel. Now that he didn't need to be at the hotel full time, Kane was considering his options. The spa extension would keep him busy for a while, and of course there was the job offer in Houston, and he knew Callum had other construction ventures on the table. But over the past week or so he'd struggled with a kind of vague restlessness that had him questioning what he was doing and where he was headed. Kane wasn't one to dwell and put his edginess down to the hotel being finished and his job with the Fortunes feeling a little too much like it was on the fringe. Kane liked being in control, liked knowing where he was headed and what he was doing at all times. Even when he'd first ventured to Texas, he'd had a plan. Work hard, get to know his extended family, keep his mind on the job. But lately, he felt as though the lines were blurring. He liked Rambling Rose. He liked knowing Adam and Brady were close by and they still had their strong family connection—but both his brothers had their own young families to think about. The truth was, Kane missed his parents and the rest of his siblings and the friends he'd left in New York.

What he didn't want to do was think that his restlessness had anything to do with Layla. For the moment they were friends and nothing more. She'd made it clear and he'd agreed.

But when he arrived at her house the following afternoon, noticing how good she looked in a long skirt and pale pink sweater, with her lovely hair flowing over her shoulders, Kane knew he was kidding himself. He had several female friends in New York, and none of them hammered at his libido like Layla did. He said the phrase *friend zone* over and over to himself as he was invited inside and greeted a chattering Erin in the hallway. She held out her arms to him and Kane glanced at Layla for permission to pick her up.

"Of course," Layla said with a smile as she closed the door. "I think we've already established that she prefers you to me."

Kane laughed. "Hey, sweetie, have you been good for your mom?"

"She's been an angel," Layla replied, and led him into the living room, where the large box still sat on the carpet. "Thank you for doing this. Grandpa is still out of action and I'm hopeless at building things."

"Well, you're in luck—I'm good at it," he assured her, and grinned.

He spent the following fifteen minutes getting the box into the playroom, taking the pieces out and setting them out on the floor—all while Erin remained at his side.

"Looks like you've got yourself an apprentice," Layla said from the doorway.

Kane looked at the toddler. "Sure does."

"Although I'm not too sure how much help she's going to be at reading the instructions," Layla said as she scooped up the instruction booklet he'd discarded.

Kane glanced at the paper in her hand and shrugged. "I think we'll manage."

She grinned. "Are you one of those men who don't read instructions?"

He stiffened, experienced a tightening knot in his chest. "Leave it on the chair and I'll look it over."

Both her brows came up. "You know, I won't think less of you for having to check them out," she said.

The tightness in his chest increased and he fought

the little voice of insecurity in his head. All his life he'd avoided talking about his dyslexia, using coping strategies and ruses. The fact that he was all out of excuses around Layla made it even harder to admit the truth. However, he had his own sizable share of ego and didn't want her to witness him potentially fumbling over the written instructions. Diagrams he could usually handle—but he'd checked out the leaflet and it was step-by-step written directions, in small, almost indecipherable font.

"I'm sure I can handle it," he said, and rearranged a couple of sections. "Construction projects are part of my brand, you know." He grinned.

She smiled. "Yeah, I'm pretty sure you could handle just about anything with one hand tied behind your back."

He figured it was a compliment and smiled back. "I think you're right."

"Well, do you need any help?"

He shook his head. The last thing he wanted was for Layla to see him struggling over the written instructions. "Nope. Erin and I have got it covered."

"I'll be in the kitchen if you need me."

"Sure. I'll call you when it's done."

"Do you want me to take her?" she asked, and gestured to her daughter.

"She's safe here."

"I know that," Layla replied. "You're good with her. I trust you with her."

"You said you had an assignment to finish," he reminded her, feeling faintly embarrassed by her praise.

She nodded. "You're right. Best I get to it."

She left the room, and he smiled when he spotted Erin toddling around, clearly quite comfortable with his presence in her playroom, and in her life. He'd always imagined he'd have a couple of kids one day. The thing was, to do that, he had to make a real commitment to someone. And despite knowing some very nice women over the years, something always held him back. He wasn't sure why commitment and marriage freaked him out so much, since he'd certainly had a good example in his parents' happy marriage. But whenever he got a few dates in, he usually backed off.

Except for this time.

It took Kane about forty minutes to put the playhouse together. He encountered a couple of problems—a few screws that didn't want to play the game and Erin moving things around—but he managed to get the playhouse finished and sat with Erin on the carpet while she investigated it. He was adjusting a couple of shelves inside when she approached and tugged on his sleeve.

"What have you got there, kiddo?"

A book, he noticed, that she was waving at him. A book with pictures of colorful dinosaurs on the front. A book she clearly wanted him to read to her.

She plunked herself down beside him and handed him the book.

"Book! Pwease!"

Kane took a breath, grabbed the book and spoke. "All right, kiddo, just don't expect too much, okay?" he said, and then turned to the first page.

Layla stayed in the kitchen for close to forty-five minutes and managed to get a good chunk of her assignment done. Every now and then she would hear Erin laughing and the sound warmed her through to the soles of her feet. Kane was so good with her and her daughter clearly had a case of hero worship. She checked on the casserole she'd put in the slow cooker, grabbed a couple of sodas and a juice box for Erin, and headed for the playroom. But she stopped in the doorway, taking in the sight before her.

They were both sitting on the floor, Kane with his long legs stretched out, Erin sitting beside him, resting her head against his arm, their backs pressed up to the side of the playhouse. And Kane was telling her a story. Not exactly the story from the book he was holding, since Layla had read the book countless times and knew every page line by line. Oh, he was still talking about dinosaurs, but this story was also about princesses and green frogs and magic dust that turned a pumpkin into a carriage and mice into prancing white horses. She listened for a moment, lost in the sound of his deep, calm voice, as mesmerized as Erin by the laid-back style of storytelling.

Finally, he looked up and stopped speaking. "Oh, hey."

"Don't let me interrupt."

"It's okay," he said, and closed the book, "we were at the end of the story."

"More, pwease," Erin said and pointed to the book.

"You know, you've just made story time really difficult," she said, and smiled. "How am I ever going to compete with that?"

He got to his feet and Erin quickly demanded to be picked up, which he did immediately. "I'm sure you do a much better job than I just did."

"Not at all," she said, her skin warming beneath his penetrating gaze. "I just read the book. I don't turn it into a fairy tale. I think you really made her day," she added when she saw how delightful Erin's expression was. "I brought sodas."

"Great, that was thirsty work."

He took the drink and she opened the juice box for her daughter. "I see you didn't need the instructions after all," she said and gestured to the leaflet, which was on the floor upside down.

"Told you," he said, and grinned.

Layla's skin warmed all over. "Are you staying for dinner?"

"Am I invited?"

She nodded, hearing the flirtatious edge to his words. "Absolutely."

They hung out for a while with Erin in the playroom and then she took off to get her daughter bathed and ready for dinner. By six fifteen they were sitting at the kitchen table and Erin was playing with her food as usual. And Layla couldn't deny the obvious—there was an intense feeling of familiarity and domesticity in the air. Like they'd done this countless times before. Like it was the most normal thing in the world to be together, having dinner, laughing at the way Erin chatted and cooed and intermittently flicked food at them.

"You'll make a really good father one day. I know, I've said that before, but you're such a natural with Erin it's hard not to think it."

The words were out before she could stop them and the moment they were she wanted to snatch them back because they smacked of way too much intimacy—and she was sure she sounded like she was recruiting him for the job.

He didn't flinch, though. "You said you and your husband planned on having more kids?"

She nodded. "We planned on doing a lot of things."

The air between them was suddenly thick and she needed to clear her head. She used Erin as an excuse and bailed, muttering something about getting her daughter ready for bed. She returned to the kitchen about ten minutes later, discovering that Kane had cleaned up.

"Wow," she said, and adjusted Erin onto her hip. "Thank you. Although you didn't have to."

"You cooked, so it's only fair."

"You put up the playhouse," she reminded him.

"I had help," he said, and motioned toward Erin. "Bedtime, I take it?"

Layla nodded. "Yes."

"Well, I'll leave you to—"

"You can stay," she said quickly. "I'll put her down and she should go to sleep quickly. We could have coffee. Or tea."

He leaned against the counter. "Okay. Night, kiddo," he said, and Erin rubbed her eyes in response and held out her arms to him. He took a couple of strides and gently kissed the baby's head, and he was so close Layla inhaled the scent of his cologne and could see the faint stubble on his jaw. He was so incredibly masculine that for a second it was hard to breathe and she stepped back, trying to regather her composure.

"I won't be long," she said.

When she returned five minutes later she could hear the kettle boiling and spotted two mugs on the counter. Stupid, but it irked her a little that he was so good at everything. She inhaled sharply and placed the baby monitor on the table.

"How do you want it?" he asked.

Layla stared at him. "Huh?"

"Your tea."

"Oh," she said. "Black with lots of sugar."

"Same," he said, and spooned sugar into both mugs.

"I wouldn't have taken you for a tea drinker," she remarked.

"Life's full of surprises," he said, and smiled and finished making the beverages.

"We could go into the living room," she suggested and grabbed the baby monitor and the cookie tin. "Oreos," she explained as she walked. "My favorite."

When they reached the living room she flicked on the heater, put a music channel on the television with the volume down low and settled on the sofa. He pulled a baby doll from behind his back when he sat down and laughed.

"Isn't this her favorite at the moment?" he asked as he inspected the toy.

"Second favorite," Layla replied as she took the doll and tossed it in the toy basket next to the sofa, still smiling. "You're not injured, are you?"

"Nah, anyway, it sure beats standing on a Lego," he said and grimaced. "Brady's boys love leaving the pieces all over the floor."

Layla curled one leg underneath herself and relaxed a little. "It must have been a huge shock for your brother when he was given custody of the children."

Kane nodded. "I think at first it was. He's settled into the role now. He's talking about employing a live-in nanny, which will help him get into a better routine with them. Naturally the boys are still grieving the loss of their parents, so the more routine Brady can provide, the better."

"I can barely manage raising one child by myself," she admitted. "I can't imagine how it must be handling two. He's lucky to have you to help."

"I do what I can," Kane said, and shrugged. "And Adam and Laurel help out. I know my mom wishes they were still in New York so she could be a part of his support network. But Brady seems settled in Rambling Rose for the moment."

"Are you?" she asked quietly, not really sure she wanted to hear the answer.

"Settled here?" He sighed heavily and grabbed the mug from the coffee table. "Honestly, I'm not sure. While I was involved in the hotel construction, I was busy and didn't have too much free time to think about the future. I know Callum has more plans for the town and I'd like to think I'll be involved in some capacity—but I'm not quite sure what the future holds."

Layla met his gaze. "I hope you do stay. I've liked getting to know you."

"You have?"

"I'm not well practiced at making friends," she

admitted. "Moving around so much as a kid, I think I put a wall up."

"Understandable."

"Is it?" she challenged, and then made a self-deprecating sound.

"You don't think so?"

She shrugged. "I think it's sort of cowardly. You know, don't let people in so you don't get hurt."

"One thing I've learned over the years is that friendships shouldn't be hard. I've got a circle of friends from high school and college and whenever we get together there's no pressure, no expectations. We simply hang out and have a good time. Then we get back to our own lives. But you got married," he reminded her. "You must have let someone in."

"Frank was easy to love," she said, her throat tightening a little. "Easy to like. Easy to trust."

"I think you have more courage than you give yourself credit for," he said quietly. "And now you're raising Erin alone—that takes strength."

"Through necessity," she said, and sipped her tea. "I love her more than anything, but I didn't ever imagine I'd be doing it alone. That's the thing about letting someone in, you can never be sure if it's going to last. I mean, I know Frank would never have believed that when he drove home that night it would be for the last time."

"None of us can know what the future holds," he said, and glanced at the photographs on the mantel.

Layla looked at them, too—saw the wedding picture she'd had framed and wondered what Kane thought when he saw it. "I guess people risk themselves because they want the chance to be happy. Well," he added, and shrugged his insanely broad shoulders, "most people."

"Not you?"

"Not me," he replied. "So far."

"What do you think you're afraid of?" she asked bluntly.

"Failure," he said, answering when she didn't think he would. "Screwing up."

She wondered if that was all, but didn't push any further. They were getting close to talking about feelings—real feelings—perhaps the ones they had for each other, and Layla suspected neither of them was ready for that. She liked him, there was no doubt in her mind about that. But was it more than simple like? Or was it simply that her attraction for Kane was making her imagine she was feeling things that weren't actually there? "I guess we're smart to keep this thing as just friendship then. That way, our fears won't get in the way."

"I guess," he agreed.

Except Layla couldn't believe how wretchedly alone that reality made her feel.

Chapter Eight

"Can you take Larkin to day care in the morning?"

Kane had just arrived at Adam's on Wednesday evening when his brother passed him a beer and asked the question. "Sure."

"Sorry to ask on such short notice, but I'm meeting a new organic food supplier at eight and Laurel has something on early at the gallery."

Brady, who'd arrived at least an hour before him with the boys, quickly cut in. "If not, I could probably—"

"I said it's okay," Kane said, cutting him off. "Just drop him off at my place on your way into work in the morning."

Adam stared at him, clearly picking up the sharpness in his voice. "Ah…is everything all right?"

"Fine."

His brother, who had also always been his closest friend and knew him better than anyone, didn't look convinced. "Girl trouble?"

Kane scowled. "No," he said quickly, then exhaled. "Yes. I dunno."

Adam's mouth twisted and he offered a knowing nod. "You like her?"

"Yeah," he admitted.

"I guess the question is, how much?"

He shrugged. "We're friends."

"That's all?" Brady queried.

Kane drank some beer. "That's all."

Adam stretched back in his seat and grinned. "You've never been friend-zoned before, right?"

The easy thing would have been to nod and shrug off the question. But he couldn't. Because as much as he and Layla were friends now, there was definitely something else brewing between them. But she was fighting it. And if he was prepared to admit it, in a way, so was he. It was quickly feeling like the fight of his life.

"Not like this. It's complicated," he replied, and shrugged.

"Because she's a single mom?" Brady asked.

"Because neither of us is in the market for anything serious." Both his brothers laughed loudly and Kane glared at them. "What?"

"You're so full of crap," Adam replied. "I saw you together last weekend." He looked at Brady. "They were like this little ready-made family. It was cute."

Kane's frown quickly turned into a scowl. "I'm not having this conversation."

"Therein lies the problem," Brady said, and sipped his beer. "You know how Dad hides how he really feels about the Fortune family by being angry and suspicious and thinking they're all not to be trusted. When we all know that he really wants to be accepted as equal to his half brothers—as being as much of a Fortune as they are. He acts that way because he doesn't want to look weak or vulnerable."

Irritation rose in his blood. "Your point?"

Brady shrugged. "Well, you never admit to anything, either."

"Like what?" Kane shot back.

It was Adam who replied. Adam who knew him best. "Like the fact that you really care about this woman and it's scaring you to death."

Kane looked at his brothers in turn, heat clawing at his chest and neck. He'd never been good at admitting his feelings—they were right. Which meant he wasn't about to start. All he really wanted to do was bail and not think about it. They were also right about Layla. He did care. He liked her. A lot. And it was more than simple "like." More than anything he'd faced before.

"I didn't come here tonight for an intervention or psychoanalysis," he said.

"Maybe not," Adam replied. "But looks like you might need it."

Kane got to his feet and paced the living room, his gut suddenly churning. He didn't want the third degree. He didn't want to admit to anything. As soon as the thought entered his brain, he stopped pacing and looked at his brothers, hands propped on his hips.

"Okay, you're right," he admitted. "I like her. I really like her. I more than like her. I want to date her. I want to wake up next to her every morning. But I'm pretty sure *she* only wants to be friends."

It hurt to say it. And since Kane wasn't usually at the mercy of his feelings, he couldn't quite get a handle on how much his conflicted thoughts pained him.

"You said it yourself," Brady reminded him. "She's a single mom, so she's got a lot to lose."

"Exactly," Kane agreed. "She hasn't dated anyone since her husband died and I'm not going to let my head get all screwed up thinking it's ever going to be anything more than simple friendship."

"Why not?" Adam asked bluntly.

"Because he doesn't want to risk getting hurt," Brady responded.

Kane's hands flew forward. "Would you both stop? I appreciate that since you've both become fathers you're more in touch with your feelings, but don't aim all that newfound sensitivity at me, okay? I gotta go."

He left without another word and drove directly to the gym, where he spent over an hour and a half lifting weights, running on the treadmill and pushing himself to near exhaustion to exorcise his demons. When he got home it was after ten and he hit the shower, changed into fresh sweats and slumped in front of the television.

The churning in his gut hadn't abated and as he sat in solitude Kane realized an undeniable truth.

His brothers, as annoying as they were, had hit one hell of a nerve.

He *was* scared. And he *didn't* want to get hurt.

It was a pattern he'd perfected over the years. Giving as little of himself as possible and getting exactly that in return. It was how he'd avoided having a serious relationship for years. Well, since Janine. That had been five months of dating and sex. Five good months, he remembered. Then he'd ended it because she had pushed for them to move in together. The next step, she'd called it. And he freaked out, convincing himself she'd be after him for a commitment and a wedding ring soon after. He winced when he remembered her reaction the day they'd broken up. Janine was a nice woman and deserved way more than he'd given her. Afterward, she'd accused him of being cold and unfeeling and he couldn't blame her. He *had* been cold that day.

Since then, Kane had managed to avoid falling hard for anyone. He'd dated on and off back home and hadn't really thought much about it since arriving in Rambling Rose, using work, his new Fortune family and the hotel as excuses to stay busy and occupied.

Until Layla.

Who had, he realized, literally knocked him to his knees.

And when she said she wanted to be friends, he had an easy out. He could stew on it, mull it over, come out thinking he was okay with the whole idea and get on with doing what he did best—which was being alone.

As he looked around the room, at the bare walls and lack of anything resembling a home, Kane realized he hadn't made any real effort to settle in since he'd arrived. He still had furniture and personal belongings in storage in New York. In limbo. Exactly how he'd been living since he arrived in Texas.

And it wasn't, he admitted to himself, any way to live.

He went to bed around eleven thirty and spent most of the night staring at the ceiling.

Adam arrived at his place just before six the following morning and Larkin was dozing in his father's arms. Kane met him by the gate, took his nephew and the diaper bag and backpack.

"Thanks again," his brother said.

"No problem."

"Ah, look, if I was out of line last night, I'm sorry," Adam said, and shrugged. "I just wanna see you happy."

"I know," Kane replied. "Don't worry about it. We're all good."

"You know," Adam said quietly, "if you like her, you should probably tell her that. I know she's a single mom and has responsibilities and maybe she thinks she needs to take things slow, but you're not a selfish jerk, Kane. You're a good man, one of the best I know. If you open up a bit," Adam suggested and smiled, "she'll see that about you."

Kane tapped Adam affectionately on the shoulder and grinned. "Thanks for the talk."

His brother nodded, kissed Larkin and then left. His nephew was such an easy and placid child, and they spent the next couple of hours having breakfast and playing. By eight thirty they were at the day care center and Kane looked around for Layla's car in the parking area. Disappointment settled in his chest when he didn't spot it and he carried Larkin into the building. On his way out about five minutes later, he saw her, standing by her vehicle parked a few spaces down from his, her upper body bent into the back seat. Kane remained by his Ranger, since she had to pass him to enter the day care center.

"Oh, hi," she said when she was on the sidewalk.

As soon as Erin saw him she held out her arms and the action twisted at his insides. "Hi."

"I take it you're dropping your nephew off?"

"I just did."

"Oh, okay."

He tried not to notice how beautiful she looked in a blue skirt and pale pink sweater. Tried not to think about how much he wanted to unpin her hair and let it thread through his fingers or how much he wanted to kiss her perfectly shaped mouth. Tried not to think about how he'd dreamed about her arms around him, her legs, every part of her pressed up against him. Tried—and failed. During the night, as he'd stared at the ceiling, trying to sleep, he'd had a lot to think about. And talking with his brothers had given him the guts to come to a decision. Maybe the biggest of his life.

Kane leaned back on the Ranger, crossed his arms and spoke. "Layla, I've decided that I don't want to be your friend."

He saw her eyes widen and then shadow over, as if his words caused her pain. "You don't?"

Kane shook his head. "No, I don't. I want more than that. I want to date you, Layla. The truth is, I would like to be your...well, for want of a better word, boyfriend." The word almost strangled him as it came out and he felt about sixteen saying it. "And then, when the time is right for us both, your lover. And then whatever comes after that."

Shock grew on her face and he saw her swallow hard, as if she was digesting his words. "Oh... I—"

"I'm not saying this to pressure you or make you do something you don't want to do. I just wanted you to know where I'm at," he assured her. "I'm very attracted to you and would really like to pursue a romantic relationship. But if you're not in the same place, that's okay, I'll understand. It's up to you."

"I'm not sure what to say," she whispered.

"The truth," he said. "What it is that you're feeling."

"I don't know what I'm feeling," she replied, as though the words were some of the hardest she'd ever uttered.

"Well, that's a start," he said. "If you want me, you know where to find me."

Then he got into his truck and left.

Layla spent most of the day in a daze. And thinking of Kane. She hadn't anticipated such an honest announcement from him. And the truth was, it simultaneously scared and aroused her. Of course, she was naive thinking she could park him in the friend zone when she was so clearly in lust with him. The man was gorgeous and her starved libido responded to that. Knowing it was mutual just about made her toes curl.

But could she?

Was she ready for something more than friendship? What if it all turned to dust after a few weeks or a few months? What would she be left with—another broken heart? But on the flip side, if she didn't, she'd never know.

Never know what it would be like to be loved by Kane Fortune…

Layla pushed the thought away. That was going in too deep, too fast.

But she knew one thing—he'd said it was up to her and she knew that meant he wouldn't pursue it any further. He wouldn't call. He wouldn't ask her out.

So what was she going to do?

By the time she collected Erin from day care that afternoon she was exhausted. And that amplified tenfold when she spotted Adam and Laurel Fortune walking out of the building with a restful Larkin.

"Hey there," Laurel said. "It's good to see you. We should arrange another playdate for the kids."

There was something so friendly about the couple and Layla was drawn into their vortex. She remembered what she'd said to Kane about friendship and realized the only way to make friends was to take a leap of faith and hold out her hands.

"That sounds lovely. You could bring Larkin over on Saturday morning," she suggested.

They quickly made the arrangements and she knew Adam was watching the interaction with keen interest. Had Kane said something to his brother about the status of their relationship? And did Adam approve? The longer she hung around the more conspicuous she felt, so she quickly excused herself and headed inside the building.

As expected, she didn't hear from Kane again that day. Nor the next. She spent a long and lonely Friday evening playing with Erin and once her daughter was in bed, she tried to get in some study time. That lasted about half an hour before she gave up and sat in front of the television and watched a comedy rerun, checking her cell phone every few minutes in case she heard a familiar ping.

But she didn't.

The following morning she made cupcakes and sweet iced tea and greeted Laurel and Larkin at ten o'clock.

"This is a lovely home," Laurel remarked once Layla had given her a short tour and they settled the kids in the large playroom at the rear of the house, and sat at the small table and chairs, sipping tea.

"It's a bit big for just the two of us," Layla said, and shrugged.

"Perhaps one day you'll…" Laurel's words trailed off.

Layla managed a smile. "Get married again and have more kids?" She finished the other woman's sentence. That didn't seem likely. But she didn't say that. "Maybe." She watched as Larkin made his way into the playhouse and then saw Laurel's concerned expression. "He's perfectly safe in there. Kane built it, so I know it's sturdy and strong."

"Like he is, right?" Laurel suggested.

Layla didn't miss the query in the other woman's expression and didn't see the point is being coy. "Yes, exactly."

"Adam said he hasn't heard from Kane for a couple of days," Laurel said, and raised an inquiring brow. "Have you?"

Layla shrugged lightly and drank some tea. "Not today," she replied vaguely.

"I probably shouldn't say this," Laurel said quietly. "But I think he really likes you."

"I know," Layla replied. "I like him, too."

"He and Adam come from a really happy family," the other woman said. "You know, like the ones you see on television shows where everyone loves and supports one another. And sometimes it's hard for them to understand that not everyone is lucky enough to have had that same start in life. Some people had a tougher time growing up."

Layla wondered if Laurel knew something about her childhood and then dismissed the idea. She trusted Kane to be discreet.

"Did you?" she asked.

"There were moments when I felt alone and

afraid," Laurel admitted. "But then Adam came into my life."

Like Frank had come into hers. But Frank was gone. And Layla had the rest of her life to live.

That thought stayed with her through the rest of the playdate, through her studying, through Erin's bedtime. Echoing in her mind, persisting. Until she couldn't ignore it any longer. Finally, she made a cup of herbal tea, sat at the kitchen table and grabbed her cell phone. She stared at the screen, knowing what she had to do as she took a breath, grabbed hold of every ounce of her suddenly dwindling courage and sent Kane a text message.

Hi. Would you like to do something with us tomorrow? L & E

She waited several minutes and sighed with relief when a message came back.

Are you asking me out on a date?

She giggled, feeling about eighteen years old, without a child, a house and a job and as free as a bird for a few crazy seconds. Then reality set in. A reality she loved. Even on the hard days.

Yes. We're going to my grandparents' for lunch. Would you like to join us?

It took a few very long minutes for the reply to come through.

Sure. I'll pick you up.

It wasn't exactly filled with thumbs-up emojis, but it was something.

11:30. See you then.

When he was two minutes late the following morning, Layla almost decided he'd bailed. But then she spotted his familiar truck pull up in her driveway and he came to the door. In dark jeans, flannel shirt and leather jacket, he looked so sexy she had to cleave her tongue from the roof of her mouth before she managed to say hello. Erin, of course, was delighted to see him and quickly demanded he take her in his arms.

"Hey there," he said to Layla.

She smiled. "Hi. She's happy to see you."

"It's mutual. Shall we go?"

Layla grabbed her tote and Erin's diaper bag and they were quickly on their way.

"I'm really glad you came today. My grandparents are looking forward to seeing you."

He glanced at her once they were driving down the street. "Shall we talk about it now or later?"

Layla stilled. "About what?"

"This. Us."

Simple words. And a loaded question. "Do you mean why I texted you?"

"Exactly."

"I thought about what you said and realized I wanted to spend time with you," she admitted, coloring hotly. "You said it was up to me and I decided I want to get to know you a little better."

His green eyes glittered. "Really?"

"That's not code for jumping into bed with you anytime soon, by the way," she said, burning from the roots of her hair to the soles of her feet, but knowing the words needed to be said. "I'm an overcautious person and I don't ever jump. But the idea of *not* seeing you again…" Her words trailed off and she sighed. "Well, let's just say I was motivated to do something that goes completely against my usual character."

"I'm glad to hear it. But for the record, like I said to you the other day, I didn't have any agenda and I certainly don't want to pressure you into something if you're not ready."

"Honestly," she said, "I have no idea what I'm ready for. I feel as though I've been in limbo for eighteen months and this is all so new to me."

"And me," he said quietly. "Don't feel alone, Layla."

She didn't—that was the thing. Around Kane, she

felt the least alone that she'd felt since Frank passed away. "What if we hurt each other?"

He took a few moments to reply. "I guess we'd both know it wouldn't be deliberate. I'm not sure we could ask any more of each other than that."

The sincerity in his voice touched her deep down and she reached across and grabbed his hand, holding it tightly for the remainder of the trip. As expected, her grandparents were delighted that she'd brought Kane and once both men and Erin were in the living room and Layla was in the kitchen with her grandmother, Maude made her approval obvious.

"He's so good with Erin," her grandmother said as she pulled an apple pie from the oven.

"I'm pretty sure he's one of those people who are good at everything," Layla remarked, and ignored the heat flaring way down, because while her grandmother was making one kind of comment, Layla was thinking something else altogether. Because if they were going to date, then they were eventually going to sleep together, and the idea of intimacy made her knees shake. Because instinct told her it would be mind-blowing and erotic and probably the best sex of her life. She'd had a loving and tender relationship with Frank, but she didn't kid herself when it came to Kane—because there was something effortlessly sexy about him. And she wasn't sure she was ready for it.

Lunch was fun and stress-free, mostly because

her grandparents clearly thought Kane had hung the moon and Erin remained either in his arms or on his lap for most of the afternoon. It was easy to see how much her daughter craved having a man in her life—a father figure—and she knew she was clutching on to Kane because he was the first man Layla had allowed into their sphere since Frank died. Plus, he was extraordinarily relaxed with her and made it look so easy.

On their way home, her grandparents had thanked him for coming to visit and welcomed him back any time.

"Thanks for coming with us today," Layla said.

"Thanks for inviting me. I like your grandparents."

She was ridiculously pleased. It was important to her that he got on with her only relatives. "Laurel said you come from a really happy and loving family."

"Laurel says a lot," he remarked, and raised his brows questioningly. "But she's right."

Layla chuckled. "We had a playdate yesterday with the kids. She's really nice."

"That she is. She and Adam were friends, and then lovers and then friends again. And then there was Larkin and that whole situation. Complicated," he added, and laughed a little. "But they worked it out."

"I'm not good at complicated."

"Me either," he said, and grinned. "So let's agree to try to not make this complicated, okay?"

"You want assurances?" she queried, smiling a little, because he was so easy to be around and her belly was loop-the-looping like there was no tomorrow. "That's a big call."

"I said try," he reminded her and grinned.

When they got home Erin was still dozing so Layla put her in her crib while Kane popped the leftovers her grandmother had given her into the refrigerator. When she met him in the kitchen he was resting his behind against the countertop. The awareness between them quickly thickened the air in the room and Layla remained by the door, away from temptation and, she suspected, damnation.

"So, would you like something to—"

"Layla," he said quietly, "would you come here?"

"I'm—"

"Please?"

She swallowed the nerves in her throat. He wasn't demanding. He wouldn't insist. That wasn't his way. If she stayed where she was, she suspected that would be the end of it. But she didn't. She walked straight into his arms.

He kissed her, long and slow and deep, and within seconds Layla forgot all coherent thought. She could only feel—his hands, his arms, the solid wall of his chest that she was pressed against, the erotic and gentle foray of his tongue in her mouth, the scent of his cologne swirling and assailing her senses. His hand strayed down her back and he drew tiny circles along her spine, urging her closer. Layla sighed against his mouth, offering him her lips, her mouth, her very sanity. While his one hand softly anchored her head, the other strayed down to her hip, curving over her bottom in a way that made her moan with pleasure. His knuckles then trailed up her rib cage and his thumb teased the underside of her breast, asking, not taking; he dipped and smoothed his palm over her with such languor she could barely draw breath.

She wasn't sure how long they stayed like that… just kissing…just touching…just getting to know each other. His hard planes and her soft curves. His insanely broad shoulders. Her aching, surging breasts. Maybe minutes. Maybe longer. But when he pulled back—when the kiss ended and he was staring into her eyes with hot burning intensity—for a second Layla thought she might pass out. But he held her upright, his strong arms resting loosely around her.

"Wow," she sighed, and then realized how foolish and inexperienced she must sound.

But he didn't mock her. There was nothing but pure, unadulterated desire in his expression. "That definitely takes us out of the friend zone."

"Where'd you learn to kiss like that?" she asked, and dropped her forehead against his chest, loving how she could hear his heart hammering behind his ribs.

"French class," he said, and chuckled.

Layla looked up and met his gaze. "I never took French class."

"Could have fooled me," he quipped, and grasped her chin.

He stayed for another hour and they had another two make-out sessions—one in the kitchen while she was making coffee, the other while they were sitting on the sofa, talking about their movie likes and dislikes. He left with a long, lingering kiss by the front door and the promise to call her the next day.

Layla waved goodbye and tried to ignore the disappointment in her heart, the heat in her limbs and the tingling on her lips. But one thing was abundantly clear.

She most definitely wanted a relationship with Kane Fortune.

Chapter Nine

Kane was amazed at how quickly and effortlessly he and Layla slipped into a routine over the course of the next week. Sometimes, it felt as though they'd known each other forever. They saw each other most days, and talked on the phone on the days they didn't. By Friday, Kane knew that whatever they were, the intensity of his feelings for Layla were stronger than any he'd had before. And of course, there was Erin, who seemed to light up whenever she saw him and who gave her affections so effortlessly it was impossible not to fall for her along with her mom.

And that was it in a nutshell.

He was falling in love. With them both.

The notion struck him with the force of a freight

train. He'd never really fancied himself in love before, not with Janine, not with the exchange student in high school. And it had spectacularly thrown him off course. He wasn't sure how such strong feelings has manifested so quickly, wasn't sure he even *wanted* to know. He did know that Layla wasn't anywhere near there yet.

"Ah, earth to Kane?"

Kane shook himself and got his concentration back to the current situation. Which was late Friday afternoon at the hotel, and a meeting with Callum and Grace. It was his last official day of work at the hotel, and he was supposed to be going through any last-minute issues. But other than the usual day-to-day dramas of running a hotel, everything seemed to be on track. Even his security team had reported no other suspicious activities, though the authorities were no closer to discovering if the balcony had actually been sabotaged last month. And because of that, Kane suspected they might never know the full story.

"Everything okay?" Callum asked.

Kane nodded. "Sure."

"New girlfriend, huh?"

He flinched. "What?"

"Adam told Wiley," Callum remarked. "Wiley told me."

"And me," Grace added with a smile.

"Small town, big family," Callum said and chuckled. "You know how it is, word gets around."

Kane was about to say something dismissive but by then it was too late because Grace was saying something about how sweet that was, and Callum was laughing softly.

"Yeah, so let's not talk about this anymore," Kane said, and got to his feet.

He made arrangements to meet up with Callum the following Monday to talk about expansion at Paz Spa and a couple of other jobs Callum had in the works, and then headed to Layla's, briefly stopping at a florist on the way.

She and Erin greeted him in the driveway and he kissed them both. Weird, he thought, how normal it all seemed. Like they were his own family. But of course, they weren't.

Not yet...

The notion settled in his stomach and instead of the usual panic he experienced when he considered anything even closely resembling commitment, Kane felt as though a kind of calming, soothing balm was smeared over his skin.

The realization shocked him to the core.

"Are you all right?" Layla asked, clearly seeing something in his expression.

He relaxed as the scent of her fragrance assailed him. "Fine. You?"

"Better now you're here," she replied, and pressed against him for a moment. "I've made tacos."

Kane smiled and grabbed the flowers from the passenger seat. "For you."

"Lavender roses," she said, and inhaled their heady scent. "Which are now my favorite flower."

They walked inside and into the kitchen, and Kane kept Erin occupied with some coloring at the table while Layla prepared dinner. He liked watching her cook. He liked the way she moved. In fact, he liked everything about her.

"How's the assignment coming along?" he asked, eager to get the image of her swaying hips out of his thoughts.

She looked up from her task. "Done. Although I have another one due soon on consumer behavior. I really need to get out and shop more," she added and grinned, "purely for research purposes of course."

"Do you like to shop?"

"I like shopping for baby things," she admitted. "Perhaps I should ask you to look over my assignment notes and get your take? You certainly have plenty of experience."

He didn't respond to her request. Didn't want her to see him struggling to read her notes. "What made you choose a marketing degree?"

She shrugged. "I've always been interested in the subject. If I could turn back the clock, I would have begun the course when I left school. But I needed to work and then one year morphed into the next and then I met Frank and my career aspirations faded for a while."

"By the sound of it, you grew up early."

She nodded. "I had to."

"What was she like?" Kane asked, knowing it was a tough subject for her, but sensing that she had something to say.

"Mom? Troubled," she said quietly. "She still is."

"Do you hear from her much?"

"No," she replied. "Once a year maybe. Some years she remembers my birthday. Other years, not so much."

Kane thought of his own parents and realized how lucky he was. "Speaking of moms," he said, and made a face, "I need to call mine. I haven't spoken to her much lately."

"Are you her favorite?" she asked bluntly, but with a broad smile.

Kane laughed. "Well, you couldn't blame her, right?"

She chuckled as she brought a tray to the table, piled high with warm taco shells and assorted fillings.

Kane quickly cleared away the paper and crayons and placed Erin in her high chair. Layla carefully placed some grated cheese, ground beef and tomato pieces on a plate and the baby immediately began eating.

"Your daughter likes her food," he said, and grinned.

"Her appetite has increased in the last couple of weeks," Layla said, nodding. "And she's been really happy lately. No crying at day care."

Kane met Layla's gaze. "That must reassure you."

She nodded. "It does. Even though she was only six months old I'm certain Erin felt her father's passing deeply—that's why she has the separation issues."

"Were they close?"

"Frank adored her. He was ten years older than me and had been married before, but they hadn't been able to have children. I know the stress of the failed IVF treatments was one of the reasons they divorced. We met about a year later."

"Was it love at first sight?"

She looked at him. "Not exactly. We were friends for a year before we started dating. Then we sort of fell in love. Then we got married and when Erin came along I'd never seen him so happy. He used to stand by her crib and look at her when she was a newborn, as though she was the most precious thing in the world."

Kane experienced something he wasn't prepared for—something that felt a lot like envy. And he wondered if he'd ever have that privilege of looking at a baby of his own. He watched Erin shove food into her mouth and it made him smile. "Well, she is kinda precious."

"I think so," Layla said, and then regarded him with a strange, almost faraway look in her eyes. "He would have liked you. He would have called you a good egg."

Kane asked a question that had been simmering inside him for days. "Do you still love him?"

"I'll always love him," she replied. "He's Erin's father and my husband. But he's gone," she added, and met Kane's gaze.

His stomach took a dive. She still loved him. Of course she did. It was exactly what he expected her to say. What he didn't expect was how uncertain it made him feel.

They began to eat and for the following hour they were entertained by Erin's antics. When they were done, Layla took the baby to get changed for bed and Kane stayed in the kitchen and cleaned up. It occurred to him that it had become something of a routine between them. It also occurred to him how easily he'd slipped into that routine.

When Layla returned, minus Erin, she was smiling. "She wants you to read her a story."

He stilled, his insides clenching. "How do you know that?"

"Because she grabbed the book from me and said *no* in a very determined voice," she replied. "I know my daughter…she wants you, not me."

Kane hesitated for a few seconds and then exhaled. "Sure."

He headed to the nursery and spotted Erin standing up in her crib in a pink onesie, her bangs falling over her forehead, and he noticed how much she looked like Layla. She was holding a book and waved it at him when he entered the room. Kane sat in the chair by the crib, took the book from her chubby hands and looked around the room, noticing the mobile lovingly hung from the ceiling, the wallpaper with tiny yellow ducks on it, the pile of teddy bears in one corner and the soft pink light on the table by the door.

"Okay, kiddo, what do you want tonight? Frogs and princesses, or bears that love honey?"

She giggled so delightfully his insides rolled over. "Book! Dada!"

Something uncurled in his chest and he realized that in a matter of weeks, so many things he'd believed of himself had changed. For one, the idea of a toddler calling him *Dada* would have sent him running for the hills. It would have scratched at that commitment-phobic part of himself he'd always held on to like a lifeline, and made him end things as quickly as they'd started. But, unbelievably, he didn't want to bail. He wanted to stay.

Forever...

Kane placed the book on the carpet and started talking. "Once upon a time, there was a beautiful princess named Erin..."

* * *

Layla wasn't sure who was more mesmerized by his deep voice—her or her utterly entranced daughter. She'd called him Dada again…and Kane hadn't corrected her because he was kind and thoughtful and obviously didn't want to upset her daughter. Deep down, she knew why Erin had been happier lately. Why she was relaxed. Why she was laughing more and sleeping better. It was because of Kane. He was such a calming presence and Layla knew her daughter was smitten with him.

As he told her a story about a princess in a castle who fell in love with a gentle woodcutter, Layla got lost in the seductive melody of his words. She looked at the book on the carpet and wondered what magic he possessed that he could make up a story so effortlessly. It would obviously have been easier for him to read the book, but he clearly wasn't a man who took the easy option in any regard.

When the story was over, Erin was lying on her belly, relaxed and ready for sleep.

She watched as he got to his feet, patted the child gently on the back and then turned, noticing her for the first time. "She's almost out."

"Thank you."

Layla lingered by Erin's crib for a few moments and noticed that Kane had left her alone to say good-night to her daughter. Once she left the nursery and met him in the living room, he was sitting on one of the single chairs and looked deep in thought.

"Something wrong?"

"No."

"She really adores you," Layla said, and noticed how his gaze narrowed. "It's amazing how quickly that's happened. She called you Dada again?"

He nodded. "Yeah."

"Well, that's one person who lives in this house who doesn't have any trouble expressing her feelings," Layla admitted with a dose of self-derision. "But I'm sorry if it makes you feel uncomfortable."

"It doesn't," he replied quietly, his elbows on his knees. "It makes me want to tell her that I'm right here and not going anywhere."

Layla's breath caught tightly in her throat. "But you can't because you don't know that. *We* don't know that."

"No," he said. "I guess we don't."

"People leave," she said, and suddenly her rib cage was shuddering. "People walk away. People die."

He met her gaze with dark, blistering intensity. "No one can promise not to die, Layla."

And then, without any warning, without her usual wall of strength coming up to protect her, tears formed and burned the backs of her eyes before quickly spilling over onto her cheeks. The lonely hollowness that always made her ache inside rose up, tormenting her for a few seconds, reminding her how alone she truly was.

But then, somehow, the loneliness was abruptly swept away. Because Kane's arms were around her and her shaking body was pressed against his. With her head buried in his neck, she drew strength from the comfort of his touch. His big hands were gentle, his shoulders broad and strong, like a shield for the ache in her heart.

"You're okay," he said softly, his voice as soothing as it had been when he'd told Erin a bedtime story. "I've got you."

And for the first time in forever, Layla cried.

Part of her wasn't even sure why, or what had caused the dam to burst. Perhaps it was the affection she'd witnessed between Kane and her daughter that made her mourn for everything Frank would miss, or perhaps it was the quiet camaraderie she experienced whenever Kane was close, or that his very presence reminded her of a life she'd once had and taken for granted. A life she sometimes could barely remember. Whatever the reason, all she knew was that in Kane's gentle embrace, she didn't feel alone. She didn't feel as though she was battling to keep herself strong and resilient and the perfect picture of someone who had it all together.

Somehow, they ended up on the couch and Layla was curled against him. One palm flattened on his chest, the steady beat of his heart so comforting she experienced a heavy lethargy in her limbs as her body relaxed. His hands were like tonic, soothing the unhappiness away, holding her nape while the other settled in the small of her back.

"I was so mad at him," she said, the words coming out in a rush of breath against his chest.

Kane was silent for a moment. "Frank?"

She swallowed hard. "Mad at him for leaving," she said, voicing the words to someone other than herself for the first time. "I know it's irrational."

"Feelings aren't irrational," he assured her. "We all experienced things we think we shouldn't in our life. Losing the one person you love above all others—that's a big deal, Layla. Give yourself a break. It's okay to be mad at him."

"Is it?" she queried. "If things had happened the other way around, I know he wouldn't be mad at me. That wasn't his way."

He reached and grasped her chin, gently tilting her face to meet his. "That's the thing when you paint someone as perfect and without flaws, it's impossible to live up to the same standard. I'm sure he would have gone through the same series of emotions, Layla. That's what grieving is. It's getting through…it's letting yourself be mad and disappointed and plain old resentful."

Layla pressed closer and kissed him softly. "Thank you," she said on a sigh. "For understanding. For being so sweet."

His eyes darkened and he returned the kiss. "Yeah, I'm real sweet," he said with a self-derisive grin. "But since all I want to do is spend the night, I'd better bail."

He kissed her softly and she held on to him.

He left soon after, and Layla was more reluctant to have him leave than ever before. The intimacy between them had gone up a few notches over the course of the evening and she felt herself getting drawn deeper and closer to him. She knew he felt it, too…knew he was thinking about the next step in their relationship. Layla wasn't under any illusions—men and women usually thought about sex differently. And the truth was, she *did* want to make love with Kane. She was achingly attracted to him, and more than that, they had developed an emotional connection that was undeniable.

But…she simply didn't know if she was ready.

And she didn't want to screw up their budding relationship.

They'd made plans to spend the following day together and it was eleven in the morning when Kane picked up her and Erin. There was a basket in the back seat of his Ranger and he quickly explained he'd stopped by Roja and Nicole had pulled together a picnic hamper for him. They drove to a park in town, one with a pond and shady trees and a lovely family vibe. It was a cool day, but the sky was brilliantly blue and clear. There were several other families already settled at the park and Layla quickly spread out the checkered picnic blanket and got Erin settled. Her daughter looked so adorable in her denim overalls, pink fleecy sweater and purple shoes, and she figured that to an onlooker, they appeared very much like your average family out for the day.

"You look nice," he remarked as he took off his jacket and sat down beside her.

In dark jeans and khaki Henley and navy sweater that did little to disguise his broad shoulders, muscular thighs and chest, and unbelievable washboard belly, Layla could barely keep her eyes off him.

"You, too," she said. "But then, looking good is probably as natural to you as breathing."

He chuckled. "Is that some roundabout way of saying you find me attractive?"

"Nothing roundabout about it," she said, and laughed. "I'm sure you know. Even my grandmother thinks you're sexy."

He laughed so loud that Erin started giggling, and Layla ignored the heat burning her ears and face and quickly checked out the contents of the basket, finding sandwiches and fruit, cheese and crackers, bottled water and soda, and a juice box for Erin.

"Incidentally," he said a little while later as they ate, and in between Erin passing him grapes, "I told my mother about you."

Layla's brows shot up. "You did?"

"She called me this morning," he explained, and

shrugged one shoulder. "Asked me why I haven't called her. I said I've been preoccupied with two beautiful girls."

Layla experienced a twinge behind her ribs. It would be so easy to fall for him. Too easy.

"And what did she say?"

"Well," Kane replied, and grabbed her hand, entwining their fingers in such a startlingly intimate way that her toes actually curled, "she was mad at first, when she thought I was dating two women. Then I explained about you and Erin and she quickly came around."

She wanted to swoon. "Have she and your dad visited Rambling Rose?"

"A couple of times. Not for a while. I know they want to see Larkin again, so perhaps Adam can persuade them to come sooner rather than later."

"I guess babies have a way of bringing families together," she said and looked at Erin. "Weddings, too."

His eyes widened. "I'm sure my mom thinks so."

Layla knew she was skirting around some suggestive ground, but she was curious. "Not your dad?"

"Depends who's getting married I suppose. If it's a Fortune wedding, not so much. He thinks bad things tend to happen when too many Fortunes get together."

Layla heard the disappointment and frustration in his voice. "Oh, I don't know about that," she said, and tried to lighten his mood, tightening her fingers for a

second before she withdrew her hand and picked at
the food on her paper plate. "I think plenty of good
can come out of it."

"You may be a little biased," he said, and flopped
back on the blanket, popping sunglasses onto the
bridge of his nose, one hand curled under his head,
the other resting on his chest. The image was so insanely masculine she caught the breath in her throat
and darted her gaze away, trying to think of anything other than his flat belly, rock-hard thighs and
unbelievable shoulders. She'd had plenty of practice
touching different parts of him over the last week
and had never known a man with such a perfectly
proportioned physique. And the thought of seeing
him without clothes had entered her mind way too
many times since they'd first met.

"How many tattoos do you have?"

He looked up. "Huh?"

"You told me you hid your first tattoo from your
parents for a year," she remarked, hoping he didn't
think she was imagining him naked—even though
she was.

"Three," he replied, and crossed his ankles.
"You?"

"None," she admitted, grinning. "So, where are
they?"

He stayed lying flat and pulled up the sleeve on
his shirt, exposing the tattoo she'd seen before—the
Celtic braid circling his biceps. Then he tugged the

shirt off one shoulder and she saw a pair of eagle wings. "The other one we'll leave for another time."

Heat surged over her skin and she swallowed hard. "I guess you have women throwing themselves at you all the time, right?"

At that instant, Erin ditched her plate and climbed across his feet. "At the moment, yeah."

She laughed, because despite the undercurrent of awareness, the companionship between them was relaxed and easy, and she loved the way he was so naturally accepting of her daughter's attention.

Loved...

The thought startled her. Was that it? Was she falling in love with him? Did she even believe she was capable of loving someone other than Frank? Did she want to? The thing was, she didn't know him that well and her overcautious mind screamed out all of the reasons why she shouldn't think she was falling for him. For starters, it was too soon. She was still missing her husband. She wasn't the kind of woman who fell hard and fast. She had a child to think about first and foremost and then quickly realized that point was moot because Erin adored him.

And despite the monologue in her head about things going too fast, she wanted more of him. She wanted to see more. To know more. To be a part of more.

"Ah, Kane," she said, hesitating a little. "Do you think that I'd be able to see your house?"

He flicked the sunglasses up. "Now?"

She shrugged. "Sometime. I mean, we always meet at my place and I just thought it would be a nice change to spend some time where you live."

"We can go when we're finished here if you want."

"Sure."

They stayed at the park for another hour, eating and keeping Erin occupied. Then they took her for a short walk, both holding one of her hands, swinging her gently in the air between them. The poignancy of the moment wasn't lost on Layla—it was exactly the kind of family day she'd longed for, and seeing her daughter so happy and so clearly enamored with Kane, she fought the battle inside her head that told her they were moving too fast. By one thirty, Erin was clearly ready for a nap and so they packed up the picnic and headed into town.

His house was small, but neat and tidy and not the bachelor pad she'd expected. For one, there was a high chair at the kitchen table and several toy boxes in the living room. She noticed a gaming console, several sporting magazines scattered on the coffee table and numerous piles of books on the sideboard.

"You like to read, huh?" Layla asked as she smoothed Erin's hair, and her daughter snuggled in her arms.

He stilled, standing rigid behind the sofa. "That surprises you?"

She shook her head. "With the way you can make

up fairy tales to get my daughter to sleep—not at all." She walked around the sofa. "You should write a book."

His mouth flattened and then he laughed humorlessly. "Well, that's the first time that's ever been said to me. It would give my brothers a good laugh."

There was something odd about his tone and she frowned, for two reasons—firstly, because she felt as though she'd said something that was somehow insensitive. And secondly, that after such a short acquaintance, she actually could recognize his reaction. It occurred to her that he considered himself the same kind of workingman as his father—good with his hands, able to fix things, the kind of man who wore blue flannel with the same stereotyping that a banker might wear a suit.

"You don't have to wear a suit to be—"

"What?" he asked harshly, cutting her off. "Smart?"

"I didn't mean anything by it," she said quickly. "If I did then I—"

"I'm dyslexic."

Layla stared at him, absorbing his quiet announcement. Again, she heard something in his tone, as though he expected disappointment, or perhaps censure. She thought about the storytelling, the way he didn't ever seem to do more than glance at menus and how he'd discarded the instructions when building the playhouse for Erin.

Her daughter stirred in her arms. "Do you have somewhere I can put her down for an hour or so? She's sleepy."

"Sure," he replied. "I've got a crib here for Larkin."

Minutes later, Erin was settled in the small bedroom in the crib. It took about thirty seconds for her daughter to fall asleep and Layla went back to the living room. There was a long silence and she watched him, standing by the sideboard, hands in his pockets.

"I'm sorry if I offended you," she said quietly.

"You didn't," he replied. "And I didn't mean to snap at you."

Layla moved around the sofa and sat down. "Would you tell me about it?"

He shrugged his magnificent shoulders. "There's not a lot to tell."

Layla saw his closed-off expression and her insides rolled over. "Kane...please?"

He met her gaze and sighed. "Okay. I was diagnosed when I was eleven. I had trouble with learning in school—poor attention span, acting up in class. And I struggled with reading and writing. I was a D student at best. My mom kept at the teachers until they realized it was more than a behavior issue. Looking back, it was very clear I was typecast as the slow kid—you know, the one good at sports but who couldn't read well. Words terrified me back then."

Layla's instinct was to stride across the room and hold him close, to soothe the obvious pain in his voice with her touch and compassion and understanding. "But you graduated from high school, went to college, got your degree, right?"

He nodded. "Yeah. Hardest thing I've ever done," he admitted. "I got into college on a football scholarship, but blew my knee out in the second year. After that, I worked two jobs to keep up with the tuition. My parents helped out as much as they could, of course, and I spent a lot of time with an occupational therapist in my teens and early twenties."

Layla thought about how easy she'd found school, even while moving around every six or so months. And how she took for granted her ability to read and comprehend the written word. Even the challenges she had with the course she was studying now was more about time management than any difficulty with the content.

"And all the books?" she asked, gesturing to the piles on the sideboard.

"I try to read every day."

"It helps?" she asked softly, eager to know more, but not wanting to push him too hard.

He nodded and walked a few steps, running a hand across a stack of books. "It keeps words in my head...makes me feel less like the dumb jock everyone called me in high school."

Layla didn't miss the way his voice lowered and it wasn't hard to fill in the gaps. "I'm guessing that a girl called you that?"

He nodded again. "Girlfriend, actually."

"It hurt you." It wasn't a question, but she said it as gently as she could.

"It made me better at disguising my flaws," he replied and smiled humorlessly.

"Like knowing what you want to order at a restaurant or story-time with a two-year-old?"

"Yeah," he replied. "Exactly. I have a voice to text app on my phone and have trained myself to use the strategies I learned when I was younger."

Her admiration for him spiked. So did everything else she was feeling. "By the way, it's not a flaw," she assured him. "You're so together," she said and smiled. "I envy that about you."

"Smoke and mirrors," he replied.

Layla's heart rolled over. "Thank you for telling me. It means a lot that you trust me with something so personal." She paused for a moment, choosing her next words carefully, and almost holding her breath as she spoke. "Kane, would you like to come over tonight?"

He smiled. "As long as you let me buy dinner."

Layla warmed from head to toe and felt as though she was standing on a precipice and about to make a monumental decision—one of the biggest of her life. She took a breath and met his gaze straight on. "In that case, I'll make breakfast."

And they both knew exactly what that meant.

Chapter Ten

In all his life, Kane had never been nervous about sex. He'd lost his virginity at fifteen with the girl who lived across the road and who had then married one of his friends a decade later. He'd had no short supply of hookups in college and since then, if he wanted to get laid, it was never too difficult to find someone he was attracted to.

But this…this was a whole lot of different.

Layla McCarthy was not a one-night, or even a one-month, stand kind of woman and he, Kane knew with certainty, wasn't that guy when he was around her. And it was a startling revelation.

They were back at her home by four and Kane carried Erin inside, who was still a little bleary-eyed after her nap. She lay on the living room carpet and Kane watched her for a moment while Layla put the remainders from their picnic lunch in the refrigerator.

"She looks so peaceful and so happy," Layla said when she joined him in the living room doorway, her head just below his shoulder. "I know she's had a lovely day. So have I."

"Me, too," he admitted. And it was the truth. Spending time with Layla and Erin had quickly become almost as intrinsic to him as breathing.

"We could sit down," she suggested, and he followed her lead, sitting on the sofa, his legs stretched out in front of him.

Once she was beside him, Kane grasped her hand. "You smell nice," he said. "Like flowers."

"I think it's only shampoo."

He rested his arm along the back of the couch and twirled a few strands of her hair around his fingers. "Still, it's nice. The again, everything about you is nice."

Erin noticed them sitting down and made her way over to the couch, standing between their knees and then holding out her arms to him. Kane lifted her onto the couch and he noticed she was holding her favorite book.

"I'll read it to her," Layla said, clearly picking up on his reluctance, and took the book from her daughter's hands.

Kane instantly saw Erin's disappointed expression and shook his head, grasping the book from Layla. "It's okay."

"You don't have to if you don't—"

"Layla." He said her name quietly but firmly. "It's fine."

He meant it. Kane was savvy enough to know that Erin had quickly become attached to him and he felt compelled to not disappoint her. And he trusted Layla. Perhaps more than he'd ever trusted anyone. He wondered how it could have happened so fast… how they had built such an incredible connection in a span of mere weeks. And then he wondered why it mattered how long they'd known one another. And with Erin looking at him with such hope and wonder, it wasn't surprising he'd fallen for them so quickly.

Once Erin was settled beside him, Kane flipped the page, took a long breath and stared at the words on the page. For a few awkward seconds, while he steeled his nerves and pulled on his guts, he thought it would be like school all over again. He would fumble. He'd feel the familiar sense of embarrassment. Humiliation. The words would taunt and mock him. His eyes wouldn't be able to see what his brain was telling him. He'd feel like a fool…or worse, like he was less than normal. Stupid. Unintelligent. Weak.

And then Layla's hand touched his thigh and strength seeped through him like water running into a dry creek bed. He also knew she wouldn't judge him. That wasn't her way.

"I have some laundry to fold," she said and got to her feet, walking into the adjoining room. He could still pick up the scent of her fragrance and it offered comfort, touching his senses in a way that nothing else seemed to do.

"Wead," Erin insisted, tapping the book. "Pwease."

It took a couple of minutes, but he eventually relaxed and it wasn't anywhere near the nightmare his humiliation barometer might have predicted. For one, he was pretty sure Erin didn't notice if he faltered over a word, or how he spoke slowly and precisely to avoid making too many mistakes. Thankfully, it was a short picture book about wild animals, and it was over soon enough.

He placed the book on the coffee table and noticed Layla was still folding laundry, even refolding from the look of the clothes stacks on the table. He left Erin playing with a collection of stuffed toys and walked into the adjoining room.

"Hey," he said and then leaned over and kissed her cheek. "Thanks."

"For what?"

"The space," he replied. "The lack of judgment."

She smiled so beautifully he experienced a tight knot in the center of his chest. "Thank you for being so wonderful with her. It means a lot."

Kane's insides tightened even further and he nodded. "Well, she's easy to love. Like her mom," he added, and then rocked back on his feet like his heels were on fire the moment he realized what he'd said. Love? It was crazy—they barely knew each other. He was imagining things because he wanted her so much. It was just his desire talking. Just what was below his belt suddenly doing the thinking. "Ah... so what do you want me to order for dinner? Mexican? Pizza?"

"Pizza sounds great," she replied, looking like she couldn't wait to get away from him all of a sudden, and gathered Erin in her arms. "I'm going to get her bathed and fed early since she's had a big day and looks really tired."

Kane ignored the way his heart hammered and nodded. "Sure."

He remained in the living room after they left, and flicked through his cell phone for the number of the pizza place. He arranged for the delivery and met Layla in the kitchen after she'd bathed Erin. He sat at the table while Erin ate her dinner, then cleaned up while Layla took her to bed.

"She's already out like a light," she said when she returned. "We wore her out today with all that fresh air and sunshine."

Before Kane could reply, the doorbell rang. "Our dinner."

He paid for the pizza and returned to the kitchen.

Layla had laid out plates and paper napkins and there was a bottle of wine and two glasses on the table.

"Red," she said, shrugging. "It's all I had."

"Red is fine," he said, and sat down.

For the following hour they ate, drank and talked about a whole bunch of things. Except the elephant that was dancing in the room. *Sex.* It was vibrating between them as though it had a life force of its own. He'd experienced desire and attraction before—but the buildup had never been as intense as it was with Layla.

"You know," he said around seven, when the tension was so high he was exhausted trying to deny it, "if you'd prefer I go home, I will."

She flipped the lid on the pizza box and grabbed her wineglass and the baby monitor off the counter. "Actually," she said, and got to her feet, "I thought I'd take a bath. Would you like to join me?"

Kane gulped. Her expression was one of pure seduction and he wasn't quite prepared for how it made him feel. He wondered if she knew her eyes darkened when she spoke and then wondered if they'd do the same when she made love. He nodded, grabbing his glass and the half-full bottle, and followed her down the hall and into the master suite, his gaze focused on the gentle sway of her hips as she moved. The bedroom was large, decorated in muted hues of blue and beige. His gut twitched when he noticed the huge king-size bed and spotted a small framed picture of her husband on the bedside table. But she was still walking, heading across the room and into the bathroom.

She placed the wineglass and the monitor on the vanity and opened the taps, adding scented bubbles to the water. Steam began to swirl around the room and he watched, mesmerized, as she slipped off her shoes.

"You know, I don't think I've ever had a bubble bath," he admitted, swallowing hard.

"You don't know what you're missing," she said, smiling. "I love them."

"Did you used to—" He stopped himself from asking the question burning on his tongue. Because he didn't really want to know what she used to do with her husband. It was none of his business. She had a life before they met, just as he had. "Sorry... forget I said that."

"I was married to a man I loved," she said quietly, sucking in a long breath. "And I used to love making love with him. But I'm not about to start comparing lovers, Kane, because he's not here. However, I am," she said, her voice a little firmer. "And you are. At the moment I think that's all that matters."

Kane remained by the door, totally mesmerized as she began removing her clothes. First she unzipped the skirt and slid it down her hips until it landed in a soft pool of fabric at her feet. Then she unbuttoned the top she wore and soon it also floated to the floor.

In her white cotton bra and panties she looked incredibly sexy, all curves and smooth, pale skin, with her hair flowing over her shoulders. She smiled, her expression so seductive he was floored by the wave of desire and longing surging through his veins. He'd never found anyone as attractive as he did Layla.

"You really are beautiful," he said.

Her hands skimmed over her hips. "I'm glad you think so. But I have all the usual insecurities and my whole body is shaking right now."

Of course, he knew that. She was the mother of a small child. Her hips were fuller than what was probably considered fashionable, but the gentle flare below her waist and the curve of her thighs were undeniably sexy. Her breasts were rounder than he'd ever let himself imagine and they almost seemed to surge forward beneath his gaze. He wanted to taste her skin, inhale the heady scent of her, trace his fingers along her thighs, her waist, her spine.

"You're beautiful," he said again, and ditched his T-shirt. Her heard her gasp softly and he smiled. Her eyes seemed to feast on him for a moment and when his hands hovered at his belt, he spoke again. "For the record, you're not the only one with insecurities."

Her brows rose. "Really?"

Kane shrugged. "I know you don't do this casually," he said above the sound of the water flowing into the tub.

"No," she said agreeably. "I don't."

"It's a lot to...live up to, you know," he admitted, a heavy flush crawling up his neck. "I want to...do it right."

"I don't imagine you've ever had any complaints?" she queried, her eyes darkening.

Kane shrugged. "No...but I get the sense that being with you will be..." He paused, looking for the right words, desperate to sound like he was in control of what he was doing and feeling, and then failing spectacularly. "I guess what I'm trying to say is that I know it will be different. I'm very... drawn to you."

"Me, too. And you're right, I don't do this casually. I never have. I've told you already that the only man I've ever been intimate with is my husband."

Kane's insides were jumping all over the place. As far as admissions went, he figured it was a huge step for Layla to admit she had feelings for him. It was a huge step for him, too. "Just so you know, this isn't some casual hookup for me, Layla. And I would never intentionally hurt you."

"I know."

He took a couple of strides and eased her against him, kissing her long and deep and harder than he had before. She moaned low in her throat and her arms looped around him, holding his hips. The steam added to the hot energy between them and soon kissing wasn't enough.

Kane ditched his jeans as she removed her underwear and within seconds they were in the tub together, her naked body sliding against him. Of course, he knew they weren't going to make love in the water; for one, he didn't have protection in place and he figured all they'd do was slosh water and bubbles onto the tile floor. But it was insanely sensual feeling her wet, slippery skin against his. He lay back, resting his head against the tub, and she settled between his legs, her back pressed against his chest. Kane's arms moved around her, anchoring her in place, his chin resting gently atop her head. They didn't kiss at first, didn't caress each other; they simply lay in the water, his hands holding steady under her breasts, her hands resting on his knees. He was aroused, and by the way her nipples were pebbled and hard, so was she, but there was something sinfully erotic and at the same time calming and companionable about the moment.

And as they talked, as they listened, it occurred to him that they had the whole making-love-and-then-talking-afterward thing backward. Then it also occurred to him that they had it exactly right.

Once the talking was over and their words trailed off, her fingers moved up and down his thighs, and Kane slipped one hand down her soft belly, settling between her legs, and he caressed her gently. She pressed back against him, arching her spine, moaning her pleasure at his touch. He didn't make her climax, although he suspected that he could have, but he continued to touch her and feel her arch against him. He wasn't sure how long they stayed like that—just gently touching, just wet skin sliding against wet skin as he gently kissed her neck.

"Wanna get outta here?" he whispered into her ear when it became too much to bear.

She nodded and rolled, sluicing water over the edge of the tub, cradled against him, her body slipping against his erotically. The ends of her hair were wet, her eyes wide and languorous. She reached up and touched his face and Kane experienced a hot, sharp pain in the center of his chest.

I love her...

The words toyed around with his mind. *It's just sex*, he reminded himself. He had her in his arms and his brain was fused with the lower half of his anatomy. People didn't fall in love in a matter of weeks. Or more precisely, *he* didn't fall in love in that amount of time. He was always in control. Always in charge of his emotions. Not this mindless, lust-charged thing he was feeling in that moment. But he couldn't ditch the feeling, couldn't quite figure out *what* he was feeling.

They got out of the tub and dried off, and he took a condom from his wallet and placed it on the nightstand when they somehow made it to the bed. The bedside light illuminated the room enough for him to see the heady flush coloring her skin. Kane kissed her hotly, drawing her down against the sheets, finding her tongue and wrapping his own around it in a way that made his libido surge. He kissed her neck, her shoulders, her breasts, drawing her hot, tight nipple into his mouth, and experienced such acute and mind-blowing pleasure at the feel of the budded flesh against his lips that he could barely stagger through a breath. Her hands were all over him, his back and shoulders, his hips, almost frantic as they moved across his skin. When he kissed her, she kissed him back and there was nothing hesitant about her touch, nothing unsure. He trailed kisses down her breasts, her rib cage, her belly, lingering at her navel for a moment before going down farther. She arched her back as he caressed her intimately with his lips and tongue, saying his name over and over as a wave of pleasure convulsed through her, her small hands gripping the bedsheets.

Kane quickly grabbed the condom, sheathed himself and settled between her thighs, holding his weight on his arms. He met her gaze, keeping the visual connection strong and intense. "So…is this okay?"

She nodded. "More than okay. Perfect."

Then she pressed closer, raising her hips to meet his erection. He entered her slowly, finding both comfort and pleasure within her. Nothing had ever felt as good. Nothing ever would, he suspected. In that moment, she was his; he was hers. They were joined together in the most intimate way and he felt that connection through to his bones and to the very depths of his soul.

And Kane knew in that moment, without a doubt, that he was completely in love with her.

Layla felt the magic of his touch and possession. She'd felt passion before and had enjoyed a good sexual relationship with Frank. Not that she wanted to make comparisons, because she didn't. But, holy heaven, Kane was so blisteringly attractive and made her yearn as she never had before. He was hard to her soft, strength to her weakness, and yet so incredibly gentle and generous. He made love like he did everything else, with concentration and quiet control. And humor, too, she thought as he kissed her mouth, her jaw, her neck. She moved as he moved, she held his back, his hips, clung to his insanely broad shoulders and experienced a connection she'd believed was lost to her forever.

"You feel so good," he whispered against her neck.

"So do you," she murmured.

Layla moved her hips in unison and felt pleasure spike again as he created a sensual rhythm that was an erotic assault to her senses. He kissed her mouth, deeply, hotly, as though he couldn't get enough of the taste of her tongue or the sound of her moans. It was wild and passionate and everything she'd known it would be. He moved above her, muscles flexing and rippling, his body so acutely masculine it defied belief. The pleasure built and she arched her spine, feeling him tense above her, and they went on a wild ride, rising up and exploding in a white-hot rush of release that left them both panting and breathless.

Kane moved, excusing himself for a moment, and headed to the bathroom. When he returned a minute later, Layla was lying on her side and he quickly rejoined her in the big bed.

"Well," she said, and traced a fingertip down his jaw. "That was quite something."

He nodded and slipped beneath the covers, quickly settling her against him. "No regrets?"

She sighed with contentment. "Not right now."

He grasped her chin and tilted it up, then met her gaze. "I'm glad. Regrets are pointless."

She knew she'd have them. Sanity would set back in and she would do her usual thing and dwell. But in that moment she simply smiled and pressed closer. "So, you *are* good at everything, then?"

"I'm pretty sure this was a joint effort."

Layla laughed and warmth pooled way down low in her belly. "You're good for my ego."

"I'm kind of hoping I'm good for all of you."

She knew what he was asking...and suspected she knew what he was feeling. He'd said as much earlier when they were talking about how fond he was of Erin. *She's easy to love...like her mom.* Layla was well aware that Kane had feelings for her. The truth was, she had them for him, too. But she wasn't ready to admit it. She wasn't anywhere near ready.

"Kane," she said on a sigh. "You know that I—"

"Don't," he said, cutting her off, placing his thumb gently against her mouth. "Let's not have any serious talk just yet, okay? How about we simply enjoy this moment and think about the rest of it later?"

He was right. They had plenty of time to worry about where their relationship was heading. Plenty of time for Layla to scurry back into her hole of insecurity and fear. But for now, she wanted to touch him some more, feel him some more, experience the pleasure of his kiss and the heat of his hands against her skin.

"So," she said and traced her fingertips along the tattoo on his chest. "Now that I know where all your ink is, I never imagined I'd like tattoos so much... but on you it's very sexy."

He chuckled. "Speaking of being good for someone's ego."

"Make love to me again," she whispered against his throat. "That's all I want right now."

The following hour was another voyage of incredible sensual discovery and Layla matched every step, every touch, every erotic thrust. She learned what he liked, knew she could drive him crazy by kissing the skin below his earlobe or the ticklish spot at the base of his rib cage. He had a lot of energy, too, she discovered, and used every ounce of it to draw as much response from her as he could. As his hands worked their magic over her, she offered her complete surrender, discovering that taking reaped its own reward. He was an attentive and unselfish lover and she reached the peak of pleasure again and again, until finally she was almost incoherent and mindless and dropped into a sublime and easy sleep.

When she woke up she saw that it was past midnight. The bathroom light was still on and she got up and padded across the room, making out Kane's masculine silhouette beneath the sheet draped up to his waist. He was asleep, and the faint sound of his breathing and the rhythmic rise and fall of his chest were hypnotic. She watched him for a moment, admiring his skin, his tattoos, his muscles, the breadth of his shoulders.

Instead of going back to bed, Layla slipped on her robe and slippers and headed to check on Erin. Her daughter was fast asleep, snoring softly, holding on to the leg of her favorite doll with one small fist. A wave of love washed over her and Layla looked at the framed picture sitting on the highboy near the door. It was of Erin and her father, taken on the day she was born. Frank was holding her as though she was the most precious thing in the world. He said it was the happiest day of his life and he would tell her stories about how he would always be there for them. But six months later he was gone.

Her heart suddenly felt heavy and Layla shook off

the feeling, along with the heat burning behind her eyes. She wouldn't let the guilt in. Not tonight. Grateful that her daughter was sleeping soundly, Layla left the room and padded down the hallway. The kitchen light was still on, the pizza box still where they'd left it. She spent a few minutes cleaning up before filling up the kettle to make tea. She was just about to pour the hot water into a mug when she heard Kane's voice behind her.

"Hey, everything okay?"

She turned and nodded, saw that he was wearing his Henley and jeans, but the button was undone and they sat low on his hips. Her mouth turned dry at the sight of him and she wondered if she'd ever had such an intense physical reaction to anyone else, or ever would again. With his unbuttoned jeans and ruffled hair, he looked like a billboard advertisement for sexy. "Yes. I just checked on Erin and then realized I wanted tea."

"Mind if I join you?"

"Of course not," she said, and grabbed another mug. "Would you like a cookie? Or chocolate?"

"I don't really like chocolate."

Her eyes widened with mock astonishment. "Oh, heavens, now you tell me."

He chuckled. "Didn't want to scare you off. What about you?" he asked as he came into the room and sat at the table. "Anything you dislike?"

"Spiders," she replied quickly. "And I'm not too

fond of heights. Cherry cola. Gladioli. And the color orange."

"And what do you love?" he asked, his elbows on the table, his chin resting on the back of one hand.

"Erin," she replied, feeling awareness quickly swirl between them. "Rain on the rooftop. Books. Quiet nights on the sofa. Dark chocolate. Lavender roses."

"That's quite a diverse list."

She shrugged and smiled. "I'm a complicated woman. What about you?"

"Dislikes?" he mused. "Musical theater. Berets. Fluffy white cats."

Layla laughed, the tension easing from her body. "And what do you love?" she asked as she walked to the table with their tea and sat down.

"Rain on the rooftop. Books. Quiet nights on the sofa."

"Smooth," she said, and looked at him over the rim of her mug. "Do you really like books?"

He nodded. "Yeah. Although over the years it's been something of a love-hate relationship."

"Can I ask you something about the dyslexia?"

"It's not off-limits to you."

But it was to others? Was that what he was saying? "Do you worry about how people might perceive you because of it?" she asked gently.

"Sometimes. Not so much these days," he replied. "But if you're actually asking if I've been judged in the past because of it, then yes, many times. At school, in college, at work. People can be insensitive and sometimes cruel. But my family has always been really supportive, so I was lucky."

Her heart ached thinking about it. "And in relationships?"

"Honestly, I've never told anyone I've dated."

Her brows rose questioningly. "Not even your last serious girlfriend?"

"Nope."

"Why not?"

"Trust," he said simply. "It's hard to explain, but when you've been judged for something you can't control, it's easier to not let people see that side of yourself. So, I don't talk about it. I don't let it define me."

She met his gaze and held it. "Thank you for trusting me enough to tell me."

"That's a big thing, isn't it?" he said, almost as though he were talking to himself. "Trust, I mean. I wonder, do we choose who we trust, or is it simply instinct?"

"Are you asking me that as a question?"

He exhaled heavily. "You know, I'm not sure. I don't ever make rash decisions."

"And this feels rash...is that what you're saying?"

"No," he replied. "That's the kicker. Nothing about you, about us, feels rash."

Logically, she agreed. But despite how good it was

between them—despite the laughter and the easy friendship and the mind-blowing sex—they *had* only known each other a matter of weeks. They couldn't be certain about anything.

He was looking at her with such blisteringly hot intensity, and suddenly she couldn't drag her gaze away. Instinctively, she knew what was coming. She didn't know how, but it was as though some internal radar switched on and she knew precisely what he was going to say. What she didn't know was why she couldn't galvanize her good sense and beg him not to say it. And when it came, it still had the power to rock her to her core.

"Layla, I'm in love with you."

Chapter Eleven

Right. First time he'd ever said it to anyone. Probably the last time, too, if the expression on her face was anything to go by.

Kane got to his feet, scraped the chair back and propped his hands on his hips. "I shouldn't have said that."

She didn't disagree. "I think we—"

"It's just the great sex talking," he said, and shrugged. "Ignore it."

But she didn't. "I'm not ready for that, Kane."

Well, that's better than being told to take a hike...

Except she suddenly looked as though she felt sorry for him, and that was worse than the notion of a full-blown rejection. "Forget about it."

Kane grabbed her hand and dragged her to her feet, bringing her close. He worked out quickly that she was naked beneath the robe, and combined with her tousled hair and reddened lips, she looked sinfully sexy. He kissed her, hoping to distract her enough that she wouldn't keep thinking about his rash statement. In seconds he figured his strategy worked because they were kissing hot and deep like a couple of mad people. Her hands slipped beneath his T-shirt and her fingers dug into his skin as Kane curved his palms over her hips. Her breasts surged against him and he kissed her neck, her throat, the sensitive skin at her nape.

"My God," he muttered raggedly into her hair. "I want you again."

She pulled the robe loose and pressed closer. "I want you, too."

"I don't…have…" The words were dragged from his throat as the feel of her hands on his skin worked like a narcotic, drugging him senseless. "Protection."

Kane felt her smile against his neck where her lips were making magic. "Let's improvise, then."

Her seductive suggestion sent all the blood in his body surging south and Kane's knees almost gave out. Improvise? Sure, he could do that. Because a baby would be unthinkable for them both at this point. Still, he thought as he lifted her onto the counter and stood between her thighs, pushing the robe aside, smoothing his hands over her belly and around her hips…maybe one day? The notion rocked him soul deep. Children. Family. And a minute ago he'd told her that he was in love with her.

What the hell is wrong with me?

Nothing, a little voice taunted. It was playing out exactly as it should. That's what people did. They met. They dated. They fell in love. They got married. They had kids.

Married?

For the first time in his life, the word slammed through his brain. Marriage had never been on his radar before. Not with Janine. Not with anyone he'd ever dated. But as he touched Layla, as her soft moans echoed around the room, as her hands dug into his shoulders and for the next hour or so, as they made love in ways that were insanely erotic and transcended pleasure, he knew it was exactly what he wanted.

Somehow, after the super sexy events in the kitchen, they'd managed to make it back to the bedroom and she lay in his arms as they slept. But when he woke up, he was alone. He could smell coffee and blinked at the ray of sunshine beaming through the crack between the curtains. He needed a shower and a shave and pushed back the duvet, spotting his clothes neatly stacked on the edge of the bed as he swung his legs around and planted his feet on the carpet.

"Good morning."

He looked up. Layla stood in the doorway and his heart skipped a crazy beat. She wore a pale green dress and flat shoes and her hair was up in a messy ponytail. But she looked fresh and rested and wholly desirable.

Kane glanced at the clock on the bedside table, ignoring the picture of a smiling Frank beside it, and saw that it was past nine o'clock. "You let me sleep."

She smiled a little. "You seemed to need it."

"But not you?" he asked, and ran a hand through his hair.

"I'm used to getting up early and surviving on five hours' sleep," she explained.

Of course she was. She had a child and a job and did it all on her own. "I'm not usually such a zombie in the morning," he offered, and met her gaze. "I think you wore me out."

She chuckled and then suddenly regarded him soberly. "Kane, I think we should—"

"Don't, Layla," he said, and waved a hand more irritably than he intended, sensing what was coming. Regret. A postmortem. Her assurance that she liked him, but that was it, and she wasn't ready for anything else. "We don't need to rehash anything. And I certainly don't need to be reminded of my foolishness. I'm sorry if I made you feel uncomfortable."

She exhaled softly. "You didn't," she said, but they both knew she was lying. "But this is happening so fast—and I don't do fast."

Neither did he. And that was the damned shock of it all. "I should get going," he said, and went to get up, then changed his mind because he was naked and in a semi-aroused state.

"I've left a towel, razor and toothbrush in the bathroom for you," she said as though it were the most normal thing in the world. "Ah—I planned on taking Erin to see my grandparents today. Would you like to come with us?"

He wanted to refuse. He wanted to stick his ego in a deep hole and ignore the humiliation making his skin itch. But the idea of spending time with Layla and Erin won out over his embarrassment. And to be fair, Layla was clearly trying to make things between them as normal as possible.

"Sure," he replied. "But I'll need to swing by my place for some fresh clothes."

"No problem," she said, and lingered in the doorway. "Kane, thank you for last night. It was amazing."

"Yeah," he agreed. "It was."

She left him then and he showered and quickly shaved and dressed. When he entered the kitchen twenty minutes later, Layla pressed a coffee cup into his hand and Erin squealed with delight when she saw him.

"Dada! Dada!"

There it was again...the *other* elephant in the room. Layla quickly met his gaze and shrugged a kind of uncertain apology and he made the effort to ignore the weird way his heart pounded. "It's okay," he assured her, and sipped his coffee.

"I don't know how to get her to stop," she said.

"Then don't," he said, sharper than he intended. "She's a kid and kids say things without a filter. We don't need to make a mountain out of it."

But he knew what Layla was thinking...what she was doing. Backtracking. Reminding him of the real status of their relationship. That he wasn't Erin's father—as much as he might want to be. He was the guy Layla had invited, probably temporarily, into her life and her bed. They were lovers. Passion like that couldn't be faked. They had a lot of chemistry and the sex was incredible. The thing was, he wanted more than just great sex.

And they both knew it.

"It's so good of Kane to help your granddad cut down that tree," her grandmother said to Layla later that day. "The neighbors have been on his back for weeks about getting it done, but it's impossible for Joe to climb that far up the ladder."

Yeah... Kane Fortune was great.

He was perfect.

Everyone loved him.

Except me.

Which she knew was a great big lie.

But she wasn't ready to admit anything...not to herself and least of all to Kane.

I'm in love with you...

Damn him for saying that. For putting it out there. For making her feel something beyond the incredible physical connection they shared. Sex she could handle. Sex she could compartmentalize into a safe place where her heart wasn't in jeopardy of being smashed to pieces.

"He told me he loved me," she blurted out, and then immediately wished she hadn't. Her grandmother was a romantic, and since she clearly thought Kane hung the moon, she would be all over the idea of them as a real couple. "But it's too soon for all that."

"Is it?" Maude queried. "You know, I fell in love with Joe the first time we met."

Layla knew the story. "You and Grandpa are an exception to the rule."

"What rule?"

The rule where a person should protect themselves from getting hurt at all costs.

"The friends-first rule," she said quickly, covering her tracks. "Like I was with Frank."

"But every relationship is different," Maude offered. "What you had with Frank isn't necessarily what you will have with someone else. And you clearly like Kane. Plus, Erin has become very attached to him."

"I know," she said, and sighed. "That's why I have to be cautious. I don't want her getting attached too quickly. What if we break up tomorrow and she'll be left—"

"*Are* you breaking up tomorrow?"

"Well, no," she replied, thinking that the thought *had* crossed her mind several times in the last few hours. Then she felt ridiculous using the words *breaking up*, because that meant a relationship and she and Kane had only known each other a matter of weeks and it was too soon to consider what they had anything more than…what? A fling? A friendship gone sideways? The best sex of her life? She didn't want to think that, either. "But there are never assurances."

"Children are amazingly resilient," Maude said gently. "So, is it Erin you're worried about or yourself?"

Layla couldn't answer. And didn't get a chance because her grandfather came through the back door with Kane in his wake and started saying how grateful he was to have someone around who could fix pretty much anything. She met Kane's shimmering gaze and her entire body went into its usual lustathon. But dammit, no man should have shoulders that broad or arms that strong or a smile so dazzling!

They ate lunch in the kitchen, just ham and cheese sandwiches washed down with copious amounts of her grandmother's famous homemade über-sweet lemonade, which she could tell Kane didn't like—but he was too polite to say so. Afterward they had cake and coffee and Layla tried not to think about how seeing Erin clamoring for Kane's attention made her feel.

Like I'm drowning...

She wanted to run. And to stay. To make sense of the thoughts running through her mind. To somehow beg Erin not to get too attached, even though Layla knew she already had.

They stayed for another hour and were back at her place by three.

"Well, I'll call you later," he said once they were at her front door and he'd carried Erin inside and dropped the diaper bag in the hallway.

Layla nodded as she took her daughter in her arms. "Sure."

He ruffled Erin's hair gently and then bent his head to kiss Layla, but she turned her face at the same time, so he only got her cheek. "Right."

She sighed. "Sorry, I didn't mean that... I'm just—"

"I get it, Layla," he said, sounding more exasperated than she'd heard before. "You want me to go."

"No," she said quickly. "Well, it's only that I have some studying to do and it's been a busy weekend and I'm sure Erin is exhausted."

"Like I said," he replied, "you want me to go. I'll talk to you later."

Layla watched him walk down the path and get into his truck and then drive off. She gave Erin a bath, put in a load of laundry and got her laptop ready for the assignment she needed to finish. Once Erin was fed and put to bed, Layla headed for her own room and was struck by an intense surge of regret when she looked at the huge bed. Had she made the biggest mistake of her life by making love with Kane? It felt like it—particularly when his words kept slamming into her brain.

I'm in love with you...

It was too much, too soon. She was still grieving, still mourning her husband, still thinking about Frank every second of the day. Only...she hadn't been thinking about Frank. In fact, she hadn't thought much about him at all for the last few weeks.

It had been Kane Fortune consuming her thoughts.

Kane, with his broad shoulders and incredible smile, who fixed her sink and gave her flowers and was such a sensational lover. Kane, who'd captivated both her and Erin. Making them quickly, and unforgivably, forget Frank.

Because that, in a nutshell, was it.

Frank's memory had faded over the past couple of weeks. The *sense* of him that she'd held on to like a lifeline since his death had diluted, become more a shadow than a force, bringing with it another, more powerful emotion. *Guilt*. A dark, relentless, all-consuming guilt that had worked its way into her blood and bones. She was sick with it.

She ignored the bed and walked into the bathroom—which was just as much of a reminder as the bedroom—and took a quick shower before changing into pajamas and stepping into the kitchen. The house seemed so quiet, the soft tick of the wall clock registering eight o'clock a pitiful reminder of how alone she truly was, and suddenly, she ached for Kane's arms around her. She ached for his kiss and the feel of his hands across her skin. He was all she wanted. All she needed. He was the tonic for her shattered heart.

She grabbed her cell and sent him a text message without second-guessing herself.

I was an idiot this afternoon. Would you like to come over?

Layla counted every second of the seventeen minutes it took to get a reply.

See you soon.

She grabbed her cell, raced down the hall and back into her bedroom, throwing off the very unsexy pajamas and finding a long black chemise and matching wrap and thong at the back of one of her dresser drawers. She brushed her hair, dabbed some fragrance to her pulse points and quickly gargled with mouthwash.

Kane arrived at ten past nine, wearing his signature jeans and blue checked shirt, and carrying a small overnight bag, and Layla greeted him by the door.

"Seventeen minutes?" she queried, brows up.

He stopped at the top step. "What?"

"That's how long it took you to reply to my text."

He shrugged loosely. "And?"

"Making me suffer, right?"

"Maybe," he admitted, and stepped toward her, to stand in the doorway and rest one broad shoulder against the jamb as his gaze roved over her with clear appreciation. "But I didn't mean to. I just... I wasn't sure what to say."

"I guess I deserved it?"

He didn't respond; instead, his eyes bored into hers. "You look sensational."

Layla pulled the screen wide and invited him to cross the threshold. He dropped the bag at their feet and she was in his arms in one long stride, kissing him a second later, and didn't think about anything else but Kane for the next two hours.

"You've been in a better mood this week."

Kane was at Adam's on Thursday afternoon, as his brother was looking for premises to start his boutique beer business and wanted to talk over his options. He ignored his brother's comment and flicked through the pages of properties on the table. "This one looks like it would suit your needs," he said.

"How are things going with Layla?"

"Fine," he replied, and flipped the page. "And this one has possibilities."

"Why don't you both come around for dinner Saturday night?" Adam suggested.

"I'll see if she's free," Kane replied, although he already knew she had no firm plans for Saturday night other than spending it with him. That's how it was. He hadn't spent a night in his own house all week. "We'll need to bring Erin."

Adam's mouth twitched. "No problem. I'll see if Brady wants to come—make it a real family night."

Kane heard the humor in his brother's voice. "Stop being a jerk, will you."

"Stop denying the obvious."

"I'm not denying anything," Kane said flatly.

I'm in love with her. She's not in love with me.

The reality was a kick in the gut. They hadn't talked about it again. Hadn't mentioned it. They talked about work, Erin, her studies, the weather and his family, and they had sex. Lots of sex. But they avoided the hard conversation—the one where she was afraid to make a commitment to the status of their relationship and where he was certain they'd break up if she didn't. Because for the first time in his life, he wanted it…needed it, like he needed air in his lungs and the ground beneath his feet. It was quite the revelation and he was feeling a mixture of excitement and bewilderment. Particularly when Layla was so obviously holding back.

"Have you talked to Mom recently?" Adam asked, changing the subject.

"Not this week, why?"

His brother shrugged. "I told Brady that we should probably think about going for a visit. She misses us and I think she's having a tough time at the moment. I'm not sure if I can get away in the next month, though. Provisions has been busy and with Laurel doing extra hours at the gallery, plus having Larkin, time is short these days."

Guilt pressed down on his shoulders. Since both Adam and Brady had kids, if anyone was going to have to drop everything to fly to New York, Kane knew it would be him. "I'll get Brady to call Brian. You talk to Josh and I'll call Arabella. Once we know if anything else is going on, I'll call Mom and try to get back home to see her."

"Tell her you've got a girlfriend," Adam teased. "That'll cheer her up."

"I've already spoken to Mom about Layla," he said flatly.

"I know," Adam replied with a grin. "I'm just dissing you. She called me up last week and asked me all about it."

Kane scowled. "How about you mind your own business?"

"Nah," Adam replied, and chuckled. "What's the fun in that?"

Kane ignored him, spent another fifteen minutes talking about his brother's business plans and then headed home. He had a meeting with Callum the following morning, so he grabbed a change of clothes, checked the mailbox, threw out a few questionable items from the refrigerator and headed to Layla's at six.

As always, Erin was delighted to see him and raced down the hallway when he arrived. He took her in his arms and kissed her forehead.

"I really am convinced she now prefers you to me," Layla said with mock disapproval as she closed the door behind him. "She's been looking out the window for you since we got home."

Kane's chest tightened. "She's a sweetheart."

"Dada!"

It had quickly become her favorite word and she said it at every opportunity. Kane knew Layla wanted to correct her, but didn't know how. Oddly, he didn't want that. He was quite happy for Erin to call him Dada, or Dad, or Daddy. Whatever she wanted. For the rest of his life.

He shifted his thoughts off the idea and told Layla about Adam's invitation. She agreed, although not very enthusiastically, and he said they didn't have to stay too long. She said she had a headache and took some aspirin after they finished cleaning up the kitchen.

There was a weird energy between them that night and when she emerged from the bathroom around ten, he noticed she was wearing a sensible cotton nightgown and did the math quickly in his head, figuring it was that time of the month for her.

"Do you take anything for period pain?" he asked quietly when he noticed her grimace as she sat on the edge of the bed and rubbed lotion into her hands.

Her eyes widened a fraction. "Ah…sometimes. I probably should have mentioned my period came this morning, in case you wanted to stay at home since we can't—"

"Is that the only reason you think I'm here?" he asked irritably, cutting her off. "To get laid?"

"Of course not."

"Then don't say that kind of stuff. Do you need anything?" he asked, calming his temper as he pulled back the covers on what had quickly become *his* side of the bed. "Maybe a heating pad?"

"I'm fine."

He took off his sweatshirt. "If you like, I could make you that chamomile tea you—"

"Do you know what I *would* like?" she snapped, and thrust back the covers. "I'd like you to stop being so damned perfect."

Kane stilled, the sweatshirt still in his hands. "What?"

"You," she said sharply, and sighed. "You're like perfect at everything. Perfect with my grandparents, perfect with Erin, perfect at knowing I feel unwell tonight because I got my period, perfect at fixing things, perfect in bed…you're like this *perfect* boyfriend. It drives me crazy," she added with a huff and got into bed, quickly flipping off the bedside light and lying on her side, her back to him.

Kane remained where he was for a second, admiring the curve of her waist and hip and long shapely legs, before she pulled up the covers. Then he stripped down to his boxers and slipped into bed, sitting up, leaving the bedside light on for the moment. "So, I'm your boyfriend?"

She let out a long and impatient breath and then turned around. "Is that all you heard from what I just said?"

"Pretty much."

She flapped her arms, and it occurred to him that it was more proof that while he'd been thinking she was quiet and controlled, Layla McCarthy actually had a pretty bad temper and a flair for the dramatic.

"You're impossible!"

Laughter rumbled in his chest. "You know, you're not exactly a walk in the park."

Her eyes darkened to a deep chocolate brown. "What does that mean?"

"I think you know."

She didn't give an inch. "Oh please, enlighten me."

Kane exhaled. "It means you're emotionally out of reach."

The words were out before he could stop them. Well, too bad. It was said and she had to deal with it. He'd been treading on eggshells all week and was tired of trying to scale the wall she had built between them.

"That's not true," she denied.

"Yes, it is," he countered. "You're impenetrable, Layla."

She didn't look happy, not one bit. "I don't know how you can say that, not after this week and all the time we've spent together."

He waved a hand between them. "You mean here? In this bed? Having sex? With your dead husband's picture staring at me every time I touch you?" The moment he said it, Kane knew he sounded petty. But there had to be some give and take, some compromise. "Look, I know you're scared, Layla, but for the record, you're not the only one. Five days ago I told you I was in love with you and you pretty much dismissed that out of hand…and all week we've tiptoed around it, pretending it didn't happen. But it *did* happen," he said. "Just so you know, I didn't say it because I like to hear the sound of my own voice."

She sucked in a breath. "You're mad at me because I didn't say it back, is that it?"

"I'm not mad at you," he assured her, seeing the tremble in her lower lip. "I'm in love with you."

For a moment he thought she was going to get up, to run from the words she clearly didn't want to hear. But she stayed and met his gaze. "I didn't dismiss it," she said softly, swallowing hard. "I know how difficult those words are to say."

"You're right," he replied. "They are. I've never said them to anyone before."

She nodded fractionally. "Then I'm sorry that I can't say them to you right now. I think you're amazing. And besides being annoyingly perfect, there's something special about you. You're kind and sweet and funny and make me feel as though I *can* be happy again. But I need time," she added, drawing in a sharp and heavy breath. "I'm not someone who rushes—and I've rushed into this thing with you because I couldn't stop myself. Just be patient with me," she pleaded.

"Layla, I—"

"Please?"

Kane grasped her hand and drew her knuckles to his mouth, kissing them softly. "Layla, I'm not about to bail on you. I'm not that guy when I'm with you. I'm not that guy who used to avoid commitment like the plague. You changed that. So of course I'll do my best to be patient."

She moved across the bed and curled up against him. He flicked off the light and took a long breath, settling her into the crook of his arm.

"I'll take the picture away," she said softly.

Kane grimaced. "Don't do that," he said, feeling like a complete jerk. "You have every right to have your husband's picture anywhere you want it. I was just being an oversensitive idiot."

"I keep it there to remember what he looked like. To remember that he always made me feel safe."

"That's important to you, feeling safe?" he asked, pushing the hair from her face.

She nodded. "I don't know why."

He did. She'd been rejected by her father, left to her own devices by an uncaring mother who allowed her to live with her grandparents at just fifteen. Kane considered his own happy childhood—his loving and attentive parents and siblings. He'd never felt unwanted or unsafe as a child. Never questioned if he was cared for. Never had to go looking for love. And Layla, he suspected, had been forced to fight for every bit of affection she got from her mother from the beginning.

"Get some sleep," he whispered against her hair. "I'll be here in the morning."

The thing was, Kane wanted to be there for her every morning for the rest of his life. He just didn't know if she'd give him, or them, that chance.

Chapter Twelve

Layla had to admit that Kane had a nice family. Picture-perfect, really. Big and robust and clearly filled with love and affection. Hanging out with them on Saturday night gave her the opportunity to get to know Adam and Brady a little better, even if she felt as though her relationship with their brother was under intense scrutiny. Laurel and Adam cooked a marvelous meal and she sensed that Erin was in her element. The truth was, her daughter was flourishing, and she knew Kane was the reason. She simply adored him and it was plain for anyone to see.

She'd borrowed the changing table in the nursery to clean Erin's face after dinner and check her diaper and was returning to the living room with her daughter in her arms when she heard the brothers talking among themselves and lingered by the doorway.

"Well, I tried talking to Dad and he brushed me off," Adam said with a sigh.

"You know how Mom gets when Dad starts on about the past," Brady said. "Dad thinks we're the only Fortunes worth a lick, and it doesn't matter what I say to him about Callum or Dillon or Steve, he just wants to think the worst. I don't think he'll ever come around."

"Perhaps it's not our place to try to make him," Kane said, clearly the peacemaker among them, and a surge of respect washed over her.

"He wants us to move back," Adam said, his voice breaking a little. "Said we were choosing sides by living in Rambling Rose."

"That's his passive-aggressive side coming out," Kane remarked. "He's more like his Fortune half brothers than he realizes. The fact is you both have lives and jobs here, and kids now, and this is your home. Dad's gonna have to accept it. I wouldn't beat yourselves up trying to change his mind."

Layla noticed the way he didn't include himself in the conversation and experienced a weird feeling in the pit of her stomach. Of course he'd talked about New York to her, about missing his family and friends, but she'd believed he was as settled in Rambling Rose as his brothers. Was she wrong? Had she been imagining it? Believing it because she didn't want to face the alternative?

That he might leave?

She plastered on a smile and entered the room and Erin demanded to be put down, and then immediately raced toward Kane. He hauled her into his lap and she snuggled close. Her daughter was weary and Layla watched in amazement at how settled she was in his arms. Erin loved him, no doubt about it.

Just admit it…you love him, too.

The truth hovered inside her, somewhere between fear and logic, if there was such a place. If she told him, the words would be out there forever and could never be taken back. And she would have nothing to hide behind, no defense.

He smiled at her and her belly did a dive. He had a way of both calming her nerves and setting her on fire. A way of making her crave as she never had before. And something else—a kind of quiet acceptance of who she was. Of course, she knew her feelings could be just the great sex putting her brain in a haze disguised as an emotional reaction. Still, she didn't want to believe she was that shallow. Sex had never clouded her judgment before.

On the way home, later that evening, she asked him about the conversation she'd overheard. "Do you think your father's feelings will ever change?"

"I don't hold out much hope. Dad is fairly set in his ways. He and Mom took a big hit in the global financial crisis all those years ago, and he's had trouble accepting that loss ever since. Added to that, finding out he's Julius Fortune's son only fueled his resentment." Kane sighed. "I don't know. Maybe it's because the Fortune name doesn't have quite the pull in New York as it does down here. We were—we *are*—a working-class family."

She nodded agreeably. "I've realized something— in your family, you're the glue, the one who keeps it all together, right?"

"At times."

"And they're missing that, with you being here."

"I guess they might be."

She sat for a moment, twisting her hands in her lap, then asked the question that had been hovering on her lips all evening. "Are you planning on going back to New York?"

He glanced sideways. "No, I hadn't planned on it," he replied quietly. "Why, are you looking for an easy out?"

Was she?

"No," she denied, but something skittered along her nerves. The deeper in she got, the less control she felt. "Are you staying tonight?"

"Probably not," he replied. "I have some chores to do around the house."

That was all he said—in fact, they barely spoke again until they got back to her house and he carried a sleeping Erin directly to her room. They lingered by the crib for a moment.

"I had a nice time tonight," she said softly. "Thank you."

"Sure," he said, and turned on his heel.

Layla followed him out, catching up with him by the front door. "So, I'll see you tomorrow?"

He nodded vaguely and crossed the threshold. "Good night." He got three steps across the porch and then turned back to her. "Damn," he said on a heavy breath.

"What?" she asked, aching inside.

"You know what," he said as he strode back toward her and took her in his arms. "You. This. Us," he said raggedly, and then took her mouth in a hot, deep, mesmerizing kiss. "For the first time in my life I'm completely at the mercy of my feelings," he admitted, dragging his mouth away from hers, still holding her close. "It's undoing me."

The vulnerability in his voice made her ache inside. "I'm sorry if I'm hurting you or confusing you, Kane. It's not intentional."

"I know," he said into her hair. "But it's still a kicker."

Then he left.

Layla went to see her grandparents the following day and Maude noticed Kane's absence immediately.

"Something wrong?" her grandmother asked as

they walked around the garden, watching Erin play with a ball.

"No," Layla lied. "We're fine. He's got things to do today. So have I," she added. "I have an assignment due and have to attack the ironing this afternoon."

"We're really proud of you," Maude said, "for going back to school and getting on with your life. We should have tried harder to send you to college years ago."

"Nonsense," Layla dismissed gently. "It was my choice not to go to college."

"And Frank was never keen on you studying, was he?"

Layla stilled, tugging on an old memory. Was that true? It was such a long time ago. But yes, she thought, remembering how he'd insisted she work until they had children and then suggesting she quit. That was the plan, until his company began downsizing due to an economic downturn and he was shuffled to another department on a lower salary. And yes, he hadn't supported her suggestion that she go back to school.

Funny, she thought, how'd she'd forgotten the way they'd argued about it.

And the last argument…the night he was killed.

She shoved the memory away where it belonged and got on with watching her daughter play, finding delight in Erin's laughter.

"Dada! Dada!"

Layla's heart rolled over and she couldn't miss her grandmother's raised brows as Erin wandered around the yard, talking to herself, calling out for her father.

But not for Frank…and they both knew it.

"She's been saying it all the time lately," Layla admitted.

"That's perfectly natural, since he's the first man to be a part of her life," Maude assured her. "She clearly loves Kane, and it's also clear the feeling is mutual. The question is, how do *you* feel?"

Confused and guilty.

When she got home she cooked a casserole and kept checking her cell for messages. Kane called later that afternoon and said he'd see her around seven thirty. Erin was already in bed by the time he arrived and Layla met him at the door and kissed him softly.

When they got to the kitchen he hung his jacket behind the chair, and as she set out plates he gestured to the laptop on the table.

"How's the assignment coming along?"

"Good," she replied, and then shrugged. "I think. I'll be glad when this semester is over."

"You know," he said as he took the plates from her, "I was thinking you should consider talking to Callum about a marketing job. He's always looking for good people and with the hotel and all the other businesses in the Fortune portfolio, there's bound to be an opportunity for you."

Layla nodded, knowing he was right, but her insecurities were sometimes overpowering. "You know, I haven't really thought a lot about exactly what I want to do when I get my degree. I think I was just so excited to get started. But you're right, I should look for opportunity and the Fortunes are good to work for." She laughed brittlely. "It's weird to talk about them as though you're not one of them. Because you are, that's obvious."

"It is?"

"Sure," she replied. "You all have that same way about you, you know. It's like it's ingrained in your DNA or something. And it's not about money or social position—it's about confidence and conviction in your values. You and your brothers have it by the bucketload and I envy that."

His brow came up as he sat. "You think you lack conviction?"

"I think I have at certain times in my life."

He disagreed. "It's easy to look like you have it all together when you have a tight family behind you, Layla. I've always felt valued and wanted by the people around me and I've never lived with any fear of abandonment."

"Like me, you mean?" she asked, and then shook her head. "You don't need to answer that. But I'm curious, if you're so switched on, why have you avoided a serious relationship all your life?"

"Because I've never met the right person," he replied. "Until now."

"How can you be so sure?"

He looked at her, then the look turned into a glare. "Weren't you sure with Frank?"

"That was different," she said hotly. "We'd known each other for a year before we started dating."

"Do you really think the length of time matters?"

"Of course it does. Relationships need time to nurture and grow. They don't just spring out of the ground in a couple of weeks. Time makes all the difference."

"That's a standard cop-out when you're on the defensive, Layla," he said bluntly, and got to his feet, his hands planted on his hips, his chest heaving.

Heat rushed to her cheeks and she stared at him, seeing the disappointment and frustration in his expression. "You don't know what I went through..." she said, her words trailing off into little more than a whisper.

"No, I don't," he shot back. "Because you don't talk about it. You keep everything inside."

"I have to," she said defensively. "For Erin's sake I need to be sure and—"

"This isn't about Erin," he said, softer, gentler. "She's not the one with the wall up, Layla."

He was right. Erin already adored him...loved him...and would welcome him into her life full-time as her father. But what would that mean? That Frank would be replaced—eventually forgotten—like he'd never existed. And Layla would drown in her guilt... in the knowledge that if she'd made a different choice that night, her husband would still be alive and she wouldn't be standing in front of another man, pulling on every ounce of strength she possessed to *not* tell him what was in her heart.

And suddenly, like a dam bursting, she couldn't keep it in any longer.

"We had a fight," she said, the words barely audible and her insides aching so much she could hardly stand up straight. When Kane frowned, she continued. "That night...the night he was killed...we'd had an argument over the phone. The truth is, we'd been arguing most of that week. The company he worked for had been downsizing. There was a reorg and Frank was moved to another department. It was a demotion with a lower salary. He was unhappy... I knew that. He'd worked for the company a long time and suddenly it was like he didn't matter. He felt devalued and a little lost, I think." As the truth poured out, Layla twisted her hands together, tears in her eyes, her throat raw with emotion. "Looking back, I don't think I was very understanding. I had Erin, and I was worried about how we were going to get by financially and deep down I was resentful that I'd given up all of my own career aspirations when we got together. I had all of these feelings going on in my head and when he called me that night and said he was staying late after work to have a drink with a couple of his work friends, I got angry and told him to do whatever he wanted."

She shuddered out a breath, pain searing through her chest. Kane was silent, listening, like he always did. "I went to bed angry. And then he didn't come home and it was after midnight when the police came to the door and told me he'd been in an accident and that he was dead. I was so numb, I simply couldn't believe it. And I knew..." She let her words trail off, sucked in some air, tried to blink back the tears. "I knew it was my fault."

"Layla," Kane said gently, coming toward her and grasping her shaking hands. "That's not true."

"It is true," she corrected, looking up at him. "If I'd asked him to come home right away, if I'd said we needed to talk, if I'd been kinder and more understanding, if I'd listened, he would never have been on the road at that time of night. He would never have been in the path of that truck."

"You can't blame yourself for an accident," he said, holding her close. "It was just timing and circumstance. No one can predict things like that."

She wanted that to be true. She wanted it so much. But she'd believed it for so long that it was etched into the very marrow of her bones.

"I can't turn it off," she admitted, shuddering. "The guilt."

"You have to, Layla," he said gently. "For your

sake, and Erin's. He wouldn't want you to feel this way."

Logically, Layla knew that and she pressed closer to Kane, absorbing the strength of his arms around her.

They didn't make love that night, although she sensed he wanted to. Instead, he held her, spoon fashion, one hand resting on her hip, the other around the top of her head. They didn't speak, either, because she was all out of words. But she felt his love through the pores of his skin, through the rhythmic beat of his heart, through the sound of his breathing as he drifted off to sleep.

And she knew what she had to do.

As usual, when Kane woke up the following morning, he was alone. He could hear Layla moving around the house, getting ready for her day, and the rich scent of fresh coffee lingered in the air. It was early, barely six o'clock, and when he got up, he noticed Erin was still asleep in her crib.

Layla was in the living room and when he joined her, she turned to face him, her shoulders tight, her back straight, and Kane recognized the look on her face instantly.

She's going to end it...right now...right here.

"Layla…"

"I think we need to take a break…or at least, step back a bit."

He didn't think any words had ever hurt so much. "I didn't peg you for a coward."

Her jaw tightened. "I'm doing this to protect all of us."

"You're doing this to protect yourself. Do you think I haven't figured out that you're scared to death at the idea of being in love again?"

She stilled, but he could see through her and knew he was right. "Try to understand that I need some time to figure it out. Just a couple of days…or a week."

The was the killer—he did understand. "Time's not gonna heal your wounds, Layla. They'll stay there until you forgive yourself for whatever it is you think you did or didn't do."

She looked stricken, and so lost he wanted to cave and take her into his arms. But she was setting new rules. Pushing him away. Devaluing everything they had become. "We could go back to being just friends for a while."

"No." He raised his hands questioningly and then dropped them. "I get what you're saying, but I'm not going to hang around and take your hot-and-cold routine day after day, week after week. It's not fair to either of us, or Erin."

"That's why I'm suggesting we be friends," she implored quickly. "You know how attached she is to you."

"Exactly," he said. "I'm not prepared to be just

some guy who drops by a couple of times a week to fix something or spend a night in your bed."

"Then what do you want?"

Kane ran a weary hand through his hair. "I want you to admit what I know you're feeling, but you're too afraid to acknowledge."

"You don't know what I feel," she refuted. "And I can't... I can't..."

"Can't and won't are two different things, Layla." He exhaled heavily, his chest so tight he could barely breathe. "I want you to know that you can rely on me to be here, with you and Erin." Kane stared at her, meeting her wavering gaze. "Do you know why I've always only given you lavender roses?" He didn't wait for her reply. "Because they signify love at first sight."

"Kane, I—"

"That's what I felt the first time I saw you, all those weeks ago when I was picking up my nephew from day care. It was as though I'd been struck by some inexplicable force. It shocked the hell out of me. I'd never experienced anything like it before. I've avoided commitment...avoided serious relationships like the plague. But then there was you and for the first time in my life I was feeling something for someone that was more than I was prepared for. More attraction, more friendship, more affection, more everything. And I can't undo it, Layla. I can't backtrack and pretend it's something else. I won't."

There were tears in her eyes...tears he knew were for him, for them, for her daughter and probably for Frank, too. He took a couple of steps toward her and rested his hand on the back of the sofa, meeting her glistening gaze.

"Layla, I love you and I want to be with you. With both of you. I know Frank will always be Erin's father, but if you let me, I would love the chance to be her dad. And I'm prepared to give this everything I have," he said, and laid a hand on his heart. "But you have to meet me halfway."

She inhaled sharply. "I'm not sure I know what that means."

He took a second, absorbing every part of her, inking her beauty into his memory for fear that they were done. "It means that I... I need the words, Layla. I didn't think I did...but I do."

Kane left moments later, his throat burning, his chest aching so much it was as though someone had taken a boot to his rib cage. With every step he took to his truck, he wanted to turn around and tell her he'd take her on any terms. Only, it wouldn't be right, it wouldn't be real, because he wasn't wired that way.

He got home and the place had never seemed so empty. He really did need to either get another place or do something with the bungalow. He showered, changed and headed to Roja at nine for a meeting with Callum. He was pleased he had something to do, something to take his mind off what had happened at Layla's.

"So," Callum said once they were seated in the restaurant and drinking coffee, "have you made a decision?"

His cousin had approached him the previous week about a new commercial project he had planned for the town—with Kane as project manager. The contract would see Kane working with Fortune Brothers Construction for at least the next few years. It was a major commitment and one that needed significant consideration. Stay in Rambling Rose for years? Without Layla by his side? He wasn't sure he could do it. But the alternative was to take the job in Houston or head back to New York.

Did it matter where he lived if Layla and Erin weren't part of his life? Probably not.

"If I can pick my own project crew," he said after a moment, mentioning a few names.

Callum nodded. "Sure. Anything else?"

"I'll need a few weeks before I can start. Personal stuff."

Callum, who was usually mostly business, regarded him with concern. "Everything okay?"

Kane didn't flinch. "Fine."

They ended with the commitment to meet at Paz Spa on Thursday, which did make him flinch. Paz Spa meant one thing—Layla.

Late on Wednesday afternoon, Kane headed to

Adam's. He and Laurel were watching Brady's kids for the afternoon. The boys were in the living room playing a video game and Kane sat in the kitchen with his brother.

"I saw Layla today at the day care center when I picked up my son," Adam said. "She waved and then left. Everything all right between you two?"

Kane sugared the coffee his brother had made. "I think we broke up."

"You think?"

"I haven't spoken to her since Sunday."

"You could call her," Adam suggested. "Just sayin'. Everything looked cozy on the weekend."

He shrugged. "Well, you know how it is, things can quickly change."

Adam regarded him soberly. "Does she know that you're in love with her?"

Heat crawled up his neck, but he didn't deny it. "Yep."

"And?"

"And...nothing. She wants to step back."

"Ouch," Adam remarked. "That's gotta hurt."

"Yeah," he admitted. "It sure the hell does."

He didn't get into it any more than that and thankfully Adam let the subject go. He hung around for another hour and then bailed, stopping at the gym on the way home, and then the supermarket. By the time Kane pulled into his driveway it was close to nine o'clock and he was glad he could simply put the groceries away, hit the shower and then flop into bed.

And not think about Layla at all. Or dream about her.

Or miss her so much he could barely breathe.

Of course, when he arrived at Paz Spa the following morning, she was the first thing he saw. She looked tired, he noticed, and he figured she'd been hit by the same sleepless train he had.

He registered the exact moment she saw him and their gazes clashed. She was on the phone and then busy with a client and by the time Kane's meeting with Callum was done she was nowhere to be seen. Kane didn't search for her. He'd said his piece and she needed to come to her own decision about them.

So when he left the building and saw her standing by his truck, he faltered midstride.

"Hey," she said, and pressed a hand nervously to her smooth hair. "How are you?"

"I'm pretty sure we both know the answer to that." He clicked his keys. "What do you want, Layla?"

"I just wanted to say that…" Her words trailed off nervously and she shrugged her slender shoulders. "Well, I wondered if you'd like to come over for dinner tomorrow."

"I can't," he replied. "I've got something to do."

"Oh," she said with a sigh. "Sure. It's just that, well, Erin misses you."

"I miss her, too," he said, his heart hammering

behind his ribs as he jerked open the driver door. "But that's not enough."

He got in the truck and drove off, seeing her figure fade in the rearview mirror the farther he got up the street, and feeling like he'd left his heart back on the sidewalk.

And loving her so much he hurt all over.

Chapter Thirteen

Layla worked late that afternoon and got her grand-mother to pick Erin up from day care. She could use the extra money and figured she owed Hailey and the spa plenty for the times she'd left early. Plus, work took her mind off things. Particularly off Kane. The way he'd regarded her before he drove off was imprinted in her brain. She didn't want to get home to a house she suspected he might never be in again. She didn't want to see Erin's disappointed look every time a car drove up the street because her daughter was looking out the front window waiting for him to arrive.

The whole week had been like that, with Erin standing watch, waiting for him, grabbing books and walking in and out of her playhouse, her little heart clearly breaking more every day. And Layla didn't know how to fix it. She didn't know if she could fix it. Fixing it meant risking herself. She knew what Kane wanted. He wanted *all* of her. And she was terrified of how raw and vulnerable the idea made her feel. Feelings weren't her strong suit.

On Friday, Layla managed to get through the morning and was in the staff room taking a break around eleven when Hailey walked in.

"You look terrible," the other woman said.

"Gee, thanks," she said, and sipped her tea. "I haven't had much sleep this week."

"Something wrong with Erin?" she asked, her brow furrowed with concern.

"No," Layla replied quickly. "She's fine. It's…you know…other stuff."

"Man trouble?"

"You could say that."

Hailey perched on the edge of the table. "Look, Layla, you can tell me to mind my own business if you want, but I'm going to say this anyway."

"Say what?"

"That I know we've only worked together for five months, but I think we've become friendly and I feel like I know you quite well. And it's been impossible not to notice how different you've been these last few weeks. Like, happy. And since that's how long you've known Kane, it's easy to make the conclusion that he's what's making you happy."

Except that right now I'm miserable.

"He does," she said quickly. "I mean is, or was, I don't know…it's sort of complicated at the moment."

"Is it because he doesn't come across as the settle-down type?" Hailey asked.

She frowned. "What do you mean?"

"Well, Kane's a great guy, right, but from what I hear, he's not known for wanting the family and white picket fence. But I'm sure that will change. Look, when Dillon and I first got together he was really hard to read and incredibly closed off. It's not always easy loving a Fortune…in fact, sometimes it's downright impossible, but it's worth it. So hang in there and let him come around at his own pace."

Layla laughed softly, the gesture hurting her ribs. "It's not like that at all."

"It's not?" Hailey's brows crept higher.

"No," she replied. "It's not him. It's me. I'm the one who's closed off. I'm the one who's hard to love. Kane has made it very clear about what he wants."

Hailey smiled. "And what's that?"

"Me," she said simply. "And Erin. And a white picket fence."

Hailey sighed. "Really? I'm so happy for you."

"That might be a little premature. To be honest, I'm pretty sure I've screwed things up with Kane."

"I'm sure it's nothing that can't be fixed," Hailey

said and touched her hand assuredly. "And you're wrong—I don't think you're hard to love, Layla. Or closed off. I've seen you with Erin—you're a wonderfully loving mother and you're so great with the customers here at the spa. That kind of thing can't be faked. Do you love him?"

She couldn't answer directly. Didn't want to admit to something she hadn't been able to fully admit to herself. "I let him go. I thought we were getting in too deep, too quick. I thought Erin was getting too attached. *I* was getting too attached," she said, and sighed. "I freaked out because I'm scared."

"Have you told him that?" Hailey asked.

"He knows," she replied. "But he's not someone to do anything in half measures."

"Sounds like you know him pretty well," Hailey commented. "Go and talk to him, Layla. If I've learned anything from falling in love with Dillon, it's that communicating honestly is the key to a good relationship."

It sounded easy, Layla thought. But she and Kane were not Hailey and Dillon. She wasn't as emotionally available as Hailey. She was as closed off as a clam. And Kane knew it.

On Sunday, after more days of simply going through the motions and nights of little sleep, Layla did something she hadn't done for months—she went to the cemetery to place flowers on Frank's grave. Erin walked around the headstone, picking up pebbles, clearly oblivious to her surroundings, and Layla stifled a sob. Erin didn't remember her father. Grief washed over her and the guilt came, rushing through her at a galloping speed.

"I'm sorry, Frank." She whispered the words to the wind.

Standing there, Layla realized what a mess she'd made of things. And then she admitted to herself how angry she'd been since his death. It was a startling revelation and not one she'd truly faced before. Because it meant facing herself. Facing all she'd lost. It meant coming to terms with everything she was afraid of. Kane had seen through her and called her out and she'd battled him every step of the way. But he was right.

She *was* a coward.

She'd learned to internalize her fears from an early age, shielded behind her wall of emotional distance. Frank had known it, too. Right from the beginning he'd been patient and considerate, courting her slowly, not making any hard demands and not asking her for anything more than what she was prepared to give. She'd wanted to be friends first, to be sure he was genuine and not going to break her heart. And he'd agreed without resistance. She wanted a small wedding without any fuss, so they eloped. She wanted to wait a couple of years to have kids, so they did. And the one time he'd needed her support, she'd failed him. She'd recoiled into her shell, using resentment to keep her distance from their problems and to keep herself safe. For the first time she wondered, if he hadn't died, would they have gone the distance? He never asked much of her, because he seemed to know she didn't want to give much. Even when he'd suggested she put off college and studying when they were first married and then planned on their family, she'd capitulated easily enough. Because she already knew what she wanted.

And then resented him for it, as it turned out.

Which made her what? Petty? Mean? Bitter and just a little self-centered? Or a lot, depending on the situation. And about as big a coward as anyone could be.

Do you think I haven't figured out that you're scared to death at the idea of being in love again?

Kane's words came rushing back with astounding clarity, and my God…he was so right.

Because she'd been scared her entire life. She'd watched her mother fall in and out of love, saw the wreckage it left in her wake, and decided from a young age that she was never going to be like that. She was smarter, tougher, stronger—impenetrable. And nothing like her mother. The flip side was, Layla knew that all her mother really wanted was to be loved for who she was.

Like I do.

Like I am.

Layla looked at the ring on her left hand. She'd

kept it in place to honor the man she'd married. To honor how much she'd loved him. But Frank was gone…and now she had a chance to find real happiness again. To be loved again and to love someone in return.

She eased the ring off and slipped it onto the finger on her right hand. Now all she wanted was to talk to Kane, to explain herself and then, if she could find the courage, ask him to forgive her for being such a fool.

And tell him what was in her heart—that she was deeply in love with him. That he was the most amazing man she'd ever known. That she loved the way he loved her and Erin. That she felt safe in his arms.

She bundled Erin in the car and drove into town, heading for Kane's bungalow, her heart racing. His Ranger was outside, but she didn't want to simply turn up unannounced on his doorstep, so she grabbed her cell and sent him a message.

Hi, I'd really like to see you.

She waited for several minutes for the reply to come through. And when none came, her insides sank. She called his number and it went to voice mail.

She looked at the truck. Right…so he didn't want to see her. Disappointment quickly churned in her belly. But she figured she deserved to be ignored a little since she'd behaved so badly.

Except when he didn't call her by Sunday night, Layla's racing heart was hurting like it had never hurt before. By then she'd convinced herself she was too late. He'd decided to forget about her. To move on. To find someone else to love. And she would be alone forever because she would never love anyone else with the depth of feeling she had for Kane Fortune.

And that night, alone in her bed, she cried. She cried tears of grief and despair. She wept for Frank and Erin but mostly, she wept for herself. Because she'd had real happiness at her fingertips and she'd been too much of a coward to reach out and take it. Even when he'd told her so rawly, so earnestly and with such profound honesty that he loved her, that he wanted her, that he needed her, that he wanted to be Erin's dad and love them both, she'd pushed back. She'd rejected him and his love.

By the time she got to work on Monday, Layla was convinced she'd ruined it for good. She managed to get through the day, making appointments, canceling appointments, handling difficult customers with a smile, and was surprised to see Laurel Fortune arrive around two o'clock.

"Hi, Layla," she said when she got to the counter. "I know I don't have an appointment, but I'm desperate for a brow shape and tint. Any chance I could be squeezed in? I have a couple of hours free this afternoon."

Layla checked the schedule and nodded. "Sure, we've had a cancellation this afternoon, so if you don't mind waiting for about half an hour, I can fit you in."

Laurel nodded eagerly. "Yes, great."

"Do you need to be out by a certain time to pick up your son from day care?"

"Oh, no, Adam is picking Larkin up at two thirty and then they're driving to Houston to drop Kane off at the airport."

Airport?

"Oh, the airport, really?" she asked in a purposely modulated voice.

"I think the flight to New York is at around five, so that will give them plenty of time. And Larkin just loves seeing the airplanes."

Layla zoned out. He was going to New York. Leaving Rambling Rose. Leaving her.

Fear swiftly clung to every cell she possessed. And she knew if she didn't do something fast, she would lose him forever. Like she'd lost Frank. Only this time, she had a chance to do something about it.

Once the panic surging through her had abated, a sense of calm washed over Layla, and she looked around for Hailey and summoned her to the reception desk. "I have to go," she said quickly, and grabbed her tote from the drawer, seeing a bewildered Hailey and equally surprised Laurel as she checked her watch. "Right now. It can't wait."

"Is everything all right?" Hailey asked, clearly concerned.

"I'm not sure," she said, and looked at Laurel. "I hope it will be. Two thirty?" she asked.

Laurel nodded and smiled warmly. "That's right."

Then she raced out to her car as though her heels were on fire.

Kane was loading Larkin's diaper bag in the rear of his brother's sensible sedan when he saw Layla's car heading into the parking area at the day care center.

"Someone's in a hurry," Adam said.

"That's Layla's car."

Adam checked his wristwatch. "Right on time."

"What does that mean?" he asked, his suspicions rising as Adam placed Larkin into the baby seat.

"It means I'm sick of you moping around like an orphaned puppy," Adam said as he closed the door. "You've been driving everyone crazy all week, pining over her. Someone had to do something about it."

"What did you do?" he asked as her car pulled up a couple of spaces away.

"Very little," his brother replied as he leaned against the hood. "Just got my wife to set this little meeting up. The rest is up to you."

He wanted to believe it. The last few days had been hell. He felt empty inside.

Nothing filled the gaping hole where his heart was.

"She's obviously here to pick up Erin."

"Obviously, you say?" Adam's grin broadened. "We'll see."

Kane scowled. He didn't want Layla being manipulated by anyone. "And you're just gonna stand there and watch?"

"Yep," Adam replied. "Should be interesting."

She got out of the car and walked toward him. In her skirt and floral blouse and low heels and with her hair pulled back in a neat ponytail, she looked effortlessly beautiful—but the flush on her cheeks and the emotion burning deep in her brown eyes gave away her mood. She wasn't there for Erin. He knew it down in his bones. She was there for him. *For them.* And his love for her suddenly intensified tenfold.

"Layla, are you—"

"Please don't go!" she said on a rush of breath, her gaze darting to the suitcase packed in the open trunk. "Please don't leave, Kane. After everything I've been through in my life, I don't think I could bear it if you left."

Kane's entire body stilled and he glanced at his brother, who was still leaning on the car and looking very amused by the whole scene. "What?"

"I know I'm afraid of getting hurt," she admitted, her beautiful brown eyes filled with tears. "I know I'm afraid of feeling anything because I think I'll end up losing what I have. I know *all* that…but I still need to ask you, no, beg you to stay. Don't go to New York. Don't leave Rambling Rose. Don't leave us. We need you."

He swallowed hard, fighting the emotion burning through him. But he pushed her some more. "We?"

"Okay," she said, and exhaled. "*I* need you."

"Why, Layla?" he asked, not sure how he was managing to speak.

"Because," she said, her hands open, her expression so raw and vulnerable he could barely stop himself from hauling her into his arms, "I'm lost without you. Because I…because I love you."

Relief pitched in his chest and warmth flowed through him like a wave. "I know you do," he said, and reached for her hand. "But I needed you to say it."

His brother cleared his throat and they both turned. "Well, you gonna catch this flight or not?"

Kane looked at Layla. "Not."

Adam grinned. "Okay," he said, and took out Kane's bag before he closed the trunk. "I have to get my son home. I'll call the folks and tell them you'll be rescheduling your visit, okay?"

Kane nodded and tightened his fingers around Layla's. "Yeah, fine."

Adam got into his car and drove out of the parking area.

"You were visiting your parents?" she asked. "That's what you were doing?"

"Yes," he replied.

"Not moving back to New York?"

"No," he said, and led her back to her car. "Just a visit, with a return ticket."

"I thought…" Her voice trailed off. "I thought you were moving back to New York for good and that I'd lost my chance. That I'd lost you."

Kane drew her toward him. "You haven't lost anything, Layla, I promise. I was planning a visit to my parents and then I was coming straight back. My life is here. My work is here. You and Erin are here. That's all I want, all I need."

"I'm sorry for making things so hard and for being so afraid to love you."

"It's okay to be afraid, Layla." He grasped her chin, tilting her face upward to meet his. "It's okay if you need to lean on me. That's what people do when they love each other. And I love you very much."

"I love you, too…so much it's terrifying."

"Layla," he said gently. "I know you're scared of loving me because you're scared of losing me, and I can't promise not to die. But I can promise that I will always love and protect you and would never intentionally hurt you."

She hugged him and neither of them noticed how

several cars were now parked in front of the center. He kissed her and she sighed, accepting his kiss as though she were starved of him.

"I've missed you so much this past week," she said against his mouth.

"I've missed you, too," he said. "But I think you needed this time apart, right?"

She nodded. "I think so. I needed to get things straight in my head. I needed to let go of all my insecurities. And I needed to forgive myself for letting Frank down."

More cars came and he suggested they sit in her car for a few minutes so they could talk.

"You didn't let him down, Layla," he assured her gently.

"For a long time it felt like I did, in here," she said and tapped her chest. "But I have forgiven myself," she said and sighed. "That's how I know that I'm ready to move on."

"I'm glad," he said gently, holding her hand as they sat side by side in the front seat. "I think you've always been way too hard on yourself. Frank knew you loved him and you didn't cause the accident that killed him. It's called an accident because that's exactly what it was. Nothing you could have said or done would have made things turn out any different. He loved you. You loved him. And you should always keep a place in your heart for the life you shared and the memories you have."

"Thank you," she said, and brought his hand to her lips and kissed his knuckles. "For being so understanding. For loving me. For not giving up on me. Although I did text you last night and when I didn't get a text back—I thought you were ignoring me."

"Larkin threw my phone in the bathtub," he explained, and chuckled.

She laughed. "Really?"

He nodded. "So I wasn't ignoring you. I wouldn't have been able to resist calling you if I'd known you'd left me a message. I can't resist anything about you, Layla, surely you know that by now."

She touched his face. "Did you really fall in love with me that first day?"

"Yes," he replied. "Right in there, through those doors. I think I knew the moment we bent down to pick up your stuff and our heads banged together."

She smiled tenderly. "I was a little smitten myself, you know," she admitted, and gave him a seductive and sexy once-over. "I mean, those shoulders of yours should be illegal."

He chuckled. "Promise me something?"

"Anything."

"Always tell me what you're feeling—even if it's hard to say."

She nodded. "You know that about me, right? That I find it difficult to admit things…to say what I'm feeling and why and how."

"I know. Trust is something we earn with the people we love."

"I do trust you, Kane."

"I trust you, too, more than I've ever trusted anyone," he admitted. "Like I told you, I've never been able to talk about my dyslexia so openly, like I can with you. For the first time in my life I don't feel judged."

"You won't ever be," she said gently. "I think you're smart and amazing and I love the stories you tell Erin. And you're right about trust, which is why I promise I'll always talk to you and be honest about how I'm feeling and what I'm scared of. Because I don't want Erin to grow up like me. I want her to feel safe and loved, like you were growing up. I want her to know that she has parents who love and protect her and will always be there for her."

Kane stilled, watching her. "Parents?"

She ran her fingers down his cheek. "Well, I was hoping that since you love me, and I love you, that you'd like to marry me one day."

His heart almost imploded. "Are you proposing?"

She smiled. "Yeah… I guess I am."

"Well," he said, and entwined their fingers. "I'm a little old-fashioned, so very soon, when the time is right, I'd probably like to get a diamond, find a nice romantic place, and get down on my knee and ask you myself." He paused, looking at her hand. "You took off your ring?"

She gestured to her right hand. "I moved it," she said quietly. "To make room for…us. Is that okay?"

He nodded. "It's more than okay."

"It felt like the right thing to do and I don't think Frank would mind. In fact, I think he would absolutely approve of you. I think he'd say that there's no man better, or with more integrity, that I could find to help me raise Erin."

Kane swallowed the emotion in his throat. "I do love her a lot, you know."

"I know. And she loves you. She's missed you so much this past week. She's been waiting by the window, looking for your truck, walking around the house with books in her hand. You know, she figured out how wonderful you are from that first day."

"Smart kid."

"I want a few more, just so you know," she said, threading her fingers through his hair.

"No problem. I look forward to making babies with you."

She smiled and kissed his cheek, his jaw, his mouth. "You're perfect, you know that?"

He laughed. "No, I'm not, but it's nice that you think so. Did you know that Adam and Laurel set this meeting up today? He said I've been unbearable this past week. I think that's why he was happy to shuffle me off to New York for a week—so he didn't have to see me pining like an orphaned puppy, I think he called it."

She laughed. "You have such a wonderful family."

He nodded. "They'll be your family, too, now. And speaking of that, I'll have to rebook my flight. My parents will want to meet you and Erin, so we can all go together. What do you think?"

"I've never been to New York."

"I'd love to show it to you. And then we'll come back here and get married and start making those babies."

She laughed. "That's a great idea. And I've decided that once I finish my degree, I *am* going to hit one of your rich cousins up for the job of my dreams and I plan on being a working career mom."

Kane had no problem with it. "I'm sure we'll manage to juggle work and parenting just fine. I should tell you that I've accepted an offer from Callum as a project manager for his newest venture."

"That's wonderful," she said and smiled. "Will you move in with me? Like soon?"

"Yes," he replied. "Your house feels very much like a home."

"Our home now," she corrected. "Although if we have a bunch of babies, we're probably going to have to build on a few extra rooms."

"I know a guy who can do that," he said, and chuckled. "I'll build you as many rooms as you need."

"I'm so happy to hear it," she said, grinning. "Erin's going to make such a great big sister."

"Layla," he said, "let's go and get her."

They got out of the car and linked their hands as they headed into the building. The receptionist recognized them both and within minutes, Erin was brought out to them. She spotted Kane and squealed with delight, racing toward him, her small arms outstretched, running on her sparkly pink sneakers. He scooped her up into his arms and she hugged his neck, holding on to him so tightly he could feel emotion burning in his chest.

"Dada!"

It was the most wonderful word—perhaps more meaningful to him because the little girl and her mom, whom he loved so much, had *chosen* to love him in return.

"I missed you, kiddo," he said, and kissed her forehead. "And I promise I'm gonna be around every day from now on."

Layla smiled warmly and linked her arm through his and he bent down to kiss her. He had everything he'd ever wanted right in front of him.

He was the most fortunate Fortune he knew.

And with his family in his arms, the future had never looked brighter.

* * * * *

MILLS & BOON

Coming next month

MATCHMAKER AND THE
MANHATTAN MILLIONAIRE
Cara Colter

"I don't need a refund. I need to be engaged!"

"That's ridiculous. And impossible."

"She hasn't done it, has she? She hasn't made me a match."

"No, I don't believe she has. I can't –

Jonas regarded her stormily for a long enough that it felt as if she was going to stop breathing.

"What about you?"

"Excuse me?"

He stepped toward her. He didn't reach out and he didn't touch her, and yet Krissy felt as if he had taken her glasses off and was planning on running his hands through her hair.

"Yes, you'll do," he decided, a touch too clinically. "There's a little of that librarian look to you. Wholesome. The girl next door. Yes, you'll do."

Krissy's heart was beating madly, as if he had removed her glasses.

"I am not going to be your temporary toy!" she said. She wanted to sound firm, but her voice had an unfortunate squeak to it. *Librarian, indeed.*

He cocked his head charmingly at her, as if he was not being completely ludicrous.

"Toy," he said, his tone mulling. "No, no I don't think so."

Why on earth would she feel vaguely insulted by his dismissal?

"That could lead to complications," he explained gravely, "That's, in part, why I turned to your aunt. No complications.

Still, we would need to get to know each other first, before we made it official. It's important to know each other."

"You think?" she asked. He seemed to miss her sarcasm.

"It's for a family reunion in the Catskills, the long weekend in July. My sister would know, instantly, if you didn't know what my favourite colour was. Restaurant. Movie. That kind of thing."

What kind of weakness was it that Krissy suddenly wanted to know what his favourite colour was? Restaurant? Movie? Plus, the long weekend in July. She had always spent it with Aunt Jane, who knew, as her own parents had not, that occasions – birthdays, Christmas, Easter, the Fourth of July – were important to families.

His invitation felt like a reprieve from the looming weekend alone, but more, it felt as if she was being invited to step into the pages of a story, a very interesting story with all kinds of twists and turns and characters she knew nothing about.

Krissy did not like temptations. She did not appreciate her sudden awareness that the nice, safe, predictable life she had so carefully constructed for herself might be slightly, well, boring.

That was her aunt's word, after Krissy had brushed off her enthusiasm about having found the perfect man for her.

You're too young to be so set in your ways, so allergic to adventure. Life is not meant to be such a bore, my dear.

"Come on," he said persuasively. "It will be fun."

Fun. So no matter what he said, there was an element of her being his toy in there. Temporarily.

What do you do for fun?

Continue reading
**MATCHMAKER AND THE
MANHATTAN MILLIONAIRE**
Cara Colter

Available next month
www.millsandboon.co.uk

COMING SOON!

LET'S TALK
Romance

For exclusive extracts, competitions
and special offers, find us online:

 facebook.com/millsandboon

 @MillsandBoon

@MillsandBoonUK

Get in touch on 01413 063232

For all the latest titles coming soon, visit
millsandboon.co.uk/nextmonth

MILLS & BOON
A ROMANCE FOR EVERY READER

- **FREE** delivery direct to your door
- **EXCLUSIVE** offers every month
- **SAVE** up to 25% on pre-paid subscriptions

SUBSCRIBE AND SAVE

millsandboon.co.uk/Subscribe

JOIN US ON SOCIAL MEDIA!

Stay up to date with our latest releases, author
news and gossip, special offers and discounts, and
all the behind-the-scenes action
from Mills & Boon...

 millsandboon

 millsandboonuk

 millsandboon

It might just be true love...

MILLS & BOON

HISTORICAL

Awaken the romance of the past

Escape with historical heroes from time
gone by. Whether your passion is for
wicked Regency Rakes, muscled Viking
warriors or rugged Highlanders, indulge
your fantasies and awaken the
romance of the past.

MILLS & BOON
MEDICAL
Pulse-Racing Passion

Set your pulse racing with dedicated, delectable doctors in the high-pressure world of medicine, where emotions run high and passion, comfort and love are the best medicine.